# RAVE REVIEWS FOR ANN LAWRENCE AND *VIRTUAL HEAVEN!*

"*Virtual Heaven* is an incomparable debut novel that shatters the soul and touches the heart with passion and high adventure. Brava!"

—Deb Stover, bestselling author of *Another Dawn*

"Ms. Lawrence paints a vivid picture of a world beyond our own with its own characters and lifestyles. This is a fantastic journey into fantasyland and one that will make your heart swell."

—*Calico Trails*

"Ann Lawrence's clever and imaginative debut novel establishes her as an exciting new talent. With a modern-day heroine and a hero perfect for any reality, *Virtual Heaven* is a nonstop romantic fantasy."

—Kathleen Nance, bestselling author of *Wishes Come True*

"[*Virtual Heaven*] is one stunning story. Ms. Lawrence is without a doubt one writer on the way to the top. Splendid! 4-1/2 bells!"

—*Bell, Book and Candle*

"*Virtual Heaven* is a perfect choice [for] Love Spell's Perfect Heroes line. Kered is a hero in every sense of the word, and Maggie compliments him perfectly. Ann Lawrence has created a spellbinding read full of colorful imagery and emotion, and characters you won't want to let go of."

—*Romance Industry Newsletter*

# A TOUCH OF DESIRE

"Come here," he said in a low voice.

"Why?" Maggie dropped her arms and hugged her chest.

"A slave must do as she is bidden," Kered replied.

"Well, I'm not a slave. If you want to make a request, say please and tell me why," she said, stalling for time.

"Your impertinence is staggering." But if Kered was angry, his soft and seductive tone did not betray it.

"And you're a cur, through and through," Maggie returned.

"Come then, please, and tend my hair."

Maggie stared in disbelief. He had said please! Her palms prickled with sweat. Rising slowly, she walked around the fire. Sinking to her knees behind him, she considered the tangled mass of his long hair. The fire lit it with streaks of gold. Heat crept up her face. When she touched his hair, he shivered.

# Virtual Heaven

## Ann Lawrence

LOVE SPELL BOOKS  NEW YORK CITY

*I dedicate this book to my perfect hero.*

LOVE SPELL®

May 1999

Published by

Dorchester Publishing Co., Inc.
276 Fifth Avenue
New York, NY 10001

ISBN 0-505-52307-8

The name "Love Spell" and its logo are trademarks of Dorchester Publishing Co., Inc.

Printed in the United States of America.

# ACKNOWLEDGMENTS

I would like to thank and acknowledge the following people for their help and support:

Judy Di Canio, Edna Frankel, Lisa Hollis McCulley, Lena Pinto, and Mary Ann Smyth for offering insightful critique.

John Paul Ferrara, a cover artist who aided me in my research, and allowed me to peek over his shoulder into the fascinating world of cover art—any errors in content are mine.

Carolyn Grayson, my agent, for guiding me through the process.

My family, for their understanding whenever I was "lost in cyberspace."

# Virtual Heaven

In peace, Love tunes the shepherd's reed;
In war, he mounts the warrior's steed;
In halls, in gay attire is seen;
In hamlets, dances on the green.
Love rules the court, the camp, the grove,
And men below, and saints above;
For love is heaven, and heaven is love.

—*The Lay of the Last Minstrel*
Sir Walter Scott (1805)

# *Chapter One*

The warrior loomed over her. His leather jerkin, open to his waist, revealed a bounty of chest muscles and a corrugation of abdominals. Tight buff breeches hugged lean hips and well-shaped thighs. Maggie O'Brien's gaze jumped from his belt buckle to his jewel-encrusted boot knife, avoiding the obvious indications of a man well endowed. Clear thought fled.

"Is the poster straight now?"

Maggie jerked to attention. "Huh?"

Gwen Marlowe scrambled down from her low stepladder. "The poster? Is it straight?"

Maggie crossed her arms and hugged herself against the chilly air in Virtual Heaven, Gwen's video game shop. "Yes. It's fine."

The two friends faced the poster that advertised *Tolemac Wars,* a virtual-reality game.

"Kinda cute, isn't he?" Gwen said.

Ann Lawrence

Maggie tipped her head back and examined the man who bristled with weapons and bulged with muscle.

"You bet." She sighed. "Why don't real men look that good?"

"Now, Mag, don't be so cynical." Gwen gave a playful tug to an unruly lock of Maggie's long black hair. "There are a few men that great, even here in Ocean City, New Jersey. Maybe if you looked up from your soldering iron, came out of your jewelry shop, you might see one."

Maggie snorted with disdain, clinging stubbornly to her viewpoint. "Some artist conjures them up to torture us wallflowers. He reminds me of those guys you see on the covers of romance novels. Those men don't exist either."

"Funny you should mention that. The artist who did the poster is a cover artist for Hearts on Fire Publishing. I just read all about him in *Video Game* magazine. The article said he uses live models, so that guy up there really exists. Now, stop gawking and come help me count my change. Haven't you seen the Tolemac warrior before? He's the hottest thing in virtual-reality games."

Maggie followed Gwen to the front counter. "No. I've never heard of him. You know I hate computer stuff."

They counted the store's earnings. There wasn't much. The summer crowds were long gone and the stormy November weather was keeping the less-intrepid Ocean City residents home. The small amount of income did not really justify the expense of keeping the game store open through the winter. Each day, another store turned its shuttered face to the nearly empty boardwalk.

As Gwen chattered, Maggie found her attention drifting to the poster and the medieval man who dominated it. She caught the tail end of a question.

"—so why did you come here tonight? You might be right next door, but it seems like we never see each other anymore. I know you didn't come to play a game."

Maggie hid a sheepish grin and went to the front of Gwen's store for a bag she'd dropped by the door. A distant roll of thunder reminded her a nor'easter was moving in. "I'm invited to a storm party—"

"A storm party? What the heck's that?" Gwen snatched the bag from Maggie's hands and spilled the contents on the counter, heaping it with clothing, jewelry, and shoes.

"You know . . . an excuse to have a party. I guess it's also to mark the end of the season. I was hoping to meet someone new."

"Finally. I was beginning to worry about you. It's time you got over Tony."

"I'm over Tony," Maggie murmured.

Gwen placed a sympathetic hand on Maggie's. "You say that, but your reclusive behavior tells me different. I want my happy, vibrant friend back. You've hidden in your jewelry shop for months. I know he hurt you, Mag, but Tony and you just weren't meant to be. Try to think of him as just another boyfriend."

Maggie dipped her head and hid behind her hair. Gwen had no idea of the depths of humiliation and pain that thoughts of Tony engendered, even now, months after their breakup. *There would never be another Tony.* After all, there couldn't be another man so mercurial anywhere on earth.

Or Maggie hoped not. "I really thought we'd eventually get married, Gwen. All those empty promises—" Maggie mentally shook herself, determined to banish the painful thoughts. She straightened and met her friend's eyes. "Help me pick something to wear. I can't make up my mind. I want to look good.'' Maggie grimaced. ''My stomach is in knots just thinking about it.''

''Maggie, you could go in those old gray sweats and you'd look good. You'd have all the dates you wanted if you'd just try a little. Bat those gorgeous blue eyes. Put on some blush. Flaunt those cheekbones.''

For a bleak moment, Maggie considered her friend's words. ''I'm not sure I'm ready.''

''Yes, you are. Think positively. Not all men are domineering womanizers like Tony. Give another guy half a chance and you might find a whole new world out there. Now, let's see these outfits.'' Gwen sorted through the pile of clothing and held up a short red dress. ''Pretty stunning, but not you.'' She cast it aside in favor of a wad of black material. Shaking it out, she said, ''You always look great in black. Let's see this on you.''

Maggie cast a regretful glance at the red dress. She'd spent a fortune on it and the matching shoes in an uncharacteristic moment of panic spending.

She looked about the long, low displays of games. ''Where shall I go? I can't change out here.''

Maggie and Gwen turned to the expanse of glass windows fronting the boardwalk shop. Rain pelted the window, obscuring their view of the wide wooden promenade and the roiling ocean just beyond a stretch of sand.

''I think the bathroom is probably freezing about now. I know! The virtual-reality booth. Come on.'' Gwen led Maggie to a freestanding chamber by the poster that had occupied so much of Maggie's attention.

Maggie paused at the entrance and stared up at the warrior. ''He is beautiful. Arrogant, I would think, but . . . powerful.''

The warrior had eyes an improbable shade of aqua.

His tangled brown hair reminded Maggie of a surfer's, with sun streaks like streams of lava running through its length. Above him, the Tolemac sun, a red nightmare in a purple sky, appeared ready to sink behind a mountain range of sharp peaks, their summits capped with gilded snow.

"Who's the woman behind him?" Maggie asked Gwen. "Why's she so indistinct? She almost blends into the background."

"I call her the Shadow Woman. She pops up at the most convenient times and saves him from some peril. She's a slave."

"How do you know she's a slave?" Maggie asked.

"No arm rings." Gwen entered the virtual-reality booth.

Maggie's gaze returned to the warrior. Three silver-hued rings encircled his well-developed upper arm. Maggie sighed, then followed Gwen. "Is she his slave?"

"Maybe. I only know she's really good at saving his butt. I suppose, after we go home, after the shop is closed, he rewards her, somewhere out there in cyber-space."

"Cyberspace? Do I know where that is?"

Gwen just shook her head. "We've really gotta work on you."

The virtual-reality booth was formed by four matte-black walls. Gwen crossed the chamber to stand behind a console on a tiny raised platform that faced a curving expanse of white screen.

"This screen lets me watch what the player is doing," she said. "When really young kids play for the first time, I give them hints. If I didn't, Mr. Warrior God out there would be buzzard bait in two minutes. Wanna try? I can walk you through the opening scenes."

"No way." Maggie cringed, her words punctuated by a loud roll of thunder. The lights flickered. Maggie grabbed Gwen's arm as they were momentarily plunged into darkness before the lights came back and steadied. Maggie gasped. "That was scary."

"Just another storm," Gwen answered, unconcerned. "Try on that dress." Gwen played with the console a moment as Maggie pulled off her gray sweatshirt and sweatpants and kicked off her sneakers. "Don't tell me you're still wearing that old underwear from college."

Maggie looked down at her faded panties and bra. The elastic was shot in the bra, and the straps repeatedly slipped off her shoulders. In exasperation, she unhooked it and tossed it aside.

She lifted the black knit dress and held it against herself. "I've worn this a million times."

"If you look great in it, who cares?" Gwen tapped a few buttons on the console. A soft glow rose from the edge of the screen and suffused to a deep indigo as it sharpened into the same background featured in the poster. The words *Tolemac Wars* flashed red on the screen and then began to drip like bloody wounds.

Gwen punched another button and the Tolemac warrior emerged.

Maggie stood gape-mouthed as the man from the poster approached on the screen. Despite a long sword and other weapons, there was nothing hesitant or clumsy about the warrior's movements. He came out of the purple shadows, his stride confident, his movements lithe and fluid. He kept his head down, watching his step on the rocky terrain.

Maggie swallowed, the dress forgotten. "He looks so real."

"That's the point. The quality of the projection is incredible, isn't it? It's even more phenomenal with the headset. Don't you feel like you could reach out and touch him?"

A flush heating her face, Maggie clasped the black dress to her bare breasts.

"He can't see you, Mag." Gwen grinned. "Go ahead, flash it for him."

Maggie didn't know what came over her. She threw out her arms and let the dress fall to the floor. Up on the screen, the warrior suddenly raised his head and paused, one boot poised to step over a tree root. He looked right at her.

And smiled.

With a gasp, Maggie flung her arms across her chest.

Gwen's full-bellied laugh drowned her cry of embarrassment. "Oh, Maggie! You should see your face! The game always starts like that. I never thought you'd actually go bare for him. You must really like the guy. Try to remember he's only a devastating combination of computer pixels."

Maggie realized she hid herself from a man who might be smiling as if he enjoyed her naked display, but in reality was only a flicker of light and shadow. "That was mean," Maggie chastised Gwen, then smiled ruefully. "I have to admit, though, you have perfect timing."

She averted her eyes from the Tolemac warrior, who now stood on the edge of a precipice, scanning the landscape, his hand wrapped about his sword hilt.

Suddenly, the screen dissolved to black. Maggie felt an intense sense of loss. He seemed so real. The warrior looked as if he could step down from the screen and sweep her up in his arms. The reality of it disturbed her.

"What happened?"

"I don't know. Damn." Gwen fiddled with the console, but there was no response on the screen. "At least I don't have to give you a refund. I guess I'll have to call the repair guy." Gwen slapped the console and the soft purple sky reappeared. "Yes!" she cried.

Reflecting shadows from the screen danced across Gwen's face as Maggie slipped into the black knit dress, an old favorite, practical yet elegant. She walked up to Gwen, who stood commanderlike at her console and offered her back, bringing her hair forward. Gwen fastened the row of covered buttons trailing down the back of the sleeveless dress.

Maggie stole another look at the warrior. He stood on the precipice, outlined in a golden glow. It touched him with a muted purple hue as the fiery crimson sun slipped behind the peaks. Just as the luminous glow faded, the Tolemac warrior unsheathed his sword. In one fluid motion, he swept it aloft and the last ray of light flashed off the blade, shooting out to cross a rusty plain of craggy rocks. The light touched a distant peak and settled there in a ball of flame.

Maggie stood open-mouthed.

"You're drooling," Gwen said softly. "Would you like to play? You can be the Shadow Woman and fight at his side, defend his back."

Maggie turned away, flipping her hair over her shoulders, feeling foolish and ridiculous. *I really need to get out more.* How else could she explain becoming mesmerized by a painting, transfixed by light and shadow, color and form? She forced herself to leave the chamber and sort through the jumble of jewelry draped across Gwen's counter.

Carefully, Maggie untangled a necklace, one she'd made for her shop, Maggie's Treasures. She lifted it over her head, then let it slide to rest between her breasts. The pendant, a lump of turquoise entwined in fine and delicate strands of silver, floated at the end of a chain like a blue planet hangs in the heavens.

She slipped on a pair of black suede flats, then returned to the virtual-reality chamber. As she approached the opening, thunder rolled again. The lights flickered and dimmed. A sensation of falling streaked through Maggie's body. She clutched the wall. Her palm flattened against the poster, touched the hilt of the Tolemac warrior's jewel-encrusted boot knife.

A spark leaped.

Maggie stifled a scream and snatched back her hand. In the flickering lights, the knife swelled and gained another dimension, each line of the knife's Celtic engravings standing out in stark relief about the gems. Then the lights steadied, came up to bright, and the knife dissolved into a collection of shadows and color, an artist's drawing, flat and unreal.

Sure she'd imagined it, Maggie hurried back to where Gwen cursed over her console. "Is it safe to be operating the game in this storm?" Maggie peered at the complicated equipment with a worried frown.

"Sure, it's got surge protection. The worst that will happen is a shutdown." Gwen looked up at Maggie and grinned. "You look great. I've always loved that dress. It flatters you."

"Do you think so?" Maggie plucked at the skirt. It flowed past her knees and fell in a sweep just below her calves. "I'm not sure." She wished for the total confidence of her friend. Gwen's red sweater, typical of her bold color choices, made Maggie's grays and blacks fade into the background.

"What about my necklace?"

"The necklace is perfect. It's probably your best work. You really expressed your Navajo background."

"I won't tell my Irish father you said that." Maggie lifted the pendant and stroked the delicate Celtic knot-work she'd designed into the chain. "It's hard to merge the two cultures."

"Matches the Tolemac warrior's eyes, too." Gwen stepped from the console. "Stand up here and let's have a look at you."

Maggie climbed the two steps to the raised platform. She twirled about self-consciously. The screen before her remained blank; the console Gwen had manipulated so expertly just resembled a typewriter missing most of the essential keys.

"How did you turn it on?" Maggie did not admit to herself that she wanted to see the warrior smile again.

Gwen joined Maggie at the console. "This is the gizmo that controls your weapons when you play." Maggie picked up a small gun-shaped object, holding the thick stock in her hand and turning it about. "You hold it like a pistol. You push these buttons when you want to fire—blue button stun, red button kill. It's super simple. The trick is, you must aim it like a real gun and have pretty decent aim. You should be a crack shot. All that practice out on the reservation with your brothers."

"I hate guns, Gwen. We shot bottles, but I always hated the feel of it, the power to hurt."

"You only hurt the bad guys with this." Gwen lifted a large, doughnut-shaped plastic headpiece from the console and offered it to Maggie. "Put this on. It puts you in the picture. If you turn your head, you'll see to the side, to the back, and so forth. It takes a little getting used to." As Maggie hesitated, Gwen pressed her point.

"It's really fun. Now, put it on. I'll talk you through the game."

Maggie shook her hair out to free the strands catching on her buttons. With the headpiece secured on her head, Maggie had the sensation of being top heavy. Her head wobbled on her neck.

"If you're ready, say so." Gwen placed the game gun in Maggie's hands, curling her fingers about the stock. "Don't accidentally shoot our stud muffin!"

As Gwen spoke, Maggie raised her head. She stood at the top of a mountain in a strange world. The title rose in the sky before her and dripped its familiar blood. The drops glistened and, involuntarily, Maggie looked down to see if they splashed on the floor. Dizziness made her jerk her head upright again.

"This is very weird," Maggie said. Her voice sounded hollow to her and far away. She experimented a moment, swinging her head about, feeling dizzy again as grass and trees spun and lurched before her. Very quickly, she took control and turned to the hill, facing the spot where the warrior would appear, barely conscious of the boom of distant thunder.

"It's so real." Maggie gasped, her heart beating a little faster, for she knew what came next. Her breath shortened as she waited for him.

*He did not disappoint her.*

The Tolemac warrior climbed the rocky hill, each boot placed deliberately. Only this time, Maggie heard the crunch of stones beneath his soles, heard the sigh of the wind in the trees. A pebble dislodged and rolled, audibly bouncing along behind him.

He came straight toward her.

A swift and heated surge swept her body as she waited breathlessly, the gun clutched tightly in her hand. She wanted to know what he would do when he met her on the hill, for she stood in his path, not leaning on the console as Gwen had, but standing rigidly in the waning light of the warrior's world. She almost felt the heat of the burning sun, did hear the eerie cry of a bird in the distance. The scrape of his boots echoed about her. Her heart pounded in her ears. Her mouth felt dry.

Thunder rolled. It vibrated in her ears, magnified to ten times its natural volume. Maggie raised her head in fear, looked from the path to the distant mountain peaks. A blinding sheet of lightning streaked across the heavens, setting the Tolemac warrior in sharp relief. The scent of ozone filled her nostrils. She shivered. Then, as the warrior raised his head and stared at her, the sky flashed a brilliant white. A sudden pain shot through Maggie's head—pulsed from one side of her skull to the other.

She moaned in agony, clasped the gun to her chest, and shut her eyes against a dazzling flare of lightning. Her head rocked heavily on her neck. She stumbled, slipping to her knees just as the white flash broke into a thousand shards of color and pain.

# Chapter Two

"By the sword!" Kered swore, staggering blindly. He stumbled over a tree root and nearly fell. The fierce white light slowly dissolved, revealing a woman stretched out at his feet.

He bent over the supine woman, his vision still blurry in the aftermath of the dazzling flash of lightning. He rubbed his eyes, making them worse. Yes, he had stepped on her, not a tree root. Through the swimming dots of color, he noted the rise and fall of the woman's breast. Alive, but badly injured.

"Kered!"

"Here, Nilrem," he called to an old man easing his way down the steep path.

"Are you hurt? Who is this?" Nilrem came to a halt at his side, planting his walking stick inches from the woman.

"I thought you might know. I tripped over her."

# Ann Lawrence

"Is she dead?" Nilrem's ancient back did not allow bending and stooping over damsels in distress.

"No, but whatever ails her, she is well gone from here." Kered ignored the stabbing flashes of color still plaguing his sight and picked up the woman's hand, seeking her pulse with his fingertips. It beat strongly.

"Do you see her pendant?" Nilrem whacked Kered on the arm with his stick.

"Curious." Kered lifted the bauble, then drew back, holding it at arm's length as he inspected it. Jewels held no interest for him, and he placed it gently back on her breast. "Her breath labors. Perhaps we should get her to shelter?" A long rumble of thunder sounded in the distance.

"Aye," Nilrem agreed, shuffling about the tree roots. "The winds will rise now; the conjunction begins."

Kered tore his gaze from the woman, a difficult task, for her exotic beauty and her deathly stillness held more allure than stellar phenomena. The Tolemac moons, four small bluish-green orbs, moved into alignment high in the eastern sky. He rose and scooped the woman into his arms. She weighed nothing. His palms caressed the unusual fabric of her gown, and he noted the supple flesh beneath. With difficulty, he forced himself to his task.

"Come, Nilrem. You may spout profundities to your heart's content when we have reached shelter."

Following the slow shambling progress of the old man, Kered climbed a steep path another hundred yards and came out of the tall trees onto a mountain meadow. Delicately scented flowers gleamed in the waning light, bowing their heads to the stiffening breeze.

He ventured a glance over his shoulder to the heavens. The conjunction was almost complete. The wind whistled through the trees, lifting the boughs, moaning like some spectral beast. At the summit of the mountain Kered turned, and holding the woman sheltered against his chest, he waited.

Nilrem raised his staff, mumbling an incantation. Kered waited with the proper respect due a man of Nilrem's age and wisdom. The wisdom drew him, the prophesies did not.

Nilrem stood for many minutes watching the heavenly conjunction before turning to Kered. "Your patience pleases me well. Come," he said. "Let us tend this slave."

Kered had not noticed her lack of arm rings. It was unlike him to be so unobservant. He blamed it on his fatigue and the remaining glitter of color in his eyes. At Nilrem's direction, he placed the woman on a fur-mounded bed in the wise man's rude hut. He went down on one knee and smoothed back her unusual hair, searching for wounds, finding a lump at the back of her head that might explain her deep sleep. Succumbing to an uncontrollable urge, he drew a callused finger along the delicate, white skin of her bare upper arm. "A slave," he murmured.

"Step aside. Let me tend her wounds." Nilrem explored as Kered had, grunted at the lump. He ran a hand over her body, touching her everywhere.

Nilrem had no sense of modesty and touched the woman's breasts and belly with pleasurable abandon. Kered turned away in embarrassment. "You are a wicked lecher, Nilrem."

"Not often I get the opportunity!" he cackled back. "Let us strip her and really see what we have found."

"No. The head wound is all that ails her. Tend it. Keep your bony fingers to the task while I see if her master is about."

Kered searched the mountainside until the light failed and the wind battered him with a relentless chill. The usual signs of the white hart grazing on the meadow or crossing the wooded slopes were all he found. There were no footprints, no broken twigs, nothing to indicate two people on the mountaintop.

The woman left only one sign of her coming.

That he tucked into the waistband of his breeches, concealing it beneath his tunic for later examination. He never allowed curiosity to overtake caution. The night deepened to inky purple and he gave up the search. The hut, ablaze with warm light, beckoned.

When he entered, Nilrem was crooning over the woman as he tied a bandage about her head.

"What do you make of her?" Kered asked as he dragged a three-legged stool across the dirt floor to the bedside. He lifted the woman's hand and held it. Her fingers were long and slim and strong. They fitted well in his.

"Her appearance is an omen."

Kered frowned at Nilrem. "Why?"

Nilrem shrugged. "The conjunction begins, there is a crash of lightning, and she appears wearing a talisman."

"The pendant?" Kered tried not to touch the woman's breast as he again lifted the necklace, holding it up for inspection. The dimming of his vision was a painful malady he did his best to ignore—and hide from the curiosity of others. "It is beautiful, but why do you think it a talisman?"

"It bears the symbols of the ancient time. If you were a believer, I would say it means you should make the ancient quest. Let her rest. When she awakens she will tell us her purpose on my mountain and all will be clear."

Kered raked his hair back from his face. "Will she awaken?" He bent over her, adjusting the furs. Her skin was like new cream, her hair glossy as a raven's wing, her brows straight and patrician.

"Oh, aye, when she is ready."

Because Nilrem said it with such confidence, Kered relaxed. "Her master must have paid a fortune for her."

"All pleasure slaves are costly." Nilrem sighed.

"You think her a pleasure slave?" Kered turned over her hand. "She bears calluses on her fingertips. Her arms are not soft; they show strength."

"Aye. She has not the soft roundness of a pleasure slave, but where have you ever seen such coloring? I have seen hair from the palest silver to the muddiest brown, but true black? Never."

"Perhaps beyond the ice fields?" Kered thought of the subtle fragrance that had teased his senses as he had carried her up the mountain. The perfume alone should have told him she belonged in the pleasure realm. His groin tightened. Her exotic beauty, her unusual coloring, and her strange, soft garment served only to remind him that it had been many months since he had taken any pleasure.

Nilrem seemed to read his mind. "If you found no sign of her master, perhaps she is a runaway. Claim her. I can step outside for the length of time it will take you to use her, or better yet, I could bear witness!"

"I need a lifemate, not another female slave. 'Tis useless to claim a woman who, by the most ancient of laws, may neither bear me heirs nor bring me power."

" 'Tis true she could never lifemate with you, but surely there is always room in a household for another female with such pleasurable attributes?"

"Perhaps in my kitchens?" Kered asked calmly. Nil-

rem loved to goad him to anger. He would not be led.
His purpose for visiting the wise man could not be lost
in side issues.

Nilrem patted his arm. "Your responsibilities have
made you sour. What brings you here?"

"The Tolemac border is again breached in two places.
I must earn a seat on the council and try to end this
useless war."

Suddenly, the woman moaned, her breasts heaving
with anxious gasps. Kered kept a tight hold on her hand,
clasping it to reassure her as she flailed about on the fur
pallet. Her moans became cries.

"Soothe her." Nilrem edged closer.

Kered obeyed, murmuring nonsense, stroking her
hands, suddenly recalling phrases his mother had used
to calm him when he was a child. Fear possessed her.
When her eyes opened, they stared wildly about, flitting
over the two men.

A red flush bloomed on her cheeks. Kered leaned forward. He watched in fascination as the red stain spread.
He wished now he had stripped her, for the color ran
under the edge of her gown. His imagination painted it
across her small breasts.

*An exotic from some distant land. Worth a fortune.*

"Calm yourself, child," Nilrem crooned. He shoved
Kered aside and made clumsy clucking sounds at her.

She struggled up on an elbow. Her eyes skipped over
Nilrem to focus on Kered. "Oh, my God!" she whispered.

Maggie stared as the poster came to life, the Tolemac
warrior rising abruptly to his feet. His head banged the
rafters and he stooped in annoyance.

An old man bent over her. Maggie pressed back into
the bed. Her stomach rolled, and she shivered, searching

the room for something familiar to anchor her senses. Either she was dreaming, or the game was more frighteningly real than she had thought.

*The game.*

Maggie sat up, then swayed as dizziness assailed her. She blinked and looked about the hut, holding her throbbing head. Her nose told her the two men could use a bath. Her eyes told her that the warrior would poke his head through the roof if he stood up straight. Right now, he slouched menacingly behind a wrinkled person garbed in rough, brown wool with a straggly gray beard that reached almost to the floor.

"W-w-ho are you? Where am I?" she stammered.

The old man spoke. "I am Nilrem. You are on my mountain, Hart Fell. Who owns you?" He held out a wooden cup.

Peeking into the cup, she sniffed. No smell. Water? Afraid to drink despite a raging thirst, she stared up at the two men. The words penetrated. "Who owns me? No one!"

"Her injury has made her forget," Nilrem said sagely.

The younger man nodded. "It makes sense. Drink," he ordered.

Maggie raised the cup. Somehow the warrior's demeanor brooked no disobedience. His voice boomed in the tiny hut. Sweet, cool water caressed her tongue as she drank. Smoke from a fire in a corner hearth stung her eyes and hung like a pall about the warrior's head. Her headache battered against her temples.

"Do you know your name?" the warrior asked.

"Please don't shout." Maggie held her head and probed the bandage encircling it, causing herself greater pain. Her stomach felt none too stable, either.

"Am I shouting?" He consulted the old man.

"A mite," Nilrem agreed.

With a nod, the warrior lowered his voice. "Go contemplate the conjunction."

Nilrem pulled a face and scuffled from the hut.

The warrior dragged a stool near, then sat down, now eye to eye with Maggie. "You belong to someone. Who?"

"I don't belong to anyone!" Maggie insisted, a prickle of fear creeping up her spine.

"Prove it," he said softly, stroking a finger along her bare upper arm, watching her as intently as a predator might watch his prey. "Free women wear at least one arm ring. You have none."

His tone added the silent word "idiot," but Maggie did her best to ignore it. Wouldn't you know Mr. Warrior God would turn out to have a nasty disposition. And where was his leather jerkin? His jeweled weapons? He wore a faded woolen tunic, long-sleeved, rough, more peasant garb than warrior finery.

"Arm ring? I . . . that is . . . what's your name?" She stalled for time. This nightmare must end, Gwen must pull the plug on the game, and soon. She was going to be sick.

"I am called Kered. What is your name?"

"Maggie O'Brien."

"You have two names?" He cocked his head to the side. "I have never heard of such a thing."

Maggie's heart hesitated before taking a beat. The planes of his face glowed golden in the flickering firelight. His skin stretched flawlessly across strong bones. She searched for some blemish, some mark, but found none. His long brown hair might be a tangled mass of knots, he might reek of sweat and wood smoke, but his skin rivaled a newborn's.

32

Kered snapped his fingers in Maggie's face.

"Stop that!" she cried, then pressed her hands to her cheeks. The pain in her head expanded and pounded.

"Forgive me. I had forgotten you were hurt." He put his hands to her shoulders and eased her back onto the pallet. "We will deal with your crime another time. Rest now."

"Crime?" Maggie struggled under his hold. He pinned her down, leaning over her. His long tangled hair tickled her bare shoulders and brushed her face.

"Aye. To desert one's master is a heinous crime. If you are a pleasure slave, the penalty will be harsh."

Maggie sputtered through indignation, disbelief, and fear, but Kered seemed not to notice. He leaned closer, his warm breath, scented with ale, washing over her face. His fingers rose and caressed her hot cheeks. "It would be a shame to mark you, to mar such a rare beauty."

"M-m-mark?" she stuttered, more from the whisper-soft caress of his fingers on her cheeks and the proximity of eyes like the rarest turquoise than from his words.

"Aye. An angry master would open your cheeks with a knife, slit your lips, remove your nipples, rendering you ugly to all."

Maggie pressed back into the furs, her arms instinctively crossing over her chest.

"You have appeared from out of nowhere at the height of a conjunction. Speak now, name your master, or Nilrem will see a prophecy in this. One may not deny a prophecy. Claim the safety of your master's name, and I will see you are not mutilated."

Angry and afraid, Maggie sat up and tried to shove him away. He didn't budge. Inches separated them.

*Reality and fantasy made it a wide chasm.*

33

"I have no master," she said into the expectant silence.

"So be it." He rose and shoved a hand under his tunic. He tossed something onto her lap. "Explain this."

# Chapter Three

Maggie stared at the game gun. Her fingers crept across her lap and poked the black lump of plastic. It lay there like a dead thing.

"I don't know what you expect," she said, stalling for time. How did one explain a gun to a man whose only visible weapons were a knife and sword? Then again, in many computer games, the heroes had strange weapons. Maybe Kered had a few she didn't know about, hidden somewhere she couldn't see.

"Nilrem will read some omen in this. 'Tis best you speak before he returns."

"All right. All right. It's a weapon. Called a gun." Maggie slipped it into her hand and smoothed her fingers over the stock. A useless piece of junk far from home. Or, if she truly was in this man's world, a potentially lethal hunk of plastic.

" 'Tis a mighty strange weapon, this . . . gun." Before

Maggie could protest, Kered had plucked it from her hand. His large fist dwarfed the stock as he wielded it like a bludgeon.

Maggie rose on her knees and grabbed his forearm. She could do chin-ups on him if he could be persuaded to hold his arm out straight. There was little chance she could persuade this man to do anything. She felt suddenly puny and inconsequential. "I'm not sure how dangerous it is. Let me have it."

"You speak as if I am some child you command." Kered turned and, with a gentle nudge, sent her flying flat onto her back.

"Of all the nerve." She struggled off the bed, ignoring the sudden hammer that rang in her head. "Didn't your mother teach you any manners?"

"My mother is dead." He turned his back to her, pointed the weapon, and studied the blue and red buttons. "How does it work? You may explain, or I will experiment."

"I think I'm going to faint," Maggie whispered. It wasn't a complete lie. Not really. If this was a dream, he couldn't hurt anything, could he?

*And if it was real, he might fry them both in a heartbeat.*

Nausea knotted her stomach and fear twisted her bowels, but her words served their purpose. Kered dropped the gun to the table and swept her into his arms. She felt as if she'd been gripped by a giant vise.

Then, with a gentleness that belied his size, Kered placed her on the bed. He touched his hand to her cheek and then encircled her throat with warm fingers. "Cool. Sweaty. You are suffering more from fear than anything else. We will not hurt you."

"Oh? Slit lips, cut off—" Maggie bit her lip.

Kered touched her arm, briefly, gently. "Your master will decide your punishment." Then he leaned back, withdrew as if he had overstepped some boundary. "Now, the weapon?"

Maggie could see he needed an explanation. But, before she gave it, he stood up, banging his head and swearing a string of strange words, then picked up the gun and pressed a button.

A large hole appeared in the wooden table. The edges smoked.

"Nilrem's beard!" Kered turned to her in astonishment. "Beyond the ice fields? Am I correct? You came through the ice fields!"

Maggie stalled. "Do they have weird weapons over there?" She massaged her temples. How could she get the gun away from him before he made Swiss cheese of the cabin?

"I have no true knowledge of the people beyond the ice fields, but legend has it they exist and have much to offer." He peered about the hut as if looking for toys on Christmas morning, searching for expendable objects to shoot.

"Then that's where I'm from." Maggie closed her eyes. Better an ice field than telling him he didn't exist, was part of a virtual-reality game—*a virtual-reality nightmare*.

He smoked a hole through a water bucket, sending a stream of steaming water rolling toward the hearth. Maggie jumped off the bed, regretting it instantly as she swayed on her feet. Just before he created a new window in the hut, she grabbed his wrist.

"You're wasting it!"

That stopped him. He accepted the comment with ill

grace, his brows drawing together over his perfect, straight nose.

"Let me have it," Maggie cajoled. She had to get the weapon away from him.

Kered shoved the gun into a leather pack by the door then stomped back to her, his boots raising a small cloud of dust. "Slaves do not bear weapons."

*Slave*. She had to go home. *Now*. Before he began to play master. If she could distract him, perhaps she could make a break for it. Perhaps outside she'd find some answers.

Without thinking, Maggie reached across the small distance that separated them and touched the sleeve covering his upper arm. The atmosphere became charged. His biceps jumped taut at her light caress.

Arm rings—under the cloth. Her fingertips explored. Three.

"You're a warrior, aren't you?" Maggie held on tightly.

*Warriors meant war.*

She felt a little faint and it had nothing to do with the blow to her head. Perhaps going outside was foolish. Maybe if she went to sleep, she'd wake from this nightmare in Ocean City, New Jersey, with Gwen hovering somewhere nearby.

Just as she slipped to the floor, he caught her. His arms locked about her waist, drawing her body against his. Her eyelids fluttered as her eyes rolled up into her head.

"Dancing?" Nilrem cackled as he opened the hut door.

Kered growled. He should lay the slave down. He should. When he placed her in the furs, he straightened her skirt, lingering over her delicate bones, stroking them with his fingertips and overlapping her ankle. He picked up his fur-lined cloak and tucked it about her shoulders. Unbidden, his hand caressed her downy cheek.

Nilrem stomped about his hut, then stuck his staff into the hole in his table. "My son, you leaned here, did you not? You broke my bucket!" Nilrem whined and whimpered over the now useless container.

"Halt!" Kered retrieved the gun from his pack. " 'Tis this curious weapon that did it!"

"She used a weapon on you?" Nilrem peered around Kered to where Maggie lay sleeping.

"Hmpf. Women do not use weapons on me."

"Ah,'tis true. Women beg you to use your weapon on them!" Nilrem slapped his knees and bent double with his chortling, then he sobered. "Let us see this weapon."

Nilrem's gnarled fingers examined the gun as closely as he had examined Maggie's body. He missed nothing. "What do you make of it?"

"The slave says she is from beyond the ice fields. The weapon is probably her master's. It makes holes in wood!"

"Ah, think of the possibilities," Nilrem gloated.

Kered snatched the gun before Nilrem could touch the blue or red button. "I have thought of the possibilities. They frighten me."

Kered and Nilrem stared at each other.

Nilrem spoke. "Your responsibilities weigh heavily?" Suddenly his demeanor changed. A subtle metamorphosis took place. His back grew straighter, his voice less rusty. "Tell me." Nilrem reached across the space and placed a hand on Kered's knee.

"The time has come for peace," Kered said in the silence, turning the gun end over end.

Nilrem merely nodded.

"Tolemac has been fighting the folk of Selaw long enough to know they raid out of starvation. It is time we aided them, instead of slaughtering them!" Kered rose and paced, head bent to avoid the low rafters. "My father will not last much longer. Peace must be made before his death, for we all know 'tis only his hand that stays a massacre. There are few on the council who would respect any peace offer from the Selaw once he is gone. They need grain. We waste in one harvest more oats than their entire tribe could use in a year! For what reason do we make war?"

"Ah, my son, you truly have earned the right to a seat on the council. Were you Leoh's true son, you would sit there already." Nilrem glowed as if he alone had raised Kered and not Leoh, Kered's adoptive father and the leader of the council.

"Seat on the council? Hah! If I cannot hold one border against starving men, what chance have I to earn the right to a council seat?" Kered struck his fist into his palm.

"Starving children make fierce warriors of their fathers." Nilrem sought to pacify Kered.

Their voices roused Maggie. For some moments she lay there disoriented, frightened. Then sense returned. She remembered. Grief cut deeply. Cyberspace, Gwen had said. Maggie faced the fact that somehow she had been transported to somewhere in cyberspace. A nonexistent thing or place—just gobbledygook from technogeeks. Until today, until this moment.

The scent of the two men seeped into her nostrils, mixing with the wood smoke that stung her eyes. She narrowed them to slits and breathed shallowly. The men's voices hypnotized her into a dreamy state until she heard the word war.

Her ears pricked; she was jolted out of her stupor.

*Tolemac Wars.* Wars meant fighting, death, and annihilation. Maggie shivered. There must be some way out of this nightmare—some way to end the game.

She poked her nose deep into the fur, then realized why the men's scent was so strong. She lay beneath a heavy fur cloak. It needed a good dry cleaning. Even a thrift store wouldn't take it in its present condition.

"What brings you here, son?" Nilrem sipped from a goblet of water. Maggie's throat scratched, but asking for a drink would alert them to her wakefulness.

"I come to seek your wisdom. By all that is holy or wise, there must be some answer."

"Lifemating?" Nilrem suggested.

Kered slumped onto the stool. It groaned dangerously beneath his weight. "Another failure. The fair Einalem rejected my proposal after Leoh spent weeks negotiating the lifemating contracts. With Einalem's wealth, I could have accomplished much. Yet she turned her hand palm down."

"By the heavens, why? You have known each other since childhood, not to mention that you are a legend from the ice fields to the Scorched Plain!"

"It seems my 'legendary' ways did not meet with her approval. The stink of blood is too strong upon my hands, she said. I am too much a man of war."

"And pleasure!" Nilrem said with jestful tones. "Hold your ire. I know you have little of pleasure in your life. So, she rejected you. 'Tis more like her father found something amiss in the distribution of wealth or power and used her option of rejection to slip out of the agreement."

"Leoh said as much, yet the end remains the same! The Selaw border is breached in two places, and I am rejected before the council. After this humiliation, what hope have I of forging a treaty or negotiating peace?''

Nilrem and Kered sat silently by the fire. Occasionally, Nilrem sipped from his cup, slurping the water and dribbling it down his beard. "My son, your father is a wise and noble leader, but old and sickly. It is time for younger heads to rule. I have watched you for many years—always you temper your words and think of others. Even as a boy you offered words first and weapons second. The council needs you. Samoht craves your father's power. He wants ice for Tolemac and the Selaw stand in the way. He will decimate them when Leoh dies. It is time."

"Time for what?" Kered rested his chin on a fist. Maggie peeked at the men from beneath her eyelashes. Kered looked discouraged and depressed, Nilrem younger and more vigorous.

"Time to make the quest. You *must* make the quest."

" 'Tis legend, a tale for children." Kered swept a hand out in dismissal.

"You bear the sign. 'Tis why Leoh adopted you. Do you deny it?"

Kered shook his head. "I bear what *Leoh and you* consider a sign. I prefer to think 'tis just a blemish, nothing more."

"I only ask you to hear my words," Nilrem said with a quiet urgency.

Kered nodded, but his face arranged itself in impatient lines, deep grooves forming about his mouth, and Maggie thought he had aged in the last few moments.

"You have come to seek wisdom. Now you must let go of your doubts and accept what you hear." Nilrem tapped a gnarled finger on Kered's chest. "There are few symbols so sacred as the one you bear. Surely, this entitles you to the legendary sword of your ancestor, the esteemed Ruhtra. If you retrieve the sword and bear it as your own weapon at the council conclave, you would earn another arm ring.''

Kered straightened on his stool. ''Four arm rings will not gain me a seat on the council.''

''A second arm ring can be earned by journeying to the Forbidden Isle of N'Olava and bringing back the sacred cup of Liarg. Both the sword and the cup are symbols of peace, not just to Tolemac, but to every neighboring chiefdom. If you can secure the two symbols and attain the status of five arm rings, your acceptance to the council is guaranteed and your peace proposals sure to be taken seriously by each councilor. Even Samoht and his cohorts will be forced to bow to your power.''

A stiff silence reined. Maggie watched Kered ball his fists on his knees before he spoke. ''And if this be just the stuff of legends or the ramblings of an old man?''

''You wound me, son. Only the one who bears the sign will successfully make the quest—gain the sword and cup. Is peace not worthy of the effort to seek the truth of the ancient legends?'' Nilrem rose. He brought the goblet of water to Maggie's bedside. ''I know you listen, child. Drink.'' He helped Maggie to a sitting position; she sipped with guilty pleasure.

Kered spoke as if she were not present, as if no interruption had occurred. ''I offer my humblest apology. I meant no insult.''

''I know.'' Nilrem nodded. ''You walked here. You abased yourself for wisdom. It is admirable. That is why I will help you. Samoht, too, has been to my mountain—will soon return.''

"No!" Kered smote the table with a fist and Maggie jumped, spilling water on the cloak.

Nilrem slapped at the drops. "Samoht, too, seeks a way—a way to eliminate every man, woman, and child of the Selaw who stand between him and the ice. You must not delay. The council will elect Samoht in Leoh's place, should he die. If you are on the council, Samoht's every decision will be tempered by your wisdom and compassion. If you are not, blood will stain the earth."

Maggie shivered despite the heavy fur about her shoulders.

"So, I must seek the sword and cup." Kered rose and paced, head bent.

Nilrem groped beneath the fur cloak and Maggie yelped as his hand touched her breast. Kered spun around and stormed to Maggie's side as Nilrem lifted the pendant. "See. This slave's appearance is an omen. The sword and the cup, they bear this image—eight rings about our earthly home hanging in the heavens. The sacred eight."

Kered went down on one knee and clasped the pendant, his knuckles grazing Maggie's breast. She froze. His nearness, the heavy weight of their words, their serious demeanor frightened her into silence.

Nilrem covered Kered's hand. "You know she must go, too."

Maggie and Kered both stared at him open-mouthed.

"Aye." The old man nodded. "She appeared at the conjunction. She is a rare, exotic find and somehow part of this. She bears the sign. It is fated."

Nilrem began to age before Maggie's eyes. Whatever vestige of youth had made him speak and move with ease now deserted him. He groaned and crabbed away, taking Kered's stool by the hearth, rocking and extending his hands to the warm flames.

Maggie and Kered studied each other in silence.

"You heard our words?" Kered asked, his hand still fisted about the pendant.

Maggie nodded. A cold hard lump formed in her throat.

"I have sought the wisdom of Nilrem the old way. I trekked here on foot, brought nothing save one pack of necessities, and wore nothing new. I ate only bread and water—abstained from meat."

Maggie nodded again. She didn't understand any of it. She would play their game—at least until she learned the rules, or woke up.

"One may not deal lightly with a prophecy. One may not scoff at wisdom from an elder who has reached the twelfth level of awareness."

He stood and, still holding the pendant, drew her up. Not wanting the chain to break, Maggie went with it.

"Will your master seek you?" His voice rasped like sandpaper in a hoarse whisper only she could hear.

"I have no master." She, too, whispered.

"So you say. But I must know the truth. Must I guard my back? Will he seek revenge if I take you?"

"I have no master. Where I come from, there are no arm rings, no slaves."

"So be it." He opened his palm, and smoothed a finger along the delicate interlocking links of the chain. "I knew, when Nilrem beheld this bauble, you would entwine yourself in my life, just as these metals entwine the stone." The pendant fell from his hand to lie between Maggie's breasts. "We will rise with the sun."

Kered dismissed her. He took a fur from the end of the bed and after a short discussion with Nilrem about the best way to set out on the quest, he stretched out on the floor. Almost immediately, he began to snore. Maggie sat huddled on the bed, watching him.

Nilrem came close, and she recoiled from his harsh breath.

"Kered has a destiny. You are somehow part of it. Aid him. I sense wisdom in you and know that in some way you are crucial to his success. Whether you have a master or not, it is an omen that you appeared at the conjunction. Take the path he sets for you. To do anything else is to deny your fate."

Maggie pictured the fates as slavering dogs or large men with knives. She would not blindly accept the old man's words. Some way must be found to return to Ocean City. Perhaps even now, a serviceman might be repairing the game. If she left Nilrem's mountain, would she miss an opportunity to return home? The possibility chilled her to the bone. No man, not even one who looked like Kered, could convince her to leave if she didn't want to!

Wearily, Maggie stretched out on the bed and tried in vain to formulate a plan. After a few minutes, she realized she needed to relieve herself. She waited until both men lay sleeping on the tamped dirt floor, singing an aphonic chorus of snores. As silent as a wraith, Maggie rose and went to the door.

She lifted the latch, pulling Kered's cloak about her shoulders. Beyond the door of the hut, the last of the red sun dipped huge and glowing below the horizon's edge. The sky was not deep black, but tinged with purple and scattered with a handful of diamondlike stars, just as it had been in the opening sequence of *Tolemac Wars*. There were no familiar constellations to tell her where she was.

Maggie stood in the clearing and stared at the same far peak that opened the game. Its jagged summit pierced the purple heavens, and off to one side, four greenish-blue orbs, not quite as magnificent as Kered's eyes, traced a straight line. Tears blurred her vision for a moment. Wherever she was, it was not home. Gwen and Ocean City might still exist, but where? She thought of her parents, her brothers, and fought a lump swelling in her throat.

Maggie sought a shadow and was glad she'd been a Girl Scout. She used a broad leaf for toilet paper and hoped it was not the Tolemac version of poison ivy. She stumbled along the path to the hut. Its candlelit windows called like home, but she turned her back. For many moments she examined the far stretching panorama of land, much like a wasteland, looking for some hint of humanity, some possible sign of habitation.

There was nothing as far as the eye could see. Standing upon a green and flowered and tree-shaded mountain, her eyes searched a plain as dry and barren and rocky as the Painted Desert of Arizona. On the distant horizon she could see white. The ice fields?

Should she hide tomorrow when Kered wished to leave? Would he force her to go on his quest—drag her if she refused? Part of her wanted to stay on Nilrem's mountain and hoped that whatever technological glitch had sent her to Tolemac would be corrected. Perhaps like an e-mail message gone astray, she had been divided up into bits or bytes, or mits or mites, or whatever they were called, and accidentally sent to this place. And just like an e-mail message, perhaps she could be retrieved, unsent, returned home.

Another part of her suspected the wise man spoke the truth when he said her appearance at the conjunction, just when Kered needed help, was an omen. Her Native American background made her open to the idea of spirits and portents. Her Navajo grandmother spoke often of heeding omens.

Maggie's shoulders sagged in weary resignation, and she rubbed her temples against the throbbing headache growing along with her fatigue. She dashed away a tear. Crying changed nothing, yet she knew it would be difficult to survive in this barren land alone, hiding from Kered and Nilrem. Should she follow the warrior and possibly discover the reason she had landed in Tolemac?

Strong hands took her shoulders and turned her. Maggie let Kered draw her against his chest. She hiccuped and choked back her fear and worry.

"Do you miss him so?" Kered asked.

"Him?" She pulled away.

Kered's grip bit into her arms. "The one to whom you belong?" Then his hands abruptly gentled. "Or did he hurt you so badly you had no choice but to flee?" His hands swept up and down her bare arms, knocking the cloak from her shoulders. The cold mountain air chilled her skin and contrasted with the warm palms soothing and stroking her.

Maggie slapped his hands away. "Hear this once more! I'm not a slave. I'm not running from anyone. I'm just lost. I hit my head. I don't know you or this place. I have no idea where I am or who you are!"

He crossed his massive arms. "Finally. The truth."

"The truth?" Maggie stuttered.

"Yes. You remember nothing, save your name. You most assuredly are a slave. I accept that you remember naught of your master, but if you cannot remember, it changes little. Your speech is like to mine, yet different. You slur your words together, but not, I think, from your head wound. You do this from habit. And . . . no arm rings have ever graced this flesh.''

He stroked a finger up her arm, sending sharp shards of sensation shooting from her navel to her groin.

''One may not wear arm rings for very long before they scar the flesh.'' Rolling up his sleeve, Kered twisted at the three silver-hued rings about his right biceps. With great difficulty, he got the narrow bands to edge out of position. The skin beneath them was callused from years of abrasion. He flexed his arm and pushed the rings back into position. ''You see now?''

A red splash of residual sunlight touched him with a fiery glow, making his skin bronze and his hair shine with streaks of copper. Maggie lost the sense of his words. He could be a god and this his Mount Olympus. His physical beauty hypnotized her. Then his demonstration made sense. No matter what she said, her undamaged skin marked her a slave to Kered and any other inhabitant of his world.

Maggie snatched up the cloak and stormed past Kered and into the hut. She wrapped herself in his odiferous cloak and curled into a little ball.

Kered likewise stretched out on the floor by the softly glowing coals of Nilrem's hearth.

''I'm not a slave!'' she whispered into the near darkness before turning her back on the warrior and his reality.

For what seemed hours she lay in stiff defiance of what her sense and senses told her. The low rumble of snores rose and fell unchanging through the night. She could not wait any longer.

She slipped from the bed. Only the soft whisper of Kered's cloak on the floor marked her progress to the door. She snagged Kered's pack from a hook and eased up the latch, gritting her teeth at the small snicking sound it made. Neither man stirred.

An icy breeze whistled around the corner of the hut, clawing at the cloak's edges. Maggie hugged them to her as she ran into the shelter of the woods, pelting down the slope of Nilrem's mountain. Her head began to pound in rhythm with her hammering heartbeat.

Kered's pack weighed a ton. She paused briefly, set it down, and opened it. On top lay the game gun. The gun represented a deadly menace in Kered's hands. She took it and a heel of bread. The bread would hold hunger at bay until Kered left on his quest, for Maggie had made her decision. She would hide from the warrior until he was gone, then explain her dilemma to Nilrem. No matter how long it took for Gwen to end the game or bring her back, she would wait. Quest or no quest, good omen or bad, no man would force her into slavery!

Maggie dragged some brush over Kered's pack. She ran and stumbled on a small stone, falling hard on one knee.

"Damn," she muttered. She rose and limped along. The trees grew dense and filtered the near-dawn light, making her progress laborious. Fresh pine and the light scent of rain-dampened earth rose with every step. The wind blew the boughs about her, misting her with drops of moisture. She prayed that her sense of direction would not fail her and that she could find her way back. Her steps slowed as the slope grew steeper and more stony. Behind her she heard something crashing through the underbrush.

*Kered.*

Panic raised her heartbeat to thundering and she put on a burst of speed, madly slipping and stumbling on the precipitous slope. She chanced a glance over her shoulder and glimpsed white through the shadowy reaches behind her. "No," she whispered, falling and going down on her side, then rising and grabbing a branch to steady herself. A whoosh of sound from behind her made her duck and scream.

A blur of white swept over her. "My God!" she shrieked, as a white deer, the size of a small horse, leaped over her huddled figure. His snowy antlers stretched an arm-span wide, snagging branches and showering her with pine needles. Just as suddenly as the deer had appeared, it vanished. Only the continuing snap of small branches and showers of stone marked its passage.

"Honestly, Maggie. Get a grip! It's just a deer," she chastised herself. Brushing her hands on her dress, she stood up straight and took a deep breath, then shook pine needles from her bandaged head. "The bread!" she muttered, searching about on the ground with her hands. The dawn did not penetrate here beneath the trees, and every stone could have been the chunk of bread. She knelt and began a systematic search. Finally, her hands touched a smooth, rounded shape.

"No!" she cried, looking up the long length of Kered's leg, past his endless torso, to his face hidden in the shadows.

"Lost something?" He dropped his pack with a thud beside her.

"No, no. Nothing," she said, her hand on her racing heart. The damn man had tracked her like a scout from a 1950s' cowboy movie.

He grasped the cloak and hauled her to her feet, heedless of the low branches. "You wished to make an early start upon the quest?" His words were mild, but clipped and spoken so softly, she needed to strain to hear them.

51

"Yes. That's it. I thought I'd get an early start."

"Or," he continued as if she had not spoken, "perhaps you have seen your folly and wish to return home to your master."

"That's it. I really want to go home," she croaked in desperation as his fist tightened on the cloak, forming a noose about her throat.

His voice rose to a near roar. "Then we go in the same direction. Let me offer you my services as escort!"

He bent and tossed her over his shoulder. As he swung about, she caught the scent of something putrid.

Then she saw it.

Leering eyes and a snarling mouth hung like a Cheshire cat grin from the shadows, so close she could almost feel the whisper of its fetid breath. Kered sensed it, too, turned, and dropped her. His sword sang from his scabbard as the thing pounced.

# *Chapter Four*

Maggie shrieked. Pain streaked up her jolted spine and into her head.

Kered dropped his sword inches from Maggie's feet. He snatched two handfuls of the beast's ruff and heaved it from side to side.

"Gulap!" Kered shouted. "You malodorous fiend."

They lunged into the shadows, tugging and pulling in a playful game of *Who's Stronger*? The creature, a cross between a leopard and a . . . Maggie had no idea what to call it—swamp thing seemed somehow appropriate—batted Kered's arms and howled. The two rolled like puppies down the hill, gathering twigs and leaves and sending small stones and sticks flying.

Maggie staggered to her feet and considered sneaking off. Kered's pack stood unattended. She wondered as she peered after them if he would impale himself on the ridiculously long knife strapped to his thigh. The thought of the first aid that might entail made her chew her nails in nervous agitation.

The combatants rolled to a halt in a sprawled pile of legs and paws.

"Come," Kered cried up at her, rising, and drawing in great gasps of air. He patted the animal on its black, spotted flank with one hand as he gestured to her with the other.

"No," she called. "Not a chance!" She backed against a tree trunk, distancing herself from the animal.

Kered bent and seemed to confer with the beast before climbing up the hill at breathtaking speed. "Surely, you are not going to be difficult?" Behind him stalked the stinking beast as if Kered were dinner and she dessert.

"That thing looks like it intends to eat you." She gulped.

Kered whirled on the beast and snarled. The "cat" retreated a few steps and clawed the air. "Stay, Gulap," he ordered. " 'Tis simple to see you terrify this slave. Nilrem will spit you and roast you should you harm one hair on her head."

Maggie, breathing through her mouth to avoid the animal's noxious odor, could see that the animal was indeed from the cat family. It weighed far more than any tiger in a zoo, and most assuredly, it was tame, for as Kered spoke, it sat back on its haunches and seemed to nod in agreement.

"Now. An explanation of your behavior." Kered crossed his arms over his chest. He might have looked forbidding except for the twigs in his hair and a leaf stuck to his cheek. The dawning light that pierced the trees bathed him in a warm glow.

Maggie mentally girded her loins. "I can't go with you. I might not remember all about my circumstances

. . . but something within me says I should remain here."

He studied her for a moment, then bent and retrieved his discarded sword, sheathing it in one smooth motion. He dropped one hand to the hilt and let the other hang loose at his side. His relaxed pose calmed her. "I see. You regret leaving your master."

"Honestly," she muttered, then smiled. *If you can't beat 'em, join 'em.* "If that's what you choose to think."

"Perhaps we may reach a compromise."

"I thought warriors only used force!"

"We warriors are occasionally known to see reason." He grinned boyishly.

Oh, dear, she thought. If he was going to be reasonable and smile like that, she'd probably agree to go along on his quest, offer to carry his pack, or maybe shine his sword.

Behind him, with tiny subtle movements, the cat edged closer, claws unsheathed.

"I believe Nilrem is correct. You must accompany me. Whatever meaning these events have, Nilrem thinks you necessary. What if we strike a bargain?"

The cat stretched and licked a paw with a studied nonchalance. Maggie kept one eye on the feline as she listened.

"You will accompany me on my quest. You will offer assistance in whatever way I deem necessary—"

"Where's the compromise?" She snorted.

The cat rolled over to its back and yawned, stretching out and pawing the air in Kered's direction.

"You interrupt. Did your mother not teach you manners?"

He had an excellent memory and used it! "I'm sorry, continue," she directed, properly chastised.

The cat rolled again, moving closer to Kered's boots, fangs bared.

"As I was saying, you will accompany me and make yourself useful, and I will return you to Nilrem's mountain at the first possible opportunity."

Maggie considered the proposition. The cat put its head on its paws and used its back legs to inch ever nearer.

"Consider, too," he continued, "this land is barren. To cross on your own would be foolhardy. To move beyond the ice fields, impossible."

"Kered!" she cried, pointing behind him as the cat nearly hooked the warrior's boots from under him.

He whirled and smacked the Gulap on the nose. "Foolish trick!" he chastised, then captured Maggie's hand. "Come. See how useful you have already proven to be. Gulap will need to seek some other prey." Grinning, he hefted his pack and moved with his now-familiar grace down the mountainside, hauling her behind him. The cat howled and screeched as if bereft at the loss of their company, but luckily did not try to follow.

"What's a Gulap?" she panted.

"Gulap? A canny beast. His name is from the Selaw, meaning claw."

"Appropriate! Is it coming with us?" she asked, stumbling after him, unable to do anything else with his tight grip on her wrist. Now that she'd seen at least one creature from the mountains, the idea of wandering or hiding there alone made her hair stand on end.

Kered laughed and shook his head. "No. His prey is on this mountain and his master, too."

"What's his prey?" she asked, peering over her shoulder.

"The white hart and hind," he answered, "and foolish folk who wander unsuspecting about these hills."

Maggie shivered and thought of snow-white Bambis being torn limb from limb. "Who's his master?" Her foot slipped and she found herself skidding on her rear. Kered turned and waited until she had righted herself and brushed off her dress.

"Gulap is his own master. Yet, if any man may command him,'twould be Nilrem. The beast wanders where he will, but I have not known him to stray much beyond Nilrem's Hart Fell." With that, Kered let go of her arm. He turned away, leading now, not dragging her.

She decided to accept the subtle change in status until something else occurred to her—something that didn't involve becoming lunch to fantastical cats with periodontal problems.

With great difficulty, she kept pace with the warrior. It did not take much imagination to calculate the speed with which he would move on a flat surface.

Maggie watched the change of crimson light as the trees thinned on the lower slopes. Hart Fell had a gentle declivity as they approached the barren stretches of plain. Taking a quick breather, Maggie leaned on the trunk of a kind of fir tree she didn't recognize. She reached down to pick up a large cone from the ground.

Where her head had been, an arrow quivered in the wood. Stunned, she stared at the trembling shaft.

Kered snatched her down. She found herself pressed face to the dirt. A hail of arrows thunked in quick succession over their heads.

"Be silent. Do not move," Kered whispered.

The heavy weight of his body made compliance inevitable. She dug her fingers deep into the cushion of pine needles and said a quick prayer, closing her eyes tightly.

Kered crushed Maggie flat. She heard the sound of his blade being drawn. Maggie only needed to hear the sound a second time to know it was permanently etched in her mind.

"Wartmen. I will return," he whispered into her ear. His weight shifted and cold air caressed her legs where her skirt had ridden up. Maggie begged him to stay, but the muttered words met empty forest air. Kered dodged among the trees.

A bloodcurdling cry sent a shiver down her spine. She had to know what was happening. Cautiously, she risked a peek and raised her eyebrows. Nothing stirred. With even greater caution, she lifted her chin, and like a groundhog in February, she looked about.

Long legs wrapped in dirty fur leaped over her. Longer legs encased in familiar leather followed, stomping down inches from her fingers. She yelped and scrambled to her knees.

The expression on the wart-and-dirt-encrusted face of Kered's opponent made her pray even harder. His gaping mouth and stumps of blackened teeth grinned with a wicked glee. The condition of his hair made Kered's tangles look merely wind tossed. Maggie could guess her fate should Kered be wounded.

Kered's smile was no less deadly than the Wartman's. The blades the men held and the concentration on their faces told Maggie whoever made a misstep was dead. With a subtle shifting of feet and hands, Kered placed himself between her and the enemy.

Kered's adversary flicked a glance in Maggie's direction. It was all Kered needed. He lunged forward and the man fell to his knees, his hand to his breast. Blood seeped between his fingers to soak the long gray tunic he wore. A bubble of blood rose to his cracked lips, and he fell forward and lay still.

Maggie reared back on her heels, her hand to her heaving chest. Kered grabbed her arm and hauled her to her feet. He drew her behind a dense deadfall. " 'Tis not over. There are three more."

"How do you know?" Maggie hissed. His fingers held her tightly as if she might run away.

"The arrows." He nodded to the tree where Maggie had been standing. "Each is fletched with different feathers."

"What will we do?" Maggie asked, frightened at the odds of three to two, or realistically, three enemies to one useful fighter. Perhaps she could improve their odds. "Should we try my gun?"

Kered studied her in the brightening light, and she became conscious of her vulnerability in his primitive world. "How far from the foe may we use it?" he asked.

Maggie bit her lip. "I don't know," she whispered. Another arrow hissed overhead to be lost harmlessly in the woods.

"Then we will stay with what I know and hold the magic for after we have tested it," he said. "I know the power of my own weapons. Stay," he ordered. Crouching low, he crept to the pack he'd dropped to the ground. In a moment he was back, just reaching the safety of the deadfall before yet another arrow whizzed by.

"They are not close. A man may shoot such an arrow for many yards," Kered instructed as he opened his pack, sounding to Maggie's ears like a pedantic English professor. "This should do nicely." He opened a suede pouch and withdrew a bouquet of eight-pointed stars. Hammered of a shiny metal, each edge was viciously honed. "Now to draw them out," he whispered. He grasped a low branch and set it to trembling.

A flash of yellow between the trees caught Maggie's eye. She flinched as Kered threw his star with a powerful flick of his wrist. A man's cry testified to Kered's accuracy.

They played a deadly game of hide and seek. Kered moved with a silence uncanny for one his size. Maggie tried in vain to move with stealth, but each twig she stepped on seemed determined to announce her presence.

The blur of Kered's throw came twice more. Each yelp made Maggie cringe. They saw a trail of thick bloody drops on dried pine needles. Each arrow they came to, Kered dislodged and snapped in two. "Why not leave them?" Maggie asked as they stalked after the bleeding enemy.

"And have them used again? Possibly planted in our backs?" Kered looked at her as if she were stupid.

"Or," she continued, determined not to let him think her completely ignorant, "or, use them yourself?"

Kered stared at her then turned away, a sheepish look upon his face. Maggie had to strain to hear his words. "I am not very accurate with the bow," he whispered, as if embarrassed by this admission of weakness. "I specialized in blades."

"Great," Maggie muttered. "I would end up with someone who needs to be up *close* to kill the enemy." Her words stopped her cold. *Kill the enemy*. She had said kill. Violence in her world was to be abhorred and avoided. Violence in his world was commonplace, and she had been accepting it far too easily. She swallowed down bile.

They came to the edge of the tree-lined slope. Kered

pointed straight ahead. "There lies the route we must take to begin our quest to the Sacred Pool. 'Tis blocked by at least one able man. I may have only wounded the other two," he stated, using a stick to indicate a confusion of footprints and bloody splotches on the ground. "If they can wield their bows from those rocks, they may hold us here past any hope of making this quest."

Maggie studied the forbidding landscape stretched beyond the rocks sheltering the Wartmen. The red surface of cracked and parched earth looked impossible to cross under any circumstances. Their sylvan shelter seemed friendlier with every moment. "Why not go up the mountain and come down somewhere else?" she asked.

"The Forbidden Isle, wherein lies the cup of Liarg, is only accessible by land on one occasion. If we do not take the most direct route, we will miss the timely turning of the tides," he snarled. "Equally, I have no wish to wait upon Hart Fell for another conjunction to come and go."

"I see." Maggie knew that Kered had only a few stars left. The thought that he might have to get close enough to the Wartmen to use a sword or knife made her mouth dry and her underarms wet. "How dangerous are those Wartpeople?"

"War*men*. They are known for their canny use of the bow and a propensity to gnaw upon the bones of their victims."

Maggie stared at him in disbelief.

Kered warmed to his subject, resting back on his haunches. "The warts are a disease from mating with their kin. Their dirty habits have expelled them from every chiefdom and thus, they have no choice but to prey upon unwary travelers." He picked up a star and it glinted in the morning sun that now bathed the parched landscape.

Trying not to retch, Maggie decided to risk offending his masculine pride. "Perhaps we should use this opportunity to test my weapon. You know, make that rock they're hiding behind disappear?" She waited for his reaction.

Kered turned and looked at her with quiet speculation. "The weapon can do that? Make their shelter disappear?"

Maggie chewed her lip. "I'm not sure. We can try, can't we?" At least he hadn't resisted outright. She watched myriad emotions cross his face.

"A good commander values even the smallest contribution of the standard bearer," he said, grinning and digging her gun from his pack. "Make the stone disappear."

Maggie took the gun. With a silent prayer, she braced herself against the bole of the tree. Her arms trembled as she sighted down the short barrel of the game gun.

She fired on blue.

The rock disappeared. Three Wartmen stared about in astonishment. Kered rose, a star at the ready.

He never threw it. A blur of black leaped over the crouching men. A confusing pile of Wartmen and Gulap stayed his hand. Blood sprayed and splattered on the dirt like a light rain.

Maggie gagged. The gun fell from her limp fingers.

# Chapter Five

Maggie looked over her shoulder again and again. She couldn't help it. No matter what Kered had told her, she kept expecting the Gulap to come bounding up, a bloody Wartman's hand dangling from its mouth.

Despite the blistering heat and blazing red sun in the purple sky, Kered's easy acceptance of the grizzly end of the Wartmen chilled her blood. His practical retrieval of his stars sickened her. It had taken grim determination to walk past the Gulap's feast and follow Kered to this stark plain.

Red dust matted the hem of her dress and rose in swirls around her ankles. Her lower legs were thick with it and her shoes were unrecognizable as black suede flats.

She paused. Ahead of her loomed jagged, red-striated mountains that reminded her of the buttes of Monument Valley. The air had a similar dry scent. There appeared to be no way up the mountains and no safe way down. Unless, of course, you sprouted wings and took flight like the blue-hued hawks that occasionally soared overhead, cawing an eerie cry into the silent landscape.

Behind her were the more rounded and softer peaks of Nilrem's Hart Fell. The gentle slopes, green with coniferous trees, struck a sharp contrasting chord to the sights before her. Yet she now knew that even that placid landscape, scented with fresh pine and delicate white wildflowers, harbored denizens more frightening than any from her imagination.

Nilrem's world retreated with every step. Their goal, the jagged red mountain before her, scarcely seemed any closer, the cave they sought for the night no nearer.

Comfortable with the long distances and monochromatic views of her parent's home in the Southwest, Maggie judged the distance as more than they could travel before the sun set. Of course, who really knew how long that ugly red orb took to orbit this Tolemac earth? Perhaps they had days of sunlight left, or minutes. She dropped her pendant into her neckline to still its annoying thumping against her chest.

Kered marched at a relentless pace. He never looked back and never spoke. Wasn't he thirsty? Wasn't he hot? His fur-lined cloak was an incongruous outfit for this desertlike environment.

From the warrior's conversation with Nilrem, Maggie knew Kered needed to earn two arm rings to sit on the Tolemac council and try to negotiate peace. Would it make that much difference to his quest if they made a pit stop or two?

Maggie swallowed against the dryness of her throat. Her mouth tasted like an old boot, or worse—like the sweat in an old boot. She wanted her toothbrush.

She frowned at Kered's large footprints stretching out before her. He needed a lifemate. One with power. What woman would want such an inconsiderate man? Maggie played a game, leaping from one footprint to the other to stem the boredom and divert her mind from her physical discomforts. Long ago, she had read somewhere about judging a person's height from his stride. She was five-feet-nine-inches and she came to Kered's armpit. That made the warrior six-foot-seven-or-eight. Taking a final hop and stomping one of his footprints to dust, she halted.

Kered marched at least fifty yards before he realized Maggie wasn't following. Turning back, he waited. She waited. With an audible sigh of resignation, he strode back to her.

"What is the problem?" He made no attempt to temper his impatience. "Darkness is falling. All manner of creatures walk the night. Surely you understand that now?"

Maggie darted nervous glances about the vast, wasted landscape. "I need to go to the bathroom!"

"You require a bath?" he roared. "Here? Now?"

"No." Maggie's voice rose to join his shouts. "I don't require a bath. Don't you have to go?"

"Go? I have been going. You are the one standing still!" he bellowed, slamming his pack to the ground and flinging off his cloak.

Maggie danced in place. Stress gave an edge to her voice. "You are the most vile cur. You have no manners despite your snotty-sounding speech. You have no consideration for women. We have been marching along for hours. Don't you have to-to-to answer a call of nature?"

Kered became aware of her fidgeting, her flushed face. He moved closer, fascinated by the change of color on her cheeks. He almost reached out and touched her, but restrained himself. Then understanding dawned.

"I see. You are a slave." He crossed his arms on his chest and nodded sagely.

"What does that have to do with this?" Maggie snarled.

"Slaves never reach the seventh level of awareness. More proof."

Maggie gritted her teeth. "What is the seventh level of awareness?"

"It is a level of control over one's mind and body. I can control those needs until a more appropriate place and time. Slaves never care to take the time to learn such control. Women slaves especially."

Maggie twisted her hands in her skirts as her need became urgent. "Look. We could argue—"

"I do not argue with slaves."

"—but I need to go now!"

"I will turn my back. 'Tis the best I can offer."

At that moment, Maggie really didn't care if he watched. She motioned for him to turn around.

A huge grin lit his face. At any other time, Maggie would have been felled by the effect. The damn man had dimples—two—symmetrically placed, of course!

Kered shouldered his pack and strode off across the dusty plain. Maggie somehow knew he would not look back. When she was finished, she ran to catch up with him. Breathing hard, she passed him, turned, and jogged backward for a moment. He arched a brow at her, but continued his relentless pace.

"What's your hurry?" Maggie asked.

"Get behind me, slave."

"Cur."

"My name is Kered. Diminution of a name is disrespectful—punishable by flogging."

Maggie stopped moving, fisted her hands on her hips, and began to laugh.

Kered halted. His swift pace carried him past her and he needed to turn back. She bent at the waist and laughed harder.

"What amuses you so?" He strode back to her, his voice rising again to a shout.

"I wasn't shortening your name! I was calling you a cur. C-U-R."

"What is a cur, pray tell?" he asked, puzzled, dropping his pack once more and raising a cloud of dust.

"A mangy, mean-spirited, ill-bred mutt!" Maggie spat out.

Kered slapped the sleeve that concealed his arm rings. "I am far from ill-bred."

"Ah, hah! So you admit, at least, that you are mean-spirited and mangy!"

"I am not . . . any of those things," he sputtered. "We have no time for this, slave." Kered swept a hand to the heavens. "The sun will set, and you do not wish to be here on The Scorched Plain when darkness falls."

A prickle of fear crept down Maggie's spine. *The Scorched Plain*. She nodded and gestured him onward. He bent to pick up his pack, but paused.

"Your feet." He knelt by her and lifted her right foot, his fingers skimming over the delicate black shoe, a frown creasing his otherwise perfect skin.

Teetering and off-balance, Maggie grabbed his shoulders. Rock slabs. Mesas of shoulders.

"Sit," he ordered.

Maggie sat. She had little choice with one foot aloft

67

and him twisting it in the air. Flailing her arms, she fell on her rear. "Yikes."

Kered drew his knife from the leather scabbard strapped to his thigh, and Maggie gulped back any other thought of chastising him for his treatment. The blade had a small dark splotch staining it on the hilt, an ugly reminder of his knife fight. In one swift movement, Kered sliced a wide strip from his cloak. He sheathed his knife and searched through his pack. The object he withdrew resembled an awl.

Maggie's mouth gaped as Kered folded himself into a cross-legged posture. He poked holes and slashed at the fur-lined strip, cutting it into two pieces. Occasionally he held the strips of cloak up for inspection, moving them close to his face and then holding them away at arm's length, scowling and muttering inarticulately as he worked. "Come here," he said finally.

"Please? Oh, never mind." Maggie scooted close to him. She stared down at his handiwork.

"Foot." Kered turned a hand palm up to her. She slapped her dirty shoe into his waiting hand, like a nurse assisting a surgeon. He clamped his fingers tightly about her ankle.

"Yow!" Maggie gasped at the strength of his grip.

Kered wrapped the strip of cloak about her shoe and then used a curved hook from his pack to thread a leather thong through the holes he'd punched along the edge. He squinted with displeasure all the while.

When he had finished and placed her foot in the red dust, she wore a furry boot. She offered her left foot and he swiftly secured the second strip of cloak.

He rose to his full height and stuffed his tools into the pack. Slinging it over his shoulder, he began to march away.

Maggie ran up to his side. "Thank you, Kered. These shoes are for dancing, not marching. My feet were killing me."

"Fourth level of awareness," he snorted, staring straight ahead.

"Fourth level? Gee, foot discomfort takes a lot of awareness to overcome, doesn't it?"

"No, the fourth level of awareness is when you learn to admit to weakness and seek solutions."

"How humiliating," Maggie murmured as she fell into step behind him, placing her furry boots in his footprints. "Cur." She stuck her tongue out at his back and determined not to say another word to him.

Darkness fell with no warning. The wind rose, swirling cold streams of air up her skirt as she plodded along. Every muscle in her body ached and her nose itched. Her shoulders drooped. They'd reached the mountain range at least an hour before and had been walking parallel to its base. Except for its color, Maggie was reminded of a string of Devil's Towers, marching arm in arm, as far as the eye could see.

"There." Kered pointed to a dark shadow fifteen or twenty yards over their heads.

"How do we get up?" Maggie tipped her head back and gulped at the sheer, ragged wall of rock.

Kered ignored her question and strapped his pack to her back. "Climb on." He turned away and went down on one knee.

Without thinking about what he intended, Maggie threw her arms around his neck and wrapped her legs about his waist. He leaped against the rock face.

She screamed all the way to the cave, in his ear, long and loud. He climbed with little pause to search for handholds or footholds, just seemed to cling to the rock and scramble up and up.

When he set her down at the cave's mouth, she collapsed in shock. "Stop grinning, you arrogant—" She swatted away his proffered hand. "I can get up on my own. Next time, warn me before you do something so dangerous. I need to say my prayers before I die! Who taught you that? Spiderman?"

"Spiderman? You babble nonsense." He shook his head and disappeared into the black interior of the cave.

It was almost as dark inside the cave as it was outside. She staggered to her feet silently and nervously. Where was he? He moved so quietly that it was as if he had vanished into thin air. Goosebumps broke out on her arms, and she rubbed them briskly to warm herself.

Kered stepped from the shadows. "Come." He paused and gripped her arm. "What is this? A disease?"

Maggie shook her head. "No, it's called goosebumps. I'm cold. Don't worry, it's not catching."

"Hm." He turned her arm over, holding it away and turning it back and forth. " 'Tis strange. Most strange." He dropped her arm, then moved swiftly into the cave.

Eagerly she followed him, snatching at his cloak and hanging on so he didn't get away this time. They wove through the silent black cave. He seemed to navigate easily despite the lack of light. Probably the fifth level of awareness, she thought, seeing in the dark, ignoring the possibilities of creatures in corners. Maggie thought of spiders and bats and bears, not to mention Gulaps and Wartmen. She grabbed bigger handfuls of his cloak and ran up his heels.

The path jogged left, then right, and emerged into a small rock chamber lit with a dim glow from an aperture overhead. Maggie stepped near the opening and peered up into the indigo sky. The four orbs of the conjunction, slightly off-kilter now, shone brightly. Their combined light just about equaled that of a quarter moon. At her feet lay a ring of small stones. The scent of charcoal embers still lingered about the long-extinguished fire.

"Sit here while I gather firewood."

"Wood? Where will you get wood?" Maggie looked about the barren chamber.

"I have stored a supply farther along the path." He gestured into the shadows and when Maggie nodded, he vanished again.

Maggie remained rooted to her spot until he returned, arms laden with short thick logs and small twigs. He stacked them neatly and reached into his pack, removing a flint. He struck a spark and held it to several small sticks. They caught immediately, and he fed twigs to the flames, gently breathing them into life.

"Tend the fire," he ordered and rose, dusting off his hands.

"Where are you going? Don't leave." Maggie didn't want him out of her sight again. The cave echoed and his brief journey to get wood had made her feel vulnerable. "Don't leave me," she repeated, ashamed of her pleading tone.

Kered grinned. "You would not want to accompany me, I think."

"Sure I would," she said, smiling back. "The fire will be fine."

"It is now time for one who has attained the seventh level of awareness to tend those needs of nature of which we spoke."

"Oh." Maggie gestured him off. "Shoo. Come back soon."

Without another word, he blended into the darkness

in the direction of the entrance. Maggie crouched by the fire. As her wait lengthened, she became aware of aching muscles. Her headache had returned, and she unwound her bandages and used her hands to comb through her hair. Gently, she probed the lump at the back of her head. Satisfied that it hurt no more than when Nilrem first bandaged it, she carefully folded the clean cloth and stowed it in Kered's pack. There was no blood visible on the cloth, and she had been taught to waste nothing.

Nilrem. Furtively, she pinched her arm. Still awake.

Dream? Game? Real life? The here and now were Kered and his quest. Should she have stayed on the mountain? No. Kered could protect her and Nilrem could not. There were no guarantees that another storm would send her home. Whoever this Samoht was, he sounded vicious and likely to return, for he, too, sought Nilrem's wisdom. Too many unknown dangers lurked about this world. She faced the glaring need for warriors.

The decision to go felt right. A peace descended and her stomach knots eased. The warrior's obvious strength was like a magnet, and she was the iron filings. She intended to stick to him. She didn't know why, only that it seemed right to do so.

Kered watched Maggie for several moments before entering the chamber. Besides taking care of his personal needs, he had dragged a supply of brush across the entranceway, a supply he had stored in a side chamber on his journey out to Nilrem. His breath caught in his throat as Maggie's hair fell down her back. The bandage had concealed its beauty. His hands itched to gather it up and hold it against his cheek. Soft it would be, he was sure, and clean—and scented with flowers, strange flowers with an erotic scent he did not recognize. A pleasure slave's scent. Only pleasure slaves danced. And only for their master's enjoyment.

*Maggie's shoes were fashioned for dancing.*

Carrying her on his back to the cave had been a torture with her warm legs about his waist and her sleek arms encircling his neck. Carrying her had proved his inadequate attainment of sensual control. Granted, warriors had no need to temper their lusts, but some discipline was necessary so one did not approach battle with important equipment unsheathed. He laughed at the thought and Maggie spun around, her hair swirling about her shoulders. His loins tightened. So much for sheathing one's sword, he thought, and sank to the ground before her.

"Food?" he asked.

"Sure. Any pizza in there?" she quipped as he rummaged in his pack.

"Pizza? What is pizza?" Kered handed her a thick wedge of brown bread.

"Pizza is a food from . . . my place." Maggie sniffed the bread, then gnawed on the chewy crust. "Hm, good, kind of a nutty taste," she said between bites.

"Water?" He held out a gourd stoppered with a wooden plug.

She nodded. When he pulled the plug she drank sparingly, wiping her chin on the back of her hand. "Thank you, Ker."

The flames leapt to consume the small sticks he fed them. His face remained impassive, but his words betrayed his curiosity. "What is a . . . cur, a mutt?"

Maggie sighed. "A mutt is a four-legged animal, a dog, from my place. It is a tamed animal, furry, a pet."

He smiled warmly. "We have dogs and pets in Tolemac. Not such a bad thing to be."

Maggie snorted in an exasperated manner.

"In what way am I mean-spirited? Mangy?" He continued to pursue the subject, poking at the fire with a stick in studied nonchalance.

She considered his smile. "I guess the truth should be okay for someone who's reached the seventh level of awareness. You treat me with contempt, without knowing if I am worthy of that contempt. It so happens I'm a well-respected metalsmith in . . . my place."

He shook his head in disbelief. "Only men work metal."

*What was the point?* But she tried again. "I assume you hold all manner of people without your beloved arm rings to be less than you. Where I come from, all men and women are created equal. In practice, many are not treated so, but still, we try."

"Men and women are not equal in Tolemac."

"No kidding," she muttered, picking at a ragged nail and wishing for a manicure.

"It is not possible for men and women to be equal. You could not best me in a fight. Want to try?"

Maggie looked up. He grinned, exposing his strong white teeth, and Maggie found herself grinning, too. "No, I don't want to try. And I'm not referring to physical equality. I'm talking about equality of life, liberty, and pursuit of happiness."

"Happiness?" Kered shook his head. "I am no philosopher. That, thank the wise men, is reserved for the twelfth level of awareness."

They sat in silence. Warmth from the fire began to creep outward to envelop them. Maggie rubbed her arms, realizing how cold she'd become. The stone floor chilled her bottom. She could see Kered's breath on the air.

"How am I mangy?" he persisted.

Maggie studied him. "Your hair. When was the last time you brushed it?"

"Brushing my hair is last on my list of priorities!"

"Fine." Maggie drew up her knees and settled her skirt down around her legs, propping her chin on her knees. "Tend to your own mangy locks."

Kered rummaged in his pack and withdrew a brush. It was like the one Maggie's father had on his dresser. It had no handle, but would nestle in one's palm. Kered tossed it to her. She ran her fingers over its dark blue bristles. They were soft and seemed made of a natural substance rather than the plastic she'd expected from the color. She bent her face and sniffed the bristles. They smelled clean and fresh.

Maggie nodded her thanks and began to brush her hair. He stared at her, watched her openly, and her hands grew stiff and her arm motions jerky as his gaze became heated. Stealing a look at him, she saw that his glance had fallen from her hair to her breasts.

"Come here," he said in a low voice.

# Chapter Six

"Why?" Maggie dropped her arms and hugged her chest.

"A slave must do as she is bidden," Kered replied.

"Well, I'm not a slave. If you want to make a request, say please and tell me why," she said, stalling for time.

"Your impertinence is staggering." But if Kered was angry, his soft and seductive tone did not betray it.

"And you're a cur, through and through," Maggie returned.

"Come then, please, and tend my hair."

Maggie stared in disbelief. He had said please! Her palms prickled with sweat. Rising slowly, she walked around the fire. Sinking to her knees behind him, she considered the tangled mass of his long hair. The fire lit it with streaks of gold. Heat crept up her face. When she touched his hair, he shivered.

It took what seemed like forever to remove the tangles. His hair fell soft and silky, thick and heavy over his shoulders. When it was done, she lingered, stroking the brush through the long brown waves.

"Enough." His voice seemed hoarse, almost rough. Maggie snatched back her hands.

"Perhaps you could tie it back?" she finally said into the silence. Maggie looked at the objects he'd spilled out on the stone floor when he'd taken out the brush. One of them was the game gun. She shoved it deep into his pack, then picked up a strip of supple leather, like the thongs he'd used to lace her boots. "What about this?"

Kered turned and looked over his shoulder. He grunted assent and then went back to his contemplation of the flames. Maggie used the brush to stroke his hair into a thick gathering at his nape, wound it with the leather thong, and tied it. She moved back to her place on the opposite side of the fire. The air practically crackled with something she didn't recognize. He exuded a power and warmth that caught at her. It had taken all her self-control not to let her hands drift to his shoulders, his neck, and his arms. Brushing his hair had been an intimate act that had set her blood rushing. Her lips felt puffy, her breasts tender against the soft knit dress.

"We should sleep." Kered stuffed the brush and his other things into his pack.

"Okay." Maggie looked about and sniffed the dry stale air. "How long do you think it will take to reach our destination?"

"Months," he said.

"Months?" she repeated dumbly. "I can't be gone months. My family will be sick with worry."

"Nevertheless, the quest could last for months." He

added several logs to the fire. "Even longer if we miss our sleep and are weary."

Maggie bit her lip. The thought of months away from home churned her stomach.

"There is no going back, only forward."

His words were ominous. She swallowed hard.

"We will rest here." Kered indicated the cloak he'd spread by the fire. He stretched out on his side and propped his head on one hand.

Maggie looked him over. In other circumstances, she would never cross that small space and lie down beside him, but her head ached. She rubbed her hands along her chilled arms to warm them. Even if she could find a way to be sent back home, that home was now months away. Kered looked warm and safe—comforting. She glanced over her shoulder. "Are there any animals in here?"

"Perhaps a snake or two," he said, the pitch of his voice dropping.

"Snakes?" That did it. She approached warily and sat next to him. He swept her down and pulled her against his body.

She lay stiff and frightened as if someone had suddenly starched her. She'd never sleep, she thought, with his body so close, his breath warming her cheek.

Kered smoothed his hand along Maggie's bare arm, raising goosebumps and causing Maggie to shake.

"I will not hurt you," he murmured against her ear. His lips pressed there briefly and his fingers stroked her skin, exploring the raised bumps as if they fascinated him.

*Beware what you wish for!* Maggie squeezed her eyes closed. She remembered many nights wasted wishing for a night with a man such as this. Her blood rushed, and her heart thumped uncomfortably in her chest.

Kered encircled her waist, drawing her even closer.

She couldn't breathe. His hand gently massaged her midriff. With infinite slowness, his hand rose and came to rest beneath her breasts. "Your heart pounds in fear," he whispered against her ear as he lightly skimmed his cheek against her hair.

Maggie clamped her hand to his wrist.

"Sleep, little slave. Sleep." He nuzzled her neck, breathed in her scent, and lowered his hand to her waist.

Maggie didn't move for what seemed like hours after Kered's breathing relaxed. It was less her circumstances that kept her awake than the press of his body against her. His thighs were now cradling hers. His arms were iron hard about her and his scent was a mysterious combination of male sweat and some spicy fragrance she assumed was a soap he used. His breath feathered against her cheek. She no longer feared that she would be cold. She was on fire.

Sometime in the night, Maggie turned. He gathered her in. A feeling, a need to protect, one he had never felt for a woman before, rose and enveloped him. He drew her against his body, a body that needed sleep, but couldn't rest.

Lust rose.

Slaves were made for manly lust, but this one, this woman, was like no slave he had ever met. She made him want to shout and tear his hair in frustration. She made him want to take her. His hand slipped into her thick, black hair. Silky and soft. Exotic. A woman from beyond the ice fields somewhere. She had hit her head, couldn't or wouldn't remember her journey to Nilrem's mountain, but it mattered not a whit. She was a slave, albeit an exotic slave, her worth phenomenal on the auction block.

He drew a knuckle down her cheek. Her skin felt like fine, precious alabaster. He had never seen a being whose skin could change color, and he wondered if the soft skin of her breasts would flush such a beguiling rose when she was aroused. His lips grazed her eyelids. Her breath caressed his cheek and he shivered, his manhood surging to even greater tumescence against her. He shifted uncomfortably.

His resolve was tested—sorely. She must accompany him on his quest. It would not do to slake his lust on her. He had no need of the entanglements of a pleasure slave when lifemating was in his future—and she did not seem amenable. She had trembled in his arms. He would not hurt her, but he sensed she did not believe that. Even in sleep, she lay guarded, not quite coming against him.

He ran a hand lightly along her arm. She murmured in her sleep, and he slipped his palm over her hip and cupped a gently rounded buttock. Her hips shifted against him and he groaned softly. Then her hand fell from her side and dropped between them, the back of her hand pressing against his swollen manhood.

He edged her away, rolled to his feet, and strode from the rock chamber. Carefully, he drew back the brush concealing the entrance and sat down against the cave wall. High in the sky, the waning conjunction shone on the barren landscape. A land without peace. He must remember his priorities—earning arm rings so that he might negotiate peace, not to mention finding a lifemate to enhance his power. Those thoughts kept him awake even more than the beguiling woman asleep by the fire.

# *Chapter Seven*

A thrashing, grunting noise startled Maggie awake.

"Ker?" she called. The fire had died and a harsh, heated glare penetrated the opening overhead. Her mouth tasted abominable. The grunting came again, accompanied by more thrashing.

Maggie shoved her feet into her fur-wrapped shoes and crept cautiously along the cave wall. She kept one hand out before her as the light grew dimmer the farther from the chamber she moved.

"Oh, my God!" Maggie cried. The beast crouching over Kered, claws clamped on his biceps, turned red feral eyes on her. It resembled a huge, reddish-brown monkey, but stood twice the size. Long fangs dripped saliva on Kered's chest. Kered took advantage of the beast's distraction to lift a knee and slam it into the creature's chest. The beast howled and gnashed at

Kered's throat, but didn't relinquish its brutal grip on his arms.

Kered's arm muscles bulged against his sleeves with the effort he used to hold the creature off. The hooked teeth slashed and Maggie knew they could sever arteries. She turned and ran back to the fire. She ripped Kered's pack open and drew out the game gun. She sped back to the entrance, skidding on the smooth rocky floor. The creature raised a clawed back foot and slammed it into Kered's groin.

She thumbed the blue button.

A scent, like that of an iron left on too long, reached Maggie's nostrils as the beast fell in a heap on Kered's chest.

Maggie held the pistol before her as she warily approached Kered, who lay writhing beneath the stunned beast. She prodded the creature and then wiped her hand on her skirt, for it came away oily. She raised her foot and used all her strength to heave the beast off Kered's body. It fell over the cliff face. When she saw the blood soaking Kered's sleeve, she did not spare a thought for its fate.

Joe and Jason, Maggie's two older brothers, had been hit in the crotch a few times, so Maggie recognized the expression on Kered's face. She stood back and let him breathe. When he'd vomited up what little he'd eaten, she approached. Placing a hand on his arm, she examined his wounds through the torn shirt. "This looks nasty. When you can walk, let's tend it."

Kered growled and let off a string of curses, rolling to his knees. He knelt there for a moment, a hand pressed to his stomach. Maggie gave him a wide berth when he staggered to his feet, a stricken expression on his face.

At their campsite, he dropped to one knee, ignoring

her. From the objects spilled from his pack, he lifted a small leather pouch. "Here. Water. Make a paste." His breath still hitched in his chest.

Maggie nodded and silently did as he directed. Lacking a bowl and an instrument to stir, she cupped her palm and sprinkled in a little of the powder from the pouch. She wasn't happy with the cleanliness of her hands, but the water could not be wasted. The gourd was almost empty. Maggie dripped some water into the gray powder and used a fingertip to mix a paste. Its pungent odor reminded her of cactus at dawn after a summer storm.

Kered stood up and lifted his shirt over his head. He tossed it to the floor and then sat gingerly at Maggie's side. Carefully, she used a bandage to wipe the blood from the wounds. Ignoring Kered's half-naked body made the effort a trial. He was all bronze skin stretched over well-defined muscles. Buffed to the max, she thought. A workout king, but not overdone with useless, bulky muscles. No, he was perfect. The hair on his chest rose from a narrow swath at his waistband and spread in dark wings across his massive chest. As she applied the salve, his chest muscles bunched and flexed.

"I guess it's a little late to say this, but I think these need stitching."

"Later." Kered gripped Maggie's wrist. "You saved my life. I thank you."

"What was that thing?"

"One of the night creatures. It is unlike me to fall asleep. I failed in my duty to protect you."

Maggie looked at his face. Anguish deepened the lines edging his mouth and creasing his forehead. "You're exhausted, Ker. Did you sleep much last night?"

He looked away. "I have not slept in five days except at Nilrem's hut."

"Five days!" Maggie gasped. "You'll be sick. The body isn't meant to go so long without sleep."

"Is it not?" He raised a dark brow.

"No, it's not. Now lie down. I'll keep watch while you sleep."

"Maggie. We must go. Now."

"What is the point in making this trek to the sacred pool if you arrive so weak that you can't find this blasted knife?"

"Sword. We seek a sword." Kered fell back onto the stone floor and stared up at the rocky ceiling. The blaze of the red sun cast a bloody gleam on his bronzed torso. "I must find the sword—the sword of Leoh's grandfather."

Maggie leaned over him, fussing at his wound, tying the bandages a second time, more neatly now that her hands were steadier. She couldn't resist tucking a few loose strands of his hair back behind his ear. "So much for brushing this mangy mess," she teased.

Kered captured her hand. "You saved my life. I know few slaves who would lift a hand to save their master, let alone a stranger. Your master must have inspired great loyalty in you. I am honored to reap the benefit."

"I saved your life because I had the means." He was so close, his hand so warm. He drew her near and she had to place a palm on his chest to prevent herself from falling over him.

"Your master. Did he teach you to use the weapon?"

Kered's turquoise eyes darkened to the color of a tropical sea. Maggie gulped. Beneath her palm his skin was warm, the hair on his chest soft, his nipple a tight point against her fingertips. Fighting an urge to stroke it, she curled her fingers into her palm.

"It's called shooting and my father taught me. In a

land not unlike this. He would set out bottles as targets. I beat my brothers, Joe and Jason, every time.''

"Father? Brothers? Joe? Jason?" Kered placed his palm over her hand, pressing it against him.

"Yes. I have two brothers. They're thirty-one and twenty-seven. I'm twenty-five." Maggie ground to a halt. He drew her closer, their lips inches apart.

"Slaves have no families." His warm breath bathed her face. His heart thumped slowly beneath her palm.

"Huh?" Maggie lost her train of thought, closed her eyes, and waited as if in suspended animation for what she knew was coming.

His lips were dry and warm. They whispered across hers, brushing lightly in a gentle caress. Maggie sighed. Kered made a low sound in his throat.

Maggie opened her eyes. Kered's eyes drifted closed, depriving her of those gorgeous turquoise pools. She puckered up for another foray into the sensual realm of Kered's mouth when an unmistakable noise issued from his throat.

Snoring!

Maggie gently shifted out of his hold, easing her fingers from his grasp. She draped his cloak over him. He couldn't possibly be comfortable lying bare-backed on a stone floor, but he looked so peaceful, she didn't dare wake him.

Questing warriors needed their beauty sleep.

Fair maidens needed questing warriors at full strength to battle slobbering night creatures and grimy Wartmen. Maggie hoisted the game gun in her hand and crept to the edge of the cave's entrance and peered over, then drew quickly back into the shadows.

Three other beasts were feasting on the one lying supine at the cliff's base. Maggie edged from the entrance, hoping they'd not seen her. Obviously they could climb as well as Kered, and she didn't want to battle three of them. She had no idea how long the gun's charge lasted. It was a miracle it worked here—wherever *here* might be—anyway.

Maggie worried that hidden entrances to the cave made them vulnerable to other carnivorous beasts, so she built up the fire and settled at the opening to their small chamber, the gun held loose and ready in her hand. She kept a silent vigil, rising only to relieve herself and to fetch Kered's shirt for mending. Kered slept the sleep of the dead, never stirring for what seemed hours. Occasionally he groaned or snored, but he never moved.

Maggie rationed herself to staring at him only once each hour. Glad she'd covered him, she shivered at her post. Better cold than torturing herself with the view.

She glanced over her shoulder every few minutes for danger. As night fell again, seeping from red to purple shadows, she kept her eye on the movement of the unfamiliar stars through the ceiling aperture.

There was little point in denying her reality. She was the Shadow Woman in the *Tolemac Wars* poster. Her black hair, her black gown, her bare arms all fit. She was fated to look after the warrior.

After all, Gwen had told her to defend his back. And she would. For during the night she'd dreamt a terrible dream, only to awaken to find Kered under attack.

In her dream, however, it was not some creature who threatened him. No, in her nightmare, Kered knelt naked in opulent surroundings. All the important male parts were foggy and indistinct, but the sensations were sharp and clear. Just as she reached for him in the dream, he was snatched from her arms. Her next memory was the stench of blood. Kered's head hung forward, his chin on his chest, blood dripping from his forehead, his arms, and his chest. The bright red blood ran in narrow rivulets down his beautiful body and pooled at his knees.

In her dream, she had raised the game gun and defended him. There was no remorse in her dream, no regret. Kered's blood slicked the hands that held the gun. The finger that moved with swift assurance to the buttons was as red as the button selected. Whoever hurt him deserved death. His face was hidden, this enemy of Kered's, but in her dream, Maggie had killed him.

Maggie shivered. She would never forget the dream.

Her Navajo grandmother would tell her the dream held meaning.

Maggie agreed.

She must watch over him.

Kered swam to consciousness, groggy from induced visions of battle, starvation, and pain. "Nilrem's knees! How long have I slept?"

"The moons are rising." Maggie pointed overhead.

He settled back on his haunches and stared at her. She sat like a guard on duty and a curious sense of unease took hold that he had surrendered himself to a vulnerable sleep state.

"You have remained thusly? Watching?"

"Yes. Some more of those things were down at the cliff base eating their friend, so I could hardly go shopping, could I?"

"Shopping? What is shopping?"

Maggie laughed as if she knew something he did not. "Shopping is a useless pastime—"

"Like attaining the fourth level of awareness is to slaves?" he interrupted, piqued by her humor.

"Grumpy, aren't we, when we wake up!" Maggie

lifted Kered's shirt from her lap. "I stitched the tear. I'm not much of a seamstress, but it helped pass the time."

He inspected the work. The stitches were clumsy and crooked. A Tolemac child could do better. Yet the fact that she had done the work without an order touched him. "Thank you. It seems I am destined to break all the laws of slavery, thanking a slave three times in one sun rising."

"Don't bust a gut over it." Maggie snatched her hand away. "Now sit down and let's see your wounds."

Kered submitted to Maggie's treatment. He willed himself not to wince as she loosened the bandage crusted to the long slashes.

She gasped. "I can't believe it. This looks almost healed."

He met her eyes. "The herbal is most effective."

She applied fresh bandages and just before he moved away, she placed her hand on his chest.

Kered froze. The gentle touch of her hand on him and his continued fatigue almost made him tremble.

"What's this?" she asked, her finger stroking over the birthmark that lay hidden in his chest hair.

He shook off her hand and pulled his shirt over his head, drawing the laces tight. " 'Tis nothing."

She drew his cloak about her shoulders. Protecting herself from more than cold, he thought, when she rubbed her arms briskly with her hands.

His groin throbbed. He had ceased thinking the ache resulted from the creature's assault and now admitted it was directly related to kissing a pleasure slave. After all, if she was twenty-five conjunctions, she had been giving pleasure for ten of them.

Kered gulped, imagining her skill after ten conjunctions of practice. With predictability, his manhood stirred. Perhaps if he concentrated on repeating the names of his adopted ancestors back to the dawn of time, he could control the ache, just as his awareness master had taught him. But, if he was honest with himself, he was bored with the recitation and happy in a most base manner with his response to the slave.

He frowned. Maggie's wildflower scent tantalized him now, just as it had when he'd carried her in his arms to Nilrem's hut. He had promised her that when the quest was ended, he would return her to Nilrem's mountain. Perhaps by then, she would not want to go. A warmth settled in his chest at the thought. Another thought intruded, driving out the tantalizing warmth.

*Lifemating.*

Shouldering his pack, Kered took Maggie's small hand, and led her along the winding path to the cave entrance. When the quest ended he would have her. That is, *if* her master had not claimed her and *if* he had not lifemated. For a moment Kered contemplated the intricacies of claiming a slave without papers. Registering her would be fraught with difficulties.

Kered turned and faced Maggie. She was frowning at the gun in her hand. "Perhaps that should be in my pack?" he suggested.

"I suppose. I was just worrying about how long it will last. There's no way to recharge it."

"Recharge? How does one recharge? I understand charging. A military tactic. But recharge? Is it a tactic from beyond the ice fields?"

"No, recharge means making sure the weapon is at full power. When it loses that power, it will be useless."

Kered plucked it from her hand. "Useless," he murmured. "We will save it as if it were the last jug of water in this dry land." He tucked it into his pack. "Are you sure it is not magic?"

"Magic? I don't believe in magic." Maggie shook her head, sending her hair tumbling over one shoulder. "Do you?"

He chafed under her scrutiny. "No . . . but strange things happen. For those who believe, those strange things may be seen to be the work of magic, or witchery."

"I'm not a witch," Maggie said softly.

Kered did not sense the presence of evil in this alluring black-haired slave. No evil, just warmth and, perhaps beneath the surface, a smoldering passion. "No, but your weapon could be proof of witchery to others who may have a less practical view of life than I." He swept a hand out to indicate the vast wasteland before them. "The Scorched Plain is often cited by the fearful as proof of strange and curious events at work in our lives."

"How so?" Maggie asked, moving up close beside him and peering over the precipitous edge.

He held her by the back of her cloak and itched to release the scent of flowers by crushing her hair in his fist. "Legend has it that an ancient chief of the Selaw lay with his friend's lifemate. In an ensuing battle, the friend struck the chief in such manner as to—" he fumbled for an inoffensive word—"as to prevent the chief from bearing heirs. With the loss of his virility, the land, too, lost its fertility, withering and wasting to what you see today."

Kered thought of heirs, heirs as unusual as Maggie. Heirs with changeable skin. First the purity of alabaster, then the blush of a new, pink rosebud. His knuckles itched to stroke her cheek or to see if, by a touch, he could raise those tiny bumps of the goose on her arms. He fought the urge. Children begotten of slaves were slaves—not heirs. "The way down is clear. We will continue our journey. Get behind me."

"Back to giving orders, Ker?" Maggie asked, a frown knitting her brows.

"Only one may lead. You, by your paltry size and strength, must follow." He grinned to soften the insult.

"Then lead on." Maggie curtsied to him, her frown vanishing. Then with a trust he sensed came hard to her, she climbed onto his back and wrapped her arms and legs about him.

He descended the cliff, leaping the final few feet in a single bound, and then dumped Maggie to the ground. Without so much as a backward glance, he struck off across the plain, parallel to the mountains. It would not do to allow a slave to become too haughty.

Hours later, Maggie hoped something would eat him. The man set a relentless pace. Her legs ached and her head throbbed. The scenery was beginning to waver before her eyes as fatigue took its toll. She decided not to walk another step. After all, she deserved a rest—saving a life and being a guardian angel took a lot out of a girl. At least if they rested, she could give him a piece of her mind! Why, at the moment, she could rival a Wartman for disgusting dishevelment.

Maggie looked up.

Kered had disappeared.

# Chapter Eight

"Oh, my God!" Maggie ran forward, then backward, then forward, then in circles. "Ker! Damn you, Ker-ed!"

Her voice echoed off the sheer rock face. "You can't just vanish." She whispered prayers and inched slowly forward, sliding her feet cautiously in case a wretched, invisible quicksand had snatched him. Then she saw it, a narrow crevice in the rocky wall. Peering through, she screeched with anger.

Turning sideways, she squeezed through the narrow gap, wondering at his ability to slip like a wraith through the crack. Before her yawned a deep chasm. It opened up on a long valley, verdant and hidden from the Scorched Plain. Kered moved across the valley, several hundred yards away—at the same Kered pace.

Maggie cupped her hands and shouted.

"Ker-ed. Oh, Ker-ed."

He stopped and turned around, then propped his hands

on his hips in what Maggie assumed was impatience. She began to slip and slide down the narrow cut to where he stood like a giant redwood in the green valley. "I suppose you didn't notice a little thing missing—like me?"

"I knew you would come."

"How? You just vanished." She fisted her hand and slugged him on the arm.

He grinned. "You are here, are you not? You found the opening. Striking a warrior is a crime punishable by flogging."

Maggie ignored him, gasping with joy as she saw the herd of horses grazing in the grassy meadow. She ran toward them, then slowed as she neared the closest. They were shaggy beasts standing on huge feet with thick hair about their hooves. Long manes trailed along their necks. Maggie knew horses. These looked like the ancient ancestors of the Clydesdales.

A mottled brown mare lifted her head and whickered at her approach. Maggie stood still a moment and let the mare adjust to her. Then she reached out a hand and stroked the long black mane.

"What charm did you use?" Kered came to her side.

"None," Maggie said as she stroked the horse's neck and murmured words in her ear. "She's a beauty, isn't she? I'm so glad you have horses here."

Kered grunted. "Tolemac may have no curs, but horses we have aplenty."

"Got any dragons?" Maggie teased.

"Of course. They are common as dust."

"Oh, my God! Dragons?" Maggie ran behind Kered and peered from around his arm, searching the horizon, remembering the Gulap from Nilrem's mountain.

93

Ann Lawrence

Kered bellowed with laughter. "Have you no dragons beyond the ice fields?"

"No," Maggie said with a sheepish grin as she slipped away from Kered's protective bulk. "Of course," Maggie's voice dropped, "there was that sixth-grade teacher—"

"You mumble. 'Tis disrespectful."

"Never mind." But Maggie found herself speaking to Kered's back. He strode away, past the horses, to a daub-and-wattle hut nestled beneath a spreading shade tree. He ducked inside and Maggie's curiosity began to gnaw as the time lengthened and he didn't return. She crept up to the hut's doorway.

"Oh, my heaven!" Maggie spun around. She clapped her hands over her face. Kered stood naked, back to the door. Gulping down her embarrassment, she marched back to the horses and moved among them, finding the brown mare and patting her flank. "Wow. You wouldn't believe what I just saw," she whispered. The mare snorted down her nose and tossed her head. "He sure is magnificent." The mare snorted again as if in agreement.

When Kered finally emerged, Maggie gaped in astonishment. He had discarded his rough clothing. His new shirt, a tunic, was of a fabric like fine linen, heavily embroidered in black and gold about the neck and hem. His trousers were supple black leather, as were his boots. The trousers clung to his thighs and hips in what Maggie considered a blatant lack of modesty.

Sheathed at his waist was a long knife. Its engraved hilt echoed the ornate swirls surrounding the gems in the dagger protruding from his boot. He had slung a blue cloak across his shoulders that looked like velvet and was shot with gold thread. As if they weighed nothing, he held a polished leather shield and a gleaming sword in one arm.

Kered ignored Maggie and strode past her to a giant black horse who trotted in their direction. It stood at least nineteen hands. As Maggie watched, the black beauty bumped its head against Kered's shoulder. The two indulged in a childish head-butting routine for a few moments, then Maggie noticed the saddle riding a low branch of a nearby tree. A deep brown leather, embossed with a design like a Celtic interlace, it surely would fit the oversized stallion.

Kered rested his shield and sword by the tree and took up the saddle, laying it over the horse's back with one fluid movement. In moments, the girth and bridle were secured. He returned to the hut for his pack and this he slung over the horse's back. Finally, Kered strapped on the shield and slid the sword into a scabbard that formed part of the saddle. He swung up onto the giant stallion.

"Come." Kered extended his hand. Maggie approached on wary feet. She felt like a homeless person from a subway next to his obvious splendor.

"If we were in such a hurry, why take the time to change?"

"I humbled myself for wisdom. You may not approach a wise man ornamented as if concerned with trifles."

"And now?" Maggie continued to ignore his outstretched hand.

"Now, we seek the sword. It is most important to display one's status to the world. Those who think you poor treat you poorly. Now. Give me your hand."

"Why can't I have my own mount?" Maggie laced her hands behind her back. She reeked of sweat and her legs and skirt hem were grimy with dust. Although she

imagined he'd not bathed, he looked clean and tidy—
even his hair lay neatly bound at his nape.

"Slaves do not have mounts." He slapped his thigh
with his palm and extended his hand.

"I am—"

"Not a slave. So you say. Mount now."

"No. I want my own horse. I ride very well, even
bareback!"

Kered sat in silence and stared down at Maggie. He
was chanting a litany of ancestors to prevent snatching
her onto the saddle.

"Stop swearing!"

"Swearing? I do not swear!" Kered blinked as if in
disbelief.

"Then what are you muttering? Sounds pretty bad to
me."

"I am repeating my father's ancestors' names, in order, back to the beginning of time. Pray I succeed in
reciting the list, else I will most likely throttle you!"
Kered swung his leg over the neck of the horse and
slipped to the ground. Before Maggie could turn away,
he grasped her by the waist and heaved her into the
saddle. Her breath whooshed out and before she could
inhale, Kered had mounted behind her.

The speed with which he galloped down the valley,
at one with the stallion, further stole Maggie's breath.
She could but grip the mane and squeeze with her thighs.

When she became used to the horse's rhythmic gait
and the press of Kered's body against hers, she relaxed
and leaned back. Immediately, Kered wrapped an arm
about her waist and drew her closer. Why not take advantage of his massive chest? Maggie nestled into the
natural space he'd made for her. "What is this boy's
name?" she asked, patting the stallion's neck.

"Windsong."

"A beautiful name," she said.

"Aye. He runs as swift as the sea breezes," he answered. "Still, he is untrained and subject to unruly behavior."

"Why untrained? I'd think an important warrior like you would have the best horse available."

His arm tightened about her waist. "This is the fastest horse available. My usual warhorse fell to a Selaw blade. Windsong will learn his duties soon enough." Windsong sidled momentarily as if to say "We'll see about that." Kered fought the horse's recalcitrant behavior.

Maggie took a peek up at Kered at the same time he looked down at her. Kered growled and bared his perfectly white teeth. She giggled. He grinned and kissed the top of her head. With a sigh, she snuggled back and drifted asleep.

Too soon the ride would end. He did not know what possessed him to deny her a mount. Slaves often rode at their master's side, rarely double with their master. If they had no mount, they walked. Riding double spoke of a familiarity, a favoritism that made him uncomfortable. She rested against him, sure of his protection. Yet, he mused, who had saved whose life the rising before? It boded ill that he had fallen asleep, leaving his little slave unguarded. Then, adding insult to injury, she had saved his life and at the same time witnessed his humiliation.

Kered flexed his fingers against Maggie's waist. How thin she was. Most pleasure slaves were well-rounded, mayhap even overfed to be sure only softness pressed against manly hardness. This slave had a lean muscularity similar to a field slave. Only a poor man took a field slave in pleasure. Even a man of modest wealth would visit a plump fornitrix before availing himself of a common laborer. Yet Maggie had come to him perfumed and garbed in a gown of soft cloth, like silk. Her changeable skin had known no extended hours laboring in the fields.

The perplexity of her condition and her beauty kept Kered happily occupied for several hours. He sniffed a lock of her hair, now dusty. He examined her ears, also dusty. Maggie needed a bathhouse—perhaps after the quest. A long sigh escaped him, waking the object of his fascination.

"Are we near?" Maggie yawned, stretching in Kered's arms. He grunted as her breasts grazed his hand. *Small and firm, not soft.* With a great effort, he resisted the urge to grasp a nipple between his fingertips. The one closest to his hand was taut against the fabric of her gown, and it tempted him badly.

He hauled on the reins and, lifting Maggie, slipped to the ground. "We will rest here."

Maggie decided to rename the warrior Mr. Surly.

She also decided her best course was to avoid him. They stood by a slow-moving brook. The water looked clear and inviting, but Maggie knew from personal experience at the New Jersey shore that appearances could be deceiving.

"Is the water safe to drink?" she asked.

"Aye. We will fill the carrier."

"Do you have any soap?" Maggie reached for his pack.

"No. It is not a necessity of travel." Kered placed a hand over the pack's flap.

"May I peek inside?" Maggie asked, her hand covering his.

"Why?"

Maggie studied him a moment. His frown was back, digging grooves along his mouth and across his forehead. "Do you think I'll take my gun, *my* weapon, and use it on you?"

His hesitation told her all she needed to know. He didn't trust her.

"No. Don't answer that. It's clear without any words." She stormed away. She had saved his life. How could he think she might use the gun on him? Tears gathered. Stress and fatigue conspired to bring them spilling over her cheeks. *Take your own advice—avoid him.*

A gnarled tree, like a witch's oak, hid her from his view. She peeked around and watched him arrange rocks for a hearth. Her skin itched with the coating of dust. She reeked. The frustration of mistrust and the grime of several days' journey needed release. Maggie whipped her dress over her head and dropped her panties. Kered could not see her. Carefully, she lowered herself into the running water. Its delicious coolness slipped over her limbs. She ducked beneath the clear surface, using her fingers to untangle her dirty tresses. The luxury of water caressing her skin vanquished her bleak mood.

Maggie kicked over to the bank and dug a hand into the sandy soil that edged the deep brook. She used the sand to scrub her skin and even worked it into her hair, rinsing it thoroughly several times. A shadow blocked the bright light of the red Tolemac sun.

"Are you mad?" Kered bellowed.

"Mad? Yes, I am. I'm mad at you." Maggie hugged the roots of the overhanging bank, blocking his view of her naked body.

"Snakes." He leaned forward, hands on hips. "Snakes."

"Snakes?" Maggie whipped around, her hands clasped over her breasts.

"Aye. Snakes abound in these streams. Out."

As much as Maggie wanted to levitate from the water, she could not just climb from the stream, dripping wet and naked. "Could you turn around?"

He grunted and obliged, although he did not step away from the water's edge. Maggie paddled downstream a few feet and scrabbled out near her dress. She shuddered before pulling its grimy fabric over her wet body; she picked up her panties. There was no way she would put them back on without a wash.

Kneeling at the edge of the brook, she ignored Kered's presence and scrubbed her underwear with sand. Just as she gave them a final rinse, a large hand reached over and plucked them away.

"You wretch!" Maggie squealed as Kered held her panties over her head at eye level.

"Nilrem's beard!" Kered whispered, as his hands stretched and turned the faded scrap of cotton. "What manner of garment is this?"

"You cur. Give . . . me . . . my . . . underwear!" Maggie bit out.

He turned to her and scratched his head. "How would such a thing keep you warm?"

"They aren't supposed to keep you warm." Maggie leaped up and tried to snag the panties, but he blocked her with his shoulder, holding them aloft.

"What purpose do they serve?" He flipped them inside out and splaying his fingers, peered inside the waistband.

Maggie's face flushed as dark as the setting red sun.

She pressed her hands to her face in mortification.

Kered raised his eyes in bafflement, then froze. "Maggie," he said, and placed a hand on her shoulder, "forgive me."

Maggie shrank from his hand, slipping away from the heavy weight of it. Kered extended her panties. She snatched them from his hand and clutched them to her chest.

In strained silence, they moved to the fire's side. Maggie knelt and spread her underwear on a smooth rock. She fussed with her arrangement to avoid speaking to Kered, who crouched at her side.

Kered lifted a hank of Maggie's wet hair and placed it gently over her shoulder. "I have shamed you. My only excuse is . . . surprise. I have never seen such a garment. But 'tis no real justification for my behavior."

"I forgive you," Maggie murmured, then she looked up at him. Tears glistened in her eyes. "It's not this." She gestured to her steaming underwear. "It's not being trusted."

"Not trusted?" Kered reached out and traced a finger along her cheek.

"Forget it. I'm just tired." She shook him off.

"We must speak of this. We may not go on a quest with rancor between us."

"*We* are not going on a quest. *You* are going on a quest. I am along for the ride. You don't speak for hours. You march like a madman. You disappear on me. You won't trust me with my gun." She stabbed the fire with a stick. The fears of being in a strange world crashed down on her.

Kered snatched the stick and tossed it aside. He manacled her upper arms with his large hands. Slowly, although she resisted, he drew her to his chest, drawing her into the vee of his thighs. They knelt together, their bodies as close as lovers, Maggie's face against Kered's heartbeat.

When Maggie relaxed against him, he spoke. "*We* are on this quest together. The omens are strong. You are as important as I on this journey. I do trust you, for you could have used your weapon on me whilst I slept in the cave. If I had not trusted you, I could not have rested. 'Tis just that at all times, I think and choose—alone. I have command of an army. I make every decision; I lead. It is not something I am used to—this having someone question me. My pack? I have no answer. It is my nature to horde my things.

"It is customary for the man to carry the weapons. I know of no women who go armed. Yet perhaps it is possible to change. You are unlike any female slave I have ever met. Perhaps you should be granted different rules."

Maggie snuffled against Kered's chest. His words brought her tears rushing back, and it was important to her that she not show him what he would consider a female weakness. She rubbed her face on his shirt; the fabric was so fine it was like rubbing her face on his bare skin. "I am not a slave."

Kered was smart enough to remain silent, but his right hand betrayed him, sweeping along her upper arm. Maggie pulled back in anger. She pounded on his chest. "You must believe me. I am not a slave! I'm a metalsmith. There are no arm rings beyond the ice fields."

He slipped his fingers into her hair, drawing her forward, his mouth crushing down on hers. For long moments he heard nothing, saw nothing.

Maggie's body molded itself to his. The thin fabric of her dress hid nothing of his aroused body from hers. She moaned softly. When he parted his lips, she thrust her tongue into his mouth.

"Nilrem's knees!" Kered flung himself back on his heels. He gripped Maggie by the shoulders, holding her off and staring at her in bewilderment. "This . . . I . . . by . . . what?" he stuttered.

Maggie reached out and pressed her fingers to his lips. "Don't you kiss like that, here on Tolemac?" she whispered.

"By the sword, no!" Kered said against her fingertips. Covering her hand with one of his, he pressed his mouth to her palm. He drew her forward until only a sheet of paper could have separated them. "It is spoken that some pleasure slaves are taught special wiles to tempt a man . . . to betray his duties. Are you tempting me to forget my quest?"

Maggie frowned. "You think I am deliberately tempting you from your mission?"

"I-I-I do not know. One moment you are like sweet innocence. The next . . . artful."

She began to shake in his arms. "No. *No.* I wouldn't do that to you. I'm not artful; I'm not tempting you to anything. You started it. *You* kissed *me.*"

Kered nodded. He pulled her so close she could feel his breath on her mouth. "Aye. I began this." He lowered his head. "Again, Maggie. Taste me, again."

Maggie froze. First his distrust, next the humiliation of having her ragged underwear inspected, and now he thought her an artful temptress, luring him from his quest. *And still, he wanted a kiss.*

She pushed him away and rose, shaking out her skirts and avoiding his smoldering turquoise eyes. "No. I won't be accused of tempting you from your sacred mission. I have no desire to kiss you, Ker. One kiss was quite enough for me."

# Chapter Nine

Maggie roused herself from the languor created by Windsong's pace. "Kered! Look! Over there!" The ground erupted in a cloud of dust. A miniature dust devil whirled along before them. Maggie stifled a scream. Kered slowed Windsong's pace as the dust devil coalesced into a child—a ragged, tiny being flying across the ground.

Escaping, Maggie thought, but not from them.

Charging across the red plain to their right came a mirage. Or, Maggie hoped it was a mirage. The creature's green, plated body and huge haunches rippled as it gained upon the child.

Windsong balked. He pawed the earth and flagged his tail and refused to move.

"By the sword!" Kered swore and leapt from the saddle. In a moment, his long legs carried him across the flat land in pursuit of the child. It was a foot race Maggie thought he couldn't win.

Maggie groped in Kered's pack for her gun. She held it firmly in her right hand and took up the reins. "How dare you betray your master?" she hissed into Windsong's ear. She kicked the horse in the flanks. He whinnied a protest, but broke into a shambling trot. Windsong's gait changed again as he approached the beast, finally faltering to a halt. Nothing she did would budge him.

Maggie's throat dried. Her palms gushed with sweat. The creature, taller on all fours than even Kered, weighed at least a ton more than the man it pursued. It opened its huge jaws and let loose a fountain of viscous liquid, spraying Kered and the ragged child.

Kered slipped. He fell on one knee, recovered, and turned to face the dragon, whose flailing tail ended in a sharp three-pronged spike.

And it *was* a dragon—as ancient and reptilian and frightening as any painting she'd ever seen. Kered and the child were almost under its snapping jaws.

Maggie tried to control the agitation of her mount, forcing Windsong to stand steady. Perhaps she could get off a shot and put the beast to sleep. Another stream of venom spewed across Kered's path. He slid and slipped, barely maintaining his footing. The child screamed and fell in the liquid patches spreading around him.

"Ker!" Maggie cried. The dragon made a quick snatch. The child eluded the clawing limb, rolling in the viscous liquid, almost swimming along the ground.

Kered used the slick surface to slide between the beast and its tiny victim. He stood his ground beneath the frenzied claws, sword in one hand, knife drawn in the other. An iridescent fountain of slime arched and fell, coating him. With a shake of his tangled hair, he parried the attacking talons.

Maggie shrieked as Windsong reared. She fell off the back of the saddle, striking the ground. Her breath whooshed from her lungs.

She lost her grip on the gun.

Quickly, she leapt to her feet and looked about. Just as she snatched up the tiny black gun, the dragon turned its liquid eye in her direction.

Maggie stumbled backward.

The slime hit her like the heavy drops of a summer storm. A rotting, acrid odor stung her nostrils. The liquid coated her face and shoulders, clung to her arms and hands. The dragon turned back to closer prey.

She raised the gun, wiping the slime from the stock. In a reflex taught long ago in childhood, she sighted on the creature and fired.

Nothing happened.

Maggie gasped and turned the gun, peering into the tiny hole that made the gun resemble a water pistol more than any other kind of weapon. She scrubbed the surface on her skirt, cleaning it again. Taking aim, she pressed the blue button.

Nothing.

Again.

In silent fear, she watched the dragon rear up on its huge haunches and throw back its head.

"Dear God, help them," she prayed and threw the useless gun. The dragon paused for an imperceptible moment and clawed the air as if to swat a pesky fly. The gun struck its head.

Kered leapt at the dragon, his sword swiping its throat and his knife blade plunging deep into the exposed breast.

In a thunder of limbs, the dragon collapsed. Maggie ran to Kered as he pulled his blade from the dragon's body. She sidestepped the twitching limbs, then bent over the sobbing child. Kered knelt at her side and plucked up the shaking bundle of rags.

" 'Tis over," he said, handing Maggie her gun after wiping it on his sleeve. She stuffed it into her boot, then pulled the hood from the child's tiny head.

Maggie stared down at the dirtiest face she'd ever seen. The chance that water had ever touched the urchin was about the same as her chance of going to the moon. The ludicrous nature of her thoughts, considering her own situation, plus the narrow escape from becoming dragon bait, made her laugh.

Kered smiled and pressed the child into her arms. "He needs a female to soothe him."

"Yikes," she gasped as an odor of excrement wafted up from the child. "Him?"

"Aye. Him. Thank you for distracting the beast." Kered patted her shoulder and rose, bellowing across the field to Windsong. "Come back, you cowardly knave!"

A warmth flooded Maggie's insides. Her gun might not have worked, but the satisfaction of having assisted the warrior was enough. Gingerly, Maggie tried to comfort the child, whose chest heaved in silent sobs. She crooned to him as she did to her brother Jason's youngest child when teething kept him awake. "Hush, hush, the bad dragon is dead."

Something in her voice got through and the shuddering sobs eased to sniffles. When Kered and Windsong trotted up to their side, she handed up the child and then, with great difficulty and less than ladylike dignity, she scrambled up in front of Kered. "We have to wash off this goop. This kid needs a bath," she said.

"Over yonder ridge is The Sacred Pool. We can bathe there. 'Tis a he, I said, not a goat." Kered kicked Windsong's flanks, and they flew across the ground.

Maggie swatted at some little bugs that hovered about the child's head and stifled an impulse to cringe when yellow, grime-rimmed nails dug into her forearm. She breathed through her mouth and tried to decide whether to explain a "kid" to Kered or just let him think she couldn't tell the difference between a goat and a child. Her skin began to itch in a maddening manner, but she couldn't scratch. The child squirmed and wriggled. His slimy garments made holding him a two-handed job.

"You know, Ker, I thought you were teasing me about the dragons," she said, rubbing her itchy chin against her shoulder.

"Common as dust. I told you."

"Still, I thought you were teasing me."

Maggie wondered if there were any animals on Tolemac she would recognize. "What's your cloak made of?"

"Wool. From a sheep. 'Tis a docile animal, soft. But 'tis also a dirty beast, stinking in fact."

"I'm familiar with sheep. And your shirt?" Maggie could not prevent her hand from touching the fine cloth on his encircling arms. It had an unusual luster despite its wrinkled condition.

His body rippled through a shrug. " 'Tis some plant. A woman would know."

"Of course," she muttered, renewing her grip on the child.

"My britches?" he asked softly against her ear.

"Your britches?" Maggie felt her cheeks heat.

"Have you no interest in my britches?" he asked, then roared with laughter.

Maggie did not deign to reply.

The terrain changed abruptly. Over one low hill the red rock changed to verdant fields dotted with small groves of trees. Here and there the red rock still showed through the long grasses. Pink clouds marched overhead, painting splotches of gray across the hills. A glimmer caught her eye.

The Sacred Pool lay like a silver skin between two folds in the hills. Kered drew Windsong to a halt and slid off the back of the saddle. He reached up and took the child, marching to the edge of the pool and dunking him like an old dust mop.

A frantic wail rose anew from the bundle of rags, and Maggie grinned as Kered swished the child back and forth. Scratching her forearms and neck, she walked into the shallows to stand at Kered's side. "Why don't I do that? You might drown the poor little guy."

"Boy. A him."

"A guy is a him—in my place."

"In this place, he is a little beggar who is certainly far from his tribe." Kered laughed, relinquishing his hold. The child fell back with a splash and came up screaming.

"Beggar? Tribe?" Maggie stepped back as the child shook himself like a dog after a bath.

"Aye. 'Tis unusual to find a little beggar separated from his elders. They are most watchful of their young." He straightened and looked over Maggie's shoulder.

She turned and followed the direction of his gaze. A cluster of black dots swarmed down a distant hill like ants escaping an ant farm. The little boy shrieked with joy and took off in their direction.

"Are they dangerous?" she asked, mentally estimating the group at greater than fifty.

"Humpf. Enough, if one is not on guard. They have been outcasts from Tolemac for generations. A scavenger people, more content to take what is not secured than hunt or plow themselves." Kered fisted his hands on his hips as he surveyed the approaching band of beggars.

As the motley band drew near, Maggie realized that even the tallest was not much bigger than a large child. She smiled when a figure separated from the group and swooped down on the boy, snatching him into her arms and hugging and kissing his little face. Then a scene unfolded like many played out each summer on Ocean City's boardwalk. The mother held the child away and smacked his bottom, her shrill admonitions readily understandable. Much loved, the child had scared his mother nearly out of her mind. The child hung his head, then tugged at his mother's arm, drawing her to stand before Kered.   .

Kered bowed stiffly to the mother. Tears ran down her face, making tracks on cheeks as dirty as her child's. The boy gibber-jabbered and gestured. The rest of the beggars encircled them in a wary ring.

The child began to act out the drama of his rescue. He swiped and stabbed the air. In the best Shakespearean tradition, he clutched his hand to his heart and collapsed on the ground as if dead. The beggars went wild with joy. They closed in on Kered, hugging him and kissing his hands. Maggie found herself cut off from him, an onlooker.

Kered took their adulation with great aplomb, bowing and nodding. They chattered in a patois Maggie didn't understand, but their sentiment was loud and clear. Kered was now their hero.

"Enough." A loud voice bellowed. The beggars parted and a tiny man approached Kered. They bowed to one another in respectful silence. As if commanded, the other beggars backed off, distancing themselves from the old man. His wrinkled skin and gnarled cane spoke of great age.

"Tolem," Kered said, bowing deeply at the waist. The incredible distance between Kered's height and Tolem's made Kered's obeisance almost ludicrous. He could have crushed the old man in one hand.

"Kered? Leoh's chosen one. Am I correct?" Tolem's gravelly voice sounded as if he hadn't used it for years.

"You have an excellent memory." Kered hunkered down on his haunches before the old man and still the old man needed to tilt his head to look up at the warrior.

"I remember the ones who matter," Tolem said. "You have rescued my namesake. How may we reward you?"

"I ask nothing." Kered gestured in Maggie's direction. "We came upon the child in a timely manner,'tis all."

"Many would say 'good riddance' and watch the sport." The old man spat into the dust.

"And many others would have done as we did," Kered said.

The old man grunted, then turned to stare at Maggie with open curiosity. His scrutiny made her itch all the more, and she rubbed her upper arms.

"For what reason do you journey through the Forbidden Lands?" Tolem asked, shifting his attention back to Kered.

"I make the ancient quest."

The old man leaned forward precariously on his cane. " 'Tis said in legend one must bear the sign to make the quest. Do you?"

"Aye. Or so Nilrem says."

"Nilrem." The old man spat again. "Show me this sign."

"No." Kered said it softly, but a ripple of unease swept the band of beggars.

A tiny hand crept up and clutched Maggie's. She looked down to find the little beggar at her side. He shot her a worried look as if to urge her to do something.

Tolem shook his head at Kered. "You are a brave man to refuse me. One against my many."

"I have dealt honorably with you and yours each time our paths have crossed." Kered stayed in his relaxed position, crouching before the indignant elder. The two men considered each other in silence.

"You do not play upon the saving of the child. 'Tis what most men would do."

Kered rose to his full height. "I am not most men."

The old man nodded and an audible gasp swept the beggars. He chattered to his band in their strange tongue, then turned back to Kered. "Camp on our land in peace, Kered." He pointed to the pool with his cane. "Take what you will from yonder water. 'Tis welcome you are."

The boy hung on Maggie's arm until his mother dragged him away. He stared over his shoulder, calling out in his language until his words were lost in the winds as they crossed over the ridge.

"What was the boy saying, Ker?" Maggie asked, scratching vigorously now that the company was gone.

Kered strolled to the water's edge and splashed water on his face. "He wished to mate with you."

"What?" Maggie cried.

Kered cupped the water and took a long drink, then rose and shook his wet hands. "Aye. He wanted Tolem to barter for—" He broke off and stared at her. Then, like an anxious bridegroom carrying his bride over the threshold, he swept her into his arms and ran to the water's edge. With a mighty heave, Kered flung Maggie into the Sacred Pool.

# Chapter Ten

Sputtering and choking, Maggie clawed her way to the surface. She rose in water to her shoulders and screamed, "How dare you? How dare—"

"The venom. Your face." Kered waded in next to her, uncaring of his splendid attire. He rubbed her cheeks and neck with his hands. "Blisters. Can you not feel them?"

In truth, Maggie now felt a burn where before she had felt only itching. "Is it bad?" she asked, peering up into his face. Anxiety was all she saw.

"Aye." He rubbed her arms. "Down." He put a hand onto the top of her head and pushed.

Maggie sucked in air just before the water closed about her head. She opened her eyes and peered about. The clear water soothed her itchy skin, but one glance showed her a muddy bottom being churned by their feet. Soon nothing would be visible.

"Stand still," Maggie ordered when she surfaced.

"You're stirring up the bottom. How will we find the sword? If it's rusty, it'll blend into the mud."

"Rusty? Ruhtra's sword will not be rusty!" Kered bellowed as he continued to rub at Maggie's arms and shoulders.

He was getting far too much enjoyment from the activity, Maggie thought. She slapped his hands away. "I'm fine." She waded very slowly to the water's edge. "Oh, damn, I lost a boot!"

Kered leaned over and swept the muddy bottom with his hand and came up with something that looked like a drowned kitten.

"My gun," Maggie wailed, stomping like a peg-legged pirate in her one boot. She shook the water off the gun's barrel, looking hopelessly around for something to dry it. "Maybe the water cleaned out the slime." She took aim and pressed the red button. A perfectly round hole appeared in a treetop, leaving a green doughnut shape behind. "At least something good came from this," she called over her shoulder. Kered's heated expression made her look down.

Her black dress might have been dusty and smelly before, but now it was hopelessly stained—and plastered to her body. Streaks of slime had bleached the color from it in long, wide stripes and splatters. Her hand groped into the neckline, then she sighed with relief. Her pendant still hung between her breasts, protected and safe.

Kered waded ashore and opened his pack. He knelt by the pool and made a paste in his palm, then approached her warily. Their tantalizing kiss had rendered all conversation stilted, at best. If Maggie's stomping and muttering were any indication of her mood, he

115

feared she might take aim with her gun and make a hole in his middle.

He urged her to the water's edge. Gently, he dotted the healing gray paste on the blisters on her cheeks and upper arms. His throat burned. Her skin might be ruined, permanently scarred by the dragon's venom. He was not sensitive to the caustic liquid, but he had seen the ugly scars on those who were. Should he tell her the sores might rot and eat away at her cheeks, burrowing like living worms? No. He could not tell her. He tipped up her chin, carefully covering each blister, hoping he was in time to save her beauty from sure ruin.

"Your gown must come off." Kered walked behind her and one-handedly plucked open the buttons on her gown. Only a few were done; she'd fastened them herself and many were out of her reach.

"Off? Are you nuts?" Maggie whipped about, her hands clasped protectively to her breasts.

"Nuts? What do nuts have to do with . . . It matters not. If I do not treat your blisters, they will suppurate."

Maggie looked at her hands. "Why should I take off my dress?"

"We must see if the slime went through." Maggie shook her head at him. " 'Tis false modesty to stand and hide yourself when as we wait, the slime could be doing damage—permanent damage." Kered wanted to rip the dress from her. He imagined the spreading blisters all too well to wait more than another moment.

She flushed red, with gray polka dots, and obliged. Bending, she lifted the dress over her head and dropped it.

Kered watched her spread her hands to shelter her breasts from his view. He tried to maintain the proper seventh level of control. He almost succeeded in keeping his blood in the right place—almost. Dabbing the gray paste on her neck and chest was not too bad. But when Maggie lowered her fingers, keeping the tips over her nipples, his hand began to shake and his blood rebelled and took the shortest path to its favorite place.

The slime had seeped through the thin fabric of her gown. Long swaths of blisters trailed along the inside of her breasts—sweet, small breasts with ripe, rosy nipples. He gulped and kept dabbing on the paste. His blood raced and flooded through him. Stealing a glance at Maggie's face, he relaxed. Her eyes were closed as tight as a sealed cask of gold. She could not see his difficulty. He peeled up one of her fingertips and soothed the salve along a nasty blister.

One touch. He slicked his fingertip with the healing herbal and swept it along the rise of her breast and under to the warm crease formed by the slight swell of her breast. He lingered there, stroking her. If he thought her nipples taut before, now they swelled like small berries, succulent and full. He wanted to taste the fruit, but his desires had not slipped entirely out of control. He smoothed the salve in long sweeps down her stomach and thighs, then hesitated. "This undergarment? Is it made of more sturdy stuff than the gown?"

Maggie did not open her eyes. She squeezed them even tighter and flushed. "It's cotton, kinda old and not too sturdy, I'm afraid."

"Take it off."

Maggie's hands shook. She opened her eyes. Kered had half-turned to the pool. She slipped her panties down her legs a few inches and saw that the skin beneath them was smooth and unblemished. She quickly tugged the panties up. "I'm fine. Nothing got through both layers."

Maggie watched him wade into the pool to his waist.

117

He stood in the cold water for a few minutes, hands on hips, staring across the expanse of silver-slick water. The sky, suffusing to a light lavender, reflected in an iridescent gleam across the water.

She groped at her feet for her dress.

"Do not touch the gown," he ordered. Maggie snatched her hands back. "Take my other shirt, in my pack."

Maggie nodded to his back and flew to the horse. She groped in the pack and drew out his crumpled shirt. Its scratchy, woolly surface would chafe her skin and set her to sweating, but it reached past her calves, offering complete concealment.

Kered left the water, pacing in long strides to her side. He unstrapped his fur-lined cloak from beneath his pack and, using his knife, sliced another strip from the hem. He neatly folded the cloak, then approached her.

"To bind the shirt." His hands were gentle as he reached about her waist and wrapped the strip of cloth twice around her, knotting it loosely. "The herbal will cling to the blisters until you bathe it off." Turning away, he lifted up her dress and inspected the damage, then whirled to face her.

"Seven," he growled.

"Seven?" Maggie repeated.

"Aye. Where once there were eight buttons, now there are seven. 'Tis unlucky." He said it as if she were to blame for their troubles.

"I-I suppose I lost one somewhere. What difference will it make?" She knew by his expression that this was important.

"Do you believe in omens?" He folded the gown into squares.

She considered her time on the Navajo reservation

visiting her grandmother. Although Maggie was only one-quarter Navajo, she had been taught to respect the ideologies of all peoples. There were mysteries and meanings unexplained in every religion.

"Yes, I do." Maggie said it simply and sincerely.

"Seven is considered a dark numeral. There are eight chiefdoms. If one rebels, there is war. You wear a pendant with the image found on the sacred sword. It has eight strands for the eight heavenly bodies circling our sun. Your gown was fastened with eight buttons. Surely you see?"

"I see that this is important to you. One button is gone. How will that change what we are doing here?"

"I do not know." He sighed. "I am weary. Perhaps I am unduly concerned." He shrugged and went to unsaddle Windsong, throwing the saddle and bridle over the branch of a low-spreading tree, whose leaves reminded Maggie of a sugar maple. He tethered the horse to graze on the tough, short grass surrounding them.

"What are you going to wear?" Maggie nodded at his squelching boots and dripping garments.

"I will dry my clothes by the fire."

With a lithe motion, he stripped his shirt off and flung it over a tree branch. Maggie stared, then groaned and spun away when he edged his trousers down his hips. A bolt of sheer lust ran through her. She heard him laugh as she marched to the edge of the pool to cool her thoughts.

After several moments he called out to her. "You may look, little slave."

She sneaked a peek over her shoulder. He had donned the worn breeches from his trek to Hart Fell. His feet were bare and he was shaking drops of water from his boots. Maggie edged near. "Aren't you cold?"

He looked up and grinned, shaking his head and sending his long hair tumbling about his shoulders. Back to mangy.

Maggie wondered how she was going to sit across from all that naked flesh when he swept his blue cloak over his shoulders. She slumped to the ground in relief. If he remained decently covered, she might be able to think—might. But he didn't remain sitting.

"Where are you going?" she asked as he shouldered his pack.

"I will hunt. Fresh meat will aid in your healing."

Maggie watched him stride away to the gently rolling hills covered in rough gorse. Tiny yellow flowers, like miniature daisies, clustered near at hand. Maggie plucked several and began a daisy chain to still her apprehension at being left alone.

When Kered returned a scant hour later, with several animals strung on a cord, Maggie tried to contain her relief. She hopped to her feet and grinned. "What did you find?" Her smile died. Hanging from the chord were three cute plump creatures. They had blue spines and Maggie knew instantly where the bristles in Kered's brush came from.

Despite growing up in a family of dedicated hunters, the death of any animal bothered Maggie. With ill-concealed distaste, she watched Kered slit the animals up the belly and in smooth, practiced strokes, separate the hide from the animal.

Kered chattered as he worked. "The blue-Goh is a delicacy and hard to trap, for they like to curl in a ball and hide in the brush. I am quite proficient with the snare; thus you will dine well."

"I wouldn't brag, if I were you, about trapping some poor defenseless animal," Maggie protested.

Kered threw back his head and laughed. "Eat or not. Suit yourself." He tended his catch, spitting it and roasting it over the fire he had built.

Maggie had to admit her mouth was watering by the time he lifted the meat from the flames.

"A taste?" He tore a limb from the blue-Goh and held it out.

Maggie took it. It felt greasy and hot, but she blew on it and tentatively took a small bite. "Delicious, I must admit." They ate in companionable silence.

When the meal was finished, they sat staring out at the Sacred Pool. The sky darkened as the Tolemac sun briefly hid behind the clouds. "What do we do now?" she asked.

"Ancient legend tells a tale that, until my visit to Nilrem's mountain, I had discounted as unworthy of a warrior's notice."

"Warriors being practical men who have no time for stories?"

"Aye." He grinned, then sobered. "It is told in legend that Leoh's grandfather threw his sword into this pool."

"Why do you refer to him as *Leoh's* grandfather. Isn't he your ancestor, too?"

"I am not Leoh's true son. He found me, an abandoned child, and raised me as his own. But we wander from the legend. Leoh's grandfather had grown weary of war, was disillusioned—"

"As are you," Maggie interrupted.

"Aye. As am I." He stoked the fire to a roaring conflagration, then sat cross-legged. "I am weary of many things, but one may not lay down one's burden because one is fatigued."

"I understand." Maggie moved next to him and

placed her hand on his long, lean thigh. "You still haven't answered my question. How do we get the sword?" He pressed his warm hand over hers.

" 'Tis said in legend that Ruhtra threw his sword into this sacred pool, proclaiming that he who bore the ancient mark, and only he, could reclaim the sword and with it, Ruhtra's might. Many have tried to call the sword—and failed."

"I heard Nilrem say you had this sign. What is it exactly?"

Kered looked off across the water. Slowly, he opened his cloak. Maggie leaned forward to see better. He hesitated, then touched his chest. There, camouflaged by the dark hair, was the faint birthmark she had noticed before.

"The sacred eight," he said.

Maggie reached out and touched the mark—the mark of infinity. No, her father would call it a lazy eight, a great brand for cattle. She thought of what Kered had said about the number of her buttons and the strands she'd soldered into her pendant.

His skin was otherwise flawless; all marks of his wounds had healed so quickly. The air between them became charged with something unspoken. Lightly, she traced the small birthmark. Her fingers strayed to explore the crisp hair that concealed it. When his chest muscles flexed beneath her fingers, she snatched them away and curled them into a fist in her lap. "How will you be different than the others?"

He pulled the cloak across his massive chest, donning at the same time a cloak of distance. "I know of no other who has this mark. The legend also states that the man must be worthy. When the time comes, I will be judged, just as the others were."

"You must believe in this very strongly," Maggie said.

"If believing in a legend will bring peace, I will believe in anything."

His vehement reply told her the depth of his desire to believe, yet she was skeptical. "Those aren't very clear instructions. Can't you be more specific?" Maggie asked.

"It is not necessary to have a plan carved in stone. Any good commander knows that one must make use of the local terrain, adjust to fit the immediate circumstances. There are other signs more important than those concerning the sword."

"What could possibly be more important at this moment?"

"Watching to see if your blisters fester."

Maggie froze. Her hand went to her throat. She wanted to see his expression because his voice was neutral, but his head was bent, his hair a concealing wall between them.

"Maybe I'll heal as swiftly as you. Your skin is perfect again," she said, enviously. "I've never seen anything so marvelous."

In answer he grunted a noncommittal, annoying sound.

Fear and anger mixed. She lost her temper, leaping to her feet. "So, we're going to just sit here and wait for me to rot?"

He tugged her gently down and placed his hand over hers, curling his fingers over her tight fist. "There is little left of the salve. You will bathe on the morrow and what is left, I will spread on the worst of the sores."

She jerked her hand away and jumped up again to pace back and forth before the fire. His words gave her no sense of time, no idea of how soon they might continue on and so eventually return to Nilrem's mountain. She desperately wanted to go home. Each day, her growing fascination with the warrior made going on more difficult and made staying distant from him less likely. Her desperation made her voice sharp. "The weather is deteriorating, Ker. We must do something."

"We must *wait* to see if your blisters fester."

Maggie tried to be calm. Her skin felt cool and the itching had vanished. He had acted quickly and loaded the salve on with a heavy hand—a warm, caring hand. It was unfair to take out her anxieties and anger on him. "You know, I'm wearing a sacred eight, too," she pointed out. "Maybe this sword will come to me."

He laughed. The sound was rich and deep and even more annoying than his inarticulate grunts.

"What's so funny? If the sword is to return to someone with your sacred number, why not me?"

"If I, a man at the seventh level of awareness, cannot call forth the sword, then by all my ancestors' graves, you will surely fail, too. Ruhtra's sword would not be called from the depths by a female slave. Only a mighty and worthy warrior may command the waters," he said, heartily amused, shaking his head in disbelief.

"Hm, is that so?" she asked. "We'll just see about that, won't we?"

Maggie ran to the water's edge. She did not need to see him to know he had come on silent feet to stand behind her. Like another sense, her body knew when he was near.

Maggie looked about. The landscape was soothingly similar to home with its rolling hills and silvery pool. Yet a red sun burned in a lavender sky streaked with dark clouds. A giant horse cropped grass nearby. How could it get any stranger? Could anything be more fantastic?

"A challenge, Maggie?" His words were soft and edged with sarcasm.

"Sure. I've always loved a challenge." She swept an arm out in a grand gesture. "Command the waters."

Kered grinned, then turned to face the pool. With a reverence Maggie suspected was not feigned, he pressed his palm over the mark on his chest and spoke. "I, the Esteemed Warrior Kered, command the sword from the depths." The water lay placid and unmoving.

Maggie laughed at the absurdity of the situation, holding her pendant in her fist. "I, the Esteemed Metalsmith Maggie O'Brien, command the sword from the depths."

As if on cue, a wind rose. Maggie reached across the space that separated them and gripped Kered's fingers. They stared across the secretive pool. A long rumble like the march of a phantom army rolled down the hills and a shiver of fear raised goosebumps on Maggie's arms. "What was that?" she whispered.

Kered gathered Maggie against his chest, drawing his cloak about her shoulders. "Just the herald of a storm. A helm wind. They come quickly across the fells. Look." He pointed to the hilltops where angry purple clouds raced the wind to hide the sun.

Maggie shivered in his embrace. In time to the beat of his heart beneath her cheek, the thunder rolled. The scent of him, his warmth, made her burrow closer to him.

The sky opened and a torrent of rain lashed them. Windsong rose on his hind legs, then pawed the dirt in a fevered protest, tugging on his tether.

"The pool," Kered cried, pulling away from her. Together they turned and watched as the sudden hail of raindrops pelted the glassy surface of the water, churning it into a seething, roiling mass, throwing waves to lap their feet.

Maggie had to shout to be heard above the cacophony of thunder. "What's happening?"

Kered did not answer.

She had ceased to exist for him.

He withdrew his hand, his fingers sliding unfeeling from hers. The rain plastered his hair to his head. He threw off his cloak and stood bare-chested before the questing waves. The blue cloak disappeared, sucked under the water and swept away.

The indigo clouds blackened the sky, blotting out the last rays of the red sun, casting them into artificial night. Maggie shrieked as a sudden bolt of lightning lit the hills, throwing Kered into sharp relief against the silver pool. Her words stuck in her throat, for he looked like a pagan god commanding the water. Without the strength of his hand, she felt small and inconsequential. She grabbed her pendant to anchor herself. The brilliant display of nature only underscored her puny stature in his world.

Waves rose and rushed to the shore, spewed foam across him, and still he stood like a statue, unaware of nature's fury.

"Ker! Kered!" She urgently cried his name. Great waves swirled about his thighs and dragged at the hem of the shirt she wore. "You'll be killed," she shrieked, wading to her armpits to save him somehow.

Another blue-white bolt struck a nearby tree, sending Windsong into a screaming frenzy. A wall of water advanced. She squeezed the pendant like a religious amulet and offered up a prayer. She dragged at Kered's waist.

When the wave hit, she lost her grip, her nails scraping across his body.

She fell and tumbled backward. Like a child knocked from her raft at the shore, she rolled with the wave, grazing her knees and scraping her hands in an effort to stand in the water. Finally, exhausted, she collapsed on the shore, gasping.

Something hard and cold dug into her side. She rolled over. A wave slapped her in the face. She coughed and blinked to clear her sight. There, lying beneath her, was a long sword, half-buried in the mud. She straddled it, grasped the hilt, and dragged it above the frothing waves to make sure it wasn't again snatched to a watery grave.

In an instant the wind died. The water slipped to oily smoothness. "Ker," she called, turning back and wading to where he stood. When he didn't respond to his name, she slapped his arm, stinging her palm against his rock-hard musculature.

Like a bear waking from hibernation, he turned and shook his head. Water sluiced in silver streams down his half-naked body.

"Maggie," he said, articulating her name as if his tongue was thick in his mouth. "Maggie?"

She threw herself into his arms, hugging his cold, wet body. "I found the sword!" She searched his face, seeing confusion in his eyes.

He raised a shaky hand and swept the wet tangles of hair from her brow and cupped her face. "You found the sword?" he said, his voice dazed.

"Come," she said, tugging him along. He went like a sleepwalker, stumbling after her. She knelt at his feet and stroked her fingers along the sword's long hilt. At the crosspiece, a hollow sphere was formed by eight entwining strands of silver. Nestled in the center sat a bril-

liant turquoise stone. "See, it's just like my pendant."
She held her necklace up for his approval, seeking some
sign that he understood. His face was deeply etched with
uncertainty and anger.

"It cannot be," he said, standing before the gleaming
blade that lay like a gift at the shore's edge. "It cannot
be." He swept up the sword and raised it high. The red
sun burst from the clouds, bathing them in a cone of
light, unearthly and hot.

The light bounced off the blade as it had done in the
opening sequence of the *Tolemac Wars* game. Maggie
choked back a cry of fear. "The waves knocked me
over. When I tried to get up, there it was, under me."
She desperately tried to explain. "The legend is true,"
she finished in whisper.

"True?" he said in a deceptively calm voice. "The
legend said the sword would come to he who bore the
sign."

Maggie floundered for words. She saw the anger in
his face and heard it in his voice. "It did, it did," she
finally said. "It came to me. I'm wearing the sign, don't
you see?"

His hand went to the mark on his chest and he rubbed
his palm there as if it itched. "I see what I see." He
thrust the sword deep into the sand. The sun gleamed
on the shining hilt as he stormed away.

# *Chapter Eleven*

Again and again she saw the gleaming blade rise, the tip cut open his chest, the blood flow down his body. His torturer would use the sacred sword. She struggled awake, cold and cramped, curled alone by a fire that offered no comfort or warmth.

Kered stood by Windsong, readying the horse for the day's ride. Maggie struggled to her feet, pushing her hair from her eyes, panic streaking through her. The words bubbled out of her mouth without restraint. "Throw it back. Throw the sword back," she begged.

Kered turned to her in astonishment. "You have obtained the blade, where others have failed, generation after generation, and you wish that I throw it back?"

"Yes," she cried. "I had a dream. Someone will hurt you. He'll use the sword on you." Her skin burned anew wherever he had applied the salve.

He placed the sacred sword on the ground and grasped

her arms. Like a summer storm, his temper had blown up and then blown over. His hands were gentle, his tone soothing. "Fear not. A dream is not reality."

"It is! *It is*. I know it. You must throw it back."

He captured her face in his hands. "Maggie. I do not know from whence you have come, but hear me. I will not throw back the sword. Your pendant, your appearance at the conjunction—it is fated. If I am to suffer from the sword . . . then so be it."

"My Gran—" Maggie began to cry.

"Gran?" He used his thumbs to smooth away her tears.

"Yes, my grandmother, from beyond the ice fields, she taught me to respect a dream. Its meaning may not always be evident, but still, we must respect it. Someone—" she choked on the words—"someone will torture you with the sword."

He drew her close into the circle of his warmth. "This grandmother of yours sounds wise. But still, we may not alter the future. What is meant to be, will be."

Maggie pushed him away, refusing solace. "You're wrong! We *can* alter the future. Destroy the sword. Fling it to the deepest part of the pool."

He exerted his greater strength, forcing her to come close, his hands soothing, sweeping back her hair, tracing the lines of her cheeks.

"Maggie, you must understand. If peace does not come to the borders of Tolemac soon, many will die. Children will starve. How can I weigh a danger to myself against sure death to others?" He released her and turned his back, returning to the saddling of Windsong. " 'Tis the children I will not betray. There are those who consider the children of Selaw expendable. The get of vermin. Of no account in the calculation of power and control. Had Leoh not taken me in, I might have been one of those children.

"When I bear the sword to the council, it will empower me with Ruhtra's legendary might. I can change the fate of the Selaw children. There is no other path." In a fluid movement of sinuous strength, he hoisted her into the saddle. "You called the sword from the Sacred Pool. What is done, is done."

Maggie gripped his strong hands, and tears flowed over her cheeks and fell on his fingers. She shook her head. She was powerless to make him understand and powerless, she knew deep inside, to change his mind or his fate.

"What next?"

Her voice was dull, lacking inflection. It had been that way now for hours. Kered pulled on the horse's reins, then slipped from the saddle. He offered her his hands, and she fell heavily into them.

"Come, we have ridden long and hard. Let us rest here."

"Here?" she asked, but her voice told him she did not care.

He kept one eye on her as he built the fire. She chewed the bread he offered her and drank from the water gourd. At one point, she rose and went off into the darkness, and he half-stood to accompany her, fearful of what she might meet in the night, but changed his mind. Perhaps she wanted to be alone. They were in a peaceful heathland. Little except a stray sheep would startle her.

When she returned, she came to him and curled in his arms. It had become their custom for him to remain on guard, his back to a tree, and for her to lie in his arms.

A bad habit. One to tempt the most resolute of men.

Her breasts now rested against his forearm, her breathing slow and deep. He wondered what he could do to raise her spirits. This dream she had described did not really trouble him. When his time came, it would come. There was little to do about it. He was trained by the finest, knew his strength, knew his abilities. Few could best him.

Maggie stretched and turned in his arms. He stroked her hair. His lust rose to taunt him, regular as the rising of the moons. He stamped it down just as often. Each time seemed to take more effort until finally, he shifted her from his arms, placed her on his cloak, and turned his back to her. Still she robbed him of concentration. She rolled against his back, hugging his waist.

Better to keep watch from a distance. With great difficulty, he disentangled himself from her arms without waking her, rose, and stood by the fire. He noted the position of the moons, close to the horizon. The sun rising was not far off. He hunkered down, poked the fire's embers until they glowed with renewed life, and began to plan their next day.

The cup of Liarg was said to lie in the depths of a cave on the Isle of N'Olava. They had little hope of reaching the island or entering the cave without combat. Maggie's weapon would perhaps speed their way, yet she had said it could not be brought back to power should it run out. He crouched at her side, reached over, and pulled the gun from her belt.

Kered stroked the gun made of a substance he did not recognize. He studied Maggie's face—beauty and courage combined. She had not run from the dragon. No, she had come to rescue him. She had made no comment about her blisters after her first horrified reaction. She was not vain.

A sigh escaped her lips. *What lips*. He could still taste their one kiss. He could still feel her tongue. When he wished to satisfy his needs, he paid coin. Most often, he used the female slaves at a pleasure house. The pleasure houses were costly in gold and time, but well worth the expense. The slave and her attendance were merely one facet of a complete sensual experience of food and wine and music.

To seek an independent fornitrix purely to relieve lust had always seemed an empty experience. At least his one time had been so. The woman had been lovely and quite adept at wringing a shattering climax from him. But the exchange of coin from his hand to hers had tainted the moment. At a pleasure house, the coin went to the proprietor and the illusion remained that the female came willingly.

Kered touched Maggie's hair. Perhaps she ran from a master who beat her. No. Her skin was nigh unto perfect. No man had abused her in such a way. But there were worse ways to abuse a woman. Words could flay the soul. Leoh had a rapier tongue. Samoht wounded with a glance and a word. Aye. Perhaps Maggie ran from a master who abused her mind and heart.

His blood beat a tattoo in his groin, and he ceased fighting it. He let his lust rise as he caressed the weight of her hair. He bunched it in his fist and let the ebony strands arouse him. He no longer detected the floral aura. Time, sweat, and his shirt's odor had overpowered her womanly scent. A cooling breeze lifted his own hair. He remembered the sensual experience of Maggie tending his hair, remembered the stroke of the brush, the nearness of her heat, the soft caress of her breath as she bent to the task.

He shook off her hair like a man wiping some noxious dirt from his hand. He shot to his feet and left the circle of fire. Her master had taught her to use her tongue to bring pleasure, something he had never experienced before. An emotion he refused to recognize as jealousy smote him—hard. If a pleasure house or common fornitrix used that exotic trick, he would have heard tell of it. His desire leapt, and he thrust aside his thoughts.

He kept his back to the fire—and Maggie—until his blood slowed and his thoughts cooled.

"Ker?" Maggie stretched. He scowled at her over the glowing coals. The harshly delineated planes of his cheeks and jaw were hard and possibly cruel. The shadows painted on his face made him seem almost evil. She shivered. Her hands shook a bit as she drew his fur cloak about her shoulders. His fine shirt, wrinkled now, the gold of its embroidery not gleaming as it had, stretched taut across his shoulders and chest. Surely, he must miss his blue cloak. "Are you cold?" she asked.

"No." He looked away from her.

"You're angry."

"No."

She huddled in the heavy cloak, no longer noticing the scent of it. It had become part of him, part of her world. The scent of his skin, of his sweat, were now an amalgam of what made up her experiences, along with the rich earth scent beneath her and the sharp smoky smell of the burning wood. Windsong snorted in the darkness, close by.

"Tell me what made you angry," she persisted.

"I am not angry."

"Then what troubles you?"

"You. You have not eaten. You sleep for many hours. You do not prick me with your taunts."

"Ah, you miss my conversation." She smiled.

He smiled in return. Dimples deepened, banishing his fierce scowl and most of her worries.

"Aye. I miss your conversation, slave."

"Please. My name is Maggie."

"Your name has sharp edges. It is not feminine."

"Say my name, Ker."

"Maggie."

The air hung heavy between them, filled with something unspoken and expectant.

"You give it an accent that is pleasing to me." She heard his professorial cadence taking over her speech's rhythm. "I like to hear you say my name."

He growled, his eyes narrowing.

"Do you make that noise in anger or from frustration?"

He didn't respond to her question. They lapsed into silence. The fire crackled and the wind blew sparks into the air, where they disappeared, floating like miniature fireworks over their heads.

"We will soon reach the Isle of N'Olava where, by legend, the cup of Liarg is said to be."

"Is that why you're so pensive?" Maggie sat up and drew the cloak about her legs. It was much shorter than before, being the source of boots and belts for her.

"Perhaps. How strong is the power of your weapon?"

She rested her chin on her knees. Of course, he thought only of the quest and weapons. Planning strategy. Too much to hope that his throaty noise signaled anything more.

Her head felt heavy on her neck and her stomach rumbled. For the first time in hours, she felt hungry. The lethargy that had stolen her will and deadened her thoughts seemed to be seeping away in the chill air. The dreams weren't gone, just softened and stored, rationalized into a compartment where she could deal with them. "I don't have any idea of the gun's capacity to hold power. It could shoot one more time or a thousand."

"Tell me of the ways in which your master used it."

She bit her tongue on a sharp retort. *Obstinate male.* "I never saw it used. I saw it demonstrated—once. I can't help you."

"So be it."

She shot to her feet. "I hate that expression. It's so fatalistic. It tells me you just accept what comes. I hate it."

"Sit, Maggie."

He scowled up at her as she paced by the fire, the cloak falling in a heap by the stones. She ignored his expression and stormed back and forth, needing the movement to calm her agitation. "You can't just say, 'So be it.' You have to seek change, try to alter events, not wait for some seventh-level thought to occur to you."

"Sit!" he thundered.

Maggie jumped and then collapsed to the ground. Kered flipped open his pack and drew out the ubiquitous heel of bread. The loaf seemed ever fresh but, by now, boring. She accepted it with ill grace as her stomach rumbled another protest.

"I have led an army since my twentieth conjunction. I am renowned for my tactics. I do not excel on the battlefield because I jump at every thought that crosses my mind. I think; I plan. I contemplate and consult those wiser than I am. Perhaps a female would perceive this as wasting time, but that is why men rule. They think first.''

"Oh, for pity's sake!''

"Do not swear!''

"Look who's talking! You swear constantly, you swear a blue streak—''

"I do not swear.''

Maggie began to laugh. She rolled to her side in hysterics. "You do.'' She gasped. She sat up and counted off her fingers. "Let's see . . . Nilrem's beard—ever popular and number one. Nilrem's knees—almost as colorful, but definitely second. By the sword—dull and number three. Your mighty ancestors—in order yet, back to the dawn of time—number four.'' Her laughter subsided into chuckles.

He unfolded his long frame and stepped directly over the fire and swept her off the ground. He held her dangling from her underarms, her feet flailing the air, their eyes level. When his mouth crushed down on hers she shook to her toes and collapsed against him. He made no attempt to be gentle. He conquered her slightest protest, his thumbs pressing painfully into the sides of her breasts.

Maggie's heart slammed frantically in her chest. She kept her lips demurely together so as not to shock him again. A lightning bolt of sensation streaked from her navel to her groin. She wriggled in his arms, her body brushing his, his heavy belt buckle rubbing the juncture of her thighs. Lying beside him, sleeping in his arms, she knew how his body felt and she craved the hard length of him, arching in his hands to get closer. Her nipples, chafed raw by his woolen shirt, burned at the contact. She cried out against his mouth.

He dropped her to her feet. Maggie's hands crept to

her breasts, pressing against her sore nipples. They stared at each other. His hands opened and closed. His dark eyes reflected the dying flames of the fire behind her.

"Would you lie down for me? Tell me your price?" he whispered.

The crack of her hand on his cheek tore the dawn quiet. He neither flinched nor moved. Her hand stung from the force of her assault and she turned away, hurrying into the tall, shrubby undergrowth, clutching her hand to her belly.

His words slashed like a knife opening a wound, drove home most graphically how little he thought of her, a paltry female. A pleasure slave—slit lips and opened cheeks her punishment for leaving her master. Probably well-deserved punishment in his mind.

She watched the dawning light pinken the indigo sky. Somewhere a bird twittered good morning. For a brief moment the pink-purple streaks and birdsong held an unsurpassed beauty. Then Tolemac's crimson sun rose and the pink diffused to copper streaks and only served to remind her again of blood. She heard the crackle of twigs under his boots when he came to stand behind her. If he touched her, she would weep. If he didn't, she would weep.

The tears edged down her face, gathering and falling as she nursed her sore hand. She wouldn't betray her feelings by raising her hand to her face. A tear dropped on a long patch of gray salve he'd so carefully, so gently, stroked on her forearm. She watched the bead of moisture travel along the herbal, then trickle onto the undamaged skin of the back of her hand.

Kered thought she was a slut. Little did he know. Tony would laugh if he heard that. Uptight virgin, he'd called her, then frigid bitch. Her determination to wait for marriage seemed ludicrous now. If Kered had not asked for a price, had merely fallen to the ground with her, she'd have made love to him with wild abandon, consequences be damned. Maybe she had sought excuses with Tony—had not really wanted him the way she now knew she wanted Kered.

But he thought she was a slave—one who gave sex for coin. A slut. No, a slut gave it away for free. A prostitute. Who cared about semantics? Both meant no respect. Just contempt.

The tears flowed and dripped off her cheeks, staining Kered's shirt and muddying the gray paste. He moved away as quietly as he'd come—to Windsong. She heard him murmuring to the stallion and knew he was saddling the horse.

Maggie wiped her eyes with her hands, then dried them on the grass by her feet. She took a long calming breath and returned to camp, doing the chore she imagined Kered considered slave duty, smothering their fire with dirt. When Windsong trotted to her side, her eyes were dry. Kered extended his hand, but she ignored it. He fisted his hand on his thigh and sat in silence.

Maggie did as she'd done since her earliest days of riding behind her father when they visited her grandmother on the reservation. She grasped his shirt and placed a foot on his boot. Her leg was extended to the cracking point, but she managed to drag herself up behind him. She sat on Windsong's broad rump and grasped Kered's belt. It was just like riding on the back of Tony's motorcycle. Kered shrugged and kicked the horse's flanks.

They flew into a gallop. No more sheltering in his arms. No more small kisses on the top of her head, or laying his cheek on hers to point out some change in the terrain. No, *she* would choose the moments of contact, *she* would choose the time to speak. When the horse slowed to a canter, she slipped her hand into his pack, retrieved her gun, and thrust it into the tie about her waist. Never again would she relinquish her safety to this man. How could she trust him to save her from some disgusting fate? How could she even sleep soundly knowing he had so little regard for her?

Kered was inordinately pleased. A stupid grin stretched his mouth, he knew, but she could not see it or comment. She had refused him. She had passed his simple test. Whatever she was in her land, giving pleasure for coin was not her way. If he had continued, lain with her, not spoken, he would never have known the truth of it. Now he knew she did not easily dispense her favors. Perhaps loyalty to her master kept her from yielding, but he was sure she had wanted him as much as he had wanted her. He touched his face. A strong little slave, for his jaw ached. Aye. He was inordinately pleased.

Windsong cropped the long grass. Kered watched Maggie crouch down and slosh the length of cloth in the clear water. For a moment she turned her face to the pure white clouds scudding across the lavender sky. Wringing out the cloth, she wandered through the thick ground cover of tiny, white star-shaped flowers. Each step she took crushed some of the petals and their strong scent came to him, sweet and, at the same time, citrus-tart.

She rubbed at the gray patches on her arms and then scrubbed at her cheeks. He knew the moment had arrived—the time to see if her sores were showing the suppuration that signaled rot, scarring, pain, and disfigurement. Kered met her in the middle of the flower-strewn meadow. He took the cloth from her hands. With gentle motions he wiped away the last of the herbal.

"Am I okay?"

He met her eyes. "Okay? You say this often. I do not know the meaning of this word." Kered smiled down at her, then touched the tip of her nose. "You are still beautiful. Some red marks, but they will soon disappear. We acted in time."

"Why didn't the venom hurt you?"

He raised and dropped his shoulders, trying to be nonchalant as he touched each red mark, turning her chin to the left and right. "I am not sensitive. I am made of sterner stuff."

Maggie swayed and staggered closer to him.

He grasped her and hoisted her into his arms. "Come, we have lingered too long in the hypnoflora. It seems you are sensitive to its seductive scent, just as you were sensitive to the venom."

"Hm?" she murmured against his neck. Her head lolled heavily against his neck and her arm fell off his shoulder to dangle at her side. She tried to lift her head, but it fell limp against him. "Ker?"

"Aye, little slave." He placed her gently near his pack on the soft carpet of grass. They should be eating, not resting.

"Ker?"

"Aye?" He stretched at her side and gathered her against him. They lay belly to belly, her face nestled in the warmth of his throat. "What is it you want to know?"

"Are you a dream? Are you real?" Her breath caressed his skin at the open neck of his shirt.

"I am real. 'Tis you who are a dream. A man's pleasure dream."

Maggie lifted her head, and he drew her up until their lips met. The kiss grew slowly from a languid foray to a deeply arousing caress. Like a pot lingering on a boil, like the tiny bubbles seeking to break the water's surface, his desires churned.

He halted the kiss. She was deeply under the influence of the floral aura. If it wore off, she might despise him for taking advantage. One last touch. He lifted his hand and for a brief instant let his fingers graze over her breast.

Her cry of pain startled him. "What hurts, little one?" He rose on his elbow and plucked open the tightly laced neck of her shirt, spreading the edges and looking down on her. His breath caught in his throat. Her breasts were small and perfect, but her nipples stood out angry and red, chafed by the coarse cloth of his shirt. "Nilrem's beard." He placed his cool palm to her. She groaned.

Kered edged the shirt up her hips. She lifted and assisted in a languid manner that seemed uncaring or half asleep. *Or inviting*. He shook off the notion and worked the shirt from her arms. She lay nearly naked before him, one hand clutched tightly about her pendant.

Her breathing slowed to a barely perceptible sigh as she succumbed to the deep hypnofloral sleep. Whatever control he had, had fled. He grew turgid with desire. Her smooth belly above the scanty scrap of cloth that was her undergarment drew him. He skimmed his fingers along her ribs and over her belly. Like a butterfly kissing a petal, he traced the borders of the unusual undergarment, traced the low band that edged her raven-black feminine hair.

He grew bolder, spreading his palm on her thigh and

caressing down its smooth length. It occurred to him that she knew bathhouses. The hair on her legs had been removed, was growing back soft as a babe's. 'Twas a common occurrence at a bathhouse to have one's body hair removed.

Was she a bathhouse attendant? The thought knotted his stomach, made his skin break out in a sweat. Her reactions did not seem those of a practiced fornitrix. No, she attended one man. Her master. He pictured this man. If necessary, he would battle the man for possession of her.

Slowly, he surrendered a tiny corner of his control, leaned forward and kissed her breast, feeling her heart beat against his cheek. She arched and moaned beneath him, moving her hand from her pendant to stroke languorously through his hair. He grew bolder, taking the sore bud of her breast between his lips and soothing it with his tongue.

Windsong lifted his head and snorted.

Kered leapt to his feet. "My mind is muddled by the hypnoflora, else I would never allow my attention to wander from my goal."

He opened his pack and searched about for the last of the herbs, then mixed a thin paste, for there was little left. In a few moments he had spread the meager amount across Maggie's nipples. He unfolded a long bandage and bound it about her breasts, then worked the shirt onto her arms. When Windsong tossed his head in a jangle of bridle and reins, Kered looked up and grinned.

"Thank you, my friend, for reminding me of my responsibilities!" He shook Maggie awake, then forced water and small pieces of bread down her throat until she pushed his hand away.

With stoic deliberation and a self-righteous sense of

accomplishment that his desires were under seventh-level lock and key, he planted his back against a tree as she regained her senses. He watched her listlessly tear bread and chew it and swallow it. Even that simple act seemed fraught with some hidden sensual meaning.

He must see his awareness master when the quest was through to retrain himself to resist these thoughts. 'Twould be for the best. Maggie would wish to return to Nilrem's mountain. Could he take her there and never see her again? Could he let her go? He shook away his thoughts. The deprivation of sleep and nourishing food were taking their toll—that was it, nothing more.

When they reached the Isle of N'Olava, he must be ready or Maggie's dream would come true. For on N'Olava, he would fight mortal men. Sly and evil men.

Blood would flow.

# Chapter Twelve

"Did I die? Are you an angel?" Maggie yawned and stretched, rubbing her back against a soft, grassy bed.

The hovering angel smiled. "Many consider me so. 'Tis true few men will fight me for fear they slay some messenger of the gods." The angel touched her cheek.

"Ker," Maggie screamed, scrambling to her feet. The man was not a dream. He was real, huge, and beautiful, so achingly beautiful that her mangy Kered looked like a gargoyle in comparison.

"Vad!" Kered embraced the angel, engulfing him in a back-breaking hug. "How did you find us?"

"Nilrem. How else? Are you truly going on the quest . . . No, do not answer." Vad broke from Kered's arms and strode to Windsong's saddle lying by the fire. He knelt and ran a hand over the hilt of the sacred sword. Reverence lit his face.

Should Kered's friend be kneeling in a chapel, Maggie

thought, he might be some visitor from heaven. His white cloak, heavily embroidered down the back with gold and black, hung from broad shoulders. His hair was a shade of blond that looked almost silver in the dawning light. His profile was breathtaking. She looked from Kered to Vad. Kered stood several inches taller, but Vad's body was leaner, slimmer.

A Warrior God and now an angel. What next?

A jingle of harness drew her eyes. An angel's horse. Maggie instantly thought of fairy tales. A white steed. A handsome prince. She searched the horizon for the evil witch. Surely a counterpoint was needed for so much dazzling perfection. She shivered as if some harbinger of evil had crossed her path.

"I did not believe," the young man said in a hoarse whisper. "May I?"

Kered flicked a negligent hand at the sword, and his friend rose and pulled it from the scabbard. With practiced ease, just as Kered had done, he swiped the air, took the sword's measure, felt its weight. " 'Tis fine. They do not make swords like this anymore. Look at the detail on the hilt. Nilrem says you will bear this as your own arms before the council and seek peace. I want to attend you at your ring ceremony." Vad presented the sword to Kered, hilt first, laying it with reverence in his friend's palm.

Kered took it and hefted it once before he sheathed it in Windsong's saddle.

"It would be an honor to have you attend me, but the blade will earn me only prestige. Acquiring the cup will gain me a council seat."

" 'Tis why I followed, my friend. One man against the guards at N'Olava? 'Tis folly. Take me with you."

Maggie studied the frown on Kered's face as he busied himself securing his saddle to Windsong's back. He jerked the girth tight and Windsong bucked his hind legs in protest.

Kered slapped him on the flanks. "No. You may not accompany me. I do not wish to be responsible for your death." Kered shook his head.

"My death? I am as able as you!" Vad strode angrily to Kered, his white cloak swinging out behind him in an inanimate protest. "Since when have we counted our safety in aiding a friend?"

"Since the friend was you." Kered turned to Vad and clasped his arm. "I thank you for the offer, but we go alone."

Vad faced Maggie. "You would take this female to assist you and refuse one of your lieutenants?" The look he shot her could boil blood.

"Did Nilrem not tell you *why* she accompanies me?" Kered swung up into his saddle.

"Aye. Some rot about omens and necklaces." Vad fisted his hands on his hips.

"Show him the necklace, Maggie." Kered's face lit like a child anticipating the presentation of something wonderful.

She drew the pendant from its hiding place against her skin. The waves of anger coming from the angel made her step back a pace as he drew nearer. Unlike Kered's, Vad's clothing was immaculate. His long white tunic with gold braiding and his trousers, black and clingy-leather like Kered's, were as perfect as his face. His high black boots could serve as a mirror. If she looked, Maggie knew she'd see her grimy face. Thank God she'd braided her hair. Vad's blond hair, swept back from his brow, fell in long waves below his shoulders, cut so perfectly he might have stepped from a Manhattan

147

salon. She continued to retreat until Kered spoke.

"Stand fast, Maggie. Vad will not hurt you. Show him the necklace." With reluctance, she stood still and held the pendant out for him.

Vad did not look at the necklace. Instead he stared, gape-mouthed. "Your skin. 'Tis red."

Kered frowned. "Attend the necklace and not my slave's skin."

Vad whirled, his scabbard knocking painfully against Maggie's knees. "Not you, too," he said.

Kered glared at his friend.

"Nilrem says she is from beyond the ice fields. A runaway. You claim her?"

"Aye. I claim her." The two men stood in silence, facing one another. "Attend the necklace," Kered repeated.

Maggie could only see Kered's face. Deep lines of fatigue and anger pulled at his mouth.

"I see." Vad turned away, his shoulders slumping.

"You see nothing," Kered said to his back.

Vad approached Maggie, his eyes locked on hers. Dejected eyes. Cerulean. Heavenly. Hypnotic.

"Nilrem thinks your master abused you." Vad spoke softly, so only she could hear.

"I have no master," Maggie said with bitterness. *This was getting tedious.*

"May I?" He asked permission, but didn't wait for it to be granted. His long-fingered hand brushed hers as he lifted the pendant.

"By the sword. 'Tis the sacred eight." Amazement banished his downcast aspect.

He turned the pendant from side to side, the red light glinting from a gold ring on his middle finger. Maggie studied it closely. The strands of gold interlocked in an ancient Celtic pattern she recognized well. Her chain echoed its twists.

"The craftsman who fashioned this is talented. No, a genius. I see no joins. And the chain—" His fingers slid up the silver links to her neck.

Kered growled.

Vad dropped the necklace as if it burned, turning abruptly away. " 'Tis fated," Vad said, moving to Kered's side.

"Fated, fated, damn it," Maggie muttered, going around the beautiful warrior and clambering up behind Kered. She settled herself, tugging his shirt as neatly as possible about her thighs.

"Lovely," Vad murmured.

Maggie blushed, for he was inspecting her legs.

"I thank you for your offer of help, but I wish to make the journey alone," Kered said. Windsong danced at his snarling tone.

Vad scowled back. "We were found together on Nilrem's mountain as orphans. We were raised together, though Leoh claimed but you as his own. We have campaigned together for a decade. I know you well enough to understand why you wish me gone. I had thought you were different from the rest, but I see I was wrong."

Vad's upturned face revealed a hurt so clearly etched it was painful to see. Maggie gripped Kered's belt to keep from falling as Windsong sidled and pranced. Kered's back was as stiff and as unyielding as a block of concrete.

"I cannot deny it," Kered said. " 'Tis the first time I have—have understood." He reached out and touched his friend's shoulder.

Vad shook off Kered's hand. "So, I do not have even you to count as friend." He turned and stormed to his waiting stallion, who, unlike Windsong, stood stock-still, well-trained and obedient. He mounted in a movement far less fluid than Kered's, then yanked the reins and rode to their side. The red sun behind him lit his silvery hair like a fiery halo.

"I meant no offense," Kered said, reaching out again.

Vad spurned his extended hand. "Yet, I am offended. I offer only arms to make your quest. Nothing else will happen."

Kered lowered his hand and fisted it on his thigh. "Nilrem's beard! You cannot control the thoughts of others."

"And what of trust? In me? And others?" Vad asked.

"Trust?" Kered's back eased, his fist relaxed, and he spread his fingers on his thigh, rubbing as if his flesh itched.

"Aye. Trust. Have we not even that between us?" Vad waited, his own hands white-knuckled on his reins.

A shudder ran up Kered's spine. Maggie's arms encircled his waist. He was making some decision, and she squeezed him to reassure him. About what, she hadn't figured out. He placed a hand over hers and returned the pressure.

"I would be honored to have you accompany us on the quest." Kered's voice was rough on the words.

"You will not regret it," Vad said, then swung his horse in a dancing circle, whooping and shouting like a crazed cowboy at a rodeo.

"By the sword, I hope not," Kered whispered, then spurred Windsong to a gallop. Maggie bent her head against the rushing wind, pressing her cheek to his back. Behind her, the thunder of hooves told her Vad followed.

\*  \*  \*

"Ker's exhausted," Maggie said, kneeling by Kered's angelic friend.

"Speak more slowly. You are most difficult to understand," Vad said.

*And you sound like an old, B-grade English movie.* She sighed. He edged away from her. Did she smell bad? Probably. She probably had bad breath, too. "I will try. I am glad you are here. Kered has pushed himself beyond his limits. He never sleeps and except for a few little blue things he caught and roasted, he has eaten only bread and water."

"He is most canny at snaring the blue-Goh." The angel looked fondly on his friend. "Not so good with the green." Kered's snores nearly drowned out their conversation, but they kept their voices low.

"Thank you for coming. He only lets me take a watch for a few hours, then he forces himself to take over. You can probably count on one hand the number of decent hours of sleep he's had in weeks. The man is driven."

"He lets you watch?" Vad's arched brows lifted in surprise. "What a thought!"

"What's that supposed to mean?" Maggie shot him a venomous glare. "I'm perfectly able to—"

"Slowly, softly," Vad waved a hand at her. "You will wake him. I meant no insult."

Maggie whispered. "You and I need to get a few things straight." She spoke slowly and enunciated every word in case he didn't understand. "I am not a slave. Neither you nor Kered can say anything to change that. Beyond the ice fields things are different. You will have to accept that."

"Kered accepts that?"

"I believe so." Maggie chewed her lip. "He promised me that when this quest is over, he will return me to

Nilrem's mountain.'' She studied the man before her. His bright blue eyes raised an ache in her chest. They vividly reminded her of the summer sky over Ocean City. ''I don't—do not—remember how I came to be on Nilrem's mountain, but in here—'' she tapped her chest—''I know that if I am ever to find my way home, I have to start there. Nilrem and Kered believe in these omens—my appearance at the conjunction and this pendant.'' She lifted the heavy weight of the necklace and slid it down into the neckline of the shirt to hide it again. ''I am not arguing the point—''

''One does not argue with Kered,'' Vad interrupted.

''You can say that again!'' Maggie grinned.

''One does not argue with Kered,'' he repeated, his face lighting with a radiant smile showing straight white teeth.

They laughed together and Maggie sensed they had just shared something important. They were bonded in an instant from the understanding of a mutual friend, perhaps of a man who was more than a friend.

''As I was saying, I am not arguing the point that my role in Ker's quest is important, but I have to go home.'' She looked about at the empty landscape shrouded in purple shadows and then up at the four moons scattered now in the night sky. ''I don't know this place.''

Vad touched her knee, briefly, lightly. ''Both Kered and I know this need for home. Nilrem found us, you know, wandering Hart Fell. He took us to Leoh. Had not Kered borne the sign . . . well, life might have been different. But Leoh took Kered as his own, and fostered me.'' He looked at his sleeping friend. ''Kered is as a brother to me.''

''He said as much.''

''Aye. I am surprised he shared it with you. Most

often, Kered shelters himself from the scrutiny of others.''

"He only said Leoh had adopted him. I sensed it was a subject closed to discussion.''

Vad nodded and looked at Kered. "Our parents were never found. We were but children and could not account for ourselves. There are those who would make an evil of that lack of knowledge and prevent Kered from taking his rightful place, no matter the sign he wears. He has always needed to fight twice as hard, be doubly strong, more valiant, more worthy, as a result of his origins.''

"I see." Maggie pulled the cloak closer about her neck. The light breeze was rising to a wicked bite. If she had a watch she could time this wind change, for it happened each night with predictability. She looked longingly at Kered's warm body.

"You look upon him as a lover does," Vad said.

"We're—we are not lovers." She felt the rush of blood to her face. Was she so transparent?

"By the sword, your skin is changing again!" Vad reached out to touch her, then hesitated and withdrew. He physically edged away from her.

"Do I offend you in some way? I know I need a bath—"

"No, no. It is just—" Vad looked at Kered. "He would not like me to touch you.''

"You should be worried about whether I like it!" Anger spiked through her, then died just as quickly at the stricken look on Vad's face.

"I beg forgiveness." He leaned forward. By doing so, the fire painted shadows on his face, defined his high cheekbones and chiseled mouth. "I cannot bear to have him doubt me. 'Tis why I draw away." Then he smiled.

"You do need a bath, though, as does he."

"Why would he doubt you?"

"This face. This damnable face," Vad snarled. " 'Tis a wicked curse. I had hoped at one time that battle might scar me, ease the burden, but even on the field, men run. No one fights me, lest they wound one of the god's angels. I am a pariah."

The vehemence of his response took her by surprise. "You don't—do not—believe that?"

"Aye. And now, Kered."

"Kered?"

"Aye, Kered. Now he looks upon me with the same loathing."

"I do not understand." She looked in confusion from Vad to Kered.

He leaned closer. "Kered was the one man who did not slay me with his jealousy. Until today."

"Jealousy? Why would he be jealous of you?" She leaned closer. Their heads almost touched as they whispered.

"In my younger days, I was often indiscreet. The women, they . . ." He cleared his throat. "Suffice to say, I have had no difficulty attracting whatever female I wish to my bed. Kered is the one who taught me that 'twas wrong to take such advantage. Yet it amused him. Most men do not wish me for a friend in fear that their lifemates or sisters or daughters will want me." He sighed. "Kered has always treated me as a brother. Never shunned me. Until now. I saw it in his eyes, heard it in his voice. He has finally found a woman he wishes to possess. He thinks I will steal away your affections. These damnable looks!" He drew the blade sheathed at his waist and stabbed its point into the dirt at his feet. "Would that I could scar this face."

Maggie reached for Vad's hand.

He snatched it back. "Do not touch me, or he will think you want me."

"No, he will not. He doesn't even like me."

"He has never looked at me like the others—until today. Now, he is just like everyone else—jealous. It can only mean he cares a great deal for you. For his sake, for the sake of our friendship, you must make me a promise. No matter how this face and form of mine should draw you, you will resist."

Maggie gasped, then choked, then ducked her head so she wouldn't offend him by laughing. "I promise," she said solemnly, raising her hand in the Girl Scout salute. "I will resist with all my might."

They sat in uneasy silence for a few moments, then Vad cleared his throat to speak. "Kered has much on his mind. It is important we not add to his burdens."

"Is there something troubling him—beyond the quest, that is?"

"Samoht. The two have been rivals for years and on many levels." Vad glanced in Kered's direction and then lowered his voice. "You know of his betrothal?"

"Not really." Maggie felt a quick pang of jealousy. "I only know of someone named Einalem."

"Ah, the fair Einalem." Vad's words didn't go with his sneer. Even Vad's sneers were alluring.

Maggie shook her head. Gwen would never believe that this man was real.

"Tell me of the fair Einalem," she urged.

"How come you to know of her?" Vad asked.

"I overheard Ker and Nilrem, but I'd like to hear about her from you."

"Einalem and Kered have known each other since they were children. Her ancestral line descends from the

155

great Ruhtra, as does Leoh's. Without those ties, a life-mating would not have been considered between them. Kered was not pleased when first her name was proposed. The council often makes these decrees without thought for those involved.''

"Did he love her?" Maggie twisted a strand of her hair about her finger, trying not to let an edge of jealousy creep into her voice.

"Love? Poet's words. I suppose Kered felt for her as one would a sister. We all learned at Nilrem's knee, as did the other children of the council members. Our companions were the same. Her brother, Samoht—"

"Samoht!" Maggie sat up straighter in dismay. "I had no idea."

"Aye. You can see how her betrothal to Kered would anger Samoht. It would bring their families into play whenever they were at cross purposes."

"Go on," Maggie urged, leaning forward into the cocoon of the fire's warmth. "Why didn't she accept Ker? How do you feel about that?"

"One question at a time. I believe Einalem's rejection was at her father's behest. The treaties gave much power to Kered. Her father and Samoht probably decided it made him too formidable a foe should Leoh die."

"Forget politics for a moment. How does he feel about the lady's rejection, personally?"

"Relieved," Vad stated emphatically. "Relieved that he would not be brother-by-mating to Samoht."

Maggie linked her fingers about her knees. "It would be hard to be lifemates under those circumstances."

"Aye 'twould test all seven levels of awareness." Vad fell silent, then he cleared his throat. "Of course, there would be compensations."

"Compensations?" Maggie wondered what Vad could mean.

"Oh, aye. They do not call her the fair Einalem for no reason." There was an easily detectable bitterness in his voice. "She is beautiful. As breathtaking as one of the ancient goddesses. Her hair is like the silver snow on Nilrem's mountain."

"But Ker doesn't really want her, does he?" Maggie tried to control her jealousy.

"It matters not. Einalem rejected him," Vad said, closing the subject.

Maggie struggled to her feet and tiptoed past Kered's sleeping form to Windsong's side. She leaned her head on Windsong's warm neck. The scent of his dusty coat raised memories of home, of currying her grandmother's horses, of sweeping out the stables.

*I hope this quest is over soon,* she thought, as she stroked her hand along Windsong's neck. *I have to go home, I have to—before I fall in love.*

# *Chapter Thirteen*

Every muscle of Maggie's body ached from the punishing pace the men set. Surely, she had calluses on the calluses on her rear from the hours of riding.

Maggie became aware of a change in Kered's posture. Where he had been relaxed, at one with his mount, now he had grown rigid, every muscle she leaned on taut in expectation. Vad rode up from his position behind them to shout, ''The sea.''

Stretched before her lay an amethyst sea. Lacy edges embroidered the waves. Gentle lapping waters met a white sandy beach. The stark contrast of colors against black cliffs took her breath away. They came to a halt at the edge of a cliff, giving her a panoramic view of the shore.

Dark shadows in the nearly black cliffs might be caves or a lichen or mossy covering. The shadows made a patchwork of the sheer rocks. They faced a horseshoe of beach, standing at one leg, looking across to the other. She put her hand on Kered's shoulder.

"Is it here? The cup?"

"No," he said, extending his arm and pointing out to sea. " 'Tis there."

Maggie looked where he pointed and saw it. A craggy island. Small and lonely in its violet sea.

"How will we get there?" she asked, gulping.

"The orbs course the sky at their farthest point tonight. 'Tis then the tides turn and a land bridge appears from this beach to N'Olava. The sea will be flat and calm. Usually, this beach is awash, the waves as high as a ship's mast. If we had delayed, we would have needed to wait for the coming and waning of yet another conjunction."

"Thank God, then, that we've come in time. Do we cross on this land bridge?" she asked.

"And be cut down by the famed N'Olavan archers? No," he said with a hint of amusement. "My plan is to make them think an army awaits the coming of the bridge."

"How will you do that?" Maggie asked.

"The turn of season leaves much debris on the shore. We will gather any dry brush we can and set fires here"—he swept out his hand to indicate the top of the cliff—"and there." He pointed to the beach far below. "Alight, they will appear as a camping army. As the guards on yonder isle await attack from many, two men will stealthily row out and come from the other side."

"Has anyone tried that before?" Maggie worried her lip with her teeth.

"Not in recorded history."

"How will we get there?" she asked him.

"*Vad and I* will use a boat, of course." There was an unstated "idiot" in his tone.

"*We* will have to get down *there* before *you men* can go anywhere."

He grinned. Reluctantly, she thought. He slapped his reins, urging Windsong along the cliff's edge. They came to a steep path and Maggie was grateful that Windsong was sure-footed and rested. Vad's white mount picked his way almost daintily behind them. Maggie squeezed her eyes closed and pressed her face into Kered's back. He laughed and she pinched his arm. What seemed an interminable time later, they reached the sheltered beach.

The wind whispered and Maggie welcomed the salt-scented air that lifted her hair and dried the sweat on her brow.

Kered wasted no time. He strode along the cliff base and finally chose a cave at the shoreline with a draped rock face that gave them a small sheltered area to spend the day. The men tethered their horses, spending time praising them for the long journey. Kered played a game of head shaking with Windsong, both tossing their tangled manes and snorting at each other. Maggie found herself laughing at the two of them. The head tossing became buffets and soon Windsong and Vad's mount were churning the sand in mock battle with Kered.

"Enough," Vad shouted. "Warok will be hopelessly soiled."

"As are you, my friend." Kered approached his irate companion, whose golden splendor had wilted somewhat. There were streaks of dirt down one side of Vad's cloak and his boots were dusty from toe to knee. "We will have need of the bathhouse on our return."

"If we return," Vad muttered, looking out at the sea.

The isle was as hidden from them in the folds of the cliffs as they were from it.

"We will prepare our fires and search for their boat," Kered instructed.

"What makes you so sure a boat is around somewhere?" Maggie asked, scanning the beach. Here and there, black rocks rose like hulking beasts, covered with a gray residue that she found on closer inspection was a crust of tiny barnacles.

Kered stood and faced the waiting sea, hands on hips. "The men who guard the cup must come and go somehow. They need provisions. Fresh water. I would imagine they have several boats. One here and at least one there."

"How many guards?" She went to his side, putting her own hands on her hips as he had, mirroring his stance and demeanor.

"Who knows? Their archers make keeping a full company unnecessary."

"Great," Maggie muttered, remembering how close the Wartmen's fletched arrows had come to killing them. "Why is the cup out there?" she asked, shading her eyes with her hand.

"The cup was stolen from Tolemac and has remained guarded on N'Olava by Tolemac's enemies. 'Tis a symbol that we are powerless against outside forces. We can only defend, not extend."

"Who stole the cup?"

"An ambitious man with help from a treacherous female."

"Ah, of course, the treacherous female. What part did she play?"

Kered turned from the sea and frowned down at her. "She played the seductress, what else?" He stomped

161

past her and hunkered down, opening his pack and tossing her his brush. She took it and began to brush her hair. It felt wonderful, but the enjoyment was tempered by his statement. Vad busied himself with their saddles and cloaks, setting himself apart from their conversation.

"Do you think all women are treacherous?"

"Hm. Enough that men must be wary." Kered scanned the sea.

Maggie remained where she was, standing, brushing her hair out in long sweeping strokes. "You don't have a very high opinion of women, do you?"

He shrugged. "They are most often a burden."

"A burden?" She clamped her hands into fists to prevent herself from hitting him over the head with the brush. Then she relaxed. Perhaps he was baiting her. "Seems to me women can be pretty useful."

"Aye, for pleasure and, of course, for barter."

Maggie pictured women lined up in rows being exchanged for swords and horses. "Barter!" she shouted.

"Lower your voice, Maggie, else the guards on the isle will have no need to see us—they will hear us!"

"I'm sorry," she whispered. She knew how well sound traveled over water. "But barter. You can't barter a human being."

"Perhaps the word offends you, yet that is what happens when a father gives his daughter as lifemate in exchange for political power. If the woman is not honorable, the bargain is ill-met. There are many examples in history from which to choose; the cup is but one example."

"Not all women are treacherous, Kered. Many are loyal, steadfast, and an asset to the man they choose."

"Choose?" He looked up. "Men choose."

"In my world, women and men choose. They both choose and they both refuse."

Kered rose and stepped close, taking the brush and giving a few quick negligent strokes to his own tangled mane. "In my world, the men choose and the women accept."

"My experience has been the opposite. The men are the seducers, the ones who don't honor their promises."

He touched her cheek. "I sense a lecture."

"No, I'm not going to lecture you, but you have to understand that every individual is different. There are loyal men and rotten men, and the same goes for women."

"What rotten men do you know?"

"My grandfather, for one. Or rather my mother's father." Maggie began to walk along the cliff face, away from Vad and the isle. "My grandmother is a Navajo."

"I do not know this chiefdom."

She swept her hand out in exasperation. "It's beyond the ice fields."

"Ah." He linked his fingers through hers.

"Anyway, Gran's a Navajo. When she was sixteen, she went with a church group to this religious retreat—"

"She was pledged to the gods?"

Maggie thought about how to describe a youth retreat of her century to a man who was medieval in thought and action. "No. Not pledged, just very active in religious work." He grunted and began to swing her arm back and forth. They could have been a couple strolling the beach of Ocean City, enjoying a summer evening. Suddenly, Maggie no longer found the white sand appealing and wished for the gray of New Jersey. "Gran met this soldier. There were many soldiers about then; a war was going on. They fell in love, or Gran fell in love. The soldier went off to war and although he made many promises, he never wrote or came back.

"My Gran's life was hard after that because she had a baby—and no husband to support them. The People, the Navajo, made life pretty hard for her. See, the soldier wasn't a Navajo. I learned a lot from my mother about intolerance and being an outcast. She grew up well loved by Gran and Gran's family, but the community never accepted her."

"Your mother, she found a lifemate, did she not? You are here." He stopped and smiled down at her.

"Yes, my father's wonderful, but not Navajo. Mother wanted that acceptance from her mother's people, but never found it until her later years. They live on the Navajo lands now, teaching, helping out."

"So this Gran, she was betrayed by a man."

"And her whole life has been doubly difficult as a result."

"I think there is more than your Gran's hard life behind these words of male treachery." He gathered her in, close to him. "Tell me what your master did to you."

Maggie grew stiff in the circle of his arms. Then before she could stop herself, she let thoughts held inside spill out. "I almost made the same mistake as my Gran. Listening to empty promises, believing in lies."

He hugged her, but remained silent.

"I was so sure that Tony loved me. So sure. We had this continuing stupid argument. I wanted to wait for— never mind. He promised me that we would get . . . life-mated. One night, this man I thought I knew so well made love to another woman." Kered gripped her tightly. She could barely breathe in his embrace. "I-I left him and went home to my parent's place. He promised me he would never hurt me again—ever. I believed every word ... then I found him with ... another woman. He made lots of promises—all meaningless.''

"This is the man from whom you run, is it not?''

Maggie jerked out of his arms. She imagined it would be easier to just say yes. "I'm sure Vad is wondering what became of us.'' She turned to run.

Kered grabbed her wrist. "Expend your fury in gathering the shore debris.''

She almost quivered with her anger. He'd heard nothing she had been trying to say. "Anything else you need done?''

"Aye,'' he answered, releasing her. "There is a rent in Vad's cloak that needs repair.''

Maggie bit her lip to keep from shrieking. She moved along the shore, bending and gathering the clumps of dry seaweed and straw that littered the beach. The hard work released her pent-up anger. As much as she wanted to fault the two men, they worked twice as hard as she hauling the debris they gathered up to the top of the cliff. When the task was done, small fires waited to be lit all along the shore and across the cliff top. Both men were sweaty and rivulets of grime ran down their faces. Their shirts clung to their backs.

Neither complained when she tossed them dry bread. They passed around the gourd and drank greedily.

The two men squatted near the horses and Maggie watched them make their plans, drawing in the sand with sticks. Occasionally, Kered looked up. Each time, Maggie made sure she was bent industriously over Vad's cloak. Her first thought when Vad had handed it to her was to tack it carelessly, so Kered would not assign her such work again, but the cloak did badly need mending. The hem might catch on Vad's sword, or on a tree at some inopportune moment. Her anger would not allow her to neglect the task and cause the blond warrior some harm. Instead, she stabbed the needle through the cloth, satisfying herself by imagining she was pricking someone else all the while.

Finally, the men rose and approached her. Vad wrapped himself in his newly repaired cloak after giving her effusive thanks.

Kered crouched near her. Maggie waited for him to speak. She longed to climb into his arms, but her disappointment over his lack of response to her emotional outpouring made her keep her distance.

"Maggie," he began.

"Yes. Is there some chore you need performed? Some women's task that needs doing?"

He frowned. "Have I done something to disappoint you?"

She met his eyes. To tell him the truth would make her vulnerable. "No. What do you want?"

"Should Vad and I die on the morrow—" he began.

She flew into his arms, encircling his neck and hugging him with a ferocious need. "Don't say it. Don't say it."

He pulled her away and shook her. "I must say it. If Vad and I die tomorrow, take Windsong. If you ride under cover of darkness and keep the moons to the east at night, you will eventually come to Hart Fell."

"I can't do it. I can't." She trembled, not from fear for her survival, but for him.

Kered smoothed her hair from her face. "Where is my worthy warrior woman who called the sword from the Sacred Pool?" His words were soft and beguiling, his hands gentle. "When the land bridge disappears, wait one sun-rising. If we are not back—go on alone. Loose Warok to find his own way."

Maggie shook her head in vehement denial. "You had better come back, because I'm not going anywhere. If I have to wait forever, damn you, I'll wait."

He drew her hands to his mouth and kissed her palms. "You will go. I command it. Wait one sun-rising, no more."

# Chapter Fourteen

Kered nudged Vad's leg with his boot. Vad shook himself awake, groaning and plucking at his wrinkled tunic. " 'Tis true, I look as woeful as the two of you."

Maggie smiled. There was amusement in his tone and she suspected that little dampened Vad's spirits.

The men began to hone their weapons. Maggie knelt by Kered and watched the easy practiced motions of his hands as he whetted his knife and his two swords—the everyday one, and the sword of Ruhtra. She was struck again by the beauty of the engraving and its resemblance to her own work. "I assume you expect fighting," she said.

"We are expecting bloodshed, aye." Kered continued at his task.

"That doesn't have to be," Maggie stated emphatically.

"Why?" Vad cocked his head to the side and dazzled her with a bright smile.

Kered looked at her belt and the weapon concealed in the loose folds of his shirt. "Maggie, hold your tongue," he ordered.

"No. This is life and death."

"Aye, *your* life or death. You will keep your weapon to yourself—for your own protection. I have no need of it," he finished.

Vad spoke into the strained silence. "Maggie has her own weapon?"

Kered ignored him. "You must hope that we are successful, else you will need your weapon—returning to Hart Fell."

Maggie grabbed his arm, alarm coursing through her. "You have to take it. I couldn't bear it if something happened to you." The gun fell from her waist.

Kered groaned, dropping his head into his hands. Vad snatched the weapon up. "Nilrem's knees. What is this?" Vad asked, crouching at Maggie's side. Unlike Kered, who had had to play with the gun right away, he gingerly returned it to her.

Kered plucked it from Maggie's hand and tucked it into her belt. " 'Tis a weapon from beyond the ice fields. It sends invisible destruction, but how much we do not know. Only Maggie is proficient in its use."

"Invisible destruction? How is it Tolemac has no knowledge of such a thing?" Vad turned to Maggie. "Is she a witch?"

His words sent a chill down her spine.

Vad looked from her to Kered and back again. "Has lust made you blind? Do you shelter some evil here?"

Kered lunged forward and grasped Vad's arm, and for a moment Maggie thought that he would strike his friend. "Maggie is not evil. You have heard the legends of the lands beyond the ice fields—fine legends, wondrous tales. Why would you think a weapon from there would be evil?"

Vad's posture stiffened. "Then show me how it works."

"Show him," Maggie urged. She wanted Kered to take it with him, and perhaps Vad could help her persuade him.

"No," Kered said, turning to her. "Since only you will use it, Vad has no need to know of it."

"Is this the trust we spoke of?" Vad fisted his hands.

"This is not about trust. This is about danger. Maggie does not know how the weapon works or how long it works. 'Tis pointless to speculate on its use. If you trust me, you will accept my word. It is a strange weapon, and 'tis for Maggie's protection, and only her protection—"

"This is so stupid." Maggie halted at the thunderous look on Kered's face. "I mean, you are being unreasonable. You could take it with you and without bloodshed—your bloodshed—bring back the cup."

"I will seek the cup with traditional weapons."

"Many have sought the cup the traditional way," Vad said, then pointed out to sea, "and it is still on N'Olava."

"That is because greedy men sought it. I seek it to bring peace."

"And Samoht and his cohorts will not covet it for its value?"

Vad snorted.

"Aye, they will covet the cup, but it will be safely in the High Priest's hands after I present it. The priests may guard it then. Samoht will find little coin in a holy relic.''

"So, you think you will succeed because you seek the cup with a pure heart?''

"Ah, Vad, what man's heart is ever pure?''

Maggie stamped her foot. The two men looked at her in surprise. "That is enough.'' She pointed the weapon at a pile of brush and pushed the red button. The pile vanished, leaving a smoking black spot on the pure white sand.

Vad stared open-mouthed. "By the sword!'' He looked at the small gun with new respect.

"Now do you understand? You must take it. I can hide in a cave if anyone comes. Convince him, Vad,'' Maggie ordered.

"May I use it?'' Vad asked, with eagerness in both his voice and his posture. "I am an expert at most weapons.''

"Yes, you take it,'' Maggie said, holding it out. Her calculation was correct. Kered's huge hand swept in and snatched it off her palm before Vad even came close.

"I will hold it.'' With ill-grace, Kered bent over his weapons. "You win this skirmish, Maggie. 'Tis a triumph that may see you dead, but you have won—for now.''


Her palms were as sweaty as her brow. Maggie fanned her shirt in the heat and watched the red sun. She held her hand horizontal to the horizon as Kered had taught her. One finger width still remained until the sun disappeared—one-quarter hour. The loneliest and longest evening would finally be behind her. She nursed the small torch behind the rocks. Kered had said to wait until the sun was completely below the horizon.

At the time they had agreed upon, she flitted from pile to pile, setting each bundle of dry sticks ablaze. Out of breath, she sought shelter in the cave where the horses were tethered. To fill the time, she tried to braid her hair, but her hands were shaky and the leather thong broke. Muttering a curse under her breath, she opened Kered's pack in search of another thong. She fell back on her heels in shock. There lay the gun, the gun he'd promised to take—and use. She ran to the cave entrance and stared out across the amethyst sea to the isle.

In her heart, she knew he'd left it for her, so she could protect herself in case they didn't return. All her dreams came to haunt her in her exhausted and nervous state. The blood on his body glistened anew. The bonds that held him now held Vad, too. Was this what the dreams had meant? Had they meant capture by the N'Olavan guards? Had they meant torture for daring to try to take the cup?

Feeling utterly helpless, Maggie sank to the sand. They had three swords and assorted knives. They had no idea of the number of guards and archers they would find.

Windsong nudged her shoulder. Through brimming eyes she looked at the stallion. He seemed to reproach her for her lack of faith. She stood on tiptoe and wrapped her arms about the horse's neck and hugged him as if he were Kered.

"Tell me what to do," she whispered. Even now the guards could be killing the man she loved. Windsong nudged her again. Her foot stumbled against Kered's pack and its contents spilled at her feet.

With shaky hands, Maggie stripped off Kered's shirt. She stood shivering and nearly naked in the chill dark cave and pulled on Kered's black breeches. She wrapped her belt about her waist and rolled the water-stiffened leather about her ankles. All Kered's shirts were white. Vad's pack held even brighter finery. There was little choice. She slung the fur cloak about her bare shoulders, then tied her boots about her neck. Lastly, she rubbed soot on her cheeks.

The tide was out. The four orbs cast a net of silver sparks on the sea, a sea so dark it lay like ebony glass before her. The shining moons magnified the glowing sandy path that lay between her and the isle—and Kered and Vad.

Maggie stepped carefully into an ankle-deep pool of purple water, gripping the gun as if it were as precious as a life preserver. She strode purposefully toward the isle, always at the dark watery edge of the sandy path. It was like trudging along the edges of a shallow sandbar. At one point, the shore dropped from beneath her feet, and she almost screamed aloud as she flailed about in the depths, regaining her balance, yet losing her boots. She stood in silence and watched them float away in the direction of the silent isle. Nothing stirred. She looked back. The fires lit along the shore beckoned her, but she knew that no one tended them, that no one was there to help her.

Sweat soaked her body as she struggled on. She felt exposed, bathed in the lambent light of the orbs as she walked. Occasionally, the path rose up from the water and lay glistening beneath her feet. Steeling herself, she would step away from safety and holding the gun aloft, sink into the black waters and swim clumsily along until the path sank again to a more concealing depth.

As she drew near the rocky isle, Maggie floated off the shoal with a clumsy crawl. Hampered by the weight of the cloak, she swam into the shelter of shadows edging the shore. Her feet touched pebbles. Her thighs trembled and her calves knotted as she crawled along an overhanging bank. The pebbles glowed like opals in the silvery shimmer of one of the orbs. A scent of wood smoke reached her.

The blood pounding in her ears made listening difficult. Finally, her heart calmed and the gentle lapping waves and rustling of leaves was all she heard. Then it came to her. A man shouted. More men joined in. She couldn't hear their words, just recognized their panic. Throwing aside her fears, she crept into the foliage in search of the men she now knew were under siege.

A stone's throw from where she knelt stood a temple. Four gleaming marble pillars shone in the orb-glow. Two guards stood alertly at their posts. Maggie knew which direction to take, for the guards both peered anxiously off to her left.

Stealthily, she made her way through the lush foliage. It snatched at her cloak and slipped along Kered's leather breeches. Her feet hurt, but she didn't have time to tend them. The smell of wood smoke grew choking, and her eyes began to sting.

Men garbed in black and purple uniforms ran about trying to put out small fires in the dense woods. Maggie assumed that Kered and Vad had set them. Quietly, she waited. The panicking men were making little headway with the flames. Grateful for their noisy efforts, Maggie slipped unnoticed past them deeper into the woods.

Maggie halted as she heard the clash of swords up ahead. She peered through the leaves and gasped as she saw Kered fighting four swordsmen. Vad circled and tried to engage two of them to draw them away from his friend. The guards, clad like devils in black, flitted from Vad's sword, eluding his efforts, and melting away to reappear from another direction.

Vad's gleaming hair and the flash of orb-light on Kered's sword were all too easily seen. Their enemies were dangerously hidden as they moved between tree trunks to keep Kered in the clearing and themselves partially shielded. The clash of metal on metal anchored her to her tree and yet, she had no clear target at which to aim.

Although Kered had but two men to worry about, as Vad once again protected his friend's back, the two guards fought with a ferocious strength that frightened her. She raised the gun, then lowered it. Vad had stepped between her and Kered's foes. She winced as a guard's sword flicked a line of blood across Kered's arm.

A hand grasped her cloak and flung her to the ground. The gun slithered from her fingers into the leafy mold beneath her feet.

A tall, bearded guard stood over her, a sneer curling his lip. "A woman." He spat. The spittle hit her face and anger heated her temper to boiling.

With a hard jab of his boot, the guard kicked her onto her back. She screamed as pain exploded in her shoulder.

Maggie heard an unearthly roar. Sure that Gulap was pouncing, she curled into a tiny ball, expecting claws. Kered leapt over her. With one sweep of his sword, Kered disarmed the hovering guard. Maggie's attacker groaned as Kered snatched him off his feet and heaved him into the two guards who had pursued him. The men lay dazed in a pile of arms and legs attempting to extricate themselves.

Maggie stifled a shriek of fear as Kered grasped the guard on the top of the pile and flung him toward Vad. Vad's two opponents, still hesitant to attack him, cowered away from their flying comrade. Kered kicked Maggie's attacker just as he'd kicked her, flinging him ignominiously onto his back, the sickening crunch of breaking bones sounding like brittle twigs snapping. Kered stepped astride the prostrate guard, pricking the epaulettes on his shoulder with the point of the sacred sword and piercing the white skin beneath the man's uniform. "So, Captain, you have made a grave mistake. I could easily kill you. Call off your men or die," Kered ordered.

"Stand off," the guard screamed as blood soaked his uniform. The other guards froze like statues with weapons drawn, wary looks on their faces. Vad used his sword to keep the other guards upon their backs.

"Have your men throw down their weapons—now," Kered commanded. The captain ordered his men to disarm with an ill-concealed hatred.

Maggie struggled to her feet. Her shoulder ached, but she could flex her fingers and lift her arm.

Kered did not take his eyes from the man at his feet as he commanded her. "Get into the trees. There are many more soldiers about."

"My gun," she whispered, going down on her hands and knees and plucking it from the leaves.

"Do as I say." Kered bent and slowly disarmed the supine guard of his remaining weapon, a long, tapered dagger. "We seem to have captured the leader. Vad, gather their arms and secure them."

Vad moved about the clearing collecting swords and knives, then thrust the bouquet of weapons into Maggie's arms. She dumped them into a pile in the black shadows beneath a tangled mass of tree roots.

"You will never take the cup," the guard at Kered's feet snarled as blood ran down the side of his throat.

Kered glanced about as Vad swiftly tied the hands and feet of the disarmed men. "It seems your men will do naught to stop us," he said.

Just then, a crackle of twigs heralded a rush of men. They charged past Maggie, shoving her aside in their hurry to aid their friends. A black horde of shadows fanned out before Kered and Vad. The two friends circled, shoulder to shoulder, swords ready.

*Kered and Vad hadn't a chance against so many.* The guards considered a woman of so little danger, they turned their backs to her.

Maggie took careful aim and just as a man charged into the clearing she fired on blue, sweeping the orb-lit ground from behind the guards. Like duckpins they fell, rolling atop each other, piling over the leader and his fellows who lay bound back to back.

Gasping for air, she looked about. A silence had fallen thick as a blanket of snow in winter.

"Are they dead?" Vad cried.

"No, just sleeping," Maggie said, her voice shaky as she stepped from behind her tree.

"Maggie!" Kered bellowed, charging her like a mad bull. He skidded to a halt.

Her heart was in her mouth. Blood soaked his sleeve and she thought she'd never seen anyone who looked so wonderful or so angry. "You're wounded," she cried, reaching out to touch the crimson stains along his arm. Her fingers came away wet and sticky. She flung herself into his arms.

Kered could feel Maggie's heaving breasts against his chest. The warmth of her and his shock at seeing the guard kick her so viciously made him squeeze the breath from her. He yanked her head back by her long braid. "You disobeyed me. You willfully disobeyed me," he growled. He tasted the metallic bite of blood as their mouths clashed. Their tongues tangled. He lifted her against him. A spiraling sensation of falling made him stagger. The press of her against him, the taste of her, his fear for her coursed in a savage pounding through his veins. A longing, held at bay for weeks, took charge of his senses. As a starving man, he feasted on her.

"When you have finished punishing her, may we get the cup?" Vad asked, stepping from the trees.

Kered dropped Maggie to her feet and pushed her away more roughly than he had intended. Her wet cloak shifted from her shoulder. A shaft of orb-glow touched her breast. Its snowy gleam and dark peak made him snatch the fur about her. His hands gentled, apologizing for his roughness as he stroked her cheek. He did not need to see the tears brimming in her eyes to know he had hurt her.

With a final silent atonement, he lifted her hand and kissed her palm. "Come. Who knows how long these men may sleep? The cup still lies under guard."

"Wait. We must know how many men are loose," Vad said, walking about the slumbering enemy, counting heads and shaking his own in open amazement. "We found their barracks," he explained to Maggie. "There were beds aplenty for a full company of men. There are twelve here. Two at the temple . . . who knows how many archers on the shoreline?"

"Then we go with caution," Kered said, taking Maggie's hand. They stealthily made their way through the dense foliage, avoiding the well-trod path. The temple guards stood in fearful alertness, their eyes trained in the direction of the rising smoke that trailed above the trees.

Kered had not spoken to Maggie, did not trust his

words, but he nodded when she raised one eyebrow in question.

She fired.

The temple guards crumpled to the ground.

"By the sword," Vad cried. He went down on one knee and kissed her hand. " 'Tis a magical goddess you are."

"Oh, Vad," Maggie said, smiling finally at the effusive gesture.

"Are you quite finished? There are more soldiers about." Kered dragged Vad to his feet. "Her weapon is the marvel, not her." No, he thought, he was lying, mainly to himself. Maggie was the marvel, her weapon but an adjunct to her. There was no way she could have come to help them but by walking. The danger of it, the knowledge that she risked much to bring him the weapon, made his stomach clench. He knew she had come to bring the weapon to him, for him. But seeing Vad on his knees, kissing her hand, smashed through his tolerance. The grinding jealousy, a choking emotion he had never experienced before, only added to his burden and made a new enemy that he must fight.

Every muscle of Kered's body screamed for rest. He quivered with a need to snap someone or something, but it must not be Vad. Wearily, he turned away.

They moved cautiously down the dark and cool cave corridor. The flickering torch lights cast eerie shadows on the walls. A half-naked warrior leapt out at them as they rounded a bend.

Maggie swallowed a shriek.

"Calm yourself," Kered hissed, grasping her arm. " 'Tis paintings of our ancestors."

The ghostly light lent a lifelike glow to the ancient

warrior, clad in a loincloth. She took a deep breath to calm herself.

Kered and Vad held their weapons ready and started at every sound. Something scurried across her foot and she stifled another yell. She would not be a coward just because the cave was dark and spooky.

As they moved deeper into the bowels of the cave, the warriors who marched along the walls became uniformed, resplendent in fancy black and purple costumes. Their spears gave way to swords and knives.

"Ruhtra," Kered whispered, his hand touching a wall painting.

Maggie studied the ancient ancestor. The resemblance escaped her. She saw a bearded man in golden robes depicted as a mighty warrior, the famed sword held aloft in one huge hand. Whatever romantic figure she'd pictured in her mind, it had not been this portly gentleman with a belly Santa Claus would envy.

"Come," he urged her. They stepped into a large chamber. On a marble altar at the center of the room stood a silver cup. Its thick neck, at least two inches in diameter, was hollow in the center. Suspended there, as in Maggie's pendant and the sword at Kered's hip, hung a lump of turquoise stone. Eight strands entwined it and held it captive in the shining base. Maggie drew the pendant from beneath the cloak and away from her skin. It had become warm, almost hot to the touch.

Kered stepped forward and stood before the cup. He hesitated and looked back at Vad. Both circled the chamber, searching the gloomy corners, sending rodents scurrying in all directions.

Vad remained reverently several steps behind Kered as he again approached the altar. "How arrogantly they leave the cup displayed."

"What are we waiting for?" Maggie whispered to the men.

"One must ask the proper questions to take the cup," Kered said. A falling rock made them all jump and step back a pace.

"And if you don't ask the proper questions?" Maggie hissed.

Kered ignored her. Vad supplied the answer. " 'Tis said that he who asks the wrong questions will surely die."

Maggie clutched the pendant in fear at his words. "Don't touch it," Maggie cried, grabbing Kered's shirt sleeve.

"Have faith." Kered gently disentangled himself and smiled at her. Gently, he smoothed back her hair that had tumbled from its braid. He took the pendant from her fingers and studied it, stepping back to do so, then clutched it tightly in his fist. "We have come this far, let it be finished."

He opened her cloak and placed the necklace inside, his hand pressing the warm metal to her heart. His fingers lingered there, then tugged the edges of the cloak closed about her throat.

Maggie's heart seemed to stop beating as he turned to the altar. Did the pendant pulse hot against her breast, or was it just the lingering touch of Kered's hand that seared her skin?

"What is this cup? Whom does it serve?" Kered asked in the heated silence. With bold confidence he stepped forward and lifted the silver cup from the marble altar. No thunder roared, no lighting struck, no blades dropped from the roof to impale them. "Much blood has been shed for this cup," Kered said in the expectant silence. "To me, 'tis just a chunk of metal."

Kered thrust the goblet unceremoniously into his shirt and laced it up tight. Then he turned to Maggie. "I do not like being in here. 'Tis eerie and has an evil smell. I sense that our luck will change. Come."

The journey back to the entrance took less time, but as they neared the light, they slowed and walked with stealthy steps in case the guards had regained consciousness. Vad darted ahead and slipped into the woods.

Kered went down on one knee and checked the life pulse of the guards. Vad circled the temple clearing and waved for them to join him in the trees. It took them little time to reach the beach, for they now knew the way. Kered practically tossed Maggie into the boat the men had hidden. Vad shoved them off shore.

The guard watched the little boat pull away. The stink of the fires made him think of burning witches. In his short life as a N'Olavan guard, he'd seen naught but boring duty. Now excitement had touched his life. He had seen a witch and witnessed her magic. The rewards for naming her would be immense. He sighed with bliss, imagining the gold coin and costly robes he would demand for pointing her out. It should be easy to find her with that black hair and pale skin.

He would demand protection. If she pointed her finger at him, he too might fall into unnatural sleep. They should strip the arm rings from the men who aided the witch. Or perhaps the warrior had been enthralled by some evil spell and been forced to take the sacred cup. He had seen the bold display of the man's arousal when he had pushed the witch away. Aye. Perhaps the warrior would also reward him for helping burn the witch and breaking her spell.

The guard swore on his ancestors' names when he saw

the boats. He ran from one to another, but each had a hole in the bottom and water sloshing about. The sun rose and the orb-path was closed to him. It would take hours to repair a boat. He stood in the shadows of the isle and watched his quarry get away.

Kered grunted in answer to Maggie's many questions and finally she fell silent. She wondered how to deal with him when next they were alone. His fervent embrace and now his anger ate at her composure. She much preferred the ardent man to this one who scowled so fiercely as he rowed them back to shore. It did not take a detective to note the tremors in his arms as he rowed or how Vad picked up the beat each time Kered missed a stroke. Perhaps his surly mood was just a result of fatigue.

Perhaps he could rest once they were far from the beach and possible retaliation. Vad had said the N'Olavan boats were as riddled with holes as a moth-eaten coat. By his grin, she knew the name of the hungry moth.

As they pulled in to shore, Maggie saw the stain of pink that signaled sunrise. Water sloshed waist-deep across the road to N'Olava. The sea began to seethe with angry waves. No one could use the path to come after them.

Kered heaved Maggie into his saddle, handing up his pack, which held the precious cup. He leapt up behind her, giving her no choice but to ride before him in the shelter of his embrace. He must tend her feet. The sight of her small bloody footprints on the boat floorboards had shaken what was left of his composure.

They fairly flew up the path to the cliff top where

Kered halted Windsong and ventured a final look out at the roiling sea. The isle lay silently off shore, smoke still curling above the trees. The smoke joined a mist that had risen along the beaches, wreathing the isle and beginning to obscure it. It seemed to be dissolving before his very eyes.

Kered shivered and drew Maggie against him, offering her his warmth. With a boldness he did not feel, he slipped his hand into the damp cloak. He pressed his palm to her heart. Her hand captured his and held him there. The beat of her heart reassured him, the warmth of her seemed made to fit his palm. Yet, he remained stiff and wary at her back. Finally, he broke the contact and gathered up the reins.

Windsong sidled and bucked occasionally as they ate the miles at a swift gallop.

"What's wrong?" she finally shouted above the wind.

"Naught!" he bellowed back.

"There is. Tell me."

He tightened the reins, and Windsong skidded to a halt, dust rising about their thighs. Vad drew up and raised an eyebrow.

"Ride ahead and scout the terrain," Kered said. Vad nodded and accepted the order, swinging his horse in a circle and cantering off to the horizon. When he was well out of sight, Kered spoke. "Aye. I will tell you what is wrong." He dismounted and paced, fists on hips. He could not really tell her how he felt or admit to the cramps that wracked his body from lack of sleep and nourishment, or mention the pounding in his skull, the throbbing in his groin. He could not apologize for his ill treatment of her or admit that fear for her had made him forget all the levels of awareness that made him rational and calm.

One small part he could admit and did. "A female procured the cup. You put them all to sleep and made a mockery of armed combat."

"Is that it? I put them all to sleep? No one died? You only got to prick one man's skin?" Maggie began to laugh. She laughed so hard, Windsong reared and tossed his head.

Kered's shoulders slumped. Words fumbled through his brain, but he could not shape them, could barely make his chest take in air.

"Come on. Surely, a man at the seventh level of awareness is able to accept a small thing like a woman's help?" Her laugh became a brilliant smile.

"Hmpf." He stomped about. Her smile, as bright as the sun at midday, made it difficult to maintain his indignation. Finally, he snatched the reins from her hand. If he did not soon mount, he might not be able to put his foot in the stirrup. He swung up behind her and drew her back against his body. "Hmpf. I suppose 'tis acceptable. Only if—"

"I never tell anyone?" She leaned back and reached up, caressing his cheek and cupping her hand about his neck, urging him down for a kiss.

"Aye, little slave. 'Tis a tale I would not soon live down."

Maggie's warm breath bathed his lips. "So be it. My lips are sealed." She pressed them to his, and he growled in his throat as he accepted her promise. "Of course, I can't speak for Vad."

# Chapter Fifteen

As far as the eye could see, nature was showing off. High rolling hills shone with the colors of the rainbow. The waning sunlight softened the masses of flowers to a rosy hue. Flocks of long-haired sheep dipped their black faces in the long grasses.

"Not all of Tolemac is forbidding and empty." Kered stood behind Maggie as she looked about. On a distant rise, a shepherd, a crook in his hand, walked among his flock. Vad, sent to determine who roamed these hills, followed him about, skirting curious ewes and their lambs.

"Are we safe here?" she asked.

"Aye. We are but a few leagues from the capital."

"How far from Hart Fell?" she asked, sheltering her eyes and peering off to the distant hills.

"Too far," Kered answered, turning away. She dog-

186

ged his footsteps as he led Windsong to a narrow, swiftly moving stream.

"I don't understand. You said we'd return there after you got the sword and cup." She helped him remove Windsong's bridle, loosen the girth, and heave the leather saddle from the horse's back.

"Maggie, it is not possible—" he began, then frowned. He recognized all too well the expression on her face. He started over. "We have not yet accomplished our task. I may have the sword and the cup, but until I present them, make my case to sit on the council, they are just worthless metal weighing down my saddle."

Her expression softened. "I understand that. But, if you take me along to your capital and we go through the folderol—"

"Fol-der-what?"

"Ceremony. I meant ceremony. If we go through the ceremony, isn't it likely to take a long time? How many weeks have we been traveling? I've lost track." She began to wring her hands in agitation. Kered handed her his pack to still her upsetting motions.

"The conjunction came at the waning of Vintage-month. 'Tis now the last of Autumn-month."

"So much time?" She turned away, his pack dangling from her hand to drag upon the ground as she walked to the edge of the running stream. He sank down beside her and watched as she opened the pack and, as if she had always done the chore, filled the water gourd.

"I am sorry, Maggie. I know you pine for home."

Tears shone in her eyes as she stoppered the gourd and placed it into the pack. "Then take me back to Nilrem's mountain," she whispered.

"Not yet," he said, his words as softly spoken as hers.

"You promised." Her hand reached out to touch his knee in a gesture of supplication.

Where she touched, he burned.

"I am not taking you back. Not yet." *He might never take her back.* He expected an explosion, a Maggie-upheaval of colossal proportions. Instead, he saw only sorrow etched on her lovely face.

"I was afraid you would say that."

Somehow he knew he had not only disappointed her, but at the same time fulfilled some preconceived idea she had of man's general faithlessness. There was no surprise or shock in her voice. A shadow crossed the sun, like the darkness on his heart, placed there by her unhappiness.

"You must understand—" he started.

"Oh, I understand." She bent her head and folded the fabric of her woolen shirt between her fingers, pleating it neatly.

Kered reached over and briefly touched her hand. "No, you do not. I am not just another male failing in some promise made to you. Nilrem claimed you have some meaning in my quest. The quest is not over until I say 'tis over. Here—" he thumped his chest—"here, I sense there is more. Should I take you back now,'twill be after Holy-month when I reach the capital. Leoh may be dead by then. I cannot delay to satisfy this ache you have for home. For all that I may sound cruel, I mean you no harm."

Maggie stood up, her posture stiff and distant. "I want to be alone."

"Do not stray. Vad has not yet returned from questioning the shepherd. Who knows who rides these hills? We travel through well-populated lands these next few days where not everyone we meet is counted friend."

She nodded. In a moment she had left him to walk along the stream's bank. The day was no longer sunny; the air rippled with something ominous. The set of her shoulders made him wish to gather her in and comfort her, but he stood his ground and let her go. How much of what he said was truth and how much fabricated argument to keep her with him? He did not know.

Vad approached, drawing up beside him. "What ails her?"

"Our direction," Kered said.

"Our direction? What is wrong with it? I reckoned it well. We are but days from the capital."

"But for Maggie, 'tis the wrong way."

"Surely she does not wish to go back to Nilrem's mountain now?" Vad dismounted and unsaddled his horse, laying his saddle in the shelter of a branching tree and snagging the edge of his cloak at the same time. Kered set him free with a slash of his knife when the branch refused to give up the strip of Vad's cloak.

"Aye," Kered said, sheathing his knife. "She wished to seek Nilrem's wisdom in hopes of going home."

"The ice fields are in the opposite direction from Hart Fell." Vad set his stallion, Warok, to graze with Windsong, then frowned at the ragged hem of his cloak.

"I know."

"So why go to Nilrem?" Vad persisted.

" 'Tis some fancy of hers. I think she says she is from beyond the ice fields because she cannot remember from whence she came. It suits her somehow to claim those lands, and perhaps if she returns to Nilrem, something there will capture her senses and point her in the right direction—point to home."

"And all her stories of her place, her family? I will

189

be disappointed to learn that her tales are just that, tales. I was quite hoping one day to meet these brothers of hers who can ride a horse more ably than you!"

"At first I thought they were fancies of hers. So much about Maggie is foreign to all we know. Her coloring—"

"Beautiful as a midnight sky!" Vad interrupted.

"She has two names."

"Two names? Nilrem's beard! What is the second one?"

"O'Brien."

"Sounds like a man's name."

"Aye." Kered turned away lest his face betray him.

"Could she be called after her master? Some form of identification of ownership? It would help if this is so. Did you ask her?"

"No."

Vad pulled on Kered's arm until he turned about. "You fear the answer, do you not? You do not wish to find her master! An unclaimed slave is nothing but trouble. And a pleasure slave, no matter your station, will not be tolerated by most lifemates."

"I know. I have always held contempt for those who dishonor a lifemate with their household slaves."

"I am worried for you. You are destined for a political alliance. Do not lose your heart to this slave, my friend."

"If half of what she says is true, she is not a slave." Kered frowned as he watched Maggie unwrap the bandages he had painstakingly placed on her feet.

"A wish or a beautiful dream. Surely, you cannot believe this?" Vad asked.

Kered looked off to the distant hills and blinked away what felt suspiciously like the welling of tears. He was so tired, he could no longer think straight. "Perhaps the blow to her head has made her conjure a better place . . . better people—''

"Better place? Than Tolemac? 'Tis unlikely.'' Vad hunkered down and busied himself making a comfortable back rest of his saddle, then stretched out and crossed his dusty boots at the ankles.

"In Maggie's world, a man may lifemate where his heart leads him, and so may a woman.'' Kered crossed his arms on his chest.

"You are in need of a retreat with your awareness master. Take her if you want her, but remember the penalties for denying your heritage. The Tolemac wars will rage on if someone does not take the peacemaking role when Leoh dies.'' Vad yawned and closed his eyes.

Kered knew that with Maggie's exotic coloring and changeable skin, she would draw every male eye for miles and most female ones, too. His belly clenched to think of other men desiring her. He wished he had obeyed the many urges crying out to him to taste of her beauty. She had resisted his offer of coin, but when faced with the opulence and beauty of the capital, would she be able to resist or would she fall to the siren song of wealth? Many might challenge him for the honor of taking her.

"Perhaps another might lead as ably as I.'' Kered wearily rubbed a hand over his face.

Vad opened one eye. "No one has Leoh's backing or your ability on the battlefield. You have proved you are more than worthy—you summoned forth the sword. Do not deny your calling. Take her and slake your hunger, but remember whence your loyalties lie.''

A double-edged sword of shame sliced through Kered's body. He had not told Vad that the sword had come to Maggie. It was a deception he could not live with much longer, and speaking so blithely of taking her, as if she had no say, made his stomach cramp. He tried to broach the topic, to make Vad understand.

"I have been thinking of Maggie's words of late, true or not. Do her tales not make you think on how we treat our slaves?"

"Hm." Vad closed his eyes. "I know that 'twould be a disaster if Anna were a free woman." He again opened one eye and peered up at his friend. "If she were not bound to your service, I might feel a need to court her."

"Court her? Since when have you courted a woman? You have but to lift a finger to have them fall at your feet. I can scarcely get a bowl of porridge if you are about. My slaves trip over me to serve you." Kered snorted in disgust, grateful for the turn of topic.

"Do not remind me. Women have no circumspection, no feminine modesty. 'Tis why I sleep in the barracks. No women allowed—free or slave."

Kered smiled, his mood lifting. "There are men there who would pursue you just as eagerly if you gave them a second glance."

Vad groaned. "Especially Ronac."

"Perhaps you could use this attraction he feels for you to swing his favor to my cause. He is one councilor who never thinks for himself. Samoht has only to nod and Ronac follows suit. His chiefdom suffers with such a weak and spineless leader. Why does Ronac not see that Samoht introduces only those measures that will benefit himself?"

"Speaking of Samoht—"

"Aye?" Kered began to pace, his eyes on Maggie sitting on the stream's bank, feet dangling in the water, the bandages in a neat pile by her side. A sudden memory of her naked in the stream so long ago came to him.

# Thrill to the most sensual, adventure-filled Romances on the market today...

## FROM ◆ LOVE SPELL BOOKS

As a home subscriber to the Love Spell Romance Book Club, you'll enjoy the best in today's BRAND-NEW Time Travel, Futuristic, Legendary Lovers, Perfect Heroes and other genre romance fiction. For five years, Love Spell has brought you the award-winning, high-quality authors you know and love to read. Each Love Spell romance will sweep you away to a world of high adventure...and intimate romance. Discover for yourself all the passion and excitement millions of readers thrill to each and every month.

## Save $5.00 Each Time You Buy!

Every other month, the Love Spell Romance Book Club brings you four brand-new titles from Love Spell Books. EACH PACKAGE WILL SAVE YOU AT LEAST $5.00 FROM THE BOOKSTORE PRICE! And you'll never miss a new title with our convenient home delivery service.

Here's how we do it: Each package will carry a FREE 10-DAY EXAMINATION privilege. At the end of that time, if you decide to keep your books, simply pay the low invoice price of $17.96, no shipping or handling charges added. HOME DELIVERY IS ALWAYS FREE. With today's top romance novels selling for $5.99 and higher, our price SAVES YOU AT LEAST $5.00 with each shipment.

## AND YOUR FIRST TWO-BOOK SHIPMENT IS TOTALLY FREE!

IT'S A BARGAIN YOU CAN'T BEAT! A SUPER $11.48 Value!

*Love Spell* ◆ A Division of Dorchester Publishing Co., Inc.

# Get Two Books Totally
# FREE —
# An $11.48 Value!

▼ Tear Here and Mail Your FREE Book Card Today! ▼

PLEASE RUSH
MY TWO FREE
BOOKS TO ME
RIGHT AWAY!

**Love Spell Romance Book Club**
P.O. Box 6613
Edison, NJ 08818-6613

AFFIX
STAMP
HERE

He remembered the light as it rippled across her skin, and he imagined the water beading like diamonds in her hair. The moment seemed fresh and raw to his senses and brought an ache to his throat.

"You are elsewhere," Vad remarked, sitting up straighter and noting where Kered's attention had wandered. "Relax, she is not in danger. Samoht is most likely in the capital by now. The shepherd said his entourage passed by two sun-risings ago."

"How did he know 'twas Samoht?" Kered dragged his attention back with great difficulty.

Vad resumed his indolent posture, crossing his hands on his belly. "He had no need to know the name. The Red Rose Warrior is all he needed to say. All his men bear the standard. How could it be any but Samoht?"

"The bastard." Kered unconsciously touched his knife hilt.

"Be careful where you say that word. He is sensitive to his ancestry—on the wrong side of Ruhtra's blankets!"

"He is a worm, no matter the side of the blanket on which he was birthed. Damn."

"Damn? You have picked up too many of Maggie's sayings. Next you will be slurring your words." But Vad spoke to Kered's back as a black cloud blotted out what little light remained.

"Maggie!" Kered ran as fast as he could. His heart thundered like a warhorse out of control and running downhill. "Stand still," he cried. "Do not move."

"I'm not moving." Indeed, she stood like a marble statue, her gun drawn and ready, fear and wonder warring for a place on her face.

Kered came to a halt about twenty feet from her. "The

puffin is a sacred bird, as is the raven. Do not use the weapon.''

Maggie tried not to be alarmed at the crowd of puffins surrounding her. One moment she had been alone; the next, a flock of birds had landed. Their great thick triangular beaks opened and closed as they turned their heads to stare at her. The red markings reminded her of blood.

''Tell them to leave me alone.''

''I do not talk to birds,'' Kered said. ''This is an ill omen, this gathering of puffins.''

''Please,'' she said softly, ''if I can't move, how will I get past them?'' Maggie looked up at him, expecting that he could solve this problem. Her trust sharpened his feeling of shame.

''Hm. Slide your foot forward and see if they peck at you or just move aside.''

The ground undulated with a mass of black glossy wings. ''Why sacred?'' she asked, sliding a bare toe ahead an inch, then moving it hastily back as a puffin made a quick move in her direction. Their bright orange feet made her think of clowns. She'd always hated clowns. Nervous laughter bubbled up in her throat and the sound agitated the surrounding birds, who ruffled their feathers and bobbed their great beaks.

'' 'Tis said the soul of Ruhtra abides in a puffin. Others claim a raven. As a result, Tolemac is overrun with both.''

''Stop talking and get me out of here.'' Maggie had seen Alfred Hitchcock's *The Birds* many times. Puffins or seagulls, the gathering flock made the hair on her nape creep. More birds darkened the sky as they joined the gathering. Ravens, this time, adding their own midnight threat. ''Do something.'' Her voice rose in panic.

"Okay," Kered said, inching his way to her. The birds pecked vigorously at his boots. When he reached her, he gently lifted her into his arms.

"Thank you," she murmured in his ear as he slowly slid his feet through the flock. The birds grew more agitated the longer he stayed in their midst. "Hurry," she urged him. She could see Vad hopping from foot to foot in his own turmoil, watching Kered rescue her.

"Think of a way to send them thither," he said. His hand was caressing her breast in an unconscious rhythm.

"Stop that," she ordered, slapping his fingers. He grinned. *So much for unconscious*. Then an idea struck her. "I have it. When we get clear, set me down."

For many slow minutes, Kered waded carefully through the mass of birds, ignoring their constant attack on his ankles and calves, grunting once as a beak penetrated the leather.

More birds were winging their way to join their friends.

"Kered. Maggie." Vad had climbed onto his saddle, which was fast becoming an island in a sea of birds as the puffins spread out to encircle him. "I think you should just stand still. There are too many and they seem to be shifting my way, following you."

Kered nodded and went still as a statue. Maggie smiled with an assurance she wasn't sure she had. "Hold your ears."

"How can I hold my ears, when I am holding you—" He didn't finish, for Maggie split the air with a shrill whistle. The puffins burst into flight in a roar of wings, splattering the three of them with excrement as they soared away in fright. A few lone, and Maggie supposed deaf, puffins remained bobbing and weaving about. She

195

let loose again, fingers to her lips, and they, too, escaped into the air.

Kered clapped his hands to his ears, dropping her unceremoniously on the ground. Well prepared, Maggie landed on her feet.

"Well, that worked great," she said.

Vad jumped off his saddle and grabbed her about the waist, swinging her about. "Teach me to make that sound."

"Oh, it's easy."

For the next few minutes as Kered scowled at them, Maggie taught Vad how to whistle. Like a child with a new toy, Vad experimented until Kered thundered at him to be silent.

"Okay," Vad said. "See, I, too, can use Maggie's words."

"Hmpf. You stood on your saddle like a female," Kered snarled, wiping bird splatters from Vad's shoulders.

Maggie patted Kered's arm. "Would you like me to teach you, too?"

"I have no need to learn this skill. I have you, my slave, to perform it for me."

"That was really low, Ker. Unworthy of such a noble warrior. Apologize."

"Forgive me," he muttered, then stomped away, leaving Vad hooting with laughter and Maggie smiling, her spirits greatly lifted.

Vad sat cross-legged by her side at their fire, tending to his stained tunic. "What else may I learn from you?"

"Can you guys read?"

"Guys? Is this a name for a warrior?"

"Actually, it just means men. Can you? Read?"

"Aye. We 'guys' can read. Kered avoids it like the

plague these days. He will not admit to having difficulty seeing the words.''

Maggie looked up the hill where Kered stood outlined against the darkening sky. ''Really?''

''Aye. He hid it from me until the treaties with Einalem. 'Twas then I noticed him holding the documents at arm's length. An affliction of great pain, this failing of his sight, to one of Kered's stature.''

''Tell me more about Einalem.'' Maggie kept her head down so Vad could not see the jealousy that painted a blush on her cheeks. Kered no longer remarked on it, but Vad still went into childish raptures over the phenomenon.

''Conniving bitch.''

''Really?'' she said. Vad was a natural-born gossip.

He frowned and picked a blade of grass, which he split with a fingernail. His long blond hair glistened in the firelight. ''Samoht will do anything to gain his ends. Einalem does as he tells her. A brainless woman who cannot make her own decisions, and she with two arm rings!''

''My, two you say.'' Maggie did little to keep the sneer from her voice.

''Aye. Two.'' Vad leaned closer, one eye on the vigilant man standing guard upon the hill. ''I think there is an unnatural love between Samoht and his sister. When she lifemates, 'tis wagered by some her man will not find a virgin in his bed, but rather Samoht's practiced lover.''

Maggie was shocked. ''Are you saying that she sleeps with her brother?''

''Sleeps? No. I am quite sure she sleeps in the women's quarters.'' He tipped his head, puzzled.

''That's not what I meant. Where I come from, to say

a woman 'sleeps' with a man, means she is making love—copulating with him.''

"Then aye. Some say she 'sleeps' with Samoht.''

"What about a baby?''

He flicked out a negligent hand. ''Any good herbalist has ways to prevent that. Do you not have such potions in your place?''

Maggie sighed. ''Some things are the same everywhere. So, how did Ker feel about lifemating with a woman who might be making love to her brother?''

"Kered's pride will not let him speak his inner thoughts on the matter. But he is my brother for all intents and purposes, and I am not blind to his faults. He often does not see the scheming behind a woman's bright smile. And then—'' Vad lowered his voice.

"Yes?'' Maggie edged closer to hear.

In the distance, thunder rumbled. She rose on her knees, her curiosity forgotten. Memory of the night she'd met Nilrem and Kered came to her with vivid, stark pain. She stood and cried out as lightning pierced the heavens, throwing Kered's silhouette against the indigo sky.

She tried to run forward, but Vad restrained her, one arm about her waist. ''Come, you will be drenched,'' he cried.

"No.'' She wrenched away and ran, oblivious to the rough turf tearing at her soles. All she could do was run, run to Kered. Each time Tolemac's thunder and lightning came, some frightening magic occurred.

She leapt into Kered's arms and he held her tightly to his chest. The rain poured down, soaking them to the skin. As she shivered in his arms, she realized that nothing had changed. She was in Tolemac despite the jagged display of nature going on over the distant hills. Reluctantly, she drew back from him. The only magic was the scent of his skin and the raw power of his strength beneath her hands.

"Come. We will need to find shelter." He lifted her into his arms and, as if she weighed nothing, loped down the hill to where Vad had gathered their belongings. Vad looked like a drowned angel at that moment, blond hair straggling on his cheeks, his tunic clinging to his muscular form.

"By the sword," Vad said, rubbing his thumb up and down Maggie's forearm.

"Just bumps of the goose," Kered answered casually as he removed Vad's hand. " 'Tis a change in Maggie's skin when she is cold. Do not touch her."

"Must you wear a knife? Even to sleep?" Maggie complained as she wriggled against Kered's warm body. The two men had made a sandwich of her in the shepherd's hut.

" 'Tis not my knife," he muttered, shifting her position.

"What did you say?" she whispered, conscious of Vad snoring at her back.

"Nothing. I said nothing. Can you not stop squirming?"

"You don't have to get crabby." Maggie curled her chilled fingers into her armpits and tried to fall asleep. In a few minutes she gave it up. If Nilrem's hut had been primitive, this was prehistoric. Across a short distance of muddy floor lay the shepherd, adding grunts and snufflings to Vad's snores. The stink of the hut was enormous, for several of the shepherd's sheep had bedded down with them. Every now and then a drop of icy water crept through the thatching to plop on her shoulder. "I can't sleep."

Kered sighed. He drew her closer and began to kiss her hair. "Perhaps I may distract you."

"That's not what I had in mind." But she edged nearer and raised her lips.

He whispered against their softness, "Touch my tongue with yours, Maggie."

The air between them sparked. Her breasts swelled with a sudden heat. She fought a maddening desire to rub like a cat against his hard chest. "I want more than touching tongues," she said into the charged atmosphere, spreading her hand on his hip.

He growled.

Their mouths met in a slow, sensuous mating of tongues. She led him and taught him, taking cues from the catch of his breath or the clench of his muscles beneath her fingertips. With deliberate finesse, she stirred his senses. That she was the one ensnared, captivated by the tastes and textures of him, eluded her. She was lost in a slow-burning fire that crept from every point their bodies touched to settle like a lance of pleasurable pain when he brushed his hips against hers. She lost track of conscious thought in the throb of her blood in her veins.

Her desire for him drove all sense away. It didn't matter that two men lay close by. At that moment no one existed except him. She breathed in the heady scent of him and savored the salty delight of his throat. He pinned her against the dirt floor, settling himself between her thighs. She lifted her hips, seeking his warmth and whatever gifts he could offer, maddened by the separating layers of leather and wool.

"Do you think you could wait until we reach the capital?" Vad complained. "I am neither blind, nor deaf."

Kered rested on his elbows and stroked Maggie's cheek with the tips of his fingers.

She wanted to scream with frustration, but instead pulled Kered's head down and gave him a wet, smacking kiss on the lips as if it were all a meaningless game. Vad snorted, then edged away, wrapping himself in his cloak.

"We can wait, can't we?" she lied.

In truth, her heart was racing, and she wanted to whack Vad over the head with Kered's sword. He had interrupted something she'd craved for so long that she felt as one must when starving and food is offered and then withdrawn.

"Aye. I can wait." Kered's tone made it a promise.

Maggie held her breath. The dim light of a few remaining coals in the shepherd's fire lit Kered's turquoise eyes with an inner glow that hypnotized her.

*She had been wrong.*

*The thunder and lightning* had *brought magic, Kered's magic.*

His body moved with subtle undulations against hers, denying his words. They danced a silent and almost imperceptible ballet, first one sliding against the other, then the other answering. It was subtle, but potent, in its arousal.

He played the game lazily, propped over her on his elbows, his fingers drifting back and forth across her cheeks, tracing her ears and teasing her neck. She played it more boldly than he, soothing the ache of her breasts against his rough shirt, caressing herself and him with deep intakes of breath. Her hands repeatedly played through the silky-rough tangles of his hair.

*This was real. He was real.*

Tears welled in her eyes and slipped over her cheeks. He caught them on the tip of his tongue and smoothed away their tracks with the tips of his fingers. Words of love clogged in her throat, unexpressed.

Where they touched, heat sprang up, flames licked along nerve endings, sending sensual messages racing along thighs and breasts. A warmth had built within her, needing release. An urgent beating and throbbing of blood snatched her breath. She caught his fingers as they moved across her lips and bit down hard to keep from screaming as wave after wave of lightning streaked through her body.

Kered dropped his head beside hers, gasping in air as if he, too, had run a race. Maggie knew they'd played the game too long and untangled her fingers from his hair. She slid her hand between them to press against his heat. He pinned her palm with his as long shudders ran the length of his body. Every muscle in his back and arms went rigid; his chest heaved. When at last he relaxed, falling to his side, Maggie rolled over him to see his face, to judge his mood, and to assess his reactions to what had passed between them.

They stared at each other.

"You have bewitched me," he whispered.

"You've enslaved me," she answered.

# Chapter Sixteen

They buried the sword and cup, along with the gun, in a narrow crevice by a beautifully blooming rosebush. Maggie thought of her mother's summer roses, full-blown, fragrant, and heady with scent. She looked about and treasured the moment, for she felt a sudden apprehension in her stomach, knew fear.

They would no longer be alone. Even the band of little beggars seemed unreal, something a dream conjured up. Other people would see her, remark as Kered and Vad did on her lack of arm rings, her unusual coloring. Vad did not delve too deeply; he respected her silences. Would others? Would she be put to a close scrutiny? Would some stranger know the land beyond the ice fields? *Would she ever see home again*?

"You are afraid?" Kered asked as he mounted Windsong before her. "Do not fear. I will say you are my slave and naught will happen to you."

They did not ride the coast for long before the city loomed before them. She gasped aloud.

He followed her pointing hand and grunted. "Some say 'tis lovely."

"Lovely? It's frightening," she said, pressing back against his chest as if to distance herself from the approaching capital. Gray stone buildings blended with forbidding rocky hills. The only relief from stark and windswept were the flowering gardens edging the street.

People hurried along, intent on their tasks. A man drove a pig with a stick, another carried two chickens squawking under his arms. Children dodged across their path.

Women stared openly at her, and Maggie found herself watching the saddle's pommel to avoid eye contact. As they neared the center of the city, gray stone gave way to stuccoed manors, trailed with flowering vines. The roofs here were thatched with elaborate designs of scallops and weavings.

She admired the artistry of each roof. Shutters were flung open to the red Tolemac sun, and it painted a copper glow on the thatched roofs. "They're beautiful," she admitted, relieved.

" 'Tis just buildings. Too many buildings, too many people."

They trotted through a massive town gate with a great toothed portcullis, and clopped across a short stone bridge over a river that flowed a deep purple, nearly black, as it wended its way along the city's edges. Ravens vied with puffins for space upon the banks. Maggie thought they watched her with cunning, craning their necks and ruffling their feathers as she rode by.

The people were very homogeneous, fair skinned, and in most cases their hair ranged from nearly white blond like Vad's to brown. No redheads, no black. The elderly were sometimes bald, but often had full heads of white hair. Kered no longer seemed gigantic to her, rather one of many.

Kered drew Windsong to a halt. He helped Maggie dismount, but she noticed a distance in his behavior as a man took the reins. When Kered bent toward her, she understood.

"Slaves walk behind their master. I do not want trouble before I present the cup and sword. Please, I ask your forbearance to tolerate the position."

She nodded and kept her head down as they climbed a steep hill next to a high stone wall. This was not the place to exert her independence.

"No," she gasped when they reached the top. There, across a narrow strait, loomed a great mountain. Atop it stood more buildings clinging to the steep slopes, resplendent with high towers and pennants snapping on the wind. The only way to the mountain was down a long wooden stair, across a short bridge, and then up another steep staircase.

"Behold the seat of Tolemac's council." Kered plunged down the steps. Maggie gulped before stepping gingerly off into what felt like open space. The steps were sturdy, but clung to the sheer wall of the cliff down which they climbed. She imagined that the defense of the council was simple. Once the stairs were burned, it would be impregnable. Her imagination placed men with clashing swords on the bridge that spanned the roiling purple sea. It didn't take much more to see them crushed against the great black boulders that rose like jagged teeth below. The beauty of it awed and frightened her.

The climb up the other side stole her breath. Her hands grew wet with sweat as they passed sentries in white and red and black who stiffened to attention as Kered and Vad passed. At the top of the stair stood a tall templelike building, this time in a soft cream color with a stone roof. A dolphin arched in the frieze and the sun dominated the peak. Tall round columns, ponderous and weighty, held the temple's roof aloft. Long narrow steps led to the portico. ''The bathhouse,'' Vad said.

Kered grasped Maggie's hand and walked with her up the narrow stairs, nodding to men and women as he went. These folk were less circumspect than those of the outer city, for they turned and openly stared at the new arrivals, and Maggie hoped it was just because of their extremely dirty appearance. All looked prosperous, their tunics of bright colors, some in jerkins, well-decorated with gold and embroidery. The women wore long-sleeved gowns with elaborate belts and brightly embroidered flat shoes. The weather was cool, so their sleeves were long, and Maggie could not see many arm rings. Those whose arms were exposed to view had an assortment of one, two, or three bands. She saw no fours and no fives.

Vad clapped Kered on the shoulder, then picked up Maggie's hand and kissed the grimy palm. ''I bid you farewell for now,'' he said, then turned and stumbled, catching himself and taking the steps two at a time in a great hurry.

Maggie smiled at his haste. ''I suppose poor Vad hasn't been this disheveled in his whole life.'' She gripped Kered's hand tighter as they followed Vad. ''What's going on there?'' Maggie asked as they passed between the central pillars of the bathhouse. Men were lined up in twos and threes on the low steps. Simple stall shelters of striped material had been erected between the pillars, and they had a drawstring curtain for privacy.

"Fornitrix," Kered said, yanking her forward. "If you have not the coin for a pleasure house, these free women will serve you for a few pennies or a chicken."

"You mean—" Maggie flushed hot and scurried after Kered. She hissed in his ear. "You mean men and women are . . . those men are waiting to—"

"Copulate? Aye." He pulled her into the chilly shadows of the bathhouse portico. "When we enter, the proprietor will ask our needs. I will answer for us. Slaves do not boldly meet a free man's eyes. Look down and do not speak. If addressed directly, look to me before replying. There is a slave chamber set aside where you may bathe. After my bath, I will meet you in a robing chamber."

"I'm very hungry." Maggie's head reeled from the myriad scents of the city, and the aroma of roasting meat made her mouth water. She had a sudden craving for a platter of steak.

"I will hurry and see that you dine well tonight. If anyone questions you, just stare blankly as if you are simple and invoke my name. I am well known and few will trespass on what is mine." He leaned down and stroked a finger along her cheek. "If you wish protection, you will do as I say. Choose another course and I cannot help you."

"Ker. Don't go! Let's skip the bath." Maggie felt a sudden rise of fear. They'd not been parted for so many weeks. She clung to him.

"Do not slur your words." He drew her inside. It was dark and cool in a lobby the size of the Capitol. Beneath their feet stretched a beautiful mosaic floor of cavorting sea monsters curled about colorful fish and amethyst waves. As they crossed the expanse of artwork, a man of great weight hurried to them. His belly, draped in a long black robe, led the way. Maggie gaped as she saw that his bare toenails were painted a bright orange to match the nails on his fingers. She thought of a great stuffed puffin.

"Kered." The man bowed as best one could with a sixty-inch waist. "A long time, a long time. How may I serve you?"

Kered bowed back. "A bath for me and my slave."

The man did not look at her, but snapped his fingers. A young girl, tall and garbed in a lavender robe, glided forward soundlessly on bare feet.

"Take our esteemed guest to the changing rooms," the proprietor ordered. The girl bent in a low bow to Kered and then walked off to an arch that opened to the right. Kered gave Maggie an encouraging smile and left. Maggie felt deserted.

"This way," the puffin-man directed, motioning for Maggie to follow. Maggie trailed his waddling figure. They passed though a small wooden door. The room she entered was whitewashed, humid, and smelled like every other health club she'd ever been in. At least this part was familiar. A tall blonde of Junoesque proportions looked Maggie up and down, her eyes widening and then becoming blank. A jerk of her chin was all the hint she gave for Maggie to follow.

At the end of a corridor, they entered a room with small cubicles, hung with brightly striped curtains. The woman handed Maggie a soft linen towel and held back a curtain.

"Disrobe."

Maggie took off Kered's shirt. She edged her tattered panties down and hung both on a hook, then wrapped the scanty towel about her as a cover-up and opened the curtain. The woman led her to a terra-cotta-lined chamber in which steamed a pit of dark water that bubbled and gave off vapors of sulfurous, lavender steam. Sweat instantly broke out on her skin. There were no other people for her to imitate or observe, so she waited.

The woman snatched away her towel and proceeded to scrub her down and rinse her off like an old wreck at a self-serve car wash.

"Who is your master?" the attendant asked, lathering vigorously.

Sense prevented the truth from tripping off her tongue. "Kered," Maggie said, gritting her teeth and hoping she'd still have skin when the torture was over.

"The warrior, Kered?" The attendant paused in her hearty scrubbing.

"Aye." Maggie was speaking as he did now, just as he was picking up her slang. She smiled, but the woman did not respond.

"He is much esteemed. 'Tis an honor to serve him." Maggie suspected the woman was not speaking of Maggie's honor but that of the women of the baths.

"Will I see Kered? Can men and women bathe together?"

The woman looked at her as if she'd grown two heads. When she spoke, her words were dripping with ice. "You think to bathe with the free men and women?"

Maggie decided on silence. Her questions had aroused more than suspicion. The woman plucked at her hair and turned her about like some oddity. A scathing remark about the service entered her mind, but Maggie held her tongue. The woman's curiosity seemed well-piqued and her hands had grown bold, touching and lingering with familiarity.

"Put this on," the attendant directed after toweling Maggie dry. Despite the rough scrubbing, Maggie felt wonderful and clean. Her skin glowed and a renewed vigor swept through her. She took the proffered shift and slipped it over her head. It came to mid-thigh and was of the sheerest lawn.

''Follow me.''

Maggie attempted to act subservient as she traipsed down a hot, dank corridor. In the distance she heard laughter and voices murmuring. Somewhere water rushed like a trapped waterfall.

At the end of the corridor, the woman turned a key and opened an arched wooden door. She shoved Maggie in and slammed the portal.

Maggie whirled around and grabbed the latch, shaking it frantically. Locked. She could only go forward. This corridor was cool and the tiles beneath her bare feet cold. She curled her toes and headed down the length of the hall. As she neared the end, the sounds condensed into male voices, arguing, chatting, and laughing. A prickling of apprehension came over her. One end was locked and the other must go to a crowded chamber. She was not ready to face a multitude of people alone. ''Damn you, Ker!'' she muttered.

She had little choice but to move forward. Within moments, she stood at the entrance to a torch-lit bathing chamber, her eyes searching for Kered in the dim interior. The room was so thick with steam, it caught at her throat and clogged her nostrils. She watched a young girl of no more than fifteen or sixteen pour an earthen jar full of water on heated bricks, sending a cloud of steam aloft to wreathe a delicate mosaic on the circular room's ceiling. The tiles depicted strange birds and flowers, a poignant reminder that she was far from home.

All the patrons were male—and naked. Some sat, some reclined on cloth-draped stone benches. Each had a young and lovely naked girl attending him.

Except Kered.

Kered had two.

He sat on a stone bench and smiled broadly at the two girls who were fussing over him, rubbing his broad chest, shoulders, and back. As they worked, they giggled and played, caressing him with oil, and bending and stroking his arms and neck.

He was aroused. Maggie, who'd imagined him in many nightly dreams, who'd felt every contour of his hard body pressed intimately to hers, had never seen him fully naked. He had always been circumspect in his personal habits. Here, he sat boldly before a roomful of strangers, aroused by the play of the slaves.

Maggie hung her head and clasped her hands to the sheer, and damply clinging, shift. It occurred to her that she'd been sent here deliberately and inappropriately. She was the only person who was clothed. A small commotion made her look up. The girls were pouring jugs of heated water over Kered to soak his hair. She realized the slave girls were twins. One stepped between his thighs and began to soap the dark hair of his chest.

She couldn't stand it.

Jealously flared and ignited. She wanted to charge the girls and fling them aside and take their place, or crack a jug over Kered's head. The jug idea sounded best. How could he do this? After their tender times together? For a moment she thought of Tony. Tony, whom she'd not thought of for many weeks. Tony bent over his secretary. This was not the same feeling. This was a deep pain, a full agony. This pain had sharper edges, honed by Kered's warm smile.

Maggie snatched up a jug and edged along the wall, her hand nearly seared by the heat radiating from the bricks. She had to escape—but not until she'd cracked his skull with the jug and not until she'd given the twins matching black eyes.

Between the gusts of steam and the resulting turmoil, no one would notice her departure. Maggie stifled a moan. One of the twins tipped oil into her hands and stood rubbing them together, staring at Kered's lap. Maggie didn't need to guess what came next. Anger roared through her. She raised the jug and charged.

A tall, fair man, handsome and commanding, blocked her way, yanking her close. "What are you doing?" he barked.

"L-l-leaving," Maggie stuttered, clutching the jar against her body.

"Attend me." The man dropped his robe. He wore only his five arm rings. Three silver on one arm, two gold on the other. Maggie knew what that signified. *A councilor.*

"No." Maggie gasped.

"You dare disobey me? You wish a flogging? Discard that shift and put down that jug."

Maggie spun toward Kered, begging him to see her and help her, but the twins blocked her view. And his.

"Please, sir. I'm not one of the . . . attendants. I've come to the wrong place." That, at least, was not a lie. She was hopelessly in the wrong place.

The man wrenched her about and thrust her across the chamber to an empty bench. Her feet skidded on the oil-slicked tiles and she fell to her knees, striking them hard as the jug shattered on the tile floor. The councilor lifted his foot and planted a kick on her buttocks. She slid forward, striking her temple on the edge of the bench, narrowly missing the broken chunks of pottery strewn about.

For a moment, Maggie lay by the bench, dazed from the man's attack. Then she shook her head to clear it. *Stand up and defend yourself*, she cried inside. She pressed her hands to the floor to gather her strength, but Kered's strong hands lifted her and wiped the blood that dripped into her eyes. He sheltered her in his arms and faced the councilor. "This slave is mine. Your abuse ill befits your station."

"You dare to question my punishment of this impertinent bitch?" the councilor snarled.

"Aye," Kered said, putting Maggie aside. "She is mine."

"You know the conventions about bringing a personal slave here."

"I know that you ill-treated her."

A hush fell in the chamber. Slaves and patrons alike waited breathlessly. Only the hiss of steam broke the silence. Maggie bit her knuckles. The councilor's face suddenly became neutral. Then he reached out, quick as a viper, and snatched her by the hair, dragging her against his side.

"Look at this hair. Exotic and erotic. You are occupied with the best of attendants . . . I will take her."

Kered leapt across the space, slamming into the councilor. They went down in a pile of arms and legs. Maggie scrambled from beneath them. Her scalp burned.

The two men got to their knees and then their feet. They circled each other like naked Greco-Roman wrestlers.

Maggie hid her face. She couldn't watch wrestling when the combatants were clothed, let alone naked. The sheer embarrassment unsettled her stomach. It wasn't just their nakedness, it was the blood, her blood, smearing Kered's hands. And the look on his face—a cold, hard, merciless look. One she'd never seen before.

The councilor kicked out at Kered's knee, connected and sent him smashing to the slick tiles. Kered hooked the councilor's leg, laying him flat. They grappled there on the floor, Kered's oil-slick body making a grip impossible. The air was filled with grunts of pain and the smacking of flesh against flesh.

The councilor, though lighter and slimmer, was quick, his fist merciless. Kered's movements were slow and ponderous and defensive.

Kered was exhausted. Maggie screamed as they locked their hands on each other's throats. Kered, his hands like a giant vise, squeezed relentlessly. The councilor's eyes bulged. He dug his fingernails into Kered's jaw and throat, scrabbling for purchase, tearing a row of furrows down his cheek.

Maggie grabbed the councilor's arm and pulled, screaming at the other patrons to stop them. Two men hauled her off.

Blood dripped from Kered's cheek to the councilor's. It scented the room. Wagers floated from man to man. The councilor jabbed at Kered's eyes, breaking Kered's hold. They slid apart, rose, and faced off again. The councilor snatched an excited twin and threw her into Kered's arms.

Kered tossed the girl away as if she were a rag doll. The councilor leapt over the steaming hearth stones, beckoning Kered to follow. Kered stalked across the stones, oblivious to their heat. They tangled again, rolling in a soapy pool of water that was dangerously close to the steaming hearth. More wagers flew and Maggie found herself man-handled to the edge of the crowd. A balding man panted against her neck as he held her still—for the winner.

Her stomach lurched. This was not a fight to the death. This was two dogs marking their territory. Winner take all. The fear she'd put aside for Kered's life resurfaced for her own fate. She stifled a scream and tried to wrench herself from her captor's arms; she was caught, like a fish on a line, reeled in and ready to be landed by the victor.

Kered pinned the councilor, his powerful arms locking the smaller man like an ugly crucifixion on the floor.

"What is this?" shrieked the puffin-man. He minced through the crowd and clucked like a mother hen when he saw the disaster of soap and oil.

"My dear friends, you must stop." The proprietor's words were not gently spoken.

Kered ignored him.

The councilor spat in Kered's face. The twins wailed. Two huge men, as fat as their master, strutted forward and dragged Kered to his feet.

Kered threw them off. His chest heaved in gulps of air. Abruptly, he turned away from the man still sprawled in the muck on the floor. The councilor did not rise. He lay there bleeding from temple and nose. Daintily, the puffin-man lifted his gown, placed his orange painted toes on the councilor's ankle, and stepped down with his ponderous weight. "I need no trouble. Concede a draw."

Slowly, the councilor rolled to his feet. He stalked to where Maggie stood against Kered's side, then wiped the blood from his mouth with the back of his hand. "Since you have no need of the twins, I will take your place." He grabbed a twin and took Kered's bench.

The slaves turned disappointed eyes in Kered's direction, then bowed their heads and began the same play they'd accorded Kered.

"Come," Kered ordered Maggie, taking her arm and leading her to the far side of the chamber. "What are you doing here?"

"I . . . a woman on the other side, she sent me." Maggie turned around to indicate the door through which she'd come. She became acutely aware of Kered's nakedness, pressed against her. And the eyes of those in the chamber, still expectant, still hoping for more bloodshed.

Kered's all-too-evident state of arousal brought a sting of perspiration—or tears—to her eyes. "I can't stay here," she whispered. She tried to yank herself from his hold, but his hands clamped like iron bands on her arms.

"What about the woman?" A muscle twitched in his jaw. She wanted to wipe a bloody smear from his face, but his expression stayed her hand.

"The attendant . . . she sent me here. Said to follow her, then she locked me in."

"She made a fool of you. Personal slaves are rare here. These slaves are specially selected to please. One does not come here to have what one may have every day in one's own home."

Maggie strained back against his hands, angry again. "Yes, I can see quite well that I'm superfluous." Just as suddenly as it had flared, her anger died. He had fought for her and defended her. This time, real tears mixed with the sweat on her cheeks. "Please, Ker, take me away. I can't stay here."

"Where do you plan to go? I am afraid your path is chosen. Our clothing, now being cleaned, awaits us at the end of the baths. It would appear most strange to go back. Would you wear only this shift and nothing else upon the streets?"

Maggie began to cry. Silently. Kered's expression

softened. He pulled her forward and held her tightly. A murmur of voices rose about them.

"Let me go," Maggie pleaded. He moved and she could feel every full inch of him. A jealous anger vied with acute embarrassment as she thought of how easily he had let the twin slaves touch him, arouse him. From the corner of her eye, she saw the councilor settle a twin in his lap, but the man's eyes watched her and Kered. "Please let me go!"

Kered picked up a large jug of water. He handed it to her, steadying it in her trembling hands.

"Rinse off these oils and soaps. We may not take substances of this chamber to the bathing pool."

Maggie raised the jug, averted her eyes from his body, and poured the water down his shoulders.

"My hair," he said, as he bent his head and scrubbed at his bloody face beneath the stream of water.

Maggie repeated the rinsing several times, watching the water swirl and run down his legs and pool around his feet. Water beaded on his well-oiled skin.

"Enough." Kered's voice sounded oddly rough and Maggie looked up at him. For a moment she thought he might embrace her, but instead he wrapped a hand about her arm and hauled her through a low arch. He walked in a measured pace, oblivious of his nakedness. At the end of a short corridor, they entered another chamber. She stopped short, shocked at the sight of a man enjoying his attendant. She groaned and scurried back into the safety of the corridor.

Kered followed her. "Enough, Maggie. This is a bathhouse. Have you not such places where you come from?"

"I don't know. Not that I know of."

"Then let me explain. One comes here to bathe, but

also for the pleasure of the experience. If you do not attend me, another such as Samoht—''

''Samoht!'' she gasped, looking over her shoulder.

''Aye. You have met my most formidable enemy. He and others will expect that you will be as agreeable as those attendants in the first cleansing room. Especially as I have claimed you so openly. Do I make myself clear?''

# Chapter Seventeen

"Yes, you're quite clear," Maggie said. "I'm not moving."

Kered sighed. "This place makes you ashamed?"

She looked away. "I think this place would be illegal where I live."

"Your customs and mine are very different. What did you mean when you said you were su-per-luscious."

Maggie burst into nervous laughter. "Not superluscious, superfluous." Her humor fled. "I meant I am unneeded, redundant, unnecessary." Her voice cracked. "Unwanted."

He touched her hair, briefly and gently. "I would not have copulated with the twins. I have come here to bathe and sweat away some of the grime of the weeks past. Vad may avail himself of an attendant, but I find I crave a raven silk," he threaded his fingers in her hair and drew her close, "and a fiery temper to warm me."

She began to tremble. In another moment she'd be sliding down the wall in a puddle.

Then he stepped away and became matter-of-fact. "You will attend me. The shift must go, for it makes you stand out. I think the woman on the slave side sought to make me angry with you. Perhaps she thought I would punish you in some way for daring to pursue me here."

Maggie felt a flush of heat run up her cheeks.

Kered stroked a knuckle down her cheek. "Does my nakedness embarrass you, or is it the thought of attending me?"

"What does attend mean?" Maggie's voice trembled.

"It means many things. It means doing whatever pleases me." He paused and laid a finger along his jaw. "I must say I am sorely disappointed. The twins are not often free."

Maggie wanted to slap his face. Then she saw his wide grin and realized he was teasing her to ease the tension. With that thought, he shattered her illusions in one swift movement, yanking the straps of her shift down her arms. He pulled the loose, damp material to her ankles. It lay about her feet, and she crossed her arms about her breasts.

"To hold yourself thusly will only draw more attention."

His amused tone only made her clench her hands more tightly over her chest. Maggie closed her eyes. He had fought for her, yet she stood naked before him, the most magnificently put together man she'd ever seen, and he seemed blithely indifferent to her. *Unlike the previous night in the shepherd's hut.* He seemed a different man, not the Kered she'd held so tightly in her arms.

Kered sighed and hauled her forward. "Who had you

planned on hitting with the jug, if I may ask? Me or the twins?''

''You,'' she muttered.

''Then I must be thankful your gun is buried with Ruhtra's sword.''

Maggie dragged her feet for she knew what waited in the other chamber. She felt as if she had been dropped into a Roman orgy. A tiled bathing pool, the size of an Olympic swimming pool, yawned at the center. Its dark purple waters bubbled vigorously, fed by hidden hot springs. Along the perimeter, men reclined on padded benches, eating, talking, and playing board games. Naked slaves of both sexes moved about with food and wine.

Several older women, still beautiful but past their prime, knelt and groomed the men, filing nails on hands and feet and plucking hair from armpits, chests, and groins. Women lounged about as freely as men, enjoying like favors from handsome male attendants.

Maggie also didn't need to wonder what had become of Vad. He was reclining at one end of the pool, almost completely hidden from her by the crowd of young women who clustered about him as if craving some invitation to heaven.

Kered selected a bench in a small alcove. ''This will shield you somewhat from scrutiny,'' he said, then beckoned to a young boy who nodded and tossed a cloth to her. She promptly clutched it across her chest. Kered frowned and tried to take the cloth. They warred a moment over the soft material, then Maggie let it slip from her fingers. Kered arranged it on the bench. He stretched out on his stomach, resting his head on his folded arms.

He saw that she fought a need to speak, smiled and

nodded. "Say what you must, for the boy will soon return."

"Your people, they-they copulate right before anyone who wants to see?"

Kered yawned. "Some do. 'Tis personal choice. I myself prefer privacy for anything more involved than play." He came up on an elbow. "I most especially like to play with twins." He grinned as Maggie's face heated.

He settled himself on his stomach just as the boy returned. He handed Maggie a tray of pots, and she heaved a sigh of relief that he didn't speak. She watched his small tight buttocks as he moved off to another bench.

"Attend *me*," Kered growled, and she went down on her knees on the warm tiles and looked over the pots before her. It was not steamy in this chamber and her duties were abundantly clear. She felt Kered's eyes on her and her blush deepened, and she noted his eyes as they followed the blush down to her breasts. Her bottom felt cold and exposed to the room and she had to fight an urge to whip about to see if anyone was watching her. She shook her hair out and tipped her head back slightly to edge it a few more inches down her back.

"Thank you for helping me back there, Ker," she said. "I was really scared."

He stared and grunted.

"Is that a 'You're welcome?' " she snapped, futilely attempting to cover everything possible with strategic curls of hair.

Kered grinned. "You are quite pleasing to me, Maggie, even if I have you to thank for a sore nose and a battered throat." He closed his eyes. Suddenly, he looked as weary as she imagined he was, the lines about his mouth deeply etched. "The blue pot first, please," he requested.

Maggie lifted the lid from the glass bowl. She dipped her fingers into the white cream. A spicy scent rose and a warm feeling penetrated the skin of her fingers. She dabbed the cream tentatively on his shoulder. It was like smoothing cream on a rock.

"We will be here for two sun-risings if you continue so."

Maggie scooped up more cream. She spread it quickly across his shoulders and began to massage his skin. He had no freckles, no scars, no marks beyond those from his recent scuffle. The slash on his arm had healed as flawlessly as his other wounds.

The cream and his perspiration combined to make a new texture, one of silk, and she became mesmerized by the soothing motions of her hands on his shoulders. She concentrated on the strange tingling sensation beneath her fingers and tried to ignore his body. It was like ignoring a rocket in your living room. The wide planes of his shoulders tapered to lean hips and taut buttocks.

"All of me, Maggie," he whispered, his voice soft and hoarse. She peered at him, but his eyes remained closed.

"I can't," she whispered back.

Kered suddenly rolled to his side, and grasped her wrist. She gasped at the pain of his grip. "All watch, Maggie. They may seem occupied, but they watch, for I have favored a personal slave and they wonder why. If you do not want trouble, spread the cream from my shoulders to my feet and make a fine showing of it." He pulled her near, his lips so close she could have kissed him. His breath washed warm across her face. "Samoht has brought the twins to the pool. He is a potent enemy with a formidable list of grievances against me. I have no wish to add his lust for you to the list. Play at the role and be the attentive slave. You act like a virgin.''

''I am.''

He stared at her, stunned. '' 'Tis not possible. You said you were twenty-five turns of the calendar.''

''I am.''

''A slave is no longer a virgin at fifteen.''

Maggie leaned close to him, her lips a paper's breadth from his, her nose touching his cheek. ''I am not a slave.''

''Were we not here, I would find out the truth of this.''

''How would you do that?'' She could see amber flecks in his turquoise irises, and his lashes were a thick sable tipped with gold.

Kered raised a hand and clenched his fist in her unruly black hair. He drew as close as she had. Anyone watching must assume they kissed. ''I would take you and prove your words false.''

He dropped her hair and lay back on his stomach. ''You test the fates. Do the work or suffer some other man's attentions.''

Maggie began the massage in earnest. She had to rise from her knees to reach all of him. By the time he shook off her ministrations, she knew every inch of his rock-hard back as well as his long legs. She had skimmed her hands over his hips and buttocks, but he hadn't complained about the neglect. Her insides churned. She knew if he tried to determine the state of her virginity, he would discover how aroused she had become from the intimate task.

''She is a fine specimen,'' Samoht said, coming to

stand before them. Tension emanated from the tall councilor. Two alert, burly attendants sensed trouble and rose from their bench.

Kered shifted to a sitting position as if he had just noted the other man's presence. "Aye," he said, drawing Maggie between his spread thighs, his arms encircling her hunched shoulders.

"Where is she from, this ebony bitch?"

Kered shrugged. "I found her, injured, on Nilrem's mountain."

"Then she is unclaimed," Samoht said, lifting a lock of Maggie's hair and rubbing it between his thumb and forefinger.

"I have claimed her," Kered growled.

"Registered, too?" Samoht arranged her hair on her shoulder, his knuckles skimming against her skin. She shivered in Kered's arms, despite the warmth of his hard body.

"Not yet."

"I will challenge you for her. I want to breed her. Think of the whelps she would produce. Look at that black hair, from head to nest!"

Maggie heard the steel in Kered's voice. "She is already breeding," he retorted.

Samoht stepped back, his fists clenching. Vad surged through the crowd in the pool, but froze in mid-stride with a lift of Kered's hand.

"Indeed," Samoht said. "Perhaps when you tire of her, we may come to some arrangement." Samoht licked his lips and moved off to another bench, one in plain view of theirs.

"How can you stand this place? I want to leave!" Maggie hissed. Her hands trembled on her knees, and she clenched her fingers into fists.

"I have no intention of granting that tyrant any pleasure. Come, Maggie, we dally overlong." Kered led Maggie from the large bathing chamber. Every eye followed them.

Cool air washed Maggie's heated body and tightened her nipples. His long strides took her through a curtained archway. She stood quietly behind him, averting her eyes as he accepted a basket containing their clothing. He entered into a heated discussion with the tiny old woman who attended this final stop in the bathhouse.

When he turned away, she knew something was wrong. She crossed her arms about her waist and shook her hair over her breasts in an unconscious effort to shield herself from his knowing gaze.

"Your garments were burned." Kered held the basket out.

She stared blankly at the cascade of blue silk that rested next to his own finery. "Burned?"

"The bathhouse replaced them. The garments were deemed—"

"Unworthy? Too weird?"

"Hush," Kered hissed, drawing her away from the old woman's avid attention. "There is naught to be done. They are ashes."

Kered steered her to a row of chambers opening off the central room and concealed by long silken draperies—no common woolen stripes for warriors and councilors.

Inside the chamber, the marble floor was veined in pink and salmon. A narrow satin padded bench stood against a wall. Masses of flowers in stone pots flooded the room with their heady fragrance.

She turned to berate him as he drew the curtain, but he pulled her into his arms.

"This has been torture, Maggie. I must know if you tell the truth." He pressed her back on the padded bench, stretching out above her. She struggled beneath him, slipping and sliding on the satin, unable to get any leverage against his relentless hold. Each of her movements aroused him to greater rigidity. Yet his mouth came down on hers with a slow gentleness that made her fall still. She lost track of his hands as his tongue caressed hers with a heated demand. He parted her thighs and placed a hot palm on her.

He lifted his head. "The truth. Tell me the truth, Maggie. You inflame my desires like the most practiced of women, then swear to your innocence."

Maggie arched, sweat breaking out on her back. His hand gently massaged her and shards of pleasure shot through her. She flailed her head on the cushion. Words were pointless, but she didn't want him to stop his caresses. She wanted his touch to continue, wanted him to finish what he had started.

He'd soon find out the truth—*or would he*?

Did women still bleed their first time? Was it just a myth of romance novels? Did it hurt? She didn't know. In fact, she was deathly afraid that all the hymeneal rituals in romance novels were overdone. What if he felt nothing? What if they made love and she didn't bleed? Where was a vial of chicken blood when you needed it?

If she couldn't prove her virginity, she'd be a liar to him forever, a fornitrix who'd spun a tale. He'd never trust her—ever. He might barter her to Samoht or another equally odious man.

Tears gathered along her lashes and her chest heaved. Kered paused over her. He snatched back his fingers as if burned.

"Forgive me." Kered struggled off her and sat at her

side. He dropped his head into his hands. "Forgive me, Maggie. 'Tis just like the undergarment. I became carried away, thought naught of your feelings, and shamed you." He turned to her and took her hand, raising it to his lips. "You have saved my life, endured much for my quest, and I have given you nothing. At least, I may give you my trust."

She knelt next to him on the bench and laid her head on his shoulder, kissing his smooth skin and linking her fingers with his. "Thank you, Ker." She was exhilarated that he would put aside his desires to demonstrate his trust. She was also heartily disappointed that they weren't going to make love.

*She had almost begged him.*

"My enthusiasm for you makes me heedless, quite like a boy with his first . . . never mind." He drew her into his arms and kissed her softly. "Maggie," he whispered.

She melted into his arms, and he drew her down against his body. Their mouths met, and she gently ran her tongue along his closed lips. He sighed and opened his mouth. She took advantage and touched his tongue with hers. She refined his kissing. She teased him, dancing with his tongue, tangling, soothing, stroking, retreating, and attacking. Her teeth nipped his chin and throat. He moved in restless agitation in her arms, his warm chest rubbing over hers. Her nipples ached and so did her insides.

If Kered wanted her, he could have her.

She wanted him beyond all reason. Her sanity flew away. In tutoring him, she'd snared herself in a trap so strong, she'd never escape. Didn't want to escape—ever.

He made deep, Kered growls in his throat. When she tried to pull back, he held her fast, drinking in her nectar.

She had taught him well, and like an able student, he did more than required, adding his own essence to the heady lessons.

Maggie knew that she loved him.

His heart thundered against her breast. "Do you feel what I feel?" he asked between shuddering gasps for air.

"Yes. Yes. Yes." She drew his mouth to hers again.

The moment was perfect.

They were finally clean.

They both wanted the same thing.

"Yes. Yes," she panted.

They fell off the bench.

# Chapter Eighteen

"Maggie?" Kered shoved himself up from the cold marble floor. Maggie remained stretched out where they'd fallen, eyes closed, her hair spread like a pool of black ink about her head. He swallowed hard. His head ached. His mouth was dry. "Maggie," he whispered.

Gently, he traced a red mark on her forehead. She did not move. With a bellow, he called the attendant, then gathered her up.

She lay like a broken bird in his arms, her limbs sprawled across his lap. Kered willed Maggie to open her eyes, speak, rail at him, anything. She did none of those things. She lay pale and silent as death.

He bent his head and pressed his face to her neck, taking solace from the beat of her blood against his cheek, the warm sweet scent of her clean skin.

The bath attendants had to speak several times before he responded and lifted Maggie to the bench. He settled her limbs neatly, crossing her hands on her stomach, but the posture reminded him of a corpse, so he arranged her arms at her sides.

"Clothe yourself, Kered," Einalem said, stepping into the chamber. Her azure silk robe, clasped with a gold chain, whispered against her long limbs as she came to Kered's side.

He spread a soft blanket over Maggie's naked body, then hastily drew on his leather trousers and laced them as Einalem shook her head ominously over Maggie's condition.

"I did not know you were here," Kered said to her as he pulled on his boots.

"You and my brother were far too occupied with this one to notice me." Einalem's long, dexterous fingers pulled up one of Maggie's eyelids. "I will not ask how this happened. If you choose to beat your slaves senseless, 'tis your affair."

Kered bit back a retort. The old crone who had summoned help for him stood watching with avid interest and would surely spread gossip. He knew Einalem was a talented healer. It would not serve to offend her and it might cause hurt if he explained that he and Maggie had been reaching for heaven when suddenly they were dashed cruelly to earth. He contented himself with a fierce scowl in the direction of the many attendants who were clustered at the chamber's entrance.

"Go about your business," Einalem commanded the gathering of curious women. "You should be about your duties, too, Kered," she said, her pale blue eyes expressionless. With slow, sensuous motions, she plaited the long, silver skeins of her hair into a thick braid. "I will tend your slave. Be gone."

"Not until she comes to her senses. This is the second

time she has suffered a blow to her head." Panic had crept into his voice so he turned away, pulling his tunic over his head to hide the telltale glitter of moisture gathering at his eyes.

"Such injuries are ofttimes fatal." Einalem shrugged and pressed her fingertips to the pulse point on Maggie's throat.

Black thoughts coursed through Kered's mind. Maggie's skin was chalk white, her lips pale. She would not die if he could help it. "I will take her to my quarters. She may rest more comfortably there."

"How unseemly—" Einalem swept a hand out in protest.

Kered ignored her and gathered Maggie into his arms, willing himself not to react to the way her head lolled against his shoulder.

Kered strode the long corridor of the councilor's palace, Vad at his side. The torches burning in iron sconces cast their shadows in a demon dance across gray stone walls damp with moisture. "You secured the sword and cup? Maggie's gun?"

"Aye. You will find them wrapped in blankets and stored with your other weapons," Vad answered, then changed the subject to the one he thought closest to his distracted friend's thoughts. "How fares Maggie today?"

"The same. It has been three days and three endless nights, and still she lies senseless," Kered said.

"Are you not surprised that Einalem is so devoted to nursing Maggie?"

"Aye. When I found my feet and discovered Maggie was senseless—not from ecstasy, as I had wished, but from cracking her skull upon the marble floor, I was too shocked to notice who came to help, or think on the consequences. Einalem camps in my chambers as if—''

"She owns them?" Vad finished.

Kered growled with displeasure.

They neared Kered's chamber door. Kered paused, his hand on the latch. He studied Vad in the smoky light. "I find that my patience with this nursing is—''

A pathetic, choking cry reached the two men. Kered flung the door open and stormed across the chamber, Vad at his heels. Einalem's silver hair entwined with that of his slave Anna's golden tresses to make a curtain concealing what went on in the bed. The cry came again, more of a whimper this time. He grasped Einalem's arm and pulled her away. Maggie lay in his bed, feebly fighting off Anna's hands. Her eyes were closed. She had no more color than her ivory pillows.

"Leave off," Kered ordered Anna, grasping at Maggie's wrists. The instant he touched her, she fell back and ceased fighting.

Einalem placed a gentle hand on Kered's arm, but her words were sharp. "She must take the potion, else she will die."

Anna, fairly new to her tasks as Kered's house slave, drew back into the shadows and away from Einalem's anger.

Kered ignored both women. Leaning with one knee on the bed, he murmured to Maggie to reassure her, gratified that she seemed to be at peace. Gently, he placed her hands on her chest. He studied her greasy hair. The room was rank with the odors of sickness.

"What is this?" He picked up the cup that Anna had abandoned on a chest by the bed, sniffed it, and reared back from the sharp scent.

"A purge," Anna piped up, then scuttled back two more steps.

Kered took the cup to his washstand. Very slowly, he dumped the contents into the basin there. He took a clean goblet from a table piled with rolled maps and documents and poured it full with fresh, cool water.

"Water will do naught but knot her insides." Einalem stepped between Kered and the bed. "I cannot allow you to interfere."

"Step aside." Kered's voice brooked no disagreement, and Einalem shrugged and did as he ordered, but not before he noted a defiant glare in her eyes. Kered sat at Maggie's side, but it was Einalem he considered. "I know only that Maggie has wasted here for three days, growing weaker and weaker. Vad, open the shutters."

"You will surely kill her," Einalem said. "Who knows what diseases this one might have? My brother said you found her on Hart Fell. She may even now be spreading some sickness to Anna or me or Vad. Leave her to my care."

Kered allowed his doubts full play, his words as sharp as Einalem's had been. "Could you have misjudged her illness? In what way does a purge help a head injury?"

In a swirl of rose silks, Einalem came to the bedside. "Are you questioning my ability to pick the best treatment?"

He fought a retort that would reveal his doubts. Instead, he spoke with calm. "I do not question your ability, just your choice of treatment," Kered continued.

" 'Tis the same thing," Einalem retorted.

"She calls oft for you," Anna said softly to Kered from a safe distance.

"Does she?" Kered felt grief catch in his throat. He

smoothed the dirty tangles of Maggie's hair from her brow. She seemed wasted and small in his bed.

"If you wish another healer . . ." Einalem began.

"I wish only that you consult your books another time and consider some other course."

A silence, broken only by Maggie's soft breathing, fell on the chamber. A raven cawed from beyond the shuttered window.

Vad encircled Einalem's shoulders and drew her to the door, his words placating. "Perhaps you could return at a later time, after you have perused your herbals? If Kered wishes to indulge himself, who are we to gainsay him?" Gently, using the charm that came so easily, Vad cajoled Einalem from the chamber. When the door closed behind her, he shot the bolt.

Kered lifted Maggie's shoulders and tipped the cup to her lips. She swallowed convulsively, water spilling over her chin to run down her neck.

"At least she kept it down," Anna said, coming back to the bedside one cautious step at a time.

It was on the tip of Kered's tongue to order Anna out, but her unobtrusive presence and eagerness to please made him hesitate. He bit back the words and instead sought information.

"Has she come to her senses at all?"

Anna wiped the water from Maggie's chin and neck. "Oh, aye. Now and then she opens her eyes. Fair wild she looks then, with all this raven hair. If I may venture an opinion?"

"Speak up," Kered said, impatience clipping his words. He tipped more water against Maggie's lips.

" 'Tis my belief that water and sweet bread would better serve than purging. What good is treating her head through her belly and bowels?"

Vad stepped forward and interrupted. "Kered, the full council is meeting now. You must hurry."

"Aye." Kered nodded, but he lingered, his hand smoothing Maggie's hair from her sweaty neck. "Anna, feed her tiny amounts as long as she can take them. And by Nilrem's knees, bathe her and air this chamber!"

With great reluctance, he settled Maggie back against the pillows. Her breathing was even and the frown had smoothed from her brow. He wanted nothing more than to gather her into his arms and beg her forgiveness for not keeping her safe. Instead, he nodded curtly to Anna, turning aside before his emotions betrayed the depth of his feelings.

Following Vad, Kered entered a small chamber that housed his weapons. Cupboard after cupboard held knives and swords and eight-pointed stars.

Vad did not allow him any inner privacy. "You displayed far too much interest in Maggie's health."

"What would you have me do—allow them to purge her until she was but bones among the covers?" Kered flung open the tall cupboard doors.

"We both know that a man of influence would never publicly show such interest in a slave. He would remember that he must lifemate for the sake of alliances—powerful alliances."

Kered busied himself pretending to assess his store of weapons.

"You would raise no eyebrows if Maggie were in the women's quarters, the proper place for ill slaves. And what of the prospects of Einalem for your lifemate? You know it is but a matter of time before the council asks her to reconsider you as a lifemate. How must she be interpreting your interest?"

Kered opened the rough blanket that wrapped the sacred sword, which Vad had hidden on the back of one shelf. Removing the woolen covering, Kered sheathed the sword at his hip. "I understand my responsibilities." Kered stowed the cup of Liarg in a soft leather pack and slung it over his shoulder.

"Do you?" Vad asked, softly. "I suspect you have lost your heart, my friend. Can you even remember why you sought Nilrem's wisdom?"

"I remember," Kered answered, avoiding Vad's eyes.

"I think not. You wanted to end the Tolemac wars. As a councilor, it is possible. This foolishness over a slave—'twill be misinterpreted as a madness. Worse, you may find yourself cast out. Who will halt the Tolemac wars then?"

"Am I the only man capable of negotiation?" Kered snapped.

"At this time? In this place? Aye."

The two men studied one another. Tension, like a brewing summer storm, filled the air.

"What of Maggie's gun?" Vad asked, stepping forward and placing his hands on his friend's broad shoulders. Then, as a personal slave would, he smoothed Kered's military tunic of white and red.

"Wrap it in the blanket and leave it where it is." Kered knew Vad's gesture was meant to appease him.

Vad gave a tug to the hem of Kered's tunic and then put the gun away, closing the cupboard doors securely. Last, he buffed the sword hilt with his elbow.

"Nilrem's beard! Leave off," Kered protested to his friend. "You are not a slave!"

"You must present the correct impression. I have hopes that you will be made one of the eight high councilors," Vad said, running after Kered as he strode to the chamber door.

# Ann Lawrence

"I have memorized my words and there is naught more to do. I do not aim so high—yet. I will be content as one of the lesser councilors. Their voting power, their oration rights, are equal with the eight chieftains. The chieftains might carry the weight of armies, treasuries, and history behind their words, but I have legend." Kered was grateful for the opportunity to put aside his own dilemmas. " 'Tis absurd, I suppose, and yet I am confident. It is a shame you will not see their faces when I present the cup."

"How can you influence them to make a treaty with the Selaw if you are not one of the eight?" Vad asked, scrutinizing his friend once more for lint or wrinkles.

"Debate. Words. Logic," Kered said soberly.

"You will need to be very good—and walk a path of propriety and level-headedness."

Kered hoped that Vad would not bring up the subject of Maggie again. "There are those who will support me outright, for they know my abilities. Others are sheep and will go as one or another councilor goes."

"Aye," Vad agreed. "Direct your words to Tol or Sallat. They think for themselves. Leoh will choose for himself, of course."

"And Samoht?" Kered asked his friend. "Where will he aim his words?"

"Aim. A good word. He has Ronac in his camp already. Ronac cannot think for himself—is besotted with Samoht's consequence."

Kered knew the sad truth of Vad's assessment. "Tarammur is Samoht's man, too, and unfortunately wavers on every issue."

Vad followed Kered back to Maggie's bedside. "Whoever offers Tarammur the most gold will have his vote and his wine."

"And Flucir is a powerful man," Kered interrupted, "but as desirous as Samoht is to take from the Selaw without treaty. He lacks compassion, lacks conscience. His loyalties are not yet established."

"He greatly admires Leoh."

Kered nodded, knowing well the difficulties and treacheries of politics. Other thoughts intruded once more on those of chieftains and loyalties. He bent to touch Maggie's brow. "Stay with Anna, my friend, and see that no one crosses my threshold, or you will answer to me."

"Do you intend to bar Einalem? A word or two from me may soften the possible insult to her healing abilities."

Kered cast one last look at the sleeping figure on his bed. "Perhaps that would be best. It sits ill with me that Einalem may be . . . delaying Maggie's recovery. You will know the words to use." With that, he left the chamber, closing the door on Vad and his inner turmoil.

Kered marched with confidence through the maze of corridors that formed the palace. His own chambers were but one of many suites of rooms that honeycombed the building. If he had been alone upon his return to the capital, he would have gone to the barracks with Vad and bunked with his men.

*Maggie had changed all that.*

He nodded briefly to two sentries who knew him well. They gave him admittance to a long corridor crowded with men. The scent of many, the washed and the unwashed, met his nostrils. Gasps accompanied his progress through the throng waiting for the council session to end. They clamored to present their personal matters to one councilor or another, and when the huge double doors at the end of the corridor opened, the petitioners would swamp the councilors. Silence fell after the gasps, for many had noticed the sacred sword strapped at Kered's side.

At the massive double doors, he stated his name and waited patiently for admission. When the sentries opened the doors, he stepped in with confidence. It would not do to display any sign of the anxiety that knotted his stomach or the fatigue that shook his resolve.

Leoh rose from his place at the inlaid table that seated the twenty-four councilors. Their status was marked by their chairs. Leoh's throne, as befit the leader of the council, dominated the group. The other high councilors sat on ornately carved chairs, gilded and fitted with plush pillows. The remaining councilors, two for each high councilor, sat on less-opulent seats.

Leoh's mane of hair was snow white—in sharp contrast to his deep ochre skin. Kered knew the yellow was a sign of disease—fatal disease. He swallowed down grief at the changes illness had wrought over the past few months in this man he called father. Where once had stood a stalwart warrior, now stood a gaunt old man, wracked with tremors, his face etched with pain.

"Come, Esteemed Warrior," Leoh called in welcome.

Kered masked his emotions and concern and walked boldly forward to stand before his father. He went down on one knee. Leoh extended a shaking hand and touched Kered's bowed head. The ritual presentation of an esteemed warrior followed, Kered kneeling before each councilor, each man touching him briefly on the head. He felt the ripple of sensation as each man noted the sword at his side.

When he had circled the table, completing the ceremony, he stood again before Leoh. "I bring to you an offering." Kered opened his pack and lifted out the cup.

Vad had personally polished it, and it shone with the light of a thousand silver stars in the glow of dozens of tapers. Kered placed it reverently into his Leoh's hands.

"The cup of Liarg." The old man's voice trembled as he beheld the sacred object. "How?"

"I sought the wisdom of the ancients and made the quest."

" 'Tis a lie." Samoht leapt to his feet and snatched the cup from Leoh.

Tol, on Samoht's right, grasped Samoht's arm. "Hold. Kered is an Esteemed Warrior. Your words challenge him."

Samoht shrugged off the older man, relinquishing the cup to Leoh with ill grace, then straightened his own ivory and red tunic. "Forgive me. I spoke in haste," he said, although his facial expression belied his words.

"Forgiven," Kered said immediately to soothe the moment. "I have trekked the Scorched Plain, called the sword from its watery grave, and visited the Forbidden Isle. I offer the cup in the cause of peace and bear the arms to enforce it."

The stunned silence following Kered's words was finally broken by the deep voice of Leoh. "What is your wish? Why have you endangered your life on this quest? 'Twas thought the sword was but a legend and the cup too well guarded to be retrieved."

"Perhaps Kered had these forged in some Selaw armory." Samoht sneered.

"Your words ill fit your station," Leoh said into the shocked babble that met Samoht's words.

Kered looked about the table, judging the moment. Hesitation would gain him naught. "I wish to sit on the council. There is no doubt what I have accomplished.

'Tis said in legend that he who bears the sword shall rule.''

"No!" Samoht cried. "No. To sit here, one of us must step down. What manner of man are you to make such a demand?''

A cacophony of sound burst around Kered. Men shouted to one another across the table. Samoht pounded his fist. Tol slapped his palm down in response. Kered's insides heaved. Words flew about him like leaves in a wind. He could not grasp them, sense their portent, good or ill.

"Hold." Leoh spoke softly, but the effect was as if he had shouted. "We will put it to the vote." Slowly, he advanced to where Kered stood. "As I have raised you as my own beloved son, I may not have a say. I had hoped and prayed for this day to come before I went to my grave." He placed a hand on Kered's shoulder and then turned and resumed his seat.

Each man settled in his chair, on edge, agitated. Kered stood aloof and calm throughout, knowing he must appear utterly devoid of nerves. Each man lifted a small book from the side of his chair, wrote upon a page, tore it out, and folded it. A uniformed sentry collected them and gave them to Leoh. He unfolded and read them one by one.

At the last vote, his hands trembling, Leoh rose and placed both hands on Kered's shoulders. "One of us must relinquish his seat. Hail, Councilor."

He fell in a heap at Kered's feet.

Pandemonium swept the chamber. Men tripped over each other to attend to their leader. Kered shoved them aside, lifting his father in his arms, tears running unashamedly down his cheeks.

# *Chapter Nineteen*

Maggie's legs wobbled. She used the furniture for support as she edged around the room to do her chores. Kered's continued absence and a lingering weakness made her grumpy. No one could see her, so she kicked Kered's boot.

She listened carefully. A whisper of cloth was the only harbinger of Einalem's bedeviling presence. When least expected, Einalem might appear to add more chores to Maggie's list.

"Maggie?" Anna called.

Maggie relaxed and kicked over Kered's other boot. "What is it, Anna?"

*When would she see him again?*

"Kered's eight-night death vigil ended this sun-rising. He will be here any moment. We must be ready." Anna swept up the boots and dashed across the room with them. Maggie sank onto a bench. When Anna returned,

243

Maggie didn't even pretend to the energy she'd been feigning for the past two days.

In the secret recesses of her mind, she associated Einalem's perfume with knotting pain and spasms of nausea. If it didn't sound absurd, she would have thought Einalem was trying to poison her. Since leaving her bed, she'd eaten with Anna and felt considerably the better for it.

"We must tend Councilor Kered's clothing and boots," Anna said. "They will hold his ring ceremony in three days, and we must be ready. The whole city will attend. Everyone will bring gifts and offerings to him. The celebration would have lasted for days if Councilor Leoh had not died."

"I wish I'd met Kered's father," Maggie said, then Anna's words penetrated the fog in her mind. "Tend his clothing? Each day you polish every pair of his boots, press his tunics, shine his swords. How could they possibly need tending?" Just watching Anna scurry about exhausted her.

"Everything must be perfect. We have no idea what he will wish to wear. His blades must shine, should he wish to draw them."

Maggie muttered a few curses and pushed herself up. Wearily, she shuffled after Anna to a cupboard. Anna loaded Maggie's arms with immaculately tended garments. "Don't you ever question your work here? This is silly. I know Kered. He probably doesn't care what he wears. I'll bet he wears the same boots every day."

"Do as you are told," Einalem ordered from the doorway. "A slave does not question her tasks."

"Maggie is just tired." Anna came swiftly to Maggie's defense.

"Then perhaps if she can be of no use here, she

should retire to the men's quarters and take her ease there, on her back, performing a task more suited to her energies." Einalem's soft voice and honeyed tone did not mask the steel in her words, or the promise of punishment for recalcitrant slaves.

"Maggie may rest here." Kered stepped into the room.

Maggie's heart thudded uncomfortably in her chest. *Her* last conscious memory of Kered had been of such intensity, she felt the blood rush to her head. The room spun for a moment, then righted itself. She searched his face, but the man standing before her was cold and controlled. No emotions furrowed his brow. There was no sign of the passion she'd felt in his arms. This was a military leader, from his stiff back to his impassive features.

"I have been instructing this one in her duties," Einalem offered.

"Thank you for your concern. I will see to her instruction now. Your brother wishes to see you concerning the ring ceremony." He stepped aside as Einalem swept away in a cloud of perfume and a swish of silks. "Go to the kitchens, Anna."

Anna took the pile of clothing from Maggie and melted away. Left alone with Kered, Maggie could think of little to say but banalities. "I'm sorry for your father's death."

He shrugged and flung open cupboards, scanning their shelves. "It was not unexpected. Has Einalem had you tending this lot?" he asked.

"Yes. There isn't a speck of lint or dab of mud on anything. You could use you dagger blade as a mirror." She thought she detected a twitch of amusement at the corner of his mouth. He closed the cupboard doors and faced her. When he spoke, her heart iced over.

"I registered you as my slave while you were sense-less. You are mine now."

She clutched at the edge of the cupboard. "I don't understand."

An uncomfortable silence fell, but he met her eyes squarely.

"You must understand, Maggie. There was trouble. The attendants wanted to know who you were, as did Einalem. You have no arm rings, and there were those who would be quick to challenge me for you. I had no choice."

"So now I have papers, like some pedigreed dog?"

"I do not know pedigreed." He came to her side and placed a gentle hand on her head. She shook him off. "You are now my responsibility. No man or woman may command you, except me. You have my protection. If this offends you, then rant and rave."

Maggie could barely swallow. The idea that he had made her officially a slave when she had been unable to defend herself was too much for her to grasp. It hurt in a place deep inside.

"Please, go away." She turned to the cupboard, fighting down her bitterness. "I have boots to polish," she said, her back to him.

"I have other duties in mind for you," he said. "Fol-low me."

The shop was dark and warm. A hearth glowed in the back. The old man at the counter bickered with a small woman about the price of a ring. Eventually gold coin slipped from one hand to another and the woman left the shop. Maggie held the cloak Kered had given her closed at her throat. With a lift of his brow and jerk of his head, Kered urged her forward.

"Ah, Councilor Kered, my condolences for your loss . . . and congratulations on your ascendancy to the council," the shopkeeper said, eyeing Maggie with open curiosity.

"Thank you," Kered said, inclining his head.

"How may I serve you?" The old man perched on a tall stool and polished his scarred counter with a dirty rag.

"I have brought you a helper."

Maggie and the old man gasped at the same time. Kered continued as if they had stood mute. "This is Maggie. Maggie, this is Mada, Tolemac's finest silversmith. Maggie is a willing worker and according to her, an able smith. If she lacks talent, train her."

Maggie grasped Kered's arm. "Why are you doing this?"

He drew her aside. "You were not meant to tend clothing. However, should you wish, you may resume those duties at any time."

"Not a chance," Maggie said, turning to the hearth. She had never worked at an open fire. Her heat had always been controlled, directed by a blowtorch. But she recognized the tools lying on a bench, chisels, hammers, files, dies for stamping patterns in metal. And ingots of silver. Her hands itched to work. She turned to thank him, but Kered was gone.

The old man smiled at her and held out his hands. They trembled. "Kered knows I am not what I used to be, but to bring me a woman . . . There will be trouble, I dare say." Then he slapped his knees and cackled with obvious glee.

Maggie smiled and drifted around the workshop. The

windows were dark with soot. A branched silver candelabrum shed the only light on a table of silver buckles, brooches, and rings for sale. She lifted a chased hand mirror and frowned at her image. An idea came to her. She turned to Mada. "May I begin today? There is something I wish to make."

Mada spat into the hearth. "I make only to order. Nothing on speculation."

Maggie slapped the mirror in her palm. "I would like to make a gift for Councilor Kered to celebrate his ring ceremony."

"You would like to make a gift?" he asked, amused.

"I know this sounds strange—"

"No more strange than the tales of a woman with black hair. Perhaps there is something here you see that would suit Councilor Kered? A dagger?"

"Councilor Kered has many daggers. No. I want to make this gift myself."

The old man studied her. "How would you pay for the silver? A slave has naught but what her master gives her."

"I have this." Maggie draped the silver chain from her necklace across the counter, pocketing the pendant in the soft purse suspended from her belt. The chain's interlocking links gleamed in the candle's glow, and the old man's hands reached out and stroked it.

"I have never seen the like," he whispered. "Who made it?"

"I did. With Councilor Kered's permission, of course," she hastened to add. "It is valuable and will amply compensate you for the small amount of silver I will need. If you don't believe I made it, you will soon discover I am telling the truth when you see me work."

"My dear, if you would teach me to make links this

fine and solders this invisible, I would give you the silver for naught!''

''Then we have a bargain?''

''Aye.'' They shook hands, as generations have done, sealing the deal.

Maggie set to work immediately. Mada gave her free rein the moment he saw her heft the hammer. They became quick friends, joined in their common love of their craft.

''We need more borax,'' she said, wiping the sweat from her brow. The small furnace licked her face with heat. ''And I'm ready for the glass.''

Mada laid a cloth on the counter and unwrapped several roundels of glass. ''I wish you would tell me what you are making. I hope the priests do not miss this glass.'' He turned away from the heat and watched Maggie clean the delicate strip of silver. She applied a fine stone powder to polish it.

Her quick, deft motions as she bent the metal and made nearly invisible piercings were practiced.

''You have done this often,'' he said. ''I am sorry I doubted you.''

Maggie grinned. ''The men of Tolemac do not often give credence to a woman's talent. Did you steal that glass?''

''Hm, borrowed, my dear,'' the old man murmured, leaning closer as she warmed beeswax and fused it onto the base of a strip of metal to aid her sawing.

Satisfied, she sat back. ''Let me see the glass,'' she said. He watched her hold the clear roundels to the light, then lay them on her drawings, dragging them back and forth over the lines, raising and lowering them. Finally, she selected one. "This will do nicely. I hope there is enough of the flux."

She worked quickly, setting the roundel in the channels she'd bent in the silver and adding details with painstaking care. At last she sat back and smiled up at the old man. "What do you think?"

Mada lifted the clear glass that formed the body of an animal. Its legs and head were intricately stamped with designs of curves within curves. "By the gods! Everything is bigger!" Mada said excitedly, raising and lowering the gift to inspect the gouges in his counter. "What manner of animal is this?"

"I call it a turtle. This turtle will crawl across Councilor Kered's maps and help him read the small print. I hope to ease the problem he has when reading so many documents."

The old man picked up a chamois cloth and began to give the turtle a final polish. He cleared his throat. "I would not let others know of his weakness, Maggie. Some might use it to say he is unfit."

"How stupid."

"Stupid, aye. But an unfortunate truth." He offered her the silver and glass turtle. "It has been an honor to watch you work."

Maggie busied herself cleaning up the work area, not meeting his eyes. Kered would soon take her to Nilrem's mountain. She would miss these daily visits with Mada.

"I cannot keep the chain," he said.

"It was to pay for all this silver and . . . borrowed glass."

"Yet 'tis a masterpiece of work. You should keep it forever. I now believe that you are the artisan who made it."

"I want to use it to pay my expenses. I can make another."

He brightened. "You could? I may truly keep it?"

Maggie looked about the shop and noted the man's worn robes. He needed every coin he earned. "I want you to have it."

"Bless you," Mada said, kissing her on the cheek. He wrapped Kered's gift in a soft cloth, and she tucked it into her belt purse.

Anna dragged Maggie out early, just as the sun was rising, to avoid the multitude who would gather for Kered's ring ceremony. They found places near the aisle of the Sacred Temple and sat on the floor to wait.

Maggie fidgeted as the morning wore on, impatient to see him. The temple became hot and stuffy as crowds gathered. She nodded off now and then. At last, horns heralded the procession, and she turned an eager eye to the temple doors. With such a tall populace, she could not see and had to jump up and down.

"Here, Maggie, here," called a small boy who carried water buckets for Anna. He beckoned her to a stool he'd dragged along. "I will sit upon your shoulders and we both may see."

Maggie grinned and let the child climb to sit with his legs about her neck. When she mounted the low stool, her view was perfect.

The tall doors opened and the priests entered, swinging incense pomanders. Maggie now knew their purpose, for the stink of the crowd was enormous. Flowery perfumes vied with perspiration, surely offensive to the High Priest's nose. The High Priest in fantastic gold robes came next.

"Look, 'tis Einalem," Anna cried, pointing.

Einalem, garbed in an ivory gown encrusted with silver beads, walked regally down the aisle as if she were a bride. "Why is she in the procession?" Maggie hissed.

" 'Twas decided a woman should carry the cup to the altar. Councilor Samoht chose her."

Maggie suppressed a bitter jealousy, turning back to stare daggers at Einalem's figure. As if it were a bouquet, Einalem held the cup reverently before her. The long train of her ivory gown swept the ground as she passed by the spot where Maggie and Anna stood. Her hair fell in a loose silver cascade down her back, below her hips. Maggie's hand crept to her own hair, concealed beneath a kerchief of wool. There had been nothing she could do about her black brows, but she'd hidden her hair to forestall staring and comments.

Twenty-three councilors paced behind Einalem. Each man wore a long purple robe, belted with a gold and black sash. Samoht led them, holding the sacred sword aloft. Eight warriors followed, Vad one of them, a white pillow in his hands. Nestled on the pillow were two open-sided gold arm rings. Lastly, two youths bore eight-branched candlesticks with thick, dripping tapers.

Maggie knew when Kered stood in the entrance, for the crowd fell silent. His tall figure took Maggie's breath away. He was garbed in a white brocaded tunic that left his arms bare for the ring ceremony. She knew the strength of those arms—and their gentleness. He looked vital and alive. No unreal game figure was this who walked so proudly to the altar and knelt at the High Priest's feet.

*She did not belong here, was not really a part of his life.* Her eyes burned with tears as the realization took hold.

Endless prayers followed as Kered remained on his

knees, his head bent, his face concealed from her by the fall of his sun-streaked hair. Maggie only took her eyes from him to watch Einalem, whose greedy gaze never left Kered. Finally, Vad stepped forward from the warriors' place and presented the arm rings. The High Priest pulled the arm rings open and clasped them to Kered's biceps, then squeezed them closed and nodded.

A brazier smoked at the altar's side and Maggie gasped, gripping Anna's arm as Samoht stepped forward and lifted an iron brand from the coals. "He'll be burned," she said.

"If he is, a warrior such as he will not flinch. Let go." Anna shook her off.

Maggie knew that the small piece of leather the bishop slipped under the arm ring would do little to prevent a nasty burn if Samoht held the brand on too long, or if Kered moved. She ran through her childhood prayers quickly and breathlessly.

The High Priest touched his hand to Kered's head, then made a sign. Samoht laid the brand upon first one and then the other ring. The crowd moaned collectively, anticipating the searing of flesh.

Samoht stepped back and thrust the brand into the coals, and Kered rose to his feet. His fluid movement belied the fact that he'd been kneeling all night and now for another hour at least.

The crowd, roaring its approval as Kered made his way down the aisle, shoved and pushed past Maggie to surge through the open door to greet their new councilor.

"Come this way, Maggie," Anna cried, tugging Maggie along. Maggie stopped long enough to let the bucket boy gain his feet, then followed Anna. "Where are we going?" Maggie asked.

"Town. The ale and wine will flow in celebration. We

may meet some warrior who will eat with us.''

Maggie pulled away from Anna. "I am going back to Kered's quarters.''

"No one will be there. He will not return tonight! The revelry will last until sunrise.''

"I do not care. Enjoy yourself,'' Maggie said, then plunged into the crowd, feeling like a salmon swimming upstream as she made her way to the palace. The townspeople filled the streets, and she kept her head down to avoid their eyes.

At the palace, she walked quickly through the deserted corridors to Kered's quarters. Her tiny cubical was doubly empty without a sound from the many other chambers. Every servant was celebrating elsewhere. Maggie pictured Kered at the banquet in his honor to be held at the great palace hall. She knew Einalem would dazzle every male eye.

She curled into a ball and focused on home. For the last few nights she'd been preparing herself to leave Kered by picturing her family's faces and imagining their joy if somehow Nilrem should find a way to send her back. But the tears that welled and fell had nothing to do with family. They were the direct result of the day's ceremony. She had no worthy part in Kered's life. If only they had not fallen from the bench at the bathhouse! Then they would have had an unbreakable bond between them.

The dream came again. Always the same. Kered snatched from her arms. Blood dripping.

"Wake up, Maggie. 'Tis naught but an evil dream.'' Kered drew her into his arms and stroked her hair. For a brief moment, she curled against him as she had so many times on the quest, then, as if sensing that things had changed, she drew away.

She bent her knees and clasped her arms around them. "I'm sorry for disturbing you. Is the banquet over already?"

Kered shrugged. It would not do to tell her he had left early to come here to watch her sleep. "I am weary. This kneeling is meant for younger men." He rose and unbuckled his sword belt. Maggie stood up, took it from him, and went before him to the chamber housing his cupboards. When she turned around, the light streaming in the chamber window glinted off his new arm rings. Slowly, Maggie reached out and traced the two gold rings. He covered her hand with his.

She slipped her fingers away, then rummaged in his cupboard and withdrew a cloth-wrapped bundle. "I made you something at Mada's shop," she said.

He held the gift, weighing it in his palm. "You are satisfied with the arrangement I made with Mada?" He hoped she was pleased and content.

"Sure. He's a dear. I guess you got lots of gifts tonight."

Kered nodded, then cocked his head to the side. The orb-glow from the window lit one side of his face and cast the other side in shadow. But the intensity of his gaze boiled her blood. "Open it," she urged.

Carefully, he pulled back the cloth and revealed the silver and glass turtle. It was large enough to cover his palm. " 'Tis beautiful." He turned it in his hands, admiring the detail.

Maggie tugged on his arm and led him to his chamber. She spread a map and took the turtle from his hand. With a few quick motions, she demonstrated.

"Nilrem's knees! 'Tis a marvel. I can read the tiniest of words, see the faintest of lines."

Like a child with a new toy, he opened roll after roll of maps, spreading them out and moving the turtle across their surfaces. Maggie enjoyed his delight. Next she would make him ketos, she thought, like the pair she'd made her brother, Joe. Ketos, which had begun as leather armbands to protect a Navajo warrior's wrist and arm when using a bow, had developed into wide, braceletlike silver bands. She could imagine them on Kered's magnificent arms.

*Stop it!* she chastised herself. *You're going home. You won't be making him any more gifts.*

Kered gathered her in and hugged her. "You are a thoughtful woman. Why is it that Tolemac has no such wonderful device?"

"I suspect few of your people have trouble with their eyes. You're the only person I've seen here who peers at things as if he can't see them clearly."

"A lamentable weakness in a warrior."

"Mada told me others might think that weakness makes you unfit to lead."

"He is correct—some might. I care not what others may say. Your gift will open a world for me that I thought was growing closed."

Kered turned away from his charts and sank down on the edge of his bed. He rubbed his temples with the heels of his palms. Maggie climbed on the bed behind him and took over the massage.

"I want to go to Hart Fell, Ker. I want to find my way home," she said and knew it wasn't a lie. She couldn't last much longer living with him, just serving him, not really being a part of his life.

He leaned his head back against her and closed his eyes. "I will take you soon, I promise."

"Okay," she said. She'd been expecting an explosion or a refusal. Part of her had wanted the refusal, part of her the answer he'd given.

"Vad has been promoted. He will take my place as head of my army. He is a good man, compassionate and fair. Maggie?"

"Yes, Ker?" She stroked her fingers along the edge of his jaw, then back to his temples.

"What do you think of a warrior who hates fighting?"

"I think he has probably seen too much bloodshed and knows the folly of it all."

He grasped her wrists and turned around to face her. "I have been raised for no other purpose—"

"Your mother raised you to be a killer?" She linked her fingers with his.

"No. My mother died long before she could shape my future. No, Leoh directed my ways. When I would lose myself in books, he would have them destroyed. He taught me bitterness and anger, impotent anger directed where I could not spend it, and I turned it on our enemies. As I buried him, I realized my mouth is bitter with the taste of my life.

"The swords in my cupboards have sent many to hell and heaven—good men and bad. Yet who can tell which is which in the heat of battle? Who can say, this man, his lifemate is ill and needs him at home? Or this man, he abuses his daughter and should go straight to his death? No one! One just thrusts the blade home and watches the blood flow. I do not want to be buried until I have weighed the scale with life and hope against the blood I have shed."

"Then I shall pray you have a long life," Maggie said, stroking his temples again.

Kered moaned softly and captured her hand, bringing her fingers to his lips. "My Maggie. What is it about you that makes me bare my soul? Tell my secrets?"

The air between them grew charged. His next words startled her. "You wish for me to make love to you, do you not? You cannot say the words, can you?"

Whatever answer he wanted, he would get the truth. "Yes. Please."

He shook his head. His hair slid off his shoulder and the silk of it caressed her bare arm. "I will not make love to you, Maggie. It would be dishonorable of me."

"Why?" she cried. Her blood was racing, her nerve endings screaming.

"I am taking you to Nilrem's mountain. A free man may not lifemate with a slave. You may love me, Maggie, but we cannot have each other." He rose, and despite the evidence of his desire for her, he turned away and flung open the long windows. The wind whipped his hair, and his silhouette blurred as her tears gathered and flowed. "The council wishes to renew the lifemating contract between Einalem and me."

The pain of it was worse than she could imagine. "And will you? Lifemate with her?" Maggie shouted.

He strode to the bed and gripped her arms, dragging her up to kneel at the edge. "No. I will not have her. If I cannot have you, I will have no one."

"Who will know what we're doing here?"

"*I* will know. When you quicken, everyone will know."

"Vad said there were potions—"

"Poisons! I will not have you sicken and die for the

258

love of me, and I will not spend myself on the sheets like some boy during a dream.''

"You found what happened between us in the shepherd's hut shameful? Is that it?''

"Aye, Maggie. I lost control of myself from extreme fatigue. I have seen my awareness master. I have renewed myself. I have regained my reason and control. I am well rested now.'' He let her go, removing his hands. "No matter how I feel, I will not succumb to these desires. You are going home.''

# Chapter Twenty

As Maggie hurried along the roadway, she saw a sight that made her smile. Not much had brought a smile to her face these past few weeks. But this did. Kered stood resplendent in his white and red tunic among a crowd of children on a green sward, the towers of the palace behind him. He tore sheets of paper into small pieces for them, so each could have his or her own. Going down on one knee to their level, he folded the paper just the way she had shown him one morning when he'd caught her idling away the time, waiting for Anna to return with water for his bath.

Now he soared his plane high, and a flurry of little planes joined it. The children's laughter delighted her and touched her with sadness. Soon she would be gone.

"Maggie," he called, leaving the children to a chorus of protests as he fell into step beside her. "Where have you been?"

"Walking," she answered noncommittally.

An uncomfortable silence fell. At his quarters, he changed his clothing and strapped on a sword. She assisted him as a squire might.

"I want to leave for Nilrem's mountain tomorrow," she said.

"Are you commanding me?" he asked, his tone sharp.

"No, of course not. I am just anxious to go. It's been ages since you promised."

"I will have duties to attend to for a few more weeks—"

"Weeks?" She turned away. She couldn't stand a few more weeks. It was all she could do to keep herself in her bed each night and not go to him and beg him to reconsider.

She paced his chambers after he was gone. When Vad arrived, she barely greeted him.

"What ails you?" Vad asked.

"Kered. He won't take me to Nilrem's mountain."

"He is negotiating the Selaw treaty now." Vad began to rummage through Kered's belongings, looking for the deck of cards Maggie had made for him during her many idle moments.

"Could you take me, Vad?"

He froze, a startled look on his face. "T-t-take you? Kered would remove my jewels with a dull knife and feed them to me for supper. Are you mad?"

"No. No. You don't understand. I didn't mean, could you make love to me. I meant, could you take me to Nilrem's mountain?"

Vad pressed his hand to his heart and heaved a sigh of relief. "Forgive me. So many women beg me to take them, it was the first thing that entered my mind." He patted her shoulder. "I most enjoy your company, Maggie. You do not pet me and pull at my clothing. Now, where have you hidden the cards?"

"I'll get them." She sighed. She fetched the box from beneath her bed, and they sat on a brightly woven rug and spread out the cards. "What did you want to play? Five-card stud? Gin rummy? War?"

"War!" Vad cried.

"I should have guessed," she said with some amusement. As she dealt the cards, he lifted the pendant from the box. "What became of the chain?"

"I bartered it so I could make a gift for Ker. A ring ceremony gift."

Vad frowned. "It is an ill deed to part with a talisman."

"It was just a chain. Now, will you take me to Nilrem's mountain?"

He stroked the edges of the cards, considering her request. Maggie held her breath.

"Why do you wish to go?" he asked.

"Kered has a life here that doesn't include me. I don't belong here. I don't fit in. The best thing for both of us would be for me to go home."

"Aye, I can see you are unhappy. I will take you. This idleness chafes at me, too. And every night some woman is lying in wait for me outside the barracks. A journey with you would be refreshing."

Maggie and Vad played cards for an hour in comfortable companionship, switching from game to game. "Kered told me you are a virgin," Vad said.

The cards flew from her hands. She fumbled about gathering them. "I can't believe he told you."

" 'Twas a confidence. He said he wants you to return home as he found you."

262

Her cheeks heated with embarrassment. "Well, I don't want to leave without knowing what it is like to be . . . with him," she said, dealing the next hand for a game of gin rummy.

"Then seduce him. Surely, all women are born knowing how?" Vad took a card from the pile in the center and cursed before he put it into his hand.

"Don't curse; it gives hints to the other player." She picked up a three and discarded a nine. "I don't think I'm much of a seductress, or something would have happened by now." She bit her lip. "Where I come from, virginity is not such a highly prized item. If I hadn't told him, we might now be lovers," she finished wistfully.

"Then do not be a virgin!" Vad grabbed a card and began to hum.

"Discard, you cheat. How do I lose my virginity?"

"The day after tomorrow is Virgin Day. Go with the virgin slaves to the god Phallus, and sit upon his rod." He tried to pick two cards, saw Maggie's face, and sheepishly slipped one back.

"Gin!" Maggie cried and slapped down her cards in triumph. "What are you talking about? The god Phallus? Are you pulling my leg?"

"Pulling your leg? As I said, Kered would cut off my—"

"No, no. Jest. Pulling your leg is making a jest."

"Your speech is most odd. Why can you not say what you mean?" He rested his elbow on an upraised knee. "The god Phallus is a remnant from the ancient times. He sits in the oldest part of town. On Virgin Day, the virgin slaves who are ten-and-five dress in white ceremonial gowns and weave flowers in their hair. They dance about the god and then sit upon the god's erect shaft."

"That's absurd." Maggie snorted.

"Perhaps, but 'tis a ritual from ancient times and still practiced. Oh, and I almost forgot, kissing the bloody prepuce is considered good luck."

"Unbelievable."

"See for yourself. Sit upon the god and shed your blood. Kered can hardly protest that he would be ruining a virgin if you are no longer intact." He clasped his hands about his knee.

Maggie shook her head over the absurdity of the conversation. "It would be easier to seduce him."

"That was my first suggestion," he said smugly. "Wear your blue gown; it clings most fetchingly to your breasts."

"Vad!" Maggie felt heat creep across her cheeks.

"'Tis true. It brightens your eyes, too."

"Thank you for the fashion advice." Maggie rose and poured Vad some wine.

He shrugged. "Should you wish to change your mind about the god, I shall bring you one of the ceremonial gowns the virgins wear and a wreath of ribbons and flowers for your hair. 'Tis best to be prepared."

She handed him the goblet and then sat at his side. "I couldn't do it. But if I tell Kered I'm no longer a virgin, do you think he will still think it's wrong to make love—if he's taking me home?"

"Maggie," Vad said, leaning forward, "Kered will not take you home if he makes love to you; he will never let you go."

"But I'm a slave in your world. We could never be together."

"That is so. You could only love here, behind closed doors. Is it enough for you? Do you know that any children you produce will be naught but slaves as well, perhaps taken away and raised elsewhere? Can you bear it should the council insist that Kered lifemate? If not, come to me and I will take you to Nilrem.''

Kered's chambers were quiet and empty in the cold afternoon's gloom. Kered stood a moment and listened. Only his boots clicking across the stone floor marked his wandering from chamber to chamber. At long last, he stood at the threshold of Maggie's small cubicle. He drew her scent into his nostrils and closed his eyes. How often had he stood here and watched her sleep, wanted to climb in beside her and feel her body curl against his?

A glimmer of white caught his eye. Conscious of trespassing on Maggie's private domain, he stepped to the foot of her bed and lifted the blanket neatly folded there. He stared down at a soft white cloth. It unfolded to reveal itself to be a flowing garment suitable for ceremonies.

Ceremonies.

Kered gripped the dress in his fist and threw up the lid to Maggie's coffer. There on top was a wreath of flowers entwined with ribbons.

Virgin Day.

He tore the wreath to shreds, scattering the blossoms across the floor as he stormed from the room.

Mada acknowledged Kered with a curt nod. When Kered jerked his head toward the door of the workshop, Mada cleared his throat and touched Maggie briefly on the shoulder.

''If you have no need of me, child, I think I will be seeking my supper.''

Maggie nodded, her eyes glued to the silver ingot she was painstakingly pounding on the metal. She had never cared for sheet silver and had hammered her own at home, so the task was one of comfort and familiarity. Sweat trickled down her temples and between her breasts from the heat of the roaring hearth.

Mada scurried out the door of the workshop, and Kered dropped the bar in place.

A prickle of sensation made Maggie look up, her hammer poised over her work. "Kered." She breathed his name.

The hearth painted a copper glow on his hair and bronzed his skin. He raised his fist and she gulped. Clutched in his hand was the ceremonial gown Vad had insisted on giving her—and a few ribbons.

"Why?" he choked out.

Carefully, so she didn't fling it at him, Maggie rested the hammer on the anvil. "I'm going home, Kered. I didn't want to leave without knowing . . . what it would be like—"

Kered flung the garment to a wooden bench. "You had but to ask."

Maggie picked up the hammer and smashed it to the anvil's surface. It rang up her arm and stunned her joints. "Ask? When? Before or after you lifemate with Einalem?"

He stepped up to her and tried to take the hammer from her fingers. "You would give yourself to a god of stone?" he shouted.

"Of course not! Vad suggested it. He gave me the gown. I told him it was stupid, but he thought that if I did, perhaps your precious conscience wouldn't keep us apart," she shouted back.

Kered let her hand go as if burned. "Ah, my precious conscience." He rubbed his hand over his face. "This,

Maggie, is what bothers me, not my conscience." He swept his hand out to the forge.

"This?" She looked about the workshop. "I don't understand."

"This is what you are. A metalsmith." Briefly, he ran a finger up her arm, raising a shiver and goosebumps in its wake. "I know you are not a slave, no matter your lack of arm rings. This strength in your arms is from your skill with the metal. What if you remember who you are? What if this activity, this work you do, sparks more than flames in the hearth? Sparks memories? How could I stand it if you wanted or needed to leave me?"

"Is that why you're so distant? In case I leave? I've been trying to leave. I've been asking you to take me to Hart Fell. Were all your excuses just that—excuses?" Maggie gulped back her emotion. The lump in her throat felt large enough to choke her. "Why didn't you just ask me to stay?"

"And have you awake one morning and remember your home and hate me for holding you here?"

"I told you all about my home. I do remember it . . . You think I made it all up, don't you?" Maggie fought against tears. "Damn it, Ker. Just ask me to stay."

He looked at the heat of the forge and watched the glow of the coals. "There is no way, in Tolemac, to change your status—or mine. I cannot bear to have you serve me when you are so much more." Slowly, he unclasped his cloak and held it in his hand. "I have nothing to offer you."

Maggie drew the leather apron over her head and draped it on the workbench. Her whole body felt hot, as if she stood too close to the hearth. "I haven't asked for anything."

Kered dropped his cloak to the sawdust covered floor.

"Would you have gone to the god?" he whispered.

"I would go to no one but you," she said softly.

He unsheathed his knife and laid it on the scarred wooden table. "Would you? Have come to me one day?"

"I can't imagine ever being with anyone but you," she said, laying aside the leather gauntlets that protected her hands.

"And I cannot imagine ever being with anyone but you," he answered, unbuckling his sword belt and dropping it on the bench behind him. "This is you, Maggie, this fire, this heat. When I come here and watch you work—" He paused at her sudden gasp. "Aye, I come here and watch you work. You do not see me, but I see you. Your beauty enthralls me. The rhythm of your hammer reminds me of the beat of my blood in my veins. All my desires are here with you."

Kered took a step forward and cupped Maggie's face in his hands. They were so close to the hearth, Maggie saw the sweat break out on his face. Her hands grew slick with anticipation. She reached out and unlaced his shirt, spreading it open, and then pressed her lips to the visible throb of his pulse beneath his skin.

"You belong to me," he said, stepping back and drawing his shirt over his head and tossing it aside. "Say you belong to me," he ordered.

"I belong to you," she whispered, splaying her hands on his chest, feeling the strength of his body. It was like touching the coals in the forge. Moisture sprang up between her palms and his chest. She dug in her fingers when his hot hands moved over her hips, drawing up the cloth of her gown, up to her waist, then quickly over her head.

He wrapped her tightly against his body, measuring

every inch of her with his hands. The heat built from within them and from without. Where their skin touched, sweat ran. Slowly she moved against him, slipping along his silky skin, moaning at the sensation of touching him without restraint. Her hands tried to know him everywhere.

When he stretched out on his cloak and drew her astride him, she pulled away, going to kneel at his feet and tug at his boots. They might never come off.

"Help me." She laughed. They bumped foreheads when he abruptly sat up. She collapsed back in laughter, then sobered as he eased his leather trousers over his hips.

*This was for real.*

"We can't fall off any benches here, can we?" she whispered when he was completely naked before her. She rose on her knees and knelt between his thighs, then reached up and stroked back his hair to study his face. Gently, she rubbed the crease that seemed permanently etched between his brows.

"No, Maggie, there are no benches to fall from, no one to interrupt us." He turned his head and caught her fingers with his teeth. The sensation was exquisite.

The workshop was an oven. Their hair stuck to their cheeks and shoulders. Maggie remained motionless on her knees. Bolt after bolt of sensation streaked through her as Kered moved his attention from her fingers to her breast, his lips and tongue gliding over her.

"You belong to me," she said, at last drawing his mouth to hers. His tongue was hot, and she moaned at the rough silk feel of him.

"I belong to you," he agreed, drawing her once again astride his hips.

The exquisite sensations of his hands on her skin and

his mouth locked to hers did not prepare her for the startling moment of his possession. She wanted to scream at the power coursing through her. He was hot metal fresh from the forge. The air grew heavy with their breathing. Her chest heaved with each breath. The scent of him rose about her. She bent her head and pressed her mouth to his chest to keep from crying out as he moved.

He was the hammer and she the metal. Each movement became a shaping of her body to his. He fit himself relentlessly, possessing her soul.

A swirl of sparks from the hearth rose and floated above them like stars in the heavens. His hands owned her, finding every sensitive spot, and just as she fashioned tiny links of a chain, each touch, each caress, forged a hold on her that was as strong as any steel.

His body reached its limit quickly, as if left too long in the flames, and he arched beneath her, his muscles going rigid. She braced her hands on his shoulders to watch him. Their eyes locked and then his fell closed. The arch of his neck drew her hands, the growl in his throat told her what would come next. He heaved against her and like a stream of molten silver, she felt him pour his passions within her.

The sensation shook her. Liquid waves of pleasure rolled from where they were joined. Her thighs went rigid, shaking against his hips.

He wrapped his arms around her and rolled her over. She shook and trembled in his arms. Without words, he touched her where they were joined and she moaned. He pressed his mouth over hers, smothering her sounds, gathering them in. Despite his swift ending, her inexperienced and unrhythmic hip movements tantalized him as nothing ever had, readying him in an instant of time that might have been an hour later or perhaps moments.

The heavy air clogged in his chest, thick with the scent of hot metal and passion. Her breasts were slick with dew and he licked across her skin, savoring the taste of her. The sounds of her passion were raw with something akin to fear, and he murmured against her lips to reassure her. Every nerve of his body throbbed with the heat of her around him and against him. She palmed his cheeks and stared, dazed, into his eyes.

He swallowed a lump in his throat. "Would that I could burn this image of you forever into my mind. Sear deep this sensation of the fire and your heat possessing me, so that this moment might never be lost. Whatever dream I might have had of taking you gently in some flower-bedecked bower, pales to what it is like to possess you here." He touched a smear of blood on her thigh. "Possession is painful."

Maggie's hand shook as she traced the shape of his face. His heart ached that she would never see her home or her family again. He could never let her leave.

*She was his soul.*

The price was high—perhaps to be paid later if he did not fulfill her dreams of love and happiness or keep loneliness at bay. But he touched her lips with his and began to move anew, and his doubts and fears burst apart with his passions. Tears ran down her face. He hoped and prayed they were caused less by the loss of home than by the joy of discovery.

Every muscle in Maggie's body ached. She tried to get up, but Kered's heavy arm kept her pinned to his bed. A gentle tickle and he groaned and rolled over, freeing her. Quietly, she left the bed, crossing the path of orb-glow that lay across the floor, and tiptoed to her dark cell and the chamber pot.

She stood in the chilly room for a moment and sighed over the loss of plumbing. Perhaps she should invent the flush toilet. Or Velcro. Or ice cream. There were a thousand little things she missed.

When she stood again at Kered's bedside, watching him sleep, she knew none of them mattered. She eased down to his side and, as if he knew she was near, he turned and gathered her in. His warm breath feathered against her cheek. She kissed him. He hardened against her thigh, and she grinned at the incredible sensation of power it gave her to know that with but a look or a touch she could engender such reactions in him.

Maggie frowned. Was it just lust? No, Kered was not ruled by lust. He had all those awareness lessons to help him stamp down those feelings. The damn man had taken months to seek her out. She smiled. She owed Vad a game of gin rummy for bringing her that virgin costume. She frowned again. Losing her virginity had been more startling than painful. "I'll never forget the moment, or the look on Kered's face, or—"

"You dream aloud now?" Kered whispered against her cheek as he stroked his fingers along her hip.

Maggie knew she was blushing and said a quick—and silent—prayer that she'd not said anything too embarrassing out loud. "I was just remembering this afternoon, Ker."

He growled deep in his throat and leaned over her, moving between her thighs with an urgency that stole her breath. There was nothing gentle about him. Like a wild storm he possessed her. He drenched her in his passions.

His madness transmitted itself to her. She trailed

stinging bites across his shoulder and chest, devouring him as if she were starving.

They fell to their backs, spent from their passions. "I love you, Kered." Maggie gasped, drawing his hand to her mouth and kissing his palm.

"I love you, too, Maggie." He rolled over onto his elbow and captured her hand. "Say the lifemating words with me, here, now."

"Why?" she asked, drawing away from him. She sat up and pulled a blanket protectively to her breasts. "You own me. I have papers, remember?" The wonderful glow of their lovemaking cooled.

"The papers protect you—nothing more. I can never own you, Maggie. You and I both know that."

He sat up and drew so close she could see the glitter of orb-glow in his turquoise eyes. "Whether we say the words in a temple or here in my bed, if we mean them, they will join us."

Maggie's heart skipped a beat. An unpleasant sensation fluttered in her stomach. "I don't need words, and I don't want any promises you can't keep. Surely, the council will demand that you chose a lifemate who offers a powerful alliance?" Pain rubbed its raw path across her heart as she waited for his answer.

"How can they force me to take a lifemate? Tie me up? Flog me? I will refuse."

"And if refusing means the end of peace or the breaking of a treaty? Perhaps a life or two?"

She could almost hear his teeth click closed on any excuse he might offer. Tears ran over her cheeks and dripped onto the blanket. "Don't say words or make promises you can't keep," she whispered.

Kered stared at her. The truth of her words stung him. "There is always something separating us." He leapt off the bed and paced the chamber. With a sudden sweep of his arm, he cleared the table, sending documents and goblets flying. The clink of metal on stone made him freeze.

Maggie's cry of anguish tore him apart. He went down on a knee and picked up the turtle. One edge was dented, but otherwise it was unharmed. She snatched it from his hand and clutched it to her chest. "That was careless of me," he said. "Forgive me."

She nodded briefly and then offered him the turtle. He took it and placed it carefully at the center of the table. A shaft of light from the window cut across the wood surface, shining on the glass. "Where is your pendant?" he asked, turning abruptly and gripping her arm. "I just realized it was not about your neck when—"

"I have the pendant." She quailed at the expression on his face, but he was powerless to change it. "But the chain . . . I bartered it." She twisted from his grasp.

"For what?" he shouted.

Maggie bent and retrieved her gown. He sensed she was hiding from him as she pulled the soft fabric over her head. A raw memory of slipping the gown off her body earlier that evening made his fists clench. She tapped the turtle on its back with one finger. "I bartered the chain to make this."

"Ah." Kered groaned, sinking to the foot of the bed and dropping his head to his hands.

"I made the necklace and if I wanted to give it away, or melt it down, I could."

"Nilrem said the pendant and your appearance at the conjunction was an omen. How could you have tampered with an omen?" Kered stared up at her in disbelief, anger consuming him. "Get the chain back."

"Mada broke it apart and sold it as small bracelets. It's scattered all over Tolemac by now."

Kered rose and went to the window, knowing words were useless. He stared up into the indigo sky. The four orbs had chased each other across the heavens and now, as if fatigued, they drew close to one another. *Aligning for the next conjunction.*

He shivered.

# Chapter Twenty-one

Maggie ignored Kered, who stood silently watching her work in a small anteroom of his chamber. She knew his curiosity would bring him near.

"May I help?" he finally asked.

Maggie grinned, rising from her seat and offering him her place. "Just give it a few extra turns," she said, showing him how to turn the handle on the wooden tub.

He did as directed. The sight of his arm muscles moving smoothly against his soft shirt sent desire through her like a bolt. Her nipples tightened against her gown. With conscious effort, she shifted her attention to his hands. A mistake, for the sight of his hands evoked memories of gentle and not-so-gentle touches.

Maggie thanked him and when he stepped away, she wiped salt and small chips of ice from her contraption. The tentative treaty with the Selaw had yielded the starving tribe much needed oats and each Tolemac councilor a sampling of the much craved ice.

She turned away and picked up one of the large alabaster bowls that Kered used when he ate. She scooped some of the pink mixture into the bowl and handed it to him along with a spoon.

"What is that thing and what is this food?" He held the cold bowl gingerly in his palms and stared at it with suspicion.

"Consider it another gift," she answered. "The bucket man constructed it for me from a drawing I made. It won't bite you!" Maggie frowned. "I hope you won't consider it a waste of the ice. You did say to help myself."

He scooped a tiny spoonful and brought it to his lips. As the chilly mixture touched his tongue, his gaze rose to hers in amazement. " 'Tis marvelous!"

Within moments, the bowl was empty and he was digging his spoon in the tub.

Maggie smiled at his delight. "There's more," she declared, pulling on his arm. He ignored her and, like a starving child, would not be deterred from scooping up more of the treat. "Kered!" Maggie punched him on the arm and he finally looked up, his tongue licking his lips.

" 'Tis . . . fresh berries and sweet cream, am I right?"

Maggie nodded, then swept a hand out to the table and pulled off a white cloth. There, arrayed in a row, stood dishes containing diced nuts and candied peel and pureed fruit. She tugged him to the table and ladled a few of the toppings into his bowl.

"It's called ice cream and when you top it just so," she said, ladling some pureed fruit over the concoction, "it's called a sundae."

Busy eating, Kered did not speak for many moments.

"I cannot remember having tasted anything so wonderful."

"You can't eat it all; you'll get a belly ache," she warned.

" 'Twill be a small price to pay," he said, rising.

Kered elbowed her aside as he hefted the tub, eschewing the bowl. His gluttony added to her mirth. Kered settled on a low bench and put the tub between his feet, then began to eat directly from it. "Bring the rest," he ordered.

"Please?" Maggie asked.

"Please!" He grinned up at her.

Maggie brought him several bowls at a time, warning him, "You'll be sick," as he dumped them into the tub. One by one they all disappeared into the mixture and then into his mouth.

"That's the most vile sundae I've ever seen," she said, tossing the last of the fruit atop the rest.

Kered ate every spoonful, then licked his spoon.

Maggie stared at him. He looked down at the tub, spoon poised in midair. "I did not save any for you!"

"You glutton!" Maggie grinned.

"What is a glutton?" he asked, then held his hand out, palm outward. "Do not explain. 'Tis an animal who eats like a pig and offers none to others."

"Very good, you're learning. You certainly inhaled that treat. I hope you won't be sick." Maggie patted his shoulder.

"I will have Einalem tend me." Maggie frowned, picking up his empty alabaster bowl. It was his turn to laugh. "Perhaps the twins may tend me, if not Einalem?" he mused.

"You cur!" Maggie banged his bowl on the tabletop.

"C-U-R!" he asked.

"Yes, C-U-R!" She smiled warmly.

He rose from the bench and wrapped his arms around her waist, swinging her high. She squealed and clutched his shoulders. "Thank you, Maggie. 'Tis a food to please the gods, or a food for making love."

There was a sudden silence between them as they stared at each other. A communication as old as time passed between them. Kered lowered her very slowly, just enough to bring her lips in line with his. He leaned to her and she to him.

He tasted sweet and sticky. Maggie used her tongue to lap the treat from his lips, and as she did he growled deep in his throat and drew her closer against his body. She let her tongue stray along his lips and then she boldly slipped her tongue in to taste his.

The kiss exploded. He lost his grip on her, and she slid down his body, their lips never breaking apart, his empty bowl dangling from her fingertips. Their tongues thrust and parried in an ancient game. Kered lifted her and carried her to his bed. With a speed that astonished her, he stripped them both.

Maggie pushed him over onto his back and leaned over him. She placed the alabaster bowl on his broad chest and dipped a finger into the remaining pool of melted ice cream. Boldly, she grinned, and as his turquoise eyes widened in surprise, she drew her wet fingertip over the tip of his arousal. "Now, let me explain a Popsicle to you," she whispered.

She had just bent her head to him when the door burst open. Men poured across the room and snatched Kered from her arms before a scream could escape her throat. It took four men to subdue him and two others to bind him. It took but one man to hold Maggie still. He bent her arm behind her back until pain streaked through her shoulder like a hot knife.

"I see you have readied your slave for me," Samoht said as he strolled in with three other warriors. Each man wore a black tunic embroidered over the breast with a red rose. Maggie knew instantly that this was personal treachery and not the doing of the council, for Samoht had brought only his own guard and none of the Tolemac sentries.

She tried to ease her posture, only to have her arm jerked higher behind her.

"I will kill you for this!" Kered snarled, heaving against the men who held him, trying to break free of the thick ropes that bound his wrists behind his back. They forced him to his knees.

Samoht snapped his fingers and a warrior drew forth a pathetic figure. Maggie gasped. The man's mouth gaped, toothless, in a swollen pulp of bruised tissue. From the ends of his sleeves, his hands hung limp, his fingers twisted into grotesque shapes.

"Do you recognize this man? Either of you?" Samoht asked, pulling the man before Kered.

Kered shook his head. "No, should we?"

Maggie didn't know how Kered could sound so calm. Then she saw his arms. His muscles bulged against his arm rings. The tendons on his neck popped beneath his skin. Her teeth chattered. She bit her lip to clamp down her fear.

Samoht shook his head sadly. "This man knows you both—well. He is a N'Olavan guard. He came skulking to me behind the council's back, seeking a reward in exchange for information. As you can see, I have tested this man quite strenuously to verify his story. I could not shake him on a single detail. Most happily, I have persuaded him to tell his story without monetary reward.'' Samoht flung the man back against a waiting Red-rose warrior. ''Such a pity he is not up to repeating his story to you just now.''

''What do you want?'' Kered snarled, heaving against his guards. They grappled a moment, lost their grip, then regained their hold.

Samoht stormed across the room, snatching down the sacred sword from where it hung on display against the stone wall. He pressed the tip to Kered's skin, piercing it and sending a stream of blood running down his chest. ''This man accuses you of using witchery to obtain the cup. How do you answer?''

Kered snorted with derision. Samoht slashed the sword across Kered's shoulder, flaying a strip of skin several inches wide. Blood welled across the patch of raw flesh. Maggie screamed.

Samoht smiled, wheeled about, and crossed to the bed. He leaned down. His light-blue eyes seemed half-crazed as they sought hers. ''Are you a witch? If so,'' he whispered so only she could hear, ''cast a spell and free him.''

''Why are you doing this?'' She gasped.

A commotion made Samoht turn away. Two guards scrambled to hold Kered still. He had gained his feet. Samoht kicked Kered in the thigh. Maggie moaned as the blow sent him back to his knees. Samoht tossed the sacred sword to the ground and drew his dagger, moving close to Kered, turning his blade side to side.

''This man claims your slave pointed at the N'Olavan temple guards and then cast a sleeping spell on them. How do you answer these accusations?''

Kered spat at Samoht's feet. Samoht touched the blade to the birthmark on Kered's right breast, etching a circle in the already blood-matted hair. "A pity you have nothing to say."

Carefully, as if he wished to prolong the moment, Samoht ran the edge of his knife down Kered's ribs, separating skin from flesh. When he reached Kered's waist, he smiled at Maggie. "Is there something important here you would miss should it be removed?" With a deft flick of his wrist he slanted the blade down Kered's thigh, scoring him in half a dozen places.

Maggie battled to remain as silent and unmoved as Kered. Samoht frowned, then stalked to her side. "Let this black-haired fornitrix go." The guard released her, and Maggie groaned at the burn of pain as she tried to straighten her arm. With shaky hands, she drew the silky sheets up to shield her body from the warriors' avid interest.

"Men, take the N'Olavan guard back to his cell. When I have examined this slave myself, I will call for him. Stand guard beyond the door."

"This warrior is dangerous. He could escape with ease," one Red-rose warrior protested.

"He will be suitably complaint should he wish his slave to live through her examination." Samoht lifted a lock of Maggie's hair and used his dagger to sever it. He held it high and chuckled. "See this? Should she be a problem, I will flay another strip from him and perhaps the sight of his blood will settle her down . . . and him." Samoht sent his men away. He slid the bar into place.

"What is the purpose in this? You will suffer grievous censure for this behavior," Kered snarled.

"Will I?" Samoht strode to where Kered knelt. He fastened a rope between Kered's wrists and ankles, making it impossible for him to stand. " 'Twill be a pity when the council learns that their favored man has lain with a witch.''

"I'm not a witch," Maggie cried. She slipped her hand beneath the pillows, searching for the game gun she kept there for protection. Her hands met nothing but smooth cool silk.

"Sit still, slave, or he will suffer." Samoht bent over Kered like a lover to give him a kiss. He slowly drew his blade along Kered's temple, and down his cheek, leaving a red welling of blood in its path. "All my life, you have gotten what I want. Einalem. The council's admiration. I may sit in the high councilor's seat, but 'tis you they listen to. I have finally found your weakness. How long can your power last if all believe a witch gained the cup?"

Maggie moved slowly, edging toward the foot of the bed.

"And if 'tis true and we know witchery? How can you protect yourself from us?" Kered asked.

Samoht pressed the point of his dagger to Kered's lips to silence him. "If I truly believed in witchery, would I be here alone?"

Samoht turned to Maggie. She froze. "Get back on the bed, slave."

Kered jerked his head away from the knife. "You will never be able to explain this brutality. Your days as a councilor are numbered," Kered said, blinking to clear the blood from his eyes.

"Are they? I think not. You see, I have but to explain that you were ensorceled by this slave. I will say you had lost your senses. 'Twas necessary, I shall say, to end your poor suffering at this wicked woman's hands. Who is to know what transpired here? There will be no witnesses.''

Samoht tested Kered's bonds, then stripped naked. He had a runner's lean body and exuded an invincible air. "Einalem might miss you—but I will comfort her." Samoht stood at the foot of the bed. "Before I kill you, Kered, you will wish that you were dead . . . and so shall your lovely little fornitrix. Come, slave. Cast your spell if you have one. Else get on your back or he suffers."

Kered already suffered. Blood ran down his thighs and pooled about his knees. Maggie turned from one man to the other. Somehow she had to save Kered. She realized that Samoht would never release either of them. "Please, a moment," she begged. "One moment with him."

Samoht laughed, turning to Kered as he tossed his blade from hand to hand. "I have wanted your slave since the bathhouse, and now I shall have her. Yet I do not begrudge her one last moment with you. Say your piece, witch. If I am pleased with your performance, perhaps I shall hear your pleas for his release—to a quick death."

Maggie slipped around Samoht to Kered. Never had she felt so exposed, so powerless. The candle's glow glinted off the blade as Samoht continued to play with it. She cupped Kered's face. The agony she saw there frightened her. It was not physical agony, it was the agony of impotence. He would die trying to free himself. Even now, sweat and blood ran down his face and body.

"Ker, hear me." She tipped up his head until his beautiful eyes, so filled with pain, looked into hers. "Hear me, please. Close your eyes, shut your ears. Don't hear this, don't watch it. It means nothing. He can't really touch me. Whatever happens, it won't be me lying there. I'll be somewhere else. He won't touch me where it matters—in my heart. I couldn't bear it if you suffered one scratch more over this. Let it be done."

He tried to break from her grasp. "No, Kered," Maggie insisted. "You must hear me. Close your eyes, close your ears." She drew his head forward and cupped his face to force him to listen. His blood flowed warm on her hands.

"The gun. Under the bed . . . card box. Save yourself," he whispered. She swallowed and nodded.

"Now, slave." Samoht yanked her away and flung her on the bed. Then he reared back. "Hm, I do not believe Kered can see quite well enough from there." He jerked her to her knees and pushed her to the cold stone floor, face down beside the bed. Maggie stifled a scream and tried not to let her revulsion show, for Kered had gone wild against his bonds. He would die for her, and she couldn't bear it.

Samoht tried to pry her legs apart. She fought him, inching forward to the edge of the bed and the black shadows beneath, her fingers stretching out, seeking the gun. If only she could reach it! She groaned as Samoht's hands clawed at her thighs. She lurched away, arms outstretched.

Her fingers touched the box of cards. Frantically, with Samoht's breath hot on her neck as he leaned over her, she ripped it open. The contents spilled, her pendant rolling away, the cards scattering. Her fingers searched and found the gun. She brought it up, twisting in Samoht's punishing grasp. Her eyes had only a moment to focus on his flushed face. She pressed the red button.

# *Chapter Twenty-two*

Samoht's head disappeared.

His torso, not understanding, remained upright on its knees, shaft erect and pulsing for a brief instant, then the body crashed to the ground, spraying blood in all directions.

Maggie began to shake. It started in her hands and traveled to encompass her whole being. With cold deliberation, she ignored the tremors, rose, and picked up Samoht's bloody knife, the one he'd used so brutally to carve flesh from Kered's body. She slit Kered's bonds, taking him against her like a mother gathers her child to comfort him. His hot breath bathed her chest as he leaned against her and gathered his strength.

He rose and took the gun from her fingers. He needed to pry them open. "Thank you, Maggie, you saved my life." He gasped. Carefully, he touched her cheek. "Did he hurt you?"

She shook her head. He was bleeding from half a dozen places and yet asked if *she* was hurt. Maggie flung herself into his arms. "I killed a councilor," she cried.

"You saved us from a painful death." Kered set her aside and stood by Samoht's still-quivering body. "I would have torn his head from his body with my bare hands if I had gotten free."

Maggie swallowed and nodded. "I'm glad he's dead. He deserved to die the moment he put that knife to you."

"Come. Quickly. Dress." Kered tossed her gown to her.

"Wh-wh-what are we going to do?" she stuttered as she pulled the silky cloth over her head and wrapped a cord belt about her waist.

Kered lifted the gun. He sighted on Samoht's corpse and fired. Samoht's remains vaporized in an instant. "Now he is missing. His men may search forever, but he is gone without a trace." He aimed at the thick streamers of blood that splattered the walls and floor. Slowly, using a sweeping motion, he used the invisible destruction to begin erasing the gory display. After a few minutes he turned to her. "It is not working."

Maggie stared about. She remembered how the gun had destroyed stone when they fought the Wartmen. If the weapon was functioning properly, surely not only the blood but also the stone floors and walls should be affected, too. Maggie took the gun and did as he had, alternating between red and blue and pointing directly at a splotch of gore by her feet. Nothing happened.

"I'll clean it; maybe it's clogged," she said, moving to the washbasin.

"Maggie, we haven't time." Kered spoke softly, catching her arm. The blood had dried in a twisted pattern like snakes writhing along his forearm. "The gun has lost its power."

She hit it repeatedly against her palm. "No. It can't be. We need it."

Kered stood before his washbasin and rinsed the blood from his wounds. "Accept it, the weapon is useless. Come help me, Maggie."

Maggie stuffed the game gun into her belt. "What are we going to do?" She quickly mixed the gray herbal and smoothed it on the worst of his wounds, then bandaged them. She began to cry as blood soaked through the salve and continued to run in rivulets along his leg.

He gathered her against him and hugged her. "Do not weep. When Samoht tired of you, he would have presented that pathetic N'Olavan guard with his story of spell casting and the council would have tried you as a witch. They burn witches here, Maggie. The High Priest would examine you first, with unimaginable torture, and then they would burn you."

Maggie pulled back. "I'm weeping for us. For you. How can we explain all this blood? His guards know he was with us. They'll know we did something to him."

"There is no time for this speculation. You are right about one thing—Samoht's men will return. We must be gone from here."

Maggie followed him to his cupboards.

Kered drew clothing from a shelf and dressed. He laced on buff breeches and a leather jerkin. Blood stained the bandages on his chest and shoulder. "We will seek Nilrem's wisdom. Surely, he can think of some solution to this. While we are gone, there will be a frantic hue and cry over Samoht's disappearance. When it dies down, we will return."

A cold apprehension settled in Maggie's stomach. "It isn't that simple, is it?"

Kered's only answer was to strap on his sword belt. He sheathed a long knife at his thigh and slipped a boot knife into place. He knelt before her, slipped his hands under her gown, and strapped a knife sheath to her upper leg. Maggie knew this arming signaled disaster.

They climbed out Maggie's window, dropping to the ground and using shadows to make their way to the barracks. Because Kered's facial wounds were bleeding again, Maggie knocked and asked the sentry to summon Vad.

Vad appeared like an avenging angel in the lighted door, a fierce frown on his face. "I have not hired a fornitrix tonight! Be gone!" he ordered angrily.

Maggie stepped into the light. "Vad, it's me. Maggie." She whirled from the door before he could answer and hurried to where Kered waited at the side of the building, away from the torchlight illuminating the barracks' doorway.

"Maggie!" Vad joined her in the shadows and his voice rose when he saw Kered. "By the sword! I thought you would never get here. I sent Tol hours ago."

"Tol?" Kered stepped into the light. Vad gasped at Kered's appearance. His cloak covered his wounds everywhere but his face. The thin, bloody line across brow and cheek stood out starkly in the bright orb-glow. "Why send Tol to me?"

"First—who did this to you?" Vad placed a hand on his friend's shoulder. Kered winced under Vad's heavy hand. "No one gets close enough to cut you without some treachery."

"Aye. 'Twas Samoht's treachery. He attacked Maggie. Accused her of witchery."

"I assume he is lying bloody somewhere if you are any indication of the battle," Vad said.

"Samoht is dead. Thank the gods for Maggie's gun. There will be no body to deal with." The two men took each other's measure in silence. "And now, Tol?"

"Have you not heard? The men bringing our second delivery of ice were attacked on the way through Selaw land. All drivers and members of the escort were massacred. Samoht called for instant retaliation. My army has been mustered to depart at dawn. Tol was to have summoned you to a special council session. The Selaw representatives swear they are not responsible and promise all-out war if we retaliate in kind without investigating this matter more thoroughly."

"Damn Samoht! What could he have been thinking to have picked such a moment to attack me?" Kered slammed his fist into the wall of the barracks.

"Don't you see, Ker, he did it deliberately. With you out of the way, who would support the Selaw emissaries?" Maggie interjected, pulling her own cloak close against the chill of fear that enveloped her.

"Maggie has it aright," Vad said. "There can be no delay in quelling what will be a bloody retribution."

"I will not be here to help," Kered said. Maggie and Vad stared at him, gape-mouthed.

"I-I don't understand," Maggie stuttered. "You must help!"

"I must return you to Nilrem's mountain," he retorted.

"What are you saying? How can you think of leaving when the wars you fought to end are starting up again?" Maggie's disbelief hardened her tone.

"Maggie." Kered gently cupped her face. "Samoht's men will come for you. We could not hide the carnage in my chamber. When Samoht cannot be found, his men will accuse you—they have the perfect witness, that hapless N'Olavan guard. Do you think he will not take the opportunity to barter his life for yours? Whatever crisis exists for the Selaw, your life is my priority."

She swallowed at the finality of his tone.

Vad, however, was not so easily silenced. "You cannot leave. 'Tis madness. Who will speak in your stead? Who will temper Ronac's marauding instincts?"

"You will." Kered addressed Vad, but stared into Maggie's eyes. "I will move with all speed. When Maggie is safely hidden with Nilrem I will return and lend the weight of my words to avert this disaster."

"Kered, you are mad. It will take three days there and three back! All the men of war will be marshaled by then."

Kered spun to face his friend, his voice sharp and angry. "Then you will need to speak in my stead. Am I the only one who sees reason? Go to Tol, appeal to Flucir. Take word from me, damn it. I will write the words if need be. Just do it."

Vad pulled himself to his full height. Maggie watched an icy calm settle on him. "As you wish." He was no longer a friend beseeching a friend; he was a soldier obeying his commander.

Maggie began to weep. "No, no. I can't let you make this journey. I'll never forgive myself if there's a massacre. Don't make me responsible."

Kered gripped her shoulders. "How dare you think I do this just for you! As long as you are here, they may accuse me of being ensorceled. My every word and gesture will be in doubt. The only way to counter the accusations of Samoht's men will be to have you gone.''

The realization that Kered might be taking her away to save his political future stabbed like a sharp dagger. "I see. Of course, you must not appear to be under any *spell*. How could I be so simple?'' She ducked her head to hide her pain. *What of the spell of love?* she wanted to scream.

"Aye. Now you understand.'' Kered turned a last time to Vad, his tone commanding, brooking no disobedience. "I will give you a written authority to speak for me. Work only to delay any action until I return. Suggest that whatever retaliation they make will be equally devastating, no matter the delay. *I will see to it.* Now fetch some paper so I may pen the words.''

Vad gave a short bow from the waist and went back into the building. When he returned, he stood at stiff attention as Kered wrote hastily on a sheet of paper. Maggie watched as he boldly scrawled his name across the foot of the paper, then rose and thrust it in Vad's direction.

Vad rolled the document, bowed again from the waist, and wordlessly left them, then stood in the arched doorway a moment before running back to them. Vad swept Maggie into his arms, kissed her soundly, and then set her on her feet. "Go with the gods. No matter what is said, I will champion you. I know you are no witch and have not an evil bone in your body. Though they lay hot coals on my tongue, or thrust burning rods up my—''

"Stop!'' Maggie cried. There was no humor in Vad's tone, no indication he was joking. She pounded her fists on his shoulders. "How can this be happening?''

Vad held her close and hugged her hard. "Look after him and send him back anon,'' he whispered in her ear. "I have not his abilities. We need him.''

Maggie sobbed on Vad's shoulder. When Kered yanked her from Vad's arms, she clung to her friend, not wanting to accept the reality of their departure, of what could happen in the next few days.

"Kered," she gasped. "My pendant. I left it under the bed."

Kered swore. "By the sword, what more could go wrong?"

"Please, Vad," Maggie called. "Get my pendant—under our bed. Keep it for me."

Vad nodded and raised a hand in farewell.

They made their way through the darkened streets, Kered avoiding all her attempts at speech. Overhead, the four orbs, close together now, cast enough light to navigate without torches. At last they stood poised at the top of the long stair leading across the strait to the stables where Windsong waited. They had not spoken once. Maggie tried to catch her breath, for Kered's relentless pace was back. He had not looked at her, nor offered her any reassurance. But when he began the steep descent, she saw him stagger. Who knew what the pace cost him?

Puffins perched along the handrails to the stair—their only escape. Kered took the steps two at a time, ignoring the agitated fluttering of wings. When Maggie tried to grasp the rail, the birds pecked at her. "Kered, wait," she called softly.

He turned about and looked back. "Hurry, the puffins sense the blood."

She nodded, slipping her hands into her cloak, and tried to steady herself for the precipitous descent. In a sudden burst of sound, the puffins lifted off, circling and swooping, brushing her with outstretched wings. She screamed and Kered halted. He swung back and leapt the stairs between them.

Kered jerked her into his arms and sheltered her as he ran down the remaining stairs. The sentries snapped to alertness when they passed by. Above a man shouted. Maggie looked up through the mass of soaring wings. A Red-rose warrior stood at the cliff top.

The birds attacked. The warrior disappeared in a black cloud. The sentries rushed to his aid, shouting as the puffins turned on them. Maggie and Kered staggered past the men who blocked their path across the narrow footbridge to freedom.

Kered placed Maggie on her feet and drew his cloak open. The guards, swatting at the birds and crying in consternation, saw the hilt of his sword and fell back against the rails in instant recognition of the ancient symbol. He swept his cloak about them both and they quickly passed the remaining sentries. The birds followed, cawing angrily, swooping and soaring overhead. Maggie felt her hair brushed countless times by wings, and yet, only the sentries seemed to be getting pecked. Their arms and faces ran with blood.

Kered took the second flight of stairs at a slower pace, his breath laboring as he ascended the steep steps. She felt a tremor run through his arm.

"By the sword," Kered swore when they reached the summit. The puffins landed in thick rows along the stone walls lining the avenue to the stable. " 'Tis grateful I am to these black fowl."

"How can you say that? They attacked us!" Maggie huddled against his side, feeling the rapid beat of his heart that was only outmatched by the pounding of hers.

"Do you think we could have crossed unchallenged without such a diversion? They attacked only Samoht's man and the sentries. Perhaps there is truth that Ruhtra's soul abides in them. Surely, he was at our side just now." Kered's words were clipped and he pulled away, reclaiming his cloak and settling it over his sword.

Maggie did not answer. She glanced over her shoulder. "Look!" she cried.

There on the palace side stood more men garbed in black. Samoht's men began the long descent, but were instantly hidden in the mass of birds that lifted and dropped on them.

"Go," Kered commanded. Maggie ran. She lifted her skirts and pelted down the avenue. He outdistanced her in an instant, startling the stableman. By the time she arrived, Kered had Windsong out of his stall and bridled. There was nothing she could do but get in the way, so she stood at the stable door and peered into the night watching for Samoht's guards. An unearthly silence had fallen. Only the sound of horses disturbed at their rest broke the night. The scent of manure and oats reminded Maggie most poignantly of her father's stables, but this was to be a ride like none she had ever taken before.

Kered brought Windsong to her side. His foot slipped in the stirrup. He paused and visibly gathered his strength, then swung into the saddle. His face was in shadow. The moons hung in a close line behind him, yet she saw the ponderous way he pulled himself up. Maggie looked at the strong hand he extended to her. A hand that made love and war with equal proficiency.

"You can't leave," she said. "The council needs you."

"Mount, or by the gods, I will thrash you." Kered slammed his fist on his thigh.

"You would hurt me?" she asked.

His face softened. "Never, Maggie. Please mount. The stableman is watching."

Maggie looked at the man who hunkered down by the stable doors. He was indeed watching, although they were too far away for him to hear their words. She looked off down the street, expecting Samoht's men to appear at any moment. Yet she couldn't climb into the saddle with Kered, either. It signaled an end she couldn't face.

"Please, there must be some way to fix this without your leaving when you're needed. Surely, Samoht's behavior is against your Tolemac laws!" she cried.

A trickle of blood ran down his cheek. "You do not understand," he said in a hushed tone. "There are no laws against what Samoht did."

"A man may flay another and it's okay?" Maggie snorted.

"No. Samoht would have suffered great condemnation for his treatment of me, if he had let me live to tell the tale. But there are no laws against abusing and using slaves—especially if that slave should later be proven a witch."

Maggie's stomach rolled. "I see. He can rape me, beat me, and go unpunished."

"Aye," he said softly.

"I hate your world," she cried in anguish.

"Good. Your hatred will ease our parting."

# Chapter Twenty-three

The Red-rose warriors descended with the sun-rising, twelve strong. They rode in a phalanx behind their leader, a black wedge coming from the capital.

Kered spurred Windsong to his top speed, leaving the specter of their pursuers in the dust. Maggie knew enough about the stamina of horses to know that Windsong could not maintain that pace for long. Great patches of foam flew off Windsong's sides. The thunder of his hooves seemed to say, "Hurry, hurry."

Maggie pressed her face to Kered's back. Her tears had long since dried. Whatever was to come, she could not force Kered to choose between her and his duty and honor. Regardless of the pain that throbbed through her, she would not beg, would not weep, would not betray the intensity of her feelings, no matter his decision.

Windsong faltered, his pace lagging. The threat behind them gained, spread out, and separated as the plain allowed them space to maneuver.

"My gun," Maggie called against the wind. She reached down to Kered's pack. "I want to try it one last time."

He gripped her wrist and held it tight against the saddle. "No gun. We will give them no opportunity to accuse you of further witchery."

Maggie stifled a sharp retort and tried reason. "There are too many of them. We don't stand a chance."

He didn't answer. She leaned her head against his stiff back and searched for something to say, something to offer. The warriors drew near enough that she could hear their hooves thundering on the dry, packed earth. Unconsciously, she gripped Kered's waist tighter. Only when he squeezed her hand did she realize he knew she was there.

Windsong stumbled then flew into a gallop again, seemingly renewed by the falter. Two of Samoht's men drew level. It occurred to Maggie that they, too, had only swords and knives. This would be a fight in close quarters. Kered's hair whipped her face as he turned and assessed the riders' positions.

They hadn't a chance against so many. Twelve guards distributed themselves around them, slowing Windsong and forcing him to fall back. Maggie felt the subtle shift of Kered's posture. In the next moment, she nearly fell off as Kered pulled Windsong to a rearing halt, then forced him into a quick turn. The horse responded. They burst between two guards. A knife thrown in vain hit Windsong's flank, the hilt doing no damage to the animal, but frightening Maggie into cowering behind Kered's broad back. The guards drew near, too close on their heels.

Their new direction led to a stretch of forest. Kered plunged into the trees. Branches snatched at their hair and dragged at their cloaks. Except for two men, the rest of the guard fell back, impeded by the density of the trees and their own numbers. The two warriors gained upon them, their horses' snorting breath loud in Maggie's ears.

A scream of pain made her turn. One guard had not ducked quickly enough and was swept from his saddle by a low-hanging branch. His companion kept coming swiftly after them, ignoring the fallen man.

Windsong dodged the trees, leaped deadfalls, charged saplings. Still the guard came on. Kered jerked Windsong to a halt and vaulted from the saddle. "Go. Hide." He tossed Maggie the reins and with a jerk of his head, turned away, sword drawn. She obeyed him, kicking Windsong and tearing deeper into the wood. She drew up, looped the reins over a branch, and snatched down Kered's pack. Blindly, she ran back. The clash of metal on metal told her Kered was under attack.

Stealthily, she crept to a vantage point. Kered fought two guards. She could tell his loss of blood had weakened him, yet he fought on. No one had an advantage, for the close quarters hampered them all. She raised the gun.

Kered's words about casting spells rang in her ears. Another horse plunged down on Kered, and she knew she had to balance the odds for him. She aimed for the horse. Nothing. She swore and shoved the gun back into her belt.

Frantically, she pawed through Kered's pack. Her fingers met his suede pouch of stars. With a deftness born of frustration and desperation, she flung the star like a Frisbee. The metal star glittered across the horse's line of vision. The mare reared and crashed into a tree, then rolled upon its rider, rose, and galloped off into the trees. The guard lay senseless on the ground.

That left two. Kered relentlessly slashed and parried their sword blows. The guards, smaller, less able, were no match for the fury that drove Kered, for he fought for his life and hers. One man fell with a gaping wound in his thigh. The other drew back, but hesitated a moment too long. Kered took the advantage, sending the man's sword spinning into the underbrush.

Maggie turned and ran back to Windsong. With shaking hands, she freed the reins and led the stallion back to Kered. There was no way she could mount unaided.

Kered had disarmed the Red-rose warriors of their knives. He tied them to a tree, the wounded and the able, ignoring their entreaties for release.

Kered heaved himself into the saddle, blood showing on his bandages in mute testimony of his injured state. He closed his eyes briefly as if to gather his strength, then reached down and dragged Maggie up behind him. Windsong vaulted the prostrate guard, and they crashed back into the trees.

*Did Kered know she'd interfered and used his stars?* Her mouth dried waiting for his condemnation or admiration. She bit her lip with nervous anticipation, wanted him to acknowledge her. Her ears strained for the sound of pursuit, but the ruckus Windsong made galloping through the woods masked any other noise. "The others?" she asked, her heart in her mouth.

"Soon on our heels," he called back.

They burst from the woods. Maggie gasped. So much for her sense of direction. They'd circled around and come out almost where they'd entered. She slapped his back in silent tribute. There was no sign of the rest of the guard.

"Nilrem's beard!" Kered swore. "Where is a dragon when you need one?" He stamped through the shallow stream, soaking his boots and the hem of his cloak. Maggie gingerly stepped from stone to stone to avoid the same result. She knew they had but a moment to water Windsong and gather their own strength. "Surely, we should be able to rouse one, even a babe," he growled.

Maggie searched the stark red horizon. Their trail lay like a bloody finger pointing to where they stood. The Red-rose warriors would have to be blind to miss it. "What do you want a dragon for?" she asked.

"I would hope to offer him dinner—roses, in fact."

She sighed. He turned abruptly and confronted her. "You used the weapon, did you not?" He fisted his hands on his hips and glared down at her.

"No, I swear it!" She held up her fingers in the Girl Scout salute. "Honest, I threw a star, that's all. You've lost so much blood . . . there were three of them," she finished weakly.

He chanted his ancestors' names, bent, and cupped the water. He splashed it on his face and turned to her, dripping. "Will you never do as I ask?"

She soaked a clean bandage and wiped his cheek. The sweat and grime had gathered along the cut on his face. "I was afraid for you." She dabbed at the ragged edges of his wound.

He shook off her hand and grunted. "We will ride through the night."

Maggie smiled. He didn't look very angry. "Why don't I put the salve on your wounds and rebandage them?"

"No time," he said, stepping from the stream. He patted Windsong's neck and praised his speed and agility. The horse bent his head and nudged Kered's shoulder.

Maggie's eyes teared up; she, too, wished for such affection and praise from him. She shoved the bandages and unwanted salve into Kered's pack and slung it up on the saddle.


They met the beggars just as the warriors reappeared on the horizon. As the horde of little folk surrounded them, Maggie searched for and found the ancient one who had spoken to Kered. Windsong picked his way daintily through the curious crowd. Kered leaned down to Tolem.

"Eight men ride hither. They are after me and my woman," he said. "We need your help."

*My woman. Not my slave. My woman.* Maggie's heart swelled.

"Eight? An auspicious number." Tolem leaned on his staff and turned a cynical eye toward the black dots advancing with breathtaking speed. "If 'twas nine or seven, who knows?" A small ragged bundle ran to Tolem and jumped up and down, pointing and grunting at Kered and Maggie. Tolem looked down at the boy. "Yet you asked nothing for this one's life."

The horde of beggars drew in, waiting, expectant. Tolem assessed the approaching riders. "Do you wish them dead or detained?"

"Detained," Maggie and Kered said in unison.

Tolem smiled, his yellow teeth sharp and singularly youthful in his wrinkled face. "So shall it be done." He raised his staff and jabbered to his band of beggars.

Kered lifted a hand in thanks. Windsong danced and

sidled at the sudden seething motion of the little people. In a moment, they had strung themselves out across the plain.

"Will they be harmed?" Maggie gasped as Samoht's guard charged the line.

"We wanted detained, not dead," Kered said over his shoulder.

"I meant the beggars," Maggie returned, clutching at his cloak.

"Perhaps." His somber tone made her shiver.

Windsong had no strength left to gallop. They cantered away. Maggie kept watch over her shoulder, biting her lip.

A wild keening wail rose from the plain. Windsong sidled and balked. The cry rose, tearing at their ears, assaulting their senses. Kered kicked Windsong to move away from the cacophony that sounded like a cry from the grave. As Windsong twisted and turned, his eyes rolling madly, Maggie saw the Red-rose warriors fighting their own mounts' fear, too. Like maggots on a carcass, the beggars swarmed the horsemen.

Maggie caught a glimpse of an upraised arm, a flash of steel before it was lost to view. The sounds of the horde grew mute, overwhelmed by the whistle of the wind across the barren landscape and the shrill cries of men under attack.

Kered honed his weapons, concentrating his attention on the rhythmic and familiar task, shutting her out.

"Let me see to your wounds." Maggie knelt before him, placing a hand on his knee.

In answer, he rose and tossed aside his cloak. Maggie stared up at him. *It was the poster.* The jerkin, the breeches, the knife strapped to his thigh. Her face must have communicated her thoughts.

He went down on his haunches before her. "What is it?" his voice commanded.

"I-I can't tell you." The tears ran down her face. *Never had he worn this particular clothing. Never.*

He gripped her chin, raising her face to his. "You will answer me. You have thought of something—perhaps life-threatening. Some mistake we have made. Tell me."

His distant behavior, his change from lover to warrior, was too much. The tears ran down her cheeks. "It's your clothes. I've seen them."

"By the sword! You speak in riddles." His fingers tightened, bruising her.

*How could she explain?* The truth might make him think her insane. "I had a dream about you. You stood on Nilrem's mountain, the sacred sword in your hand. You wore these clothes."

"And?" he asked. His turquoise eyes hypnotized her to obey him, answer him, regardless of cost.

"And you drew the sword, pointed it there—" she gestured to the sky—"and a fireball appeared, flew through the sky to that mountain." They both looked where she indicated. The gilded peak loomed ominously near.

Kered abruptly stood and turned away. Maggie watched his back as he considered the distant landscape. When he spoke, her stomach clenched. "You dreamt this before coming to Tolemac, did you not?"

"Yes," she whispered, nausea rising. It was a small lie. A prevarication to preserve what little remained to bind them together.

"Mount up," he ordered. In a moment he had

sheathed his weapons. He strapped his cloak to the saddle.

Maggie remained kneeling. "We have to check your wounds." She thought he would refuse. Instead, he turned to her and in a blatantly sensual motion, stripped off his jerkin. With trepidation, she approached. Her fingers were clumsy on the knots of the bandages, but she concentrated and tried to ignore the rise and fall of his chest as he breathed, tried to ignore the sudden liquid heat of her insides.

The salve had worked wonders, yet the flayed patches over his ribs still looked like raw meat. She secured the bandages and dropped her hands to his waist. "The rest?"

Kered didn't say a word as she unlaced his breeches. Maggie's hands traveled over his warm skin as she peeled the supple leather from his hips, savoring the hard feel of his bones beneath resilient flesh. She wanted to touch him, arouse him to match her own desire, but she didn't. Instead, she clinically removed the bandage about his thigh, and seeing that the wound looked clean, she retied the cloth and gently pulled his breeches back into place.

He shoved her hands away as she tugged the laces together. In silence, she picked up his jerkin and offered it. He belted it, open to the waist. A lump formed in her throat. But for the stark white cloth wrapping his midriff, he looked as he had in the poster. *Beautiful. A warrior from another time and place.*

"Mount up." He linked his fingers and she placed her foot in his palms, swinging up into the saddle. The familiar feel of his thighs about her liquefied her insides again. Her blood heated and thrummed in her veins as he wrapped his arms around her and pulled her against him. The odors of his leather clothing, his sweat, and the oil he used on his weapons enveloped her. She closed her eyes and shut out the world to drink in his heat, his touch, and his scent.

Kered woke her at the base of Hart Fell. The Tolemac sun still ruled the sky. He tethered Windsong and offered his arms so she could dismount. "We made it in two days, didn't we?" She tried for a neutral conversational tone.

"Aye," he said, linking fingers with her and striding up the steep slope.

"Wait," she cried. He let her go and she ran back to Windsong, encircling his neck and whispering against his black hide. "Good-bye, precious boy."

Windsong raised his head and tossed his mane. With a last wistful look at the stallion, she returned to Kered. They stepped into the trees and began to climb.

At the summit, smoke drifting from the thatched roof told them Nilrem was home. Kered did not knock, just flung the door open. Nilrem looked up from his contemplation of the fire. A black, sinuous cat rose to stand at his side, the flames lighting his feral face.

"What brings you to invite the Gulap inside?" Kered asked, slamming the door.

"The whisper of unrest," Nilrem said, stroking the Gulap's flank.

Maggie clung to Kered's hand. The Gulap yawned.

Kered removed Maggie's cloak and ran a knuckle across her cheek. She sensed that Nilrem had noted the caress and her skin heated in a deep flush. The Gulap opened his mouth wide in a jack-o'-lantern grin.

"How did word of unrest reach you? I have just now left the capital." Kered placed his hands on Maggie's shoulders and steered her to the far corner of the hut and Nilrem's bed.

"It came with the winds." Nilrem lifted a goblet and drank.

Maggie huddled on the heavy furs of Nilrem's bed. Smoke wreathed the rafters, twisting into an opening in the thatch. Kered, slouching, paced about the small hut, pouring out the story of Samoht's treachery from beginning to end. Each time he passed the cat, it took a swipe. Nilrem finally slapped the beast's flanks, sending a miasma of stink in Maggie's direction.

"What do you suggest we do?" Kered asked.

"There is little to say. Had you chosen death for Samoht's men, you would have had more time. But you were merciful—far more merciful than they would have been to you. 'Tis too late to wish for their blood. I know Tolem. Detained means a day or two, perhaps three at most." He laughed into his goblet of ale, dribbling some of it down his beard. "Eight warriors, you say? When Tolem's women are finished with them, they will scarce be able to crawl up Hart Fell."

Kered frowned. "His women? I fail to see what the beggar women have to do with this."

"Tolem's men may subdue the warriors, but Tolem's women will keep them on their backs!" He slapped his knees, then wiped the back of his hand across his mouth. "Just imagine—only eight red roses for so many women to share! Of course, the warriors may be further delayed if some of the men are desirous of those red rosy buttocks for themselves. All that clean flesh at the beggars' mercy, oh my."

"Stop it," Maggie said. "Can't you be serious?"

"Ill-tempered, is she not?" Nilrem cocked a gray eyebrow in question, then slapped the Gulap's hindquarters.

"Range the hills, my friend. Warn us of intruders. Feel free to taste of any who displease you." The Gulap paced to the hut door and when Kered opened it, the ebony feline melted into the twilight.

Kered sank to a three-legged stool. "Maggie is correct to wish that we cease this speculation. How may we be together?"

"Together!" Maggie rose on her knees and threw off the furs. She climbed off the bed and knelt before Kered, encircling his waist and laying her cheek on his chest.

Kered tenderly stroked her hair from her face and lightly kissed the top of her head. "Aye. How may we be together?"

"My son, your father is dead. The council is in shambles. Renewal of war is imminent. 'Tis unlikely that you will be together for many months. Most likely, six or seven, and then only if you can wipe out all hint of this idea of witchery."

Maggie turned in Kered's arms, riven with anger. "I am not a witch!"

"Perhaps not, but the taint of the accusation will spread to eat away at this man's reputation. Can you deny that? How many saw you together? Sensed your ardor for one another? The N'Olavan guard has but to accuse you of casting a spell over Kered, the Red-rose warriors have but to implicate you in Samoht's disappearance, and poof—you are smoke and ashes, your bones ground and scattered on the road to the capital as a warning to all."

"By the sword." Kered's arms tightened about her.

Maggie bent her head, her hair curling over Kered's strong forearms. "Kered's needed, isn't he?"

"Aye, my child. Would you deny him his destiny now that he has gained the sword and cup?"

" 'Tis *my* destiny to deny," Kered snapped. "I will decide. Hear the truth—Maggie secured the cup and sword."

"Perhaps you did it together," Nilrem suggested.

"Or not," Kered returned.

Nilrem spoke softly. "Then look to the heavens before making any decisions."

On that cryptic remark, Maggie shivered. Kered drew her up and led her back to the bed. "I want you to rest, Maggie."

She nodded. Her eyes felt heavy and the bed, though likely flea-ridden, was soft and inviting.

Kered stepped out of the hut, drawing the crisp air into his lungs to clear out the smoke. He looked up. The orbs had aligned. The winds would rise, cutting to the bone with icy fingers. An intangible longing to shed his life and responsibilities nudged at his conscience. All that he had ever dreamt or desired in a lifemate lay sleeping behind him. All that he loathed—war, brutality, the underhanded intrigues of politics—lay ahead. 'Twas the height of vanity to think that only he could cut through the treachery and restore the Selaw treaty. The agony of his decision coursed like a river of fire through his veins. He silently raged at the gods for setting Maggie in his path and him in Leoh's.

He touched his new gold arm rings. His hand dropped to the sacred sword at his side. The gesture pulled against the bandages about his ribs. A riffle of wind stirred the leaves at his feet.

An awareness that Maggie stood behind him made Kered turn and face her. The night breeze molded the light silk of her gown to her body. Her gaze caressed him before dropping to his hand on the sword.

She looked to the heavens. ''No,'' she whispered as if beseeching him for mercy.

Her denial shredded his resolve. The wind blew her hair in a glorious raven cloud about her shoulders, tearing at his insides. He knew what he would do.

He snatched her against his chest with his free arm, crushing her delicate bones against his own. The sacred sword's hilt burned like molten metal in his palm—searing his decision into his body. His mouth sealed hers for an instant of time. ''You are my soul, Maggie O'Brien.''

He thrust her away. Duty and love warred in his heart.

The gleam of the sinking Tolemac sun caught the ancient blade as he whipped it from the scabbard. A red flame dazzled his eyes as he inscribed an arc in the indigo sky, casting a fireball on the distant mountain. Lightning tore the fabric of the newly birthed night.

The orbs blurred before his eyes.

He smote the blade to the ground.

''No-o-o-o.'' Her scream echoed across the mountains.

# Chapter Twenty-four

Maggie woke entombed in velvet darkness. She lay disoriented, her stomach churning. Tentatively, she lifted her hand. Heavy. She let it drop.

Blackness pressed down on her. Breathing shallowly, she rolled onto her side. Pain shot through her head. She moaned, gulped down nausea, and curled into a protective ball.

Slowly, she became aware of her surroundings. A distant glow might be light, perhaps from a candle in Nilrem's window. The ground pressed against her cheek was rough, smelled medicinal. She idly stroked her fingertips along it.

*Carpet.*

A moan escaped her as she forced herself to her knees. Bent over, she explored with her hands. The near-total blackness told her nothing, but her fingers and nose said new carpeting, its chemical scent heavy in the air. Another scent came to her—the scent of plastic.

And she knew. Knew without a doubt where she was.

She staggered to her feet then fell back down. Her hands grazed along something solid. She wept, silently, in great, body-shaking gulps.

"Kered." She whispered his name tentatively, hopelessly, not really believing he would answer. Silence was all she heard.

The pain in her head pulsed and throbbed. On hands and knees, she crawled toward the faint glow. It coalesced into the gleam of a streetlight shining into the front window of Virtual Heaven.

Maggie knelt in the doorway of the game booth and stared at the light. Rain ran in sheets down the plate-glass windows. Her ears picked up the harsh whip of wind. She shivered, now aware of the flimsy protection of her gown. She listened intently, seeking some sign that Kered was with her. Only storm sounds filled her ears.

"No, no, no," she chanted, more alone than she'd ever felt in her life.

As her stomach settled, she grew frightened. What if he lay unconscious in the game booth? Gathering her strength, she stood up and turned back into the small chamber behind her. She thrust her hands out and shuffled her feet carefully along the floor, her fingers searching for the light switch. Her legs trembled. The switch was where she remembered it to be, but she stood for several long moments without using it. Finally, taking a deep breath and offering up a silent prayer, she thumbed the switch. Light flooded the chamber. Instantly, she flicked the light off again. She sank to her knees and leaned her cheek against the wall in the comforting darkness.

She was alone.

She did not want to see the empty chamber, did not want to face the reality of what she knew to be true.

*Kered had sent her away.*

The ebony shadows of the room filled her eyes, seeped into her soul, and helped her slip into oblivion.

Maggie regained consciousness the second time with sharp-edged clarity. The pain in her head lingered, but had subsided to a manageable level. Her stomach no longer heaved. When she stood up, the world only tilted for an instant before righting itself.

Taking a deep breath, she turned on the light in the booth and refused to look about or make a pointless search. She approached the control platform of the game with resolute steps. The keyboard still meant nothing to her. At her waist, the game gun dug into her side. She pulled it out of her belt and placed it gingerly on the console. Her gaze swept the wide, white screen.

"Why?" she whispered to it. To him. Wherever he was.

She had thought her tears done, but new ones dripped down her face. Grief-stricken, she touched the keys, tapping combinations, seeking a way to turn the game back on.

A whir and hum filled the chamber in a sudden burst of sound and vibration. Maggie flinched away from the controls. Her back came up against the railing. The headpiece, resting there, dropped to the floor with a thud. Then the game fell silent.

Fingers hovering above the slick plastic keys, Maggie hesitated. Could she bear to see him climb that hill? Smile as if he cared. And know he was out of reach. Had sent her away—no, thrust her away. She rubbed her arms. They ached where his fingers had grasped her. She imagined the bruises that would develop there in a few days. Her hands fell to her sides.

Thunder muttered in the distance.

On unsteady legs, Maggie walked out into the main room, using the wall for support. She scanned the shop. Dimly lit by a streetlight across the boardwalk, the shop looked comfortingly familiar. Until she gazed at the south-facing wall. The wall that had separated Virtual Heaven from Maggie's Treasures was gone. Virtual Heaven stretched twice its former width.

Maggie stumbled down the aisles of video games and came to a breathless halt. Hands out like a mime, she touched empty space. Crossing into what was once her shop, Maggie rubbed her temples. Maggie's Treasures had been swallowed up, had ceased to exist.

Turning back, she headed to the door of Gwen's shop. She shook it blindly, feeling like an animal trapped in a cage. The small red light of the security console mocked her. If she opened the door, the police would come. And Gwen. Maggie desperately, unreasonably, needed to escape the shop and the reality of her situation.

Maggie took a deep, shuddering breath and forced herself to be calm. She had killed a man to save Kered. She could find a way out of a simple shop. Quickly, she scanned the door, the security box. Short of breaking the window, she had no idea what to do.

A curious lethargy settled over her. She leaned her face against the cool glass and stared up and down the deserted boardwalk. How dull and colorless the world looked. It could be midnight or five in the morning. The dense cloud cover and heavy rain prevented her from reading the stars or the position of the moon, prevented her from knowing whether Gwen had just locked up a moment ago or had shut down the shop weeks ago for the winter hiatus and gone to sunnier climes.

By the front door stood a revolving stand of periodicals. The store must still be open, Maggie realized, otherwise the rack would be empty and covered. In fact, the aisles of games would be shrouded against sand and dust as well.

One magazine caught her eye. The cover story of *Video Game* froze her to the spot, one hand outstretched.

TOLEMAC WARS—NO PEACE.

She grabbed the magazine and flipped quickly through the pages, moving closer to the windows and the meager light shed by the outside streetlamp.

Her hands trembled as the magazine fell open to a long article that spanned several pages. But it was the photograph of a poster in the right-hand corner, not the text, that drew her.

*Kered.*

The opening paragraph of the article stated that Townsend Creations, the company that had created the virtual-reality game *Tolemac Wars,* was undergoing an internal upheaval that might result in the demise of the immensely popular game.

*What would happen to Tolemac if Townsend Creations pulled the plug?* Maggie thought, her pulse throbbing in her throat. Her head felt stuffed with cotton, her hands suddenly ice cold. She scanned the rest of the article to discover that the reclusive D. W. Townsend could not be reached for comment. Stock prices were plummeting. A sidebar article asked the question in a bold headline: WILL THERE BE A *TOLEMAC WARS II*?

Maggie slapped the magazine closed. She stared at the date. October. Not quite a year since she'd walked through the door of Virtual Heaven to choose an outfit for a November storm party.

All around her, Ocean City was inundated with another nor'easter. The waves snarled and snapped at the boardwalk, spewed their foam up through the boards. The wind, muffled by thermal glass, still whined about the gutters. The scent of damp and mold overwhelmed even that of the new carpeting.

Maggie turned slowly about. What was it Gwen had said so long ago? The poster artist, who also painted book covers for Hearts on Fire Publishing, used live models. That meant the Tolemac warrior might exist . . . somewhere.

She didn't want some poster model. She wanted only Kered.

She thrust the thought away even as her feet took her to the game booth and the large poster next to it. The magazine fell from her fingers as she approached *his* poster with slow, dragging footsteps.

With a complete loss of composure, she slammed her fists into the poster, pounding out her frustration and pain. Energy surged up her arms, through her shoulders, and burst like a gunshot in her head. She staggered back. An ozone scent filled the air.

She gazed in wonder at her hands, then up at the poster. It, too, showed no hint of what had just happened to her. With less anger, she spread her shaking hands. Her fingers touched the poster's glossy surface.

"Just paper," she whispered. With the lightest of touches, she skimmed her fingers over his face. Nothing. Over his well-muscled torso. No spark. No jolt. But when her hands reached the jeweled knife strapped to his thigh, the knife strapped to hers flashed red hot. She screamed and fell back. Frantically, she clawed the knife from its sheath. It glowed like molten metal. She dropped it to the carpet. It lay there, blade gleaming, in the faint light from the boardwalk.

Maggie paced a wide circle around the knife, her eyes glued to Kered's face. Nothing changed. Her world tipped and she sank to the stool Gwen kept behind the counter. Her thigh burned.

As she kneaded the sore spot on her leg, she worried her lip between her teeth. A connection still existed. But could she go back? Could she find him again?

She rose and touched a mere fingertip to the flat glossy knife. A tremor swept through her. Grief and something else, something vague and disquieting, filled her being. Reluctantly, she dropped her hand.

A terrible thought again intruded on her grief. What if Townsend Creations stopped making the game? Did that mean the path to Kered's world would cease to exist? Did it mean *he* would cease to exist?

She looked over her shoulder at the rain-swept sky. What did it take to get to Tolemac? A fluke of lightning at the right time? As if in answer, there was a luminescent flicker over the horizon.

"What should I do?" she whispered to Kered, who stood as he had when she'd first seen him and as he had at the last—impervious to all around him, powerful and silent.

She hung her head and slipped down to her knees. Maybe he needed her *here*. Maybe he needed her to keep the game going. The Shadow Woman still merged with the trees behind him, a wraith, ready to defend his back.

Maggie looked to where her shop had once stood. Her life, here in Ocean City, had changed drastically in the time she'd been gone. What must everyone think had happened to her? What did Kered think had happened to her?

How long she sat looking up at Kered she could not later say, but her legs had gone to sleep, and her back ached when she finally stood and entered the game booth.

She stepped up to the controls just as she had that first time—unsure, yet lured by a man's smile.

"I need you," she said to the empty screen.

The keys blurred. She dashed at her tears with the back of her hands before bringing her fists down on the keyboard with a resounding crash.

The whir and hum filled the game booth. Maggie gripped the railing to anchor herself. Anguish clawed at her resolve.

*They burn witches,* he'd said. Had he sent her away to protect her? Had he sent her away because the question he'd posed to Nilrem—How may we be together?—had no answer in a slave society? Or had other factors conspired against them?

"It takes a while to warm up."

Maggie shrieked and whirled around. Gwen stood in the arched entrance to the game booth, her hair sticking up like a rooster tail, an old chenille robe knotted over her sweatpants.

They fell into each other's arms, sobbing and gasping out unintelligible words of joy and disbelief.

Gwen shoved Maggie out to arm's length and chastised her as one would a lost child, dearly loved. "Where have you been? Everyone has been worried sick about you! How could you do this to us?"

Maggie hugged Gwen close to forestall an answer. "I'm sorry. So sorry." She glanced over Gwen's shoulder, like an addict who knew her fix might appear at any moment. The screen remained blank.

"Look at me!" Gwen shook Maggie, then reached around her and tapped a few keys. The hum of machinery fell silent.

Biting her tongue, Maggie allowed Gwen to drag her into the shop and force her down onto the stool. "Please, Gwen, don't ask me to explain." Maggie folded her hands tightly in her lap.

"I'm sorry, but you have to," Gwen said softly. She briefly touched Maggie's shoulder. "For the past year, everyone thought you were dead—or almost everyone." Gwen squealed and hugged Maggie tightly once more. "Oh, God. You owe me an explanation. You owe your mom and dad an explanation—"

Gwen stopped short. She reached down and picked up the dagger Maggie had thrown to the floor. Light glinted off the blade. Gwen's gaze swept over Maggie, and she seemed to see her for the first time. "This costume, this knife—" Gwen shifted her gaze to the *Tolemac Wars* poster. "I don't get it. Halloween's not for two weeks."

Maggie bit her lip and tasted blood. There was nothing she could say that would not sound insane.

"You're involved in that damned game convention in Atlantic City, aren't you? Don't tell me you've become a game groupie!"

"Game groupie?" Maggie tried to keep her voice neutral.

Gwen slapped the dagger into Maggie's lap. "Take your stupid prop." She stomped to the doors, came back, and stood before Maggie with her hands on her hips. "You damn well better explain yourself because with what I'm thinking—" She stuttered to a halt.

"I don't know what you're thinking. Why don't you

319

tell me?'' Maggie was amazed at the calm sound of her voice.

"No. You tell me. Start with the night of the fire.''

"What fire?'' Maggie found her gaze drifting to the place where her shop ought to be.

"You know what fire I mean.'' Gwen jerked her thumb over her shoulder toward the missing jewelry shop. "Lightning hit your shop, remember? My shop filled with smoke in a flash. I passed out trying to save your butt, so you'd better explain. Where in hell have you been?'' Gwen's voice rose to a shout.

Maggie leaped off her stool and embraced her friend's rigid body. "Forgive me, Gwen. Forgive me. I didn't know. I didn't know. I was gone. Just gone.''

Gwen tore herself out of Maggie's arms and gripped her shoulders. "Gone? Where? The rescue squad looked everywhere for you! We thought you'd collapsed somewhere from smoke inhalation, had staggered the wrong way, fell in the ocean, drowned, for God's sake!''

Maggie had nothing to say. She imagined the anguish of her friend and parents. She'd thought of her mom and dad often in Tolemac, but had put those thoughts aside.

The irony that she'd been practicing the fourth level of awareness control without even realizing it made her smile. She had put thoughts of home aside until it was time to deal with them.

*It was not yet time. There were other priorities.*

Maggie met her friend's eyes. "If I tell you what happened to me, do you promise not to tell anyone?'' They'd shared much in their friendship. Successes, heartaches, bereavements, secrets.

Gwen sighed as if someone had let the air out of her. She dashed tears from her eyes. "Tell me anything, Maggie. Just explain where you've been.''

Maggie stepped past her friend. She lifted her hem and sheathed the now-cold dagger as she stared up at the poster, locked her eyes on the hypnotic lure of Kered's gaze, steadying herself for what she was going to say. She did not wish to confront the disbelief in Gwen's eyes. "I guess if my store's gone, my house is gone, too, isn't it?" she stalled.

"No," Gwen said. "Your Gran wouldn't believe you were dead. She's been paying the mortgage since the fire."

"Good for her," Maggie said to the poster. "Good for her."

"Yeah. Your Gran swore she felt your spirit in your house. Your folks went nuts about it. You know how they are. They couldn't say you were dead, couldn't quite accept you were gone, but they felt it was just plain foolishness to be paying the mortgage for a ghost. Your Gran couldn't handle the shop rent on top of the house, and your parents couldn't either, so I took over your space. It was nothing but a burned-out shell anyway."

Maggie did not flinch at the angry sarcasm in Gwen's voice. Grief had always made Gwen angry. Eyes locked on Kered's, Maggie took a chance. "Do you believe in other worlds?"

"Yeah, Captain Kirk convinced me years ago."

"Unfair," Maggie said, turning and facing her friend. "You asked me to explain. So shut up and listen." And Maggie needed to test how Gwen would cope with her resurrection. After all, if she wanted Gwen to turn on the game again, make it work so she could return to Tolemac, Gwen must believe.

"Sorry. Go on." Gwen's voice was low and soft, barely audible.

Maggie tried again. "I've been in Tolemac. Trapped

there, actually. Somehow, this equipment in here," she patted the wall of the game booth, "can send you into the game."

Silence fell between them. The soft murmur of thunder sounded very far off and weak. Maggie felt a quiver of urgency—the storm was moving away. A glance at the window showed her that the wind and rain had subsided.

She raised a hand in the Girl Scout salute. "I swear. Look at me. I'm the Shadow Woman."

She read the disbelief on Gwen's face. She also read wary speculation. When Gwen nodded and murmured, "Sure," Maggie knew that she'd gambled and lost. Whatever Gwen would say, it would be an attempt to "handle" the situation until some authority could step in—or some doctor.

A thought made Maggie's stomach clench. *Maybe I am mad. Maybe I hit my head in the fire and have been wandering in madness for almost a year.* "Could you turn on the game? I can prove it to you! Just turn it on."

Gwen nodded slowly. "Uh. Sure. But—"

Maggie took an urgent step forward. Gwen backed up, hands raised as if to ward off a blow. Maggie froze. She forced herself to turn away and pick up the game magazine and idly flip through it as if playing the game was not particularly important. She resisted the urge to drag Gwen to the game booth and twist her arm until she turned on the game. "But what, Gwen?"

"Well," Gwen flicked out a hand in the direction of the game booth, "it takes forever to warm up."

Maggie noted how Gwen's eyes no longer met hers. Unfortunately, Maggie did not know enough about virtual-reality games to know how long they took to start. "How long?" she asked.

"Uh, oh, maybe, that is, a couple hours. It's been off for a few days, you know." Gwen bit her lip, still not meeting Maggie's eyes.

How could Maggie accuse her friend of lying? She had to accept whatever Gwen said. And why was Gwen lying? Another, equally painful, thought flitted through Maggie's mind. Gwen was humoring her the way one humored an unreasonable child.

Gwen cleared her throat and shoved her hands into the baggy pockets of her robe. "I'm only open on weekends now. The game's off during the week. That's why I came down here. I was just going to bed when I heard the game come on. I thought maybe my weekend clerk had come over to play. He does that sometimes." Gwen's laughter sounded strained. "I was going to chew him out for scaring me. What a shock, seeing you at the controls."

Maggie's shoulders sagged. Gwen might turn on the game, but Maggie wasn't going to get to play. She could tell. Gwen was stalling, trying to decide how to lace the straightjacket.

"You're sure dressed to play the game," Gwen continued.

"Yes, I am," Maggie said softly, stroking her fingers over the glossy surface of the magazine cover.

"I know what . . . I'll start the game, and while it's warming up, we can go over to your house and get you something else to wear. Then we can call your folks." Gwen's eyes gleamed with tears. "They'll want to know. Especially your Gran. She's waited so long."

Maggie nodded and followed Gwen into the game booth. She watched intently as Gwen touched a few keys and the equipment hummed to life. Maggie stood by passively. She'd do anything to get the game turned on.

And the storm was moving off even as they spoke. Her time was limited.

"Let's go," Gwen said. "The game won't warm up any faster with us watching it."

Gwen unlocked the rear door of the shop and stood waiting while Maggie kneaded and twisted the magazine in her hands. Should she go? Should she insist they stay?

Cold, tidal-scented air swirled through the shop.

Impulsively, Maggie dashed back into the game booth. She snatched up the game gun and tucked it into her belt. It was another link to Kered—however tenuous.

They both ignored the light rain that still fell. How incongruous a pair they made, Maggie thought, Gwen in her robe and sneakers and Maggie in her long, flowing gown, as they walked the short block to Maggie's house. It stood dark and small between two tall duplexes—summer rental properties whose windows were as blank looking as Maggie's.

Gwen fished the key from under an empty flowerpot. The air inside the house was stale and cold, colder than the stormy atmosphere outside.

Maggie rubbed her arms and from long habit, turned the thermostat up, hearing the familiar click of the gas heater as it responded. It was as if she'd just opened the door and come home from work. She sank into a well-worn maple rocker.

Gwen paced. "Maybe we should call your folks now. It's only eleven here. It's not that late out in New Mexico, is it? Three hours earlier? Or is it two?"

Maggie looked up at the battery-powered clock. Its hands had stopped at half-past six. Probably months ago. "Two." She picked up the phone on the small table by her side. At least she knew what she would *not* say to her mom and dad. She would not mention Tolemac, that was for sure.

The phone was dead. She raised an eyebrow in Gwen's direction. "Nothing."

"Oh. I guess your Gran didn't keep the phone going. Look. I'll just zip back to my place and make that call for you."

*And tell my parents to bring a straightjacket with them when they come.*

Maggie nodded and remained where she was, slowly rocking, hugging her magazine. Gwen pointed a finger at her and smiled. It was a smile one offered to small children right before telling a lie. "Now don't go anywhere! Sit right there and wait for me. I'll just be a moment. I'll check and see if the game's warmed up for you."

Gwen backed out of the door. Maggie counted to ten, then shot from the chair and flew up the narrow staircase to her bedroom. She skidded to a halt before her closet, flung open the door, and yanked down a duffel bag. In moments, she had stuffed it with whatever came to hand.

Maggie ripped her gown over her head and shoved it into the bag along with the game gun. She placed Kered's dagger and the magazine on top of the gown. Hunting in a drawer, she grabbed a set of underwear, wasting a moment moaning over the feel of fresh, clean clothing. Next, she jerked on black jeans and a black silk shirt. Her fingers fumbled over the familiar task of lacing up an old pair of paddock boots.

Her good leather shoulder bag was just where she always draped it, over the linen closet doorknob at the top of the stairs. She hooked it off on the way down, taking the stairs two at a time.

In the kitchen, Maggie thanked God for her Gran,

who'd left things just as they'd been. She reached into a coffee can and extracted the plastic bag of bills she'd stashed there so long ago, too lazy to make a deposit of store receipts more than once a week.

Finally, with her purse over one shoulder and her duffel bag over the other, she hesitated. Would she be better off waiting for Gwen's return and trying again to explain?

A murmur of voices, one Gwen's, one male, came to her from outside. Maggie eased the back door open. She slipped into the night just as footsteps sounded on the front porch.

# Chapter Twenty-five

Maggie spent most of the next day in a Spartan room at the Seaview Motel just outside Ocean City. The taxi driver she'd flagged down at the Chatterbox Restaurant on Ocean City's main street hadn't cared if Maggie was a runaway from a virtual-reality game. The driver had only cared about getting paid.

Likewise, the motel clerk had yawned through Maggie's explanations about car trouble and flooding as he'd slapped her key on the counter. In truth, no one seemed to care who she was or what she was doing.

Almost involuntarily, she picked up the phone and punched in her grandmother's familiar number. Her heart throbbed uncomfortably in her throat. But before her Gran could answer, she dropped the receiver back into its cradle.

"I'm not ready," she said to herself. Instead, she pulled a pen and a small tablet from her purse. Although it took three long hours, she composed a letter that reassured her family of her love, offered plausible reasons for her year-long absence, and yet explained her need to stay away in terms her Gran would understand and convey to her parents.

How could she "come back to life" when her quest was not yet finished? And as the hours passed, she felt more and more as if she was on a quest—a quest to find a way back to Kered and Tolemac. Just as Kered had said his quest was not over until he said it was over, so she must see this task through as her warrior lover might.

Her Gran would understand.

*If only she understood herself.*

Maggie paced her small motel room, tapping the letter in the palm of her hand. Her gaze fell on the game magazine. The picture of Kered stared up at her, drawing her, torturing her with what could have been.

"Courage," she said to herself. She slipped the letter into her purse for later mailing and drew out her credit card, which luckily would not expire for another month. In the next few moments, she charged a plethora of phone calls and a round-trip ticket to Colorado Springs, the home of Townsend Creations.

Unfortunately, she had no luck learning the identity of the model for the Tolemac warrior. The fact that the cover model would probably have little influence in determining the game's fate didn't discourage Maggie from starting her search with him.

The burden of saving the game loomed like a dark spectre over her shoulder. What would happen if Townsend Creations stopped the game? She couldn't bear what her imagination conjured up—a Tolemac running with blood as red as the ugly Tolemac sun, the children starving along with their Selaw brethren.

## Virtual Heaven

*The way to Kered gone forever.*

She propped the phone between her ear and shoulder. Her pen circled a line in the *Video Game* article. The story contained a wealth of information about an upheaval among the board members of Townsend Creations, a hostile takeover bid by a Thomas Rawlins that had failed, and wary stockholders, but not one word of the man who was the personification of the Tolemac warrior.

The reclusive creator of the game, D. W. Townsend, couldn't be reached for comment. All she could glean about the man were quotes from a previous issue in which the game's creator had lamented the lack of respect he and other cover artists received for their work in the romance field.

A truck rumbled past outside, grinding its gears as it slowed for a turn into the motel. The semi idled right outside Maggie's window, filling the small room with the thick scent of diesel exhaust.

Maggie waited with nervous impatience. She'd been shuffled from one secretary to another in search of the cover model. He was as elusive as a bath among the Tolemac beggars. Mr. Townsend, the artist, was her best and last hope.

On the fifth ring, a brusque female voice answered. "Mr. Townsend's office."

Maggie sat upright, fumbling her pen. "Hello, my name is Maggie O'Brien. I'm trying to track down the model for the Tolemac warrior." She wished she could think of some creative story. As it was, she felt like a groupie hunting her hero.

"I'm sorry, miss, but the model wishes to remain anonymous. He is available for neither interviews nor photographs. He does not make personal appearances or attend conventions or signings.''

"Wait, wait, don't hang up! I didn't realize he'd be so inaccessible. Is it possible to talk to Mr. Townsend?''

"Honey, we'd all like to talk to Mr. Townsend. Unfortunately, he doesn't much like to chat. Now, what's this about? We're quite busy, you know.''

"Of course. Forgive me for taking up your time. You see, I-I'm writing an article and would like to interview the model, but perhaps Mr. Townsend would consent to an interview instead?'' Maggie frantically searched the magazine article for inspiration.

"I'll give you Mr. Townsend's personal assistant. Just a moment.''

Maggie leaned back, suddenly weary, and waited to be connected. She doodled swords and knives on the margins of the article. She embellished Kered's photo with hearts.

"This is Ms. Whitcomb, Mr. Townsend's personal assistant. How may I help you?''

"I'd like to know if it's possible to set up an interview with Mr. Townsend on his latest project—'' Maggie began.

"You mean the covers for the *Apache Bride* series or are you talking about *Tolemac Wars*? He's not doing anything on *Tolemac Wars,* you know. No interviews. He's not seeking any further publicity for that project.'' Ms. Whitcomb's clipped tones discouraged any further discussion.

Maggie prayed for inspiration. "No, no, I don't want to talk about the game.'' *Not much.* "I want to ask him about a quote in *Video Game* magazine in which he said illustrators of romance novels don't get the respect that other illustrators do.''

"Well now, honey, that happens to be a topic near and dear to Mr. Townsend's heart. Fax me your credentials, and I'll see what I can do. Mr. Townsend is rather capricious, sets his own schedule, you know." Ms. Whitcomb rapped out a fax number, which Maggie scrambled to write down. She never got to say thank you before the phone went dead.

Maggie gently replaced the receiver and fell on her back against the pillows. "Oh, God," she said to the empty room. "I have no credentials. And what good is it to interview this artist?" She crumpled the fax number and pitched it away, tears welling up again.

She curled up on the bed in a fetal position and willed herself to sleep. Perhaps rest would help her think of another way to get to see Mr. Townsend. Once she met him, she'd tell him all the reasons why he had to keep the game going—Kered and Vad, Tolem's beggars, the starving Selaw children.

*And she needed to worm the cover model's name and address out of the man.*

The only alternative was to find another *Tolemac Wars* game booth, wait for a storm, and then play until her money ran out or she was sent back into the game. The thought of never seeing Kered again, never touching him, never lying in his arms, made the tears run down her cheeks and a stonelike lump form in her throat. She fell into a restless sleep.

Maggie woke hours later, feeling no more refreshed than when she'd fallen asleep. She washed her face and stared into the bathroom mirror. Sun streamed between the limp brown drapes in the bedroom behind her. The nor'easter had passed. She leaned on the sink and hung her head. Had all hope of returning to Tolemac passed with the storm? She thought of her life with Kered, the violence of their last few days together. She thought of Vad and hoped he had not suffered in any way trying to retrieve her pendant.

Maggie stroked her fingers down an imagined pendant. *Navajo silversmithing.* Suddenly, she knew what credentials she would present to Mr. Townsend's assistant.

Half an hour later, Maggie was filling in a fax sheet at the desk of her motel. It seemed even cheap motels had moved into the technological world.

With a large dollop of exaggeration, Maggie presented herself to Mr. Townsend's assistant as a woman who wrote freelance articles, her latest one on Navajo silversmithing techniques. She did not mention that the Navajo article was all she'd ever written, or that she'd written it in college, for an obscure metalsmith journal.

With a flourish, she gave the phone number of her hotel in Colorado Springs. She'd be there by the next day. After all, there was no storm to hold her in New Jersey.

Maggie put her new totebag on the floor beneath her airplane seat. Inside it, a stenographer's notepad and a small tape recorder bought at the Philadelphia International Airport nestled between three game magazines. During the flight she would read up on Townsend Creations. She would go through the farce of pretending she was a freelance writer. Somehow she must trick the poster model's name out of poor Mr. Townsend and convince him to save the game. She looked out of the window at the distant horizon.

Fighting dragons and decapitating evil councilors had made her merciless when she thought of this artist and his refusal to talk about *Tolemac Wars.* She pictured him at his easel, a Norman Rockwell sort of man.

He hadn't a chance.

The pain in Maggie's heart grew and mutated like a cancer with each passing hour. Doing the interview would be like an analgesic. It might not cure the disease, but at least she would be doing something concrete to help assuage the mental agony of being apart from Kered. If she never saw him again but saved the game, she'd know he was alive and safe.

Outside the window, her plane floated in the azure sky. Who in the nineteenth century would have believed man would routinely travel above the clouds? How could she convince people that Tolemac existed?

Desperation accompanied her everywhere. Her hopes and dreams all hinged on this one interview. Her sanity depended on this one small meeting.

She slipped her hand into her totebag. The airport security had accepted her excuse for carrying a knife. Just an example of her work, she'd said. She needed the knife with her. Kered's knife. The knife represented tangible evidence that Kered and Tolemac existed. The knife sheath, a finely wrought piece of hand-stitched and oiled leather, was comforting to her hand. Her fingers stroked along the engraved and jeweled hilt. With her eyes closed, she could picture it in Kered's hand, see him slide it into his boot. She didn't need to close her eyes to remember the feel of his hands as he had strapped the sheath to her thigh beneath her dress.

No, the touch of his hands was memorized forever.

"Good morning." The heavy-set woman stood blocking the door of Mr. Townsend's house. Her broad features and impassive expression immediately reminded Maggie of her Gran. Behind the woman, Mr. Townsend's home looked inviting and warm in the glow of sunshine. On either side of the house, aspen trees shivered their bare arms in the autumn wind.

Her fear made her stammer. "Good-good morning. I've come from New Jersey to interview Mr. Townsend. His personal assistant gave me his address and set up this appointment."

"Ah, Maggie O'Brien?" The woman smiled warmly.

"Yes." Relief swept in. She wouldn't be turned away.

"Come in. I'm Consuela, Mr. Townsend's housekeeper." The woman led the way down a glazed tile hallway with whitewashed walls. There were no paintings about. The walls held excellent examples of Navajo rugs of various sizes, but no canvases by Mr. Townsend. Maggie recognized the fine artistry of the rugs; some she could tell were old, woven by hand from naturally dyed yarns. The hallway floor gleamed with the soft peach of old terra-cotta. It led past a large airy living room of muted colors.

The woman did not pause, but opened a door and led the way through a large arch. Maggie had a brief glimpse of a kitchen outfitted with gleaming white appliances, scented with cinnamon and cloves and baking bread, before she was directed to a doorway. For the first time in days, she felt hungry. Much to her shame, her stomach growled.

"Mr. Townsend said you were to wait in his studio." Maggie's guide threw open the door and gestured Maggie in.

For a moment, Maggie thought she had stepped outside. A wall of glass gave her a soaring sensation of open space. As her eyes adjusted to the dazzling light, she realized she now faced the mountains, with Pike's Peak dominating the landscape. The room tilted, then righted itself as she recognized the view from Hart Fell, the opening sequence to *Tolemac Wars*. But the colors were all wrong.

She barely registered the housekeeper's words. "Mr. Townsend, he often forgets the time. He's out hiking."

Maggie nodded, looking quickly away from an array of canvases to her right as she removed her jacket and draped it over a chair. She still wore her black jeans and black shirt. She'd packed her duffel bag with nightgowns and an unfortunate jumble of the clothing she wore when making her jewelry. She could no more do an interview in a flannel nightgown than she could in overalls with holes.

She smoothed her French braid and adjusted the cuffs of her shirt, then examined the room. A deck beyond the windows, cantilevered over open space, gave the impression that you could step off into air. A vapor trail cut the stark blue sky and reminded her that somewhere in the distance, the Air Force Academy was nestled at the foot of the mountains.

"Wait here. I'll bring Mr. Townsend as soon as he gets back." The housekeeper went off in the direction of the kitchen.

Maggie wrung her hands. Mr. Townsend was her last hope. His return might mean the end of her love, the end of something precious, something she needed as desperately as her lungs needed air. She had to shake off this fear.

Maggie stood by the door for a few moments and peered about. A large drawing board stood at one end of the room. A long table, cluttered with the tools of an artist, sat next to it. There were coffee cans loaded with brushes, sheets of paper, pencils, and templates. But they held no interest for her. Cheek by jowl with the artist's

335

tools were two computers and a bevy of electronic equipment she couldn't identify.

Maggie slipped her hands into the pockets of her jeans as she approached the computers. A well-worn chair on wheels stood askew before one computer whose screen showed a kaleidoscope of colors twisting and moving in fascinating repeating patterns.

She was only prolonging her pain.

She wrenched her attention to the other end of the room, walking slowly past a tan leather couch sitting squarely in front of the windows. A low coffee table crouched before it. Books piled there showed interests other than art. She touched one, open face-down. *If I Never Get Back*, by Darryl Brock. Curiosity, an itch she scratched far too often, made her lift the book and read the front flap. She slammed the book closed and dropped it on the table. *A time-travel.*

Finally, she could no longer avoid the right end of the room. She squared her shoulders and held her hand to her queasy stomach.

This side of the room held three easels. Stacks of canvases leaned against the wall and many hung helter-skelter across the white spaces. They were pictures of the mountains beyond the windows, painted in all seasons, all lights, and all moods. They were Tolemac in summer, Tolemac in winter, Tolemac in earthly colors, and unearthly.

One oil painting caught and held her attention. She walked to it like an automaton, for there, front and center on an easel, sat a painting of Kered.

Her eyes burned with unshed tears. He had been painted face to the wind, his hair blowing wildly behind him. A kilt molded his thighs. Heather-covered hills filled the background.

Her hand reached out to the canvas, clutching the wide wooden frame that held the painting. A single bold word—Townsend—had been stroked across one corner.

Every detail of Kered was perfect. Every hair on his chest. Every shadow of his beautiful face.

She couldn't bear it. "No," she practically shouted. *Her Kered did not dwell in the Highlands.* She clutched the edge of the easel and it tipped. The painting crashed to the floor.

A door behind her opened and closed.

Frantically, Maggie tried to right the easel and replace the heavy oil painting, while wiping her tear-blurred eyes. She felt caught in some demonic slapstick routine.

"Do you have something against my Highlander?" called a voice filled with laughter.

Maggie felt heat flash up her cheeks and she ducked her head in embarrassment. She settled the painting in the easel and tried for nonchalance, "Actually, I've never much cared for half-naked men in kilts." She pasted a smile on her face and turned to face the artist.

The room stretched away from her as if viewed through the wrong end of a telescope. The man standing in the wash of brilliant sunlight cast a huge shadow across the white wall.

Maggie took one halting step toward him, hand out, throat as dry as the Scorched Plain. "Kered. Oh, God, I've found you," she whispered right before slipping into oblivion.

Derek Townsend made a valiant attempt to catch her. He almost made it. Luckily, she did not strike her head on anything more solid than a pile of folded drop cloths. He knelt at her side. Unable to resist, he reached out and smoothed the hair from her cheek. "Yes," he said softly, "you've found me. And it seems I've finally found you."

# *Chapter Twenty-six*

Maggie woke stretched out on the long leather couch. She moaned, then sat up. She swung her legs over the side and her gaze frantically searched the room. Rising, she saw him standing with the housekeeper by his computers. He turned toward her, his face blank. The pulse in Maggie's forehead throbbed. Her body was cold and hot at the same time, for she saw no recognition in the artist's expression.

Consuela bustled forward. "Are you feeling better, my dear?"

Maggie nodded to the woman, but it was the man who stood by her shoulder that held Maggie's eyes.

"This is Derek Townsend," Consuela said, her hand on Mr. Townsend's arm.

The sunlight glinted off the artist's wire-rimmed glasses so Maggie was unable to see the color of his eyes. "Forgive me for that little episode," she said, rubbing her arms with her hands. Why didn't he recognize her? Or say something? "You really look like . . . I mean . . . I thought you were . . . I'm so sorry."

The housekeeper clucked with concern and felt Maggie's forehead and said, "I think you'll be all right now. And he is that warrior fellow. He doesn't much like to be reminded, but he is. I'll make you some tea." With that, she bustled off and left the room. Left them alone.

Maggie stood up and faced him. He came forward and offered his hand. She took it in hers. The urge to tug him close was almost overwhelming. His words prevented her from making a fool of herself.

"Miss O'Brien? Right? You're here to interview me about cover art?"

Despite the impassive expression on his face, the complete lack of recognition or any sign that he knew her, he was Kered. She would know him anywhere—in any world.

He wore his brown, sun-streaked hair pulled back at the nape of his neck. Although he wore a faded flannel shirt and jeans, he was every inch her lover and friend.

They spoke as strangers. "Yes," Maggie said softly, "and I apologize again for my behavior. I never expected—"

He gave a rueful laugh and withdrew his hand, which Maggie realized she still held.

"I get strange reactions all the time," he said. "In my pauper days, when I was designing the game, it made sense to use myself as the Tolemac warrior. Now, let's just say, it's inconvenient."

They stood in awkward silence for a few moments. Then he swept an arm out to indicate the computers. "Why don't we get started, Miss O'Brien?"

"Maggie," she offered.

He nodded.

She sat at his side. Near enough to touch. A feeling of being at sea without a sail, in a boat that just swirled along with the current, made her dig in her totebag for a notebook and pencil and hide her embarrassment.

And as if it really mattered, Maggie consulted her list of questions. Just as she had not told Kered the truth of where she had come from, she would not tell Derek Townsend the truth of why she was interviewing him. She'd consider it a two-fold quest—for now—a quest to discover how she could ensure the game continued, and, at the same time, a quest to discover who this man really was.

Consuela entered with a cup of tea and insisted Maggie drink it. "Don't pester Miss O'Brien," Derek said, taking the cup and placing it at Maggie's elbow. "I think Miss O'Brien, I mean Maggie, seems quite recovered." The housekeeper left with further admonitions that Maggie drink.

"So," Maggie said, trying to regain some semblance of a professional demeanor, "you do cover art for Hearts on Fire Publishing. Do you paint any covers other than romance?" How was she going to bring up the game?

"Not often. Hearts on Fire keeps me busy—"

"Excuse me. The British accent. Are you from England?"

Derek Townsend tipped his chair back and Maggie's heart skipped a beat. He was so large and familiar.

"My mother was British, my father a colonel in the American Air Force." He swiveled his chair to face the sheet of glass and gestured at the distant mountains. "My father taught military history at the academy. I bounced around a bit from England to here as a kid." When he swung his chair around to face her, she bit her

340

tongue to keep from screaming out her frustration.

Why didn't he recognize her? What cruel trick had life played on her? Instead, she kept her tone as neutral as his. "How did you come to be the model for the covers?" She pointed over her shoulder with her pencil in the direction of the half-naked Highlander.

Flags of color appeared on his cheeks. "It's a long story, but basically, I'd made up this *Tolemac Wars* game as a kid and thought it might be a lark to fashion it into a computer game. I found some backing, did the art work and so on, but it wasn't making enough money to feed me . . . so my agent suggested I do cover art. Hearts on Fire gave me my first commission, and the rest is history." He fiddled with his keyboard. "Of course, I don't paint the covers in oils anymore."

Maggie found herself staring at his face. He had beautiful skin for a man whose tan told her he spent many hours outdoors. "Why don't you tell me how all this computer stuff works? And why don't you paint in oils?"

She sat on the edge of her chair, barely able to follow what he said. She kept searching his words for some sign he recognized her, for some opening to mention her fears for the game's demise.

"For years," he said, "I did the paintings the traditional way, but now I use the computer for everything. I go through a photo shoot with the models in costume, then I scan in the photos I like and . . . paint."

"Paint?" Maggie tried to concentrate on her notes. "Whoops, excuse me." She hastily dug in her totebag for the mini tape recorder. How unprofessional she must appear. What if he threw her out? He had a temper.

No. *Kered* had the temper—like a swift summer

341

storm. She started the recorder. She could listen later, bring back each word he had said.

"Watch. This is called a stylus," he said, holding up what looked like a thin plastic pencil. She thought of those doodle boards from childhood where you could lift the plastic sheet and make your drawing disappear. "I use the stylus just like a pencil." He moved the stylus across a hard plastic pad lying by the computer's side, and on the screen an image appeared.

Maggie stared, agog, as he sketched a face. Her face. "Now, I can pick different options, depending on which software I'm using, and vary the medium." He moved the stylus to select from a drop-down menu on the screen. As his hand moved, blue shading appeared as if rendered by chalk. "As soon as I get the information from the art director, I start to sketch—"

"Are your sketches computerized?" Her voice was barely a croak as she watched him work.

"Sure. Then I fax them to the art director, who changes things to suit himself, and when I get approval, I start to work on the final product."

"How long does it take you to complete a cover?" Maggie watched his deft hand as he added detail to his sketch of her. The speed with which he worked took her breath away. In moments, she had come alive on the screen. He drew her hair loose and flowing across her shoulder, not in a French braid as she wore it today.

"Used to take me maybe four or five days to do a traditional oil painting, once the art director approved the sketches." He grinned. "*Now* it takes me . . . four or five days. You see, the principles are the same. The computer isn't doing the art work, I am. Whether I'm using the computer or not, it's still a composition. I need to plan the same way, balance the values, and so forth.

There's a structure underneath, a design. That doesn't change just because I'm using a computer.''

He added color to her hair, highlights he could not know existed. Maggie swallowed hard. There was a sensual aspect to the drawing, almost as if . . .

"Watch." He played with his keyboard and she disappeared from the screen. The opening sequence of *Tolemac Wars* appeared instead—in earthly hues. Pike's Peak. Her heart lurched.

"This is one of the landscapes I did for *Tolemac Wars*. I can choose to leave it the way I've painted it here, or I can make it otherworldly by changing the color values. All the *Tolemac Wars* scenes are my favorite places, altered to fit the game. I love the red rocks of Monument Valley." He used his stylus to make more changes. The mountain colors shifted through various shades as he demonstrated. At red, he stopped.

"More brown." She said it softly and he spun to face her. They stared at each other for several long moments. Finally, he lifted the stylus and altered the color.

"I can tint the sky, too," he said with a touch of hesitation. The heavens on his screen deepened through the blue scales to deep purple.

"Darker," Maggie instructed. "Like velvet on an ancient king's robe."

He did as directed, but slowly, his head turned away so she could not see his expression. A pulse throbbed in his temple.

Maggie desperately wanted to know if the people of Tolemac were figments of his imagination. "How do you know what the characters should look like?"

He rolled his shoulders a moment, then faced her again. "Hearts on Fire always sends me a few pages of the book describing the characters. I read them and when

343

the photo shoot is set up, I make sure the costumes are correct. The little details, like hair color and eyes, I take care of later. And I buff the pecs—"

"No," Maggie interrupted. "The beggars. The warriors. How do you know? I meant in . . . Tolemac."

"I think them up in my head, Maggie. That's it. I decide."

She had nothing more to say. Her mind was blank.

He thought them up. Was she insane? Had she suffered some collapse after the fire and simply imagined it all?

Sitting next to this man made her doubt her sanity far more than when she'd tried to explain it all to Gwen.

"But you didn't come to discuss *Tolemac Wars*, did you?" His words challenged her. His expression remained as neutral as before. He moved his head, and the sun's glare on the lenses of his glasses concealed his eyes as effectively as a blindfold.

Maggie shook her head. She had to get out of here. Yet the thought of leaving him hurt. She consulted her notepad. What other excuse had she to stay? "Do you mind discussing the issue of respect? Are you pleased to be known as an illustrator of romance novels?" She'd almost forgotten the question that had gained her the interview in the first place.

Derek busied himself loading another program into the computer. "To do a cover, I need to know everything a painter doing fine art knows. My training is classical, by the way. I'm a romantic at heart. Doing these covers allows me to work with figures in many historical settings. It gives me an opportunity to time-travel, so to speak. An artist must put many elements together in a composition. If he likes what he's doing, it shows, regardless of the medium."

He grinned at her. The smile reminded her of other smiles.

"I love the authors," he said. "They're great. They treat me with respect. They'll let me know if I get any details wrong, too." Then he frowned. "If I did science fiction covers, my work would probably be collected. I know the *Tolemac Wars* poster gets stolen off shop walls. But when I say I do romance covers, there isn't the respect there."

Maggie nodded. "I suppose the writers feel the same way. I understand many romance authors feel they don't get the respect writers of other genres do."

"I wouldn't do anything else right now. If I can only convince the board of directors to let me do *Tolemac Wars II*, I'll be busy for years."

He wanted to keep the game going. "You have to!" Her voice rose to a squeak. She forced herself to be calm. "I mean, everyone loves the game. You can't end it."

"Yes, well, I just draw the game. I don't control the corporate heads."

"Will you be the model for *Tolemac Wars II*?" she asked with trepidation.

"No," he said abruptly and drew a file folder toward him. He shuffled through a neat pile of sketches. "I can't play the part anymore," he said. "I'm getting too old, and the publicity is stifling." With a flick of his wrist, he pitched a sketch onto the desktop.

Maggie picked up the page. The Shadow Woman. The character blended with the lights and darks of the forest in the background, her hair almost a part of the leaves. The pendant about the woman's neck, however, gleamed from the dappled shade and drew the eye. "Nice." Maggie handed it back without further comment. If he expected a reaction, he wouldn't get one. Her heart and mind were frozen in a state of shock, mixed with the fear that some madness possessed her. She could be as impassive as he.

"Mr. Derek?" Consuela stood in the doorway, a large tray balanced on one arm. "Lunch?"

"Oh, my, is it lunch time?" Maggie's chair slid away as she leaped up. "I have to go." She reached for her totebag on the leather couch.

"Why not stay for lunch?" Derek suggested. "I'd like to show you how the computer records my sketches. I can run them back like a movie from the very first line." He sounded exactly like an eager child wanting approval.

How could she refuse?

Consuela arranged the lunch tray on the coffee table as Derek Townsend worked and Maggie pretended to listen. In truth, her mind whirled like a storm over the Sacred Pool, preventing rational thought.

Half an hour later, Maggie perched in the center of the couch and selected a chicken salad sandwich and a glass of iced tea.

"By the way, what software do you use for your writing?" Derek asked, offering her a dish of lemon slices for her tea.

"None. I don't own a computer. I hate them." She fumbled the lemon wedge into her glass.

He grinned and laughed. "You must have a hard time living in the real world."

"Yes," she said. *So much so, I want to leave it.*

The artist settled far too close to her on the tan couch. "What made you decide to write this article?" he asked, stretching out his long legs. Maggie imagined them encased in black leather and felt her body heat.

She averted her eyes and studied Pike's Peak before answering. "I have a friend who owns a video game store and subscribes to *Video Game* magazine. When I read about your concern over the lack of respect accorded romance illustrators, it piqued my interest."

They ate in silence for a moment, or he ate—she just arranged and rearranged the sections of her sandwich. Abruptly, he stood up, stretching his long frame. The sight was torture.

"Why don't you stop by tomorrow? I'm doing a final photo shoot for *Tolemac Wars*. The very last one. We'll be doing a final piece that will be used on a home computer version that will be in the stores for Christmas."

Maggie jumped to her feet. "Yes. Thank you. I'd love to. What time?" The last one? What did that mean? How would that affect the game? She had to find out.

"Three o'clock?" He offered his hand. She took it. His fingers clasped hers, and she remembered all the times Kered had touched her with love. She gave his hand a perfunctory shake and walked away to gather her jacket and bag.

Maggie took a final look over her shoulder at Derek Townsend as she left the room. Everything about him was hauntingly familiar, the way he cocked his head, the way he unfolded from the chair. Her vision blurred with tears, her head ached with confusion.

He was Kered.

*And he was not.*

Derek Townsend placed the lunch tray on the kitchen counter. He put the dishes in the dishwasher. He wiped the tray, carefully placing it on top of the refrigerator. The whole time he cleaned up, he frowned. When the kitchen was practically hospital-sterile, he slumped at the round oak table in one corner and propped his chin on his hand.

"Maggie O'Brien," he mused aloud. Now he knew her name. He had put her in the game. Or suggested her. Never had he felt such an uncontrollable urge to hug someone. She needed hugging. Damn it, he needed hugging.

She acted almost frightened.

People often reacted strongly to him—ever since kindergarten—but they never fainted. That's what happens when your mother is six feet tall and your father tops her by several inches.

He tipped the chair back on its legs, but when it creaked, he thought better of it. He let it drop with a thump and whacked the table. If Maggie O'Brien didn't arrive for the photo shoot tomorrow, he'd go get her. After all, he needed to know if she was just a woman with an undefined aura that drew him, or if she was the woman he'd put in the game—the Shadow Woman—a protectress, a warrior in her own right.

Consuela strolled in and sat down across from him. "Where'd that sweet child go?"

"Back to her hotel," Derek said. And maybe out of my life forever, he thought.

"So, explain yourself. Poor child looked as if she'd lost her best friend. And don't make up some fairy tale. I clean the studio, you know. You can turn pictures to the wall or bury them behind others, but eventually they gotta be dusted."

"Snooping doesn't become you," he said, rearranging the sugar bowl with the salt and pepper shakers.

"All I know is you've painted that poor girl without her clothes, yet you two acted like you'd never met. Never could understand why you can't just paint a nice bowl of fruit or a vase of flowers—"

"So you've said. Many times." Derek grinned, then he frowned. "Consuela, do you believe in ESP or precognition or any of those things?"

"I believe in the PTA and the CYO. What do you mean?" She put the sugar and salt and pepper back where she liked them.

"Two years ago, I did a *Tolemac Wars* convention in Santa Fe. I was browsing around the Palace of the Governors when I saw this woman in the square." He looked off into a distant place. He could almost feel the heat of the sun coming off the buildings in waves. He did feel the same intense jolt of knowledge he'd felt then. He shifted uncomfortably in his seat. "The woman fascinated me. I tried to discover her name. She wore a distinctive piece of jewelry that I thought might identify her, but no luck."

Derek took a deep breath. "I sketched the woman, and her necklace, to help me remember. She stood in the square with two children, twirling in a circle. The look of joy on her face . . . mesmerized me." In fact, he'd raced back to his room to commit her to paper. And had been drawing her ever since.

"So, you had to come home and paint her all bare?" Consuela said with disgust, then rose and attacked the already clean countertops.

"No, I did not paint her nude—then. I did sketch her, though. It seemed important at the time to meet her, but I looked away for a moment, and when I turned back, she was gone. She had disappeared. No one knew her name. I lost sight of her—until today."

Consuela paused, sponge in hand. "That's mighty creepy. How'd you come to paint those other paintings of her?"

"Dreams, Consuela. Dreams."

# Chapter Twenty-seven

Maggie stood in Derek Townsend's doorway and gaped in disbelief. The artist stood before the great glass windows garbed only in buff breeches and high leather boots—and arm rings. His hair lay in a tangled mane about his shoulders. His glasses were nowhere to be seen. Every inch of his bare arms and naked chest were as she remembered. Her body reacted. She took a deep, steadying breath.

Derek abruptly turned as if sensing her scrutiny and impaled her with an intent look. He lifted a leather jerkin from the hand of a small woman whom Maggie had not noticed before, so mesmerized had she been by Derek Townsend's near-nakedness.

She felt the heat of embarrassment sear up her cheeks. "Hi. Consuela told me to come on back."

"Hi, yourself," Derek said, slipping on the jerkin. He belted it, concealing from her the opportunity to see if he, too, bore a birthmark shaped like a sacred eight on his chest. She sidled near and perched on the arm of the couch. "This won't take long," he said.

The photographer, a woman in her early forties, bustled about the end of the room that had held the stacks of canvases Maggie had abused the day before. Now the area was crowded with a white backdrop and what appeared to be umbrellas on poles.

Fascinated, she watched as the photographer maneuvered Derek Townsend around until he stood just as she wanted. It was like watching a Great Dane being led about by a very small terrier. Six-foot-eight to five-foot-nothing.

The photographer posed him as he had been in the poster. Last, she slapped the sacred sword in his hand. Maggie itched to snatch it away and examine it. Was it the real thing? Was it made of finely tempered steel with a turquoise stone entwined in silver, or was it just a replica? The way the photographer used two hands to heft the blade told her it weighed quite a bit.

"Where's your boot knife?" the photographer asked him.

Derek Townsend raked his hair back with one hand. "I can't find it. I've looked everywhere."

The photographer swore. "Probably stolen by some groupie at that convention in Denver."

"It's okay. I can scan it into the pictures," the artist said.

Maggie walked away. She opened the sliding door in the wall of glass and stepped out onto the deck despite the chill in the air. She could not watch the photo shoot. She had thought she could, but he was too close to the real thing.

Derek Townsend's house stood on a rise, isolated

from his neighbors, surrounded by aspens and juniper trees and the rocky terrain.

Eyes on the distant peaks, Maggie mourned. How colorless and washed-out the world now appeared. How frightening her future.

She had lain awake all night contemplating her options. She could go home to her parents. They loved her. No matter how insane she might sound to them, they would take her in. Without a good story to offer them in explanation of her disappearance, however, she would face months of psychiatric treatment. Her mother would see to it.

Another option was to go back to Ocean City. Maybe she'd tell Gwen some tale of following video game conventions, panting after the Tolemac warrior, and then suddenly coming to her senses.

Or she could say she'd had amnesia. After all, it worked in soap operas and horror novels. Eventually, when the furor died down, there would be another empty shop to rent, and she could settle into her old business of making jewelry. She supposed she could make jewelry anywhere. Even here in Colorado Springs. No. Derek Townsend was here. And Pike's Peak would loom over her life and taunt her.

Last, she could try to get back into the game.

The door slid open behind her. Maggie inched along the deck until she stood at the corner, rubbing her arms with her hands to warm herself.

"What's wrong?" Derek spoke close by her shoulder.

Maggie turned to face him.

He loomed over her. His leather jerkin, open to the waist, reminded her quite well that she had lost her mind. "I have something to give you," she said, "and then I have to go."

The chill wind rose and whipped his hair about his shoulders. He was the quintessential Tolemac warrior. Her heart ached. Head down, she stepped back into the house and went to her totebag. She dug deep into the bottom and pulled out the boot knife.

The photographer was gone. The house was still. The scent of paint and leather filled her nostrils. Across the coffee table, its blade gleaming in the afternoon sun, lay the sword. The turquoise stone in the hilt echoed that of her pendant, which was still in Tolemac, under Kered's bed.

Maggie skimmed her fingers along the blade before turning to the doors. He waited there, leaning back against the deck railing, as out of place in Colorado Springs in his medieval garb as she had been on Nilrem's Hart Fell.

She extended her hand. "This is yours."

He pushed off the railing and stood staring at her outstretched palm.

Maggie memorized his face. She wouldn't see it again. He took a tentative step toward her, but did not move to take the knife. "Here," she said, nearly shouting. "Take it." She jerked the blade from its sheath and thrust it at him.

His hand closed over hers, imprisoning it about the hilt. A fierce and powerful surge of energy ran through her arm. Pain and flames licked up to her shoulder and coursed along her spine. Her hand felt fused to the metal and his flesh.

In agony, she fell against him, her hand engulfed in his, metal burning palm to palm.

The knife fell with a clang to the deck. Derek wrapped his arms about her and held her tightly against his chest. Her arm hung limply at her side; her whole body quivered against his. Heat ran from his hands and arms along her spine and back. The air sang with energy. The smell of ozone filled the air.

He lifted her chin with one hand, his breath warm on her face. His lips touched hers. Maggie's mind rebelled. Gasping, hand cradled to her chest, she shoved herself away from him. "No, don't," she said, panting. She reeled away to grip the deck railing. She could not look at him. Her mind churned with the knowledge that when he'd touched his mouth to hers, the taste of him had been one she craved.

*Kered's taste*.

He shook his head as if waking from a trance, then took a deep breath.

"No. Don't speak," she practically shrieked at him. "I know I'm crazy. Just let me go," she begged when he moved in her direction.

"You're not crazy. Now stand still."

The imperious tone of his voice made her stop.

"Pick up the knife," he ordered.

She shook her head and edged away from him.

"Pick it up." He softened his tone and took another step in her direction. The wind had died. They seemed to be standing in a pool of heat. The bright sun gilded his hair. The sight of him, and the gentle tone of his voice, made her look at the knife where it lay on the deck. She knelt and studied it. It looked no different. He crouched next to her. He linked his fingers with hers and, hands joined, placed their fingers on the knife.

Her body sang with a pulse of sensation. She swayed and collapsed into his arms. He held her tightly against him, then lifted her and carried her into the sun-flooded studio. He placed her on the couch and knelt beside her. Her eyes watched him with wary fear. Gently, he combed her hair from her eyes. "You're not crazy. And if you are, so am I."

Derek watched Maggie close her eyes. Her tongue licked over her lips.

"If I tell you what's going through my mind, you'll call the police," she whispered.

"Open your eyes, Maggie, and look at me." She did as he asked. He shoved the Tolemac sword aside and picked up his glasses and put them on. "There's no one here but you and me. I say we tell each other fantastic stories over tea. Later, if you feel the need, you can deny every word you said."

An hour later, Derek Townsend sat across from Maggie, once again garbed in his jeans and a flannel shirt. He was numb. He took a final swallow of cold tea and carefully placed his mug on the coffee table. He cleared his throat. "I guess it's my turn for telling tales."

"I don't suppose you can top mine," she said.

She sat on his couch, feet tucked up under her, hair in a tidy braid over one shoulder. He wanted to undo the orderly plait and spread her hair over her shoulder and breast. "Actually, I think I can," he said.

"I'm all ears." Her tone had turned impish, but her eyes were wary. It was as if telling him her tales of being lost in the *Tolemac Wars* game for about a year had cleansed her of something. She seemed almost light-hearted. But the wariness told him she did not trust him. And why should she?

He rose and paced the long length of his studio. "I haven't shared what I'm going to tell you with anyone since I was about seven years old. I told it once and my father brought in the head doctors."

Maggie nodded. Her silence encouraged him.

355

"I had a friend once. We were quite the little swords-men. We were always battling some evil knight or other in our games. This was in England, by the way. We were visiting my mum's family at the time. My friend was a boy of five from down the lane. We had a lot in common because his father was an American serviceman like mine. Well, one day, while playing our game, we de-cided to lay siege to this old cottage filled with rubbish. His mum had warned us away from the abandoned cot-tage, but you know small boys . . .''

He sat at Maggie's side and leaned his head back and closed his eyes. "Armed with our swords, we attacked. Inside we found a pile of junk—metal, coils, an assort-ment of what looked like radio parts. A mountain of fun for small boys. I don't remember, or *won't* remember, what happened next.'' He took a deep breath. "I only know that my friend disappeared. We had been holding hands and jumping about on the rubbish when he tripped and . . . and suddenly he was gone. I could feel his hand in mine, but he wasn't there. Then my arm disap-peared.'' He met her eyes as an old familiar grief filled him. "I did something I've been ashamed of all these years. I let go of my friend's hand.''

She touched his knee.

He warily covered her hand. No power surge, no shock, no sear of desire swept up his arm. He felt only a warm wash of comfort. "I woke up in my bedroom. My father told me my friend was missing. The police questioned me over and over. It was quite a sensational case. I told my father what had happened and, of course, I was sent to a psychiatrist. I learned the value of silence there.

"I still have clippings from the case. My friend was

never found. I know where he went, but after a while, I stopped talking about it.''

Her fingers were warm and soft. He savored the feel of her hand lying trustingly in his. How long had it been since he had trusted someone enough to confide? "I started dreaming that same night. Now, I live one life by day and another by night." He lifted his head and met her gaze. "You're part of my night."

Derek Townsend devoured a mountain of chili. Consuela had cooked, served, and disappeared. Outside, the night sky was ink black. The house was quiet, warm, and scented with spices and corn bread. Later, he'd regret the spicy meal, but for now, he savored every moment it gave him to observe Maggie O'Brien. The longer the meal lasted, the longer she would stay. She rose and fetched them each another bottle of beer.

"What are we going to do about our 'tales'?" she asked. "If what you say is true, you think you're Kered. Or part Kered." Her eyes and words challenged him.

"I don't know what's true. But I want to find out." He ignored the glass she had given him and drank directly from the long-necked bottle. "I no longer know whether I'm drawn to the places I paint because they remind me of Tolemac, or if I draw Tolemac like my favorite places."

Maggie picked at her bowl of chili. "I've been there. They're the same . . . but different."

He reached across the table and touched the sheathed knife that lay between their bowls. "I knew you were no figment of my imagination when you corrected my drawings. I was deliberately changing the color values. You noted each time I got it wrong."

She nodded, her eyes watching his long fingers trace the edges of the knife sheath.

"No matter how sure you are that something exists," he continued, "if you can't access it, I guess it doesn't exist."

"You can access it." A drop of water falling from the kitchen faucet rang in the silence that followed her words.

Derek cleared his throat. His heart thumped in his chest. "I'll have heartburn after this." He rose and carried the empty bowls to the sink, concealing his emotion with activity. He rinsed the dishes and stacked them in the dishwasher. His hands were shaking.

He desperately needed to know if he was mad. He'd spent almost his whole life unsure. He'd spent over twenty years in steadfast silence, broken only this night, with this woman. To know, to understand, would mean the bringing together of his fragmented life. He swallowed and nailed her with his gaze. "How can you access Tolemac?"

She frowned. "I'm not sure of how it works—or not completely. There was a lunar conjunction in Tolemac when I arrived. And when I left. I know that there needs to be a storm. Or possibly the game needs the boost of energy from a storm."

Derek leaned against the kitchen counter and crossed his arms on his chest. He grinned. "There's bad weather on the way."

# Chapter Twenty-eight

Maggie shivered in her gown, the same gown she'd worn the last time she'd stood on Nilrem's mountain. She rubbed her hands up and down her arms. Hail pelted the windows of Bits and Bytes, the equivalent of Virtual Heaven in Colorado Springs. Cars whooshed by outside on Academy Boulevard. The rattle of the hail seemed freakish to Maggie.

It was long after business hours at Bits and Bytes, but apparently the creator of *Tolemac Wars* had little trouble getting a game store opened for just his pleasure.

Behind her, Derek was involved in a spirited negotiation with the shop owner. In exchange for exclusive rights to *Tolemac Wars II* in the Colorado Springs area, the shopkeeper would give Derek the key to his store for the night. No questions asked. Of course the lewd glances the man shot in Maggie's direction told her his imagination had painted a hot time in the game booth for Derek and his groupie girlfriend.

She hugged her arms across her chest. She was acutely conscious of the press of her breasts against the filmy gown.

Finally, Derek obtained the key. He locked the shop door and placed the key on the counter. "It isn't too late to back out."

She couldn't back out. Her mind said this man was Kered, but her heart wasn't sure. "What if he comes back tomorrow and finds his game on?" she asked to distract him.

"He'll assume I didn't turn it off." He walked the length of the shop to the familiar freestanding booth that Maggie recognized from Gwen's shop. She tagged along, reiterating every point of their night-long discussion—and argument—on how the game booth might have worked to send her into the game.

Derek rounded on her before entering the booth. He held his hands palm up and stemmed the flow of her words. "Look. We've checked on conjunctions. There are dozens. Pick any date and you can find a conjunction—at least in *this* place. We have all the bad weather we could wish for; it might even snow by morning. Who knows how long we'd have to wait for another storm like this one? If there's anything else we've missed, well then, it won't work." An edge entered his voice. "But I have to know, Maggie. You can stay here, if you want. But I'm going." His tone softened, and he avoided her eyes as emotion tinged his words. "I feel a gnawing desperation. I have to know. I have to make some sense of my life."

Maggie whirled away from him and looked out the shop window. The world was a dismal gray. The man of her dreams was waiting for her. Somewhere. *Perhaps right here.* Why prolong the agony? Why hold back? Because Kered had pushed her away. Could she bear to know the reason why? Not knowing had led her to a small deception, one she hoped would not have deadly repercussions.

Derek's dreams of Tolemac were not always specific. His last dreams were of carnage and blood, but not of the actual events of Samoht's last days. Maggie had not provided those missing details. Instead, she had told him over and over only of the dangers that Tolemac held for *him.* After all, if Kered had sent her away to protect her, might not Derek refuse to take her into the game if he knew she, too, was in danger?

She had to go with Derek—to protect *him.* Whatever perils existed in Tolemac when she'd left, still existed. Derek was determined to face them—with or without her. He was as stubborn as his counterpart.

Another fact made it imperative she go. Without Kered, the most important part of her life was missing. Once in the game, she'd find the real Kered and come back—with him this time. And if Derek was Kered and he seemed to be in any danger, she'd be there to help.

With resolute steps, Maggie followed Derek Townsend into the game booth as he put on the lights. He stood with his hands on his hips. He wore his Tolemac warrior garb; the engraved knife was in his boot and the sword was strapped at his hip. He looked magnificent and worried.

"I've been dreaming of this place all my life. I draw it. I think about it. I feel as if half of me is missing. I have to know where I belong. I need to know how hard I must fight to preserve the game."

His thoughts so echoed her own feelings that she relaxed. "I've read a little science fiction," she said. "What if you *do* get into the game and meet yourself?"

He gripped her arms and drew her near. "This isn't fiction. You've been there. What will be will be."

She gasped. His fatalistic words struck like a dagger to her breast. "No. Don't say that." She pressed her fingers to his lips. They stood very still, their breath the only sound in the booth. Slowly, Maggie skimmed her fingers down his throat to his chest. She parted the leather of his jerkin. How many times had she touched this distinctive mark on his chest with her fingertips, anointed it with her kisses during lovemaking?

Derek gripped her elbows in his palms and drew her against him, but she pulled away.

"You can't accept who I am," he said softly. "Look at me, Maggie. Really look."

She was afraid to look, afraid to have him see the doubt in her eyes. It was like having a lover who'd gone away on a long journey—on an Arctic expedition or something—and while he was away, inadvertently discovering the lover had a twin brother. Her attraction to Derek was as powerful as to her attraction to Kered. Yet she was filled with ugly sensations of betrayal, as if she had lustful thoughts for a boyfriend's brother. She, too, needed to know who this man was. A mark on the chest, a taste, a magnetism that drew her was not enough to quiet the fearful treachery she felt in her heart.

Derek felt more than the stir of his blood. He felt an urgency that was ill-defined. She marched to the raised platform like a soldier going off to war. He admired her courage. She touched the weapon at her waist, a game gun she'd brought with her from her friend's shop.

He had another reason for trying to access Tolemac that he'd not shared with this mysterious woman. He was

uncomfortable with his deceit, but he needed to know if
she was the woman he'd put in the game; he needed to
know if she was worthy of the position he'd created for
her.

He joined her on the raised platform. Together, they
lifted the head pieces. Derek glanced about, then rolled
his shoulders, a sheepish look on his face. "I hate to say
this, but I don't know how to start it up."

Maggie smiled and shook her head at him. The smile
sent a flood of relief through him. "You created this
game and you don't know how to start it? Lucky for us,
I watched my friend Gwen start hers. She said it takes
hours to warm up."

Derek hooted with laughter. "This is the latest version. It's incredibly quick, or so I'm told. I plot it, I
draw the scenes; I never play."

*So, Gwen had been humoring her.* Maggie knew she
might lose her nerve if she didn't act quickly. She
touched the sequence of keys she'd watched Gwen press
and a hum and whir filled the air. Her heart throbbed in
her throat. She lifted the headpiece.

Derek stayed her hand. He placed the headpieces on
the railing and faced her. He lifted his hands and held
them close to her cheeks. "May I?" he asked, his voice
soft and low.

Maggie nodded, unsure what he intended.

He cupped her face and stared into her eyes. "Whatever happens, Maggie, you must know the truth as I see
it. I believe all you told me. I dream it. I live it each
night. If this fails, I still believe you."

Just as she had when Derek kissed her, Maggie desperately wanted to fall into his arms and embrace him
as her Kered, her Ker, embrace him as her lover, not
just because he trusted her, but because he had asked

permission to touch her. Something held her back. Trust?
One part of her wanted to trust in this man as she had
learned to trust in her Ker. Part of her just didn't know.
No words seemed worthy as a response to his declaration. She nodded her head.

His fingers lingered along her cheek. Then he dropped
his hands. At the same time, they lifted the headpieces
and faced the screen. They linked hands, and Derek
placed their joined hands atop the hilt of his sword.

Maggie gasped as the sword heated beneath her palm.

The storm outside howled its approval and, fingers
laced with Derek's, Maggie opened herself to pain and
other worlds.

Derek shook himself awake. The scent of wet stone filled
the air. His head hurt like a dozen hammers beating on
one anvil—just as Maggie had described.

*Maggie*. He squeezed her fingers, still curled in his.

He stared up at the night sky. A stunning array of
constellations dazzled his eyes. Not one was earthly. He
rolled to his knees and stared about, a groan issuing from
his lips as nausea joined the pain.

Maggie lay curled on her side, eyes tightly closed.
Gently, he stroked her cheek. It was ice cold. His head
pounded with images that made him want to close his
eyes and lie down for a week. He forced himself to focus
on Maggie. He lifted her head into his lap and said a
silent prayer that she would wake.

Pain and confusion possessed him. Images that had
been nothing but dreams in his head until today stretched
before him in vivid reality—the blue-green orbs nestled
in the star-studded indigo canopy that hung overhead,
the scent of flowers whose names he could recite as if

he'd known them all his life, the warmth of the woman he held in his arms.

Perhaps an hour later, perhaps five minutes, he couldn't tell as his mind grappled with his new world, Maggie stirred in his arms.

"Kered?" She whispered his name and reached up to touch his face.

He nodded. He could not explain what was roiling through his mind, so he helped her to her feet in silence. They stood facing each other, both panting as if they'd sprinted a mile.

Then she leapt into his arms. He hugged her tightly, tears running down his face. He kissed her mouth, hungry, but couldn't lie to her. "Maggie. Stop." He pushed her to arm's length.

She shook her head and fought against his staying hands. "Please, I need you." She burrowed into his chest.

He gripped her arms as tightly as he could without hurting her and placed her at arm's length. "*Stop.*"

He had a desperate need to make her understand. Immediately. She had to know who he was.

She fell still. The expression on her face made him feel as if he'd kicked a kitten. He gentled his hold. "Look about you."

She did as he bid.

"Do you know where we are?" Kered asked.

Maggie nodded. They stood on the gentle slope of a meadow, one she knew well. Where Kered had flown paper airplanes. She had walked it numerous times on her way from Kered's to Mada's shop. To her left, Tolemac lay spread out. Flickering candlelight gleamed in a few windows, but most were dark.

She pointed away from a grove of trees whose black

shadows told her it was hours before dawn. "Mada's shop is that way."

He nodded. He remembered everything—everything—with a sharp-edged clarity that made his head sing. For the first time in two decades, he felt healed, whole. His gaze followed the direction of Maggie's outstretched hand.

"That way is the bathhouse," she said.

"Aye." Exaltation choked his voice. She abruptly turned from the contemplation of their surroundings to face him. Her hand lifted, stretched out to him, then very slowly, almost haltingly, she came close. Inside him, every nerve of his body was strung taut.

She stood on tiptoe and stared up into his eyes. He bent to her, skimmed his mouth across hers to silence her words. Flames of want and desire—the want and desire of two worlds—raced through his system.

He pulled her swiftly to the concealment of the trees. Into the dark shadows he hurried, his heart pounding, his need great.

She was sweet and eager, pliant in his arms. He stroked and savored the feel of her hair as it tumbled down her back. He touched her lips, then kissed her.

The sweetness of her taste exploded in his mouth. He was hungry, starved for what he knew was his alone. With little thought for the consequences, he pulled her to the cold earth, to the cushion of leaves and ferns that would make an ample bed. He drew up her gown, sliding his hand along her warm thigh, taking in the gasp of her breath, the soft moan in her throat.

He tasted her and knew if he did not have her he would expire with the wanting.

She stiffened in his arms, planted her hands, and

shoved. "No," she gasped against his mouth. Her fingers kneaded his chest but held him off.

"Maggie?" He fell still, his hands wanting to seek further beneath her gown, yet he felt the resistance, heard the pain in her voice.

Maggie struggled from his arms. She pressed her hand to his where it lay on her thigh to hold him still. "We can't do this, Derek, we can't."

He fell back and flung his forearm across his eyes. His breath burned in his chest. His body throbbed for release, but he knew what was wrong. She had given her heart and loyalty to only Kered.

Maggie rose onto her knees. The dark shadows did not allow him to read the expression on her face, but her quick breath, her occasional sniff communicated quite effectively.

He groped for her hand in the dark. It lay small and still in his. "Listen to me, Maggie. You must believe in me." A lump in his throat made it nearly impossible to speak. "I remember every moment in Mada's shop that first time with you. I can taste you in my mouth, even now. Your scent fills my head."

She gripped his hand in the dark, her fingernails digging into his palm.

"I wake in the middle of the night with those images burned into my mind and my body ready for you. I can feel the heat of Mada's forge, the sweat that slicked our skin. And now, I even remember the fear I felt when Samoht attacked you."

She groaned and shook her head, her hair sweeping down to brush like a cobweb across his bare arm. He shivered.

"Aye. You understand." He used both hands to hold her, for he sensed she would bolt. "I also remember the taste of Consuela's chili that gave me heartburn last night.''

"No. No.'' Maggie tugged violently against his hands. He held her captive.

"Accept it. I am Kered. And I'm Derek, too. Ask me anything, any detail. Something only Kered would know.''

Maggie's mind refused his words. Her head and heart ached with equal agony. Try as she might, she could not stop the words that were barely audible in the sylvan silence. ''When did you first kiss me?''

Maggie heard the smile in his voice. ''You kissed me first, or perhaps I dreamed it was so. In the cave. On the Scorched Plain. I remember falling asleep with your taste on my mouth.''

Then his voice grew somber. ''Now. Something only Derek Townsend would know. I saw you first in Santa Fe two years ago. In the square by the Palace of the Governors. You were looking at the jewelry. There were two children with you, and I remember your necklace, its design, both Navajo and Celtic at the same time. I put you in the game.''

"Why?'' she whispered. ''How? How could this be?''

He clasped her hands and brought them to his mouth. ''I do not wish to explore the hows or the whys. I wish to explore what is still between us.''

Maggie went into his arms. He growled as he clasped her near. She buried her face against the warmth of his throat and breathed deeply of the scent that was Kered and only Kered.

They slid closer in the bracken, bodies touching along their lengths, and she craved all she had thought lost forever.

In the mad darkness his hands were the same—soothing, arousing. His touch was at once rough and gentle as he explored her body from knee to hip. The sound he made in his throat was the same Kered growl.

His mouth was hungry and insistent on hers. She groaned at the familiar and knowing touch of his hands, the feel of his aroused body pressed to hers.

The words he uttered in breathy gasps at her ear turned her inside out. "I know you," he said. "In any world. The way your hips lift against me to tell me you want this, too. Open to me."

She wrapped her arms about his neck. The scent of him was intoxicating, the heat of his hands melting all resistance. Cool air bathed her legs as he lifted her gown. "Ker," she cried out as he touched her.

"Maggie," he said, moving between her thighs. He could not control the violence of his need. He crushed her in his arms and barely worked the laces of his breeches open to shove them from his hips. Her mouth feasted on the frantic throb at his throat and the same throb drove him to hurry, hurry, hurry to join himself to her.

She dug her fingers into his shoulders and held on. Memory swirled through her. As if stabbed by the molten knife he'd strapped to her thigh, she felt the heat of him sear into her. A scream rose in her throat. She felt the familiar fullness, the hot liquid desire to somehow make herself part of him as he was part of her. She gasped his name again and again, hanging on for the wild ride.

She was scorching heat. He knew how she would move with him, meet his rhythm and take him beyond mere physical sensation. Her legs clasped his hips and a brilliant flare of memory coursed through his brain. His release was the echo and reverberation of each time he had met ecstasy with this woman. It stopped his breath and tore apart his insides. With a mighty shout, he collapsed across her.

Maggie lay there beneath his weight, lungs heaving, body alive as if an electrical wire had been placed against her wet skin. "Oh, God. Kered. Ker. Ker." He didn't respond.

She heaved him off. He rolled heavily onto his back and lay like the dead. She knelt over him and cupped his face. "Kered. Derek. Wake up." She slammed her fists into his chest and slapped his face. "Don't you dare die just when I've found you!"

His hand whipped out and gripped her arm. "Enough. Would you kill me twice?" With a groan, he sat up.

Maggie frantically searched him with her hands. Sweat slicked his body, and she realized as she explored in the darkness that he was enjoying her ministrations far too much. "Okay. What happened there?" She sat on her heels and tucked her gown back down over her knees. Her body throbbed from head to toe.

Kered rose, and from her place at his feet, he loomed like a giant pine in the dark, faint light gleaming off his naked skin. He pulled up his breeches and laced them, then crouched before her. "I cannot explain it. When-when I gave myself to you, it was as if I was experiencing each time I have loved you, again, all at the same time. My mind went red. I would imagine a lesser man might have expired from such joy."

Maggie stood up and dusted off her skirts. "Yeah, well, we both know you're not a 'lesser' man."

With a wild whoop, he scooped her into his arms. Her stomach lurched as he twirled her about, danced her among the trees.

"You are mine, Maggie. Mine and mine alone."

His joy and exuberance could not be denied. She found herself laughing and kissing him with a fervor that matched his own. Whatever explanation these events had, she would think of them later. And later, she would ask him why, if he loved her so much, he'd thrust her away.

Finally, he stood still. She slid slowly down his long, hard body.

"Do you have doubts?" he asked. He realized that her answer could kill him. The pain of her rejection would be more devastating than any defeat a warrior might experience.

"Come." She drew him to the edge of the grove. The orbs overhead gleamed down on them. In the wash of light, she examined him. He rubbed his hands up and down her arms to maintain contact with her. Goose-bumps broke out on her skin.

"There are a thousand small ways a woman knows her lover. It's in the touch of his hands, the way he moves as he loves her. No one tastes like you, or has your scent." She half-turned away from him, heat rising in her cheeks. "I have to call you Kered."

Warmth swept his body. Relief and joy mingled in equal measures in his mind. He enfolded her in his arms and kissed the top of her head. "I understand and am filled with joy that you recognize me."

Suddenly, Maggie knew she had ceased to exist for him as he dropped his hands from her shoulders and turned his face to the Tolemac heavens. His voice was awed. "I feel as if some part of me was lost and now is found."

Maggie followed his gaze. She gripped his arm and pointed heavenward. "Look. Look at the moons!"

"What of them?" he asked, turning to look heavenward.

"Don't you see? We're early. My God. We're early."

"Early? For what?"

His exasperated tone made her stutter through her explanation. "The conjunction—when I left. It hasn't happened yet. Can't you see?"

He nodded slowly. He understood what she meant. The conjunction was yet to come. Unconsciously, he gathered her into his arms and held her tightly. "It makes no sense. The movement between Tolemac and . . . home is—I can't explain it." The familiar sight of the moons' alignment raised a raw fear in him, a fear he could not set aside. "We must speak of Samoht, how we may protect you against—"

"Do you know what this means?" she whispered.

Kered squeezed her tightly. "I can think only of how you may be in danger."

Maggie pushed away and pounded his arm. "Think! Think of how the orbs were aligned when Samoht attacked us."

Kered strode to a position on the meadow where he could overlook the capital. He surveyed the shadows, the position of the stars and moons overhead. "Aye. I see what you are saying. By all the gods, there is still time!"

He grabbed Maggie's hand and began to run across the green sward. Maggie stumbled along behind him. She could barely get her breath to gasp out, "We could stop the N'Olavan guard from accusing you." It was then she realized Kered had taken a direction away from his quarters—and Samoht's. "Where are you going? You're headed in the wrong direction." She dug in her heels. "We should be looking for the guard and stopping him, damn it!"

Kered skidded to a halt and rounded on her. He gripped her hands. "There is no time for that. I can stop the massacre of the soldiers who guard the ice shipment. That must come first."

"Sweet heaven," Maggie whispered. Why was she surprised? Of course he would think of others before himself. Maggie realized that this concern for others was what she loved most about him—what made him Kered. "Please. Oh, God. Please stop the guard. Then see to the ice shipment."

"Seek the answer to that suggestion in the heavens." He shook her off and strode away.

Maggie stifled her grief. She then knew he still needed her protection. She had no need to look overhead.

# Chapter Twenty-nine

The die was cast. Kered would act whether it endangered his life or not. He strode past the councilor's hall impervious to Maggie's presence. She walked quietly as any good slave would do, head down, several paces behind him. He only became aware of her again when they passed the palace and the rising wind whipped her skirts in a sharp snap against her legs.

Kered stopped and looked about. She stood there, silently. As if bidden, she raised her hand and offered it to him. He lifted her fingers to his lips. His breath was warm and his touch gentle. "I want you badly, and we have no time."

Maggie nodded. He crouched down in the bright orb-glow by the side of the road. He drew his dagger and quickly sketched a map with the tip of the blade. "I can't wait to see Vad. I know 'twill seem to him as if we left him but a day ago, but in a way—" he looked up, a twisted grin on his face—"to me 'tis twenty-odd years ago and one bloody night with my heroine defending my life. I must conceal what I know—for now. And you must put your fears aside. We know where the treachery lies. We can guard our backs this time. I will need all my levels of awareness."

Maggie watched him shake off his emotion with a visible shudder of his shoulders. He peered at his drawing, then groped at his chest where a pocket might be if he were garbed in other clothes. "How I wish I had my glasses." He added a few more details to the map. "Here is the most likely place for an ambush—" Maggie's gasp interrupted him. "What is wrong?"

She knelt and surveyed his drawing. "You should conceal this sudden ability to draw. This is extraordinary." The map he'd rendered was but a few lines, yet it conveyed the terrain with uncanny accuracy.

"Aye. I see what you mean."

Maggie duck-walked closer to his side and pondered the drawing.

"Too bad there's no United Nations army to protect the ice shipment," Kered said. Abruptly, he shot to his feet. "That's it! The U.N. Why didn't I think of it before? It's perfect."

He strode off, leaving Maggie crouched in a swirl of dust. She had to run to catch up to him. "How's it perfect? And watch the contractions. You're Derekizing your speech."

"Aye. I must be cautious. Hm. Do you not see that if I can convince the council to make up an escort of, let us say, two men from each chiefdom, Selaw included, there could not be any accusation of treachery? I must share this with Vad."

Maggie considered his words. "I see what you mean.

And if Samoht had any hand in the massacre—''

''Hush.'' Kered raised his hand and swept her behind him. They had reached the barracks. Kered left her with an eagerness she knew stemmed from his friendship with Vad. Left in the shadows, Maggie bit her lip, waiting for the men. Apprehension filled her.

Vad joined them moments later. He gave Maggie a quick, friendly squeeze, then ignored her. After all, he could not know what had transpired in the last few days. Grinning, Kered hovered close at Vad's side and said, ''I have shared my plan with Vad. He thinks it as marvelous as I do.'' Kered's grin of satisfaction made his teeth gleam in the torchlight of the barracks entrance. ''Come, we shall take it to the council.''

The men bantered back and forth as they headed for the palace. They included her occasionally, but Maggie had difficulty responding or meeting their eyes. She had to shake off the weird sensation that prickled her spine. She could not respond to Vad's gentle teasing about her suddenly humble demeanor. He rolled his eyes at her as Kered waxed on about his marvelous scheme.

Every now and then Kered stopped walking and stopped to stare at Vad as they spoke. Maggie knew he looked at Vad with a different eye, as did she. The men's enthusiasm filled her with both apprehension and admiration.

Maggie tugged at the back of Kered's jerkin. ''Kered. We have a problem.''

The men faced her. ''What problem?'' Vad asked. The glow of the orbs silvered his hair and made him look like a marble statue—unreal.

''A N'Olavan guard is going to accuse Kered of being ensorceled. He'll accuse me of witchery. To Samoht.'' There, it was out. She didn't care that she couldn't explain how she knew. She only knew that Kered would suffer, and the carnage of Samoht's death would repeat itself, if she did not speak up.

"Maggie—" Kered began, but Vad interrupted him.

"Where did you hear this ill news?" He dropped his hand to his sword hilt, his eyes searched the shadows as if ready to challenge some unseen enemy.

"It does not matter where I heard it. Slaves know stuff."

Vad nodded. "Aye. Anna often knows some curious information."

Thank God Vad was open-minded, Maggie thought. "A guard on the island must have seen me use my gun. He might convince Samoht that the weapon is evil. That I am evil."

"We cannot stand here in debate," Kered snarled. "Come. We must not waste time. If we cannot convince the council to send the proper escort, worse ill will befall the men who bring the ice."

Maggie gripped Vad's tunic. "Please, Vad, please. You must hear me. What good is Kered's plan if Samoht accuses him of being under my spell? They'll never accept his ideas if it's believed they stem from evil—foreign evil."

"She is right, Kered. Perhaps she should use the weapon on Samoht." Vad laughed—alone.

Kered avoided Maggie's eyes. She dragged a toe through the dirt. "The gun doesn't have much power left. It will be useless after, maybe, one more shot."

Vad smiled and patted Maggie on the shoulder. "You could not hurt a fly, my friend." He turned to Kered. "Does not the idea of Maggie using her weapon on Samoht make you want to laugh?"

This time, Kered joined Vad in laughter, but the sound

was hollow. Maggie shrugged away their mirth. Anger and fear made her tart. "I would protect Kered with my life. He knows that."

They sobered immediately. Kered touched her cheek. "Aye, my Shadow Woman. You would defend me as fiercely as the worthiest of warriors."

Vad smiled. At another time, Maggie would have been dazzled. "I have an idea of my own," he said. "One that will put Samoht in his place without bloodshed."

Vad crossed his arms on his chest. The council stared at the game gun lying by Kered's place on the council table.

Samoht shot to his feet. "What is the meaning of this?"

With a confidence Maggie admired, Vad said, "It is a weapon from beyond the ice fields. This slave was abused by her master, dragged across the barren wastelands. Even when her master perished of the cold, she kept going. She brought his weapon to us. Our esteemed councilor, Kered, tested this weapon on N'Olava."

"This is absurd—" Samoht sputtered.

The councilor Tol interrupted Samoht's indignation. "I wish to know more of this weapon."

Samoht subsided in his seat. Kered rose. He nodded to Vad, who stepped back from the table. "We suspect it may harm the user." He paused for dramatic effect. It was important that he cover all the possible accusations of the N'Olavan guard. "It is for this reason we took this slave to the Sacred Isle to demonstrate it— slaves being expendable."

Maggie had to bite her lip as several councilors made

lewd remarks and nodded their agreement with the final statement.

Tol gestured to her. "Step forward, slave."

Maggie did as bid. She kept her head down and her hands clasped reverently before her.

"Your master had this weapon?" Tol asked.

She nodded without lifting her head.

"Did he teach you to use it?" Samoht asked, skepticism in his voice.

"No, Esteemed Councilor. I only saw it when he used it to hunt. He kept it close until his death."

She stole a glance at Kered. He sat silent and aloof at his place at the magnificent table, the flicker of torchlight bronzing his features—practicing all his levels of awareness, she imagined. How he must be suffering. They were taking such a chance. It would be nothing for Samoht to order her tortured to determine the truth of her words. She bit back bile as she pictured the guard's mutilated hands and mouth.

Samoht rose and circled the table. He lifted the weapon from where it lay before Kered and brought it to her. "What is this material?" Samoht's pale blue eyes bored into hers.

Maggie dropped hers, feeling her face flood with heat, remembering how he had challenged Kered for her in the bathhouse. "I do not know. Many things are made of this material beyond the ice fields. I am but a slave. I have not been taught such things." She made herself sound as ignorant as Vad had suggested.

Kered came forward from his seat. He plucked the weapon from Samoht's hand. "Shall we have my slave demonstrate its use?"

The cacophony of sound swept the room as the councilors variously protested a demonstration and eagerly promoted it. Tol banged the hilt of his dagger on the table to restore order. "How do we know the slave will not turn this weapon on us?"

Samoht laughed and answered before Kered or Vad. "And face the tortures of treachery? She must surely know that to disobey her master will bring her naught but prolonged agony. Do you not know this, slave?"

His eyes glittered with an unholy pleasure. Maggie knew that he had put the N'Olavan guard to the test himself. He would savor her pain, too, if given the opportunity. "I know of what you speak. I shall demonstrate the weapon if it is Councilor Kered's wish." She hoped she had put the proper amount of soppy devotion to her master in the final words. She looked at her lover with blatant adoration.

Tol and the other councilors moved away from the table in a rush. Kered walked toward her. He stepped close and placed the gun gently in her hands. "I love you, in your world and mine," he said softly, so softly that no one but she could hear. "I will defend you—at all cost."

Her eyes filled with tears and she nodded. Swallowing, she stroked the gun. Kered moved back to join the councilors. "I am ready," she said. Lifting the gun, she did as Vad had suggested she do. She aimed it at the tapestry of silk that hung from the back wall of the council chamber. Thumbing the blue button, she vaporized the wall hanging.

A thunderous silence fell. A roar of excitement burst around her. But she had eyes only for Kered. She knew her lines.

"The power of the weapon is almost gone," she said into a lull in the din. "It will soon be useless."

* * *

The councilors questioned her for two hours. Maggie tried to maintain an aspect of mental dullness. No, the weapon could not be made to work once its power was used up. No, she did not know how the weapon worked, she was a kitchen slave. She knew only that at the end, when he had anticipated his death, her master had told her to use it sparingly, for once it ceased functioning, it could not be made to work again.

Eventually, the councilors grew bored of the interrogation and chatted among themselves as if she were no longer in the room. Vad was given the weapon for safe-keeping and ordered to deliver it to the deep vault that held the Tolemac gold reserves.

Kered rode the triumph of the weapon demonstration with his proposal of a joint escort to bring the next shipment of ice.

Samoht was forced to take a back seat as Tol and others took up Kered's ideas. But Samoht's hot eyes never left Maggie, and the cold in the pit of her stomach rivaled that of the ice fields.

Kered woke her just before dawn. He gathered her close to his body. The heat of his skin warmed her as no blanket ever could. He whispered his hopes and dreams in her ear. She knew the man who bubbled over with peace plans was Derek, too. The occasional reference to a "slam dunk" of a plan reminded her that she must caution him again to guard his speech.

Eventually, his well ran dry. Maggie rose and threw open the shutters. The sky was tinged with the first streaks of pink, rendering the horizon a multitude of lavender hues. She lit a candle, walked back to the bed, and looked down on Kered. Sleep had erased the care from his face. His hair lay in a tangled disarray across her pillow. "I love you," she whispered and kissed his mouth.

He wrapped an arm around her and flipped her to her back. "No more than I love you," he growled.

The touch of his hands ignited a fire within her. He slid down her body and worshipped every inch on his journey. The sight of him was a visual feast. Candlelight gilded the muscles of his back and highlighted the flex and extension of his biceps as he embraced her thighs. She was the glutton who must sit at the table.

She buried her fingers in his hair, drew him up, and fed upon the joy of his kiss. He whispered that she had made him whole, that she was all he needed, in any world.

*Except peace,* her mind whispered back, but then she gloried in the moment when his touch was too much, his kiss too intense, and all her senses flashed into overload, and so the elusive thought was lost.

Kered moved within her. Slowly, quickly, teasing her, trying to draw her out. He feared a return of her doubts. It was only with his body that he felt he could convince her of who he was and how much he needed and loved her. She had claimed to know his touch. Claimed to know his taste. He gave her both. Endlessly. He stroked and kissed and made love to her until she lay weeping in his arms. He wanted her to go beyond simple satiation. He wanted her sure of who loved her, who was lying at her side.

Finally, she closed her eyes and fell limp as a rag doll in his arms. Her breath heated his chest as she lay asleep. The room filled with the song of dawn birds.

Never in his life had he felt so complete. But the feeling of wholeness did not come from finding that his night dreams existed as a real world or that some part of him had lived another life. No. He felt complete because Maggie was in his arms.

# *Chapter Thirty*

Maggie waited impatiently for Kered. Each hour without him dragged. But it was Vad who appeared at the door just as twilight painted the indigo heavens with streaks of red. She shooed Anna away.

"What is it?" Maggie asked, a small frisson of fear running down her spine.

"I came to bid you good-bye. The council has selected me to lead the escort for the ice shipment. It is a great honor—one I have waited for my whole life."

She embraced him. "I'm so proud of you. I know everything will be well now."

He preened and Maggie momentarily saw the small boy that Kered had described.

"But where is Kered?" Maggie asked. "Why didn't he come with you?"

Vad paced the room. "Kered was called into a special meeting of the council." He turned and faced her. His

383

military stance made her think of someone facing a firing squad. "They have great news for him. News I feel you should know," Vad finished.

"What is it? Tell me!" Maggie begged, half-afraid to hear what he had to say.

His expression was kind, his words devastating. "It seems that in reward for Kered's service in securing peace without bloodshed—a lifemate has been chosen for him."

Maggie reeled away. She staggered to the low window and leaned on the cold stone sill. The shutters banged softly in the wind. "A lifemate. Einalem?" She could barely say the name.

Vad touched her lightly on the shoulder. "No. The council sees a means to make a peaceful alliance, a more valuable one than that of Samoht's house and Kered's. It is rumored the mate will be the daughter of the Selaw chief—an equal to Kered in status."

Numbly, Maggie shook her head. *Lifemating.* The thought destroyed her hope of happiness but, at the same time, preserved Kered's precious peace.

"We both know you would not do well taking orders from Kered's mate." He cleared his throat. "I know you once asked me to take you to Nilrem's mountain, and I am sorry I may no longer perform that service."

She had no answer, could not answer, as a myriad thoughts clamored in her mind for attention.

"If you wish it—" Vad cleared his throat again and ducked his head—"I will offer to buy you from Kered—"

Her gasp interrupted him. He raised a hand as if to ward off her anguish and finished in a rush. "Not for my bed, for my household. I do not think you would last here. I could give you a worthwhile life."

Maggie sank to a stool and tried to take it in. How could she have forgotten so easily the world in which they were living? A slave society. Where she could be bought and sold. His next words brought the goose-bumps out on her arms.

"I have seen the way Samoht looks upon you. I believe he will eventually challenge Kered for you. My new duties will take me from the capital. You could go with me—"

"Thank you, no." Maggie offered him her hand. "I understand what you are doing, and it is very sweet of you."

He squeezed her hand. "Think what your life will be as Kered rises in power."

She squeezed back. "I know what my life will be." *Agony.* How could she have thought she could come and go at will? Or believed that Kered needed her? The Shadow Woman was no longer necessary. She squared her shoulders and forced a bright smile. "Is there a way I might get to Hart Fell by myself?"

"Alone?" Vad scratched his chin and wandered about Kered's quarters. "Hm. The best I can offer you is safe conduct—of a kind."

"Safe conduct?" Maggie watched him rummage in one of Kered's chests. He held out a small silver square about the size of a credit card. It was gilded and engraved with the symbols of the Tolemac moons in alignment.

"You may show it to anyone who challenges you. It will stand as guarantee that the horse I am giving you is yours. I cannot provide an escort. 'Tis not done to offer such to slaves."

Maggie stared at the smooth, metal plaque, cold and hard as her decision. She gripped his hands. "Take me to Hart Fell, Vad. Come with me. The world is different beyond the ice fields. You will find it more home than this place,'' Maggie begged.

Vad shook his head. ''I have worth here. I will be a councilor one day. I see it in my dreams.''

Impulsively, Maggie ran to the bed. She swept her hand beneath it until she found the small wooden box that held her pendant. She extended the box to Vad. ''Take this. You could teach a few of your friends to play cards.''

He opened the box and withdrew the deck of cards. ''I am grateful for your tutoring.'' He dug out the pendant and held it up. ''What of this?''

She pressed it on him. ''Keep it. If you ever change your mind . . .'' She hoped what she was about to say would be true. ''If you ever change your mind about crossing the ice fields, take this to Nilrem. He'll know what to do.'' She folded his hand about the silver piece.

''I am honored.'' He lifted their hands and kissed her knuckles.

Maggie hugged him about the waist. ''Tell Kered I love him. Tell him—'' she bit her lip and swallowed hard on her grief. ''Tell him I know how important he is here. But tell him I had to go. He'll understand.''

With a brisk nod, Vad set her aside. ''It is doubtful he will understand, but this is best for you, Maggie— and for him. I cannot imagine that you would be content to serve Kered's mate. Oh, he would always see to your care, for he is an honorable man. Your children by him would be given meaningful work, might even have status above other slaves, but—''

''Stop.'' Maggie felt the tears hot on her cheeks. ''We both know I cannot live with the idea of Kered and another woman. I cannot live in your world.''

And she knew that outside the orbs were rising, moving closer together.

Tol stepped forward. He placed his hands firmly on Kered's shoulders. "I wish that Leoh had survived to see this day. You and your lieutenant have crafted a plan that will see us into a new age of prosperity and peace. Who would ever have dreamed we would make peace with the Selaw? And without so much as a drop of blood?"

Kered solemnly acknowledged the compliment with a bow.

The councilor's heavy hand held him in place. "It is with that in mind that we have searched for a suitable lifemate for you. One that will be worthy of a man who, I am sure, will one day head this council."

His mind reeled. *A lifemate*. It was all he could do to hold himself still and not roar with the pain of it. Reality and all its many thorns and pricks wrapped around him.

"Aye," Samoht said from his place. "The council has selected a worthy mate for you. The daughter of the Selaw chief. The contracts are being drawn as we speak. We shall benefit greatly from the alliance, and so shall the Selaw."

Kered tried in vain to force his way through the crowded palace corridors. He had to get to Maggie. He had to break this news to her in just the right way. Together they would think of a solution. After all, had not Maggie been there and helped him along each step of his quest?

At nearly every turn of the cool stone hallways, someone pulled him to a stop to congratulate him or to ask for confirmation of details on the next day's convoy to fetch the ice. The good wishes he could brush off, the concerns for the morrow he could not. So he ground his teeth in mute agony and answered with a patience he did not feel.

Surely, if the news of his marriage alliance had reached so many, so soon, Maggie would hear it as gossip—hurtful gossip. Finally, unable to pretend any longer, he put a man aside and raced the length of a corridor, then burst through the doors to his quarters.

Torches lit the chambers and wreathed the ceiling with smoke. He searched the many rooms for Maggie. Her neatly made bed, her small chest of possessions, might mislead another man to believe she'd stepped out for a moment. But he knew her better than he knew himself. After all, how could he not know the woman who linked him to another world, who was bound to him heart and soul?

He could smell the bleakness of her chamber. Beneath his bed he found the empty box that had held Maggie's pendant and Vad's cards. With a roar of grief, he flung the box away.

He raced to the barracks and hauled Vad from his bed. "Where is she?" he demanded, his desperation shredding his composure.

"What makes you think I know where Maggie has gone?" Vad wrenched himself from Kered's grip, then hastily drew on his clothing.

Kered raked his fingers through his hair and stomped in a circle. "Why do I think you know? Who else would help Maggie? Einalem? Anna? She has no one else in this world!"

"Control yourself," Vad ordered as he pulled on his boots. "And lower your voice. Ears are everywhere. You have need to see your awareness master. Maggie is a slave. Nothing more. By all the gods, you have lost your heart to a slave—one who will cause you naught but grief. It is best you lifemate now, before you do something foolish.''

Kered clenched his fists against the grinding reality of Vad's words. ''She is not just a slave.''

Vad slammed a hand against a nearby table. ''No, my friend. You are wrong. She is naught but a slave. You can sell her. You can lie with her. You can breed children off her, but still, she will be a slave. Your children will be slaves. There is nothing you can do about it.''

*At least in this world,* Kered thought.

''You are wrong. I can do something.'' Kered strode past Vad. He took the barracks' steps two at a time.

Vad caught up with him, breathing hard, half-running to keep pace with Kered's long strides. ''Do not be foolish, friend. Accept what is inevitable. She has.''

Kered jerked to a halt in the wide thoroughfare. ''She has? What does that mean?''

''I spoke to her. Told her of the great honor the council offers you. She agreed it would be best for you both if she left. I gave her safe conduct.''

''Safe conduct!'' Kered cried. ''There is no such thing for a slave. By Nilrem's knees, can you not understand? I love her. All this—'' he swept his hand out to encompass the sprawling capital—''is meaningless to me without her.''

Kered looked up at the sky. *As purple as an ancient king's robe.*

The moons silvered Vad's hair as he, too, looked about. ''I cannot understand. There is no place I would wish to be besides Tolemac. We are about to enter a new age of peace. Peace you brought about. How can you throw it away for a slave?''

Kered placed his hands on Vad's broad shoulders.

## Ann Lawrence

"Come with me. Help me find her. Tol will see our work is carried out. Another may guard the ice shipment." He could barely contain himself. "By the sword, let Samoht mate with the Selaw daughter! We will cross the ice fields and see this place Maggie describes, a place without slavery!" But Kered knew that all his words would not make a difference. Vad knew only this world and this reality. "I am sorry, my friend," he said softly. "The council will have to find another mate for the Selaw daughter. I am going after Maggie."

He studied the sky. He would need to ride both day and night to reach her in time. Swiftly, he embraced his friend. Tears ran unheeded down his cheeks. He had wondered at his friend's fate for more than twenty years. This leave-taking was more painful, more final than he'd ever imagined.

Vad shook him off. They cleared their throats and looked everywhere but at each other. Kered tried a final time. "I must go. Come with me."

Vad shook his head, his own eyes alight with the gleam of emotion. "Go with the gods, my friend," he said.

"Aye," Kered returned. "You, too, go with the gods." He grasped his friend's hand and, as he had twenty-odd years before, he let it go.

Kered tore through his cupboards, tossing garments aside as he searched for certain articles of clothing—buff breeches, his leather jerkin. He wasted precious time hunting for the turtle Maggie had made for him. When he held it in his hand, he paused a moment to consider the remarkable woman who had used her skills to aid him. With great care, he slipped it inside his jerkin, where the cold metal and glass could rest against his

390

skin. Finally, he sheathed the sacred sword of his ancestors. Time was flying—and so must he.

An hour later, mounted on Windsong, he cantered across the meadow that overlooked Tolemac. He had known she would not be standing in the center, awaiting a conjunction still a day and a half away. One did not need safe conduct to a meadow on the outskirts of the city. But still, he had come.

He gripped his reins and wheeled his mount in another direction, toward hostile country. Windsong sidled beneath him, turning and objecting to the direction his master seemed determined to take. Overhead, the heavens told him he would be too late. He gripped the hilt of his sword and vowed to try anyway. He leaned forward and whispered in Windsong's ear. "Get me there, my fine friend. Give truth to your name."

She journeyed as quickly as her mount would allow, frightened at every turn by the slightest noise or hint of humanity on the horizon. She rather doubted that her small metal pass would protect her from anyone who wished to claim an unescorted slave. Even Kered's boot knife, which she touched frequently to reassure herself, would be of little use against a Wartman, or even a determined beggar.

Occasionally, she imagined that the dagger grew warm against her thigh, but she shook it off as imagination—and desire for what could not be. Still, in those moments, she looked over her shoulder at the barren land behind her and kneaded the spot where the metal hilt lay warm against her skin.

Nilrem expressed no surprise when she appeared on his doorstep. He asked no questions, just set a wooden cup of water before her and offered her a thin broth from a pot set over the flames. They spoke little of anything save the coming conjunction.

She napped and to pass the time, mended a woolen blanket for the wise man. Finally, she knew from the shadows cast that it was time.

She kissed the old man on his head.

"Do not be so sorrowful, my child. You are doing what is best," Nilrem said, patting her hand. "Kered will do what is best for him, too."

"I am doing what is right for Kered. I was wrong to think one could come and go, or dwell in more than one place. He feels complete here, so here he belongs."

"I imagine Kered feels complete wherever you are, child."

She shook her head. She remembered the look of joy on Kered's face when he'd stood on the meadow, surveying the world around him with new eyes. "Goodbye." With that, she lifted the latch and stepped out into the cold night.

The moons were almost in alignment. A flicker of lightning on the horizon made her hurry to the edge of the mountain meadow. The wind rose. As in the opening of the game, she stared along the path to the grove of trees and the way to the Scorched Plain.

He was safe.

He no longer needed her protection.

She no longer wondered why he had thrust her away. He had known there was no place for her in his world. She hung her head and hugged the engraved knife to her chest. Even without Derek to draw the game, Tolemac still thrived and moved on. And so must she.

A shower of pebbles made her head jerk up. Her breath hitched in her chest. The sound of a boot on the loose stone of the path made her heart swell. He climbed the rocky hill, each foot placed deliberately. She heard the crunch of stones beneath his soles, heard the sigh of the wind in the trees. The sweet scent of mountain flowers drifted on the breeze.

Kered came straight toward her.

Maggie flew into his arms. He hugged her close, then wrapped his arm about her waist. The heady taste of his kiss told her all she needed to know.

"Hold me tightly," he said, his gaze locked to hers.

She hugged him close.

The orbs aligned.

His sword sang from his scabbard. "Where you are, Maggie, there I must be."

A ball of fire lit the sky as his sword traced an arc against the heavens.

# More Than Magic

## Kathleen Nance

Darius is as beautiful, as mesmerizing, as dangerous as a man can be. His dark, star-kissed eyes promise exquisite joys, yet it is common knowledge he has no intention of taking a wife. Ever. Sex and sensuality will never ensnare Darius, for he is their master. But magic can. Knowledge of his true name will give a mortal woman power over the arrogant djinni, and an age-old enemy has carefully baited the trap. Alluring yet innocent, Isis Montgomery will snare his attention, and the spell she's been given will bind him to her. But who can control a force that is even more than magic?

___52299-3                          $5.99 US/$6.99 CAN

**Dorchester Publishing Co., Inc.**
**P.O. Box 6640**
**Wayne, PA 19087-8640**

Please add $1.75 for shipping and handling for the first book and $.50 for each book thereafter. NY, NYC, and PA residents, please add appropriate sales tax. No cash, stamps, or C.O.D.s. All orders shipped within 6 weeks via postal service book rate. Canadian orders require $2.00 extra postage and must be paid in U.S. dollars through a U.S. banking facility.

Name_____
Address_____
City_____State_____Zip_____
I have enclosed $_____ in payment for the checked book(s).
Payment <u>must</u> accompany all orders. ❑ Please send a free catalog.
      CHECK OUT OUR WEBSITE! www.dorchesterpub.com

## Bestselling Author of *The Mirror & The Magic*

Elinor DeCortenay hails from a world of castles and conquests, sorcerers and spells. So she has no trouble accepting the notion that a magic charm can send her to another time and place, where leather-skinned demons ride noisy beasts. What she can't believe is that the devilishly handsome man she mistakes for Satan's minion is really a knight of the present.

Since the death of his wife, Drew has become a virtual recluse, showing interest in little besides his passion for motorcycles. Then, while riding his souped-up Harley through the California countryside, he chances upon a striking beauty dressed like a resident of Camelot, and despite his misgivings, she wakens his lonely heart to a desire for the future. A medieval maiden and modern motorhead, Elinor and Drew are both trying to escape painful pasts—pasts that will haunt them forever unless they can share a love timeless, tempestuous, and true.

___4273-8                                     $5.50 US/$6.50 CAN

**Dorchester Publishing Co., Inc.**
**P.O. Box 6640**
**Wayne, PA 19087-8640**

# Heart's Magic

## Flora Speer

### Bestselling author of *ROSE RED*

In the year 1122, Mirielle senses change is coming to Wroxley Castle. Then, from out of the fog, two strangers ride into Lincolnshire. Mirielle believes the first man to be honest. But the second, Giles, is hiding something–even as he stirs her heart and awakens her deepest desires. And as Mirielle seeks the truth about her mysterious guest, she uncovers the castle's secrets and learns she must stop a treachery which threatens all she holds dear. Only then can she be in the arms of her only love, the man who has awakened her own heart's magic.

\_\_\_52204-7 $5.99 US/$6.99 CAN

The Magician's Lover — Fiora Speer

Determined to locate his friend who disappeared during a spell gone awry, Warrick petitions a dying stargazer to help find him. But the astronomer will only assist Warrick if he promises to escort his daughter Sophia and a priceless crystal ball safely to Byzantium. Sharp-tongued and argumentative, Sophia meets her match in the powerful and intelligent Warrick. Try as she will to deny it, he holds her spellbound, longing to be the magician's lover.

___52263-2                                        $5.99 US/$6.99 CAN

**Dorchester Publishing Co., Inc.**
**P.O. Box 6640**
**Wayne, PA 19087-8640**

Please add $1.75 for shipping and handling for the first book and $.50 for each book thereafter. NY, NYC, and PA residents, please add appropriate sales tax. No cash, stamps, or C.O.D.s. All orders shipped within 6 weeks via postal service book rate. Canadian orders require $2.00 extra postage and must be paid in U.S. dollars through a U.S. banking facility.

Name_____
Address_____
City_____State_____Zip_____
I have enclosed $_____ in payment for the checked book(s).
Payment <u>must</u> accompany all orders. ❑ Please send a free catalog.
CHECK OUT OUR WEBSITE! www.dorchesterpub.com

# *Love* Once & Forever
## Flora Speer

Laura has traveled here, to this time before the moon has come to circle the earth, to embrace Kentir beneath the violet-and-ochre brilliance of the Northern Lights. In his gray-blue gaze, she sees the longing he cannot hide. His lips seek hers and find them. In his kiss she tastes the warmth of amber wine and the urgency of manly desire. She drinks deeply, forgetting that for them there can be no past, no future; for he is of a time that is ending, while she belongs to one that has yet to begin. Closing her eyes to the soft shadows of the lantern lights, she gives herself to him, determined to live out her destiny in this one precious night.

___52291-8                                    $5.99 US/$6.99 CAN

**Dorchester Publishing Co., Inc.**
**P.O. Box 6640**
**Wayne, PA 19087-8640**

Please add $1.75 for shipping and handling for the first book and $.50 for each book thereafter. NY, NYC, and PA residents, please add appropriate sales tax. No cash, stamps, or C.O.D.s. All orders shipped within 6 weeks via postal service book rate. Canadian orders require $2.00 extra postage and must be paid in U.S. dollars through a U.S. banking facility.

Name_____
Address_____
City_____State_____Zip_____
I have enclosed $_____ in payment for the checked book(s).
Payment <u>must</u> accompany all orders. ❑ Please send a free catalog.
CHECK OUT OUR WEBSITE! www.dorchesterpub.com